A Thousand Years
of
Johnny Von

Edith M. Cortese

TRUMPET BOY PRESS

LOS ANGELES

Published by Trumpet Boy Press

Los Angeles, CA 90020, USA

A THOUSAND YEARS OF JOHNNY VON.

Illustrations by Marcia Adams Ho
Cover and text design by Delaine Ulmer

Library of Congress Control Number 2013946345

ISBN 978-0-9898869-0-1 (paperback edition / 2013)
ISBN 978-0-9898869-2-5 (ebook edition / 2013)
ISBN 978-0-9898869-3-2 (audio / 2013)

Trumpet Boy Press Hardcover ISBN : 978-0-9898869-1-8

PRINTED IN THE UNITED STATES

Introduction

"And we are put on earth a little space,
that we may learn to bear the beams of love."

~ *William Blake*

I t was the best of times, it was the worst of times.

No, that's silly, I'll never pass that off as mine. It's not that kind of story, anyway.

It was a dark and stormy night.

Well, see, that's just a lie, and frankly, hard to pull off if you're not a cartoon dog.

Call me Ishmael!

It's the pressure. The pressure of that crucial opening

line, the first impression I'm trying to make with you —
wanting it to be good, it's my Achilles heel. Look, I'll just
tell you this: it's important to me, telling you this story. It's
important to my heart, and when things are important to
me, sometimes I choke and sputter and stumble all over
myself without a word in my head. I can't come up with
anything that articulates what is bursting inside to get out.

How about this...

All of this happened, more or less.

Would Kurt Vonnegut really mind if I used his opening
line? It's an homage. Everyone likes that, right?

Or even better, Billy Pilgrim (aka Johnny Von) has
become unstuck in time.

That could work. I could just change the name. Besides,
you always have to change the names...so lawyers and agents
and movie stars don't get upset.

Oh, hells-bells. I'm going to come up with something,
because I want you to see what I see. I want you to know
what I know now, how the universe dances and converges
and brings events that answer the call of your heart. How
the mystical behind the mundane came to change me. And
how Johnny Von fits into all of it.

Tall, beautiful, Johnny Von.

I'd like to tell this story so that by the end, we'd
understand what the poet William Blake is talking about in
all his lovely writings. We would know that a story, even
just the ones you tell yourself, can help move you forward

and give you courage — that a story has tangible power to change who you are. And while poetry may no longer have the power to spark a revolution, or attract the attention of the masses, in a world that has YouTube and TMZ, I know it can spark a revolution inside a person. Even a person who didn't do well in 10th grade English, a woman who still doesn't know what iambic pentameter is.

I'd like to tell you this story so that by the end we'd understand that outside of the 10th grade, poetry is trying to say what is pushing from inside you, bursting to get out. And like William Blake, with the close of this story we'd all understand the power of desire and imagination, the birthplace of love and art. We'd seek it out; knowing its value to a life well lived. Rank it up there with good food, great sex and big money. That's my hope, outside of just having a good time.

Don't get me wrong, I think just plain having a good time is also very important. I don't want to mislead you already with all this grandiose talk of poetry and the power of desire; words like "birthplace." I'm not a dramatic person. I'm not full of big words. I'm not like that at all. I should tell you now before we start, I'm more "comfort fit," more t-shirts, worn jeans and bare feet. Quite possibly, my toenails are painted red. But that's about as fancy as I go on a regular basis. So look, I'll just stop now and make it easy. I'll start where it all started.

In the beginning, God created the heavens and the earth.

And then some time after that, God made me.

About 33 years after that, God made Moochie, my brown Labrador, and we were walking up Valley Glen Drive in the Hollywood Hills to get the other dogs when the first thing happened.

Chapter 1

"Man's Desires are limited
by his Perceptions; none can desire
what he has not perceived."
~ *William Blake*

It's a day like any other day over the past three
years. I'm walking my dog route, same dog-walking
schedule I'd had for a while. Moochie is new, but
it's not his first day. He's bouncing off the end of a
red nylon leash, the two of us on our way to Jackie
Sheppard's house to get Rocky and Theodore on Valley
Glen Drive. I'm a little self-conscious, making a mental
note as we progress up the street, "I really need to train this
puppy to walk." I'm making kiss-kiss sounds along the way

to coax him on. "What are people going to think? What kind of dog-walker can't get her own dog in a forward motion?"

He is only a little thing now, a round brown teddy bear-looking Labrador, so I can pull him along, but he's expected to top out at 90 pounds or so. By the rate he is growing in just the short time he's been with me, Lord only knows how big this little chunk of chocolate could get.

I remember thinking that.

Otherwise I didn't feel anything strong afoot in the universe. In fact, the very idea that nothing was different was starting to weigh me down. I moved to L.A. from London convinced that things would be different, if for no other reason than the sheer distance around the earth that was between my old life and my new one. Regardless of my shipwrecked heart, I was determined my life in L.A. would be different. But so far nothing had happened, and three years was starting to feel like a really long time. Maybe it was when I opened the door, and watched as the dogs did what dogs do, that the signal went out from my heart to the universe at large.

Moochie bounds inside the Sheppard's front door and becomes a wagging maniac, kissing up one side and down the other on both Rocky and Theodore. Rocky, a bulldog who is unusually bouncy, starts popping in the air, eye-level. And Theodore, a short black mutt who smiles when he looks at you, zips out the kitchen and starts circling the courtyard like a greyhound. Then all three are outside, whipped up into a love frenzy. Pure glee. And not just "nice to see you" glee, but unbounded, romping, full speed tackles of joy. Clouds of mirth and happiness are rising off of the three little guys as they tumble in the grass. I guess if you weren't a dog-walker you'd try to calm them down, but this is what I'm paid to do, so I let them go for it, full force. I sit on the step at the kitchen door, put Jackie's daily dog note in my pocket, and watch the happiness rushing out of them.

It must have been then, in watching the pure glee, in having the impulse to call someone and say, "You gotta come see these dogs play!" and not having anyone to call that set it all in motion. Or, maybe it was feeling the contrast inside me as I put Theodore back in the kitchen and leashed Moochie and Rocky for the walk, of how badly I wanted to experience unbounded, romping, full speed tackles of joy.

I don't mean physically tackling and rolling in the grass, necessarily. Or, maybe I do. But what I really want is that feeling — all the connected, uncensored play-with-me feeling. What's the word for it I'm trying to find, you know, that feeling of freedom and abandon?

I'm suddenly heavy as the word pops into my head, shutting the door behind us.

Love.

Damn it.

My soul heaves a sigh as Moochie, Rocky and I head out and round the big tree at the bend in the street.

I need a love.

No sooner do the words form in my brain than I hear a rustle of commotion from the branches that canopy over the street at the far end. I turn to see falling green leaves. I call the dogs along and take a step in the direction of the noise. Just as I move forward, a large red-tailed hawk breaks from the leaves.

Hawks are my favorite.

Given the amount of time I spend as a dog-walker looking up to the sky, lost in my daydreaming, it's not uncommon for me to see a hawk or two floating majestically high in the air. And it's not uncommon for me, while lost in my daydreaming, to imagine myself in a long, flowing white dress with my hair loose in the wind, my cheeks naturally rosy and my cleavage perfect, even though I'm bra-less. In my imaginings I put my hand in the air, clad in a big leather-cuffed falconer's glove. In one sharp motion, I reach to the sky. The hawk screeches in, claws first, and alights on my wrist.

Hawk-Tamer! Humbly commanding the forces of nature. Generous and wise, I don't keep the hawk like a pet. We only admire each other for a moment. Communicate with our eyes the respect, power and beauty innate in the other. Then I send the hawk on its way... at which point I hike up my imaginary white dress, kick-start my imaginary motorcycle with the heel of my cowboy boot, give it some gas and ride off.

Only in real life, a hawk never gets that close.

I don't know how to call a hawk to me; I'm just a dog-walker. I have no idea how to get close enough to pet it and love up on it like I do with Moochie. He always stays far away. With a hawk you only get moments, in patches of sky.

As this hawk breaks from the tree at the bottom of the street, it does something that hawks don't normally do. Instead of breaking high and flying out, this hawk swoops low and heads straight for me and Moochie, flapping its wings.

"Wow. That's beautiful," is my first thought, followed by a split second of exaltation "this is what it must feel like for a hawk to come to you."

"Whoa, what the hell? That hawk is coming straight at me," is my panicked second thought as I duck on reflex. Perhaps I look silly scrunched down in the middle of the road, the hawk nowhere near my head, but I can only tell you how it feels to me.

It swoops up, I'm sure mere inches from my person, spikes in the air, turns and dives toward the vacant hill at the top of Valley Glen Drive.

I straighten up.

Something different is afoot.

Moochie, Rocky and I make haste to the top of the street. I peer out over the vacant lot. I scan the sky, sure the renegade hawk that almost took me out is somewhere close, but it's nowhere in the clouds and blue overhead. I follow the tree line, focus my eyes to each of the big pine branches of the house below, looking for a perched silhouette, but still no hawk. I move my vision systematically to the manicured lawn, through the tall bushes and flowery plants and there …there in the lush green grass of the backyard, he stands.

My heart thumps in my chest. "Is that, is that…?" I hear the startled words in my mind, but I'm not sure. He's tall, bare-chested with a scruffy beard, like a man who's been out in the forest a few days chopping firewood to keep his family warm, except it's bright and sunny, and he's wearing only silky white pajama bottoms. And then, though it's a distance, I hear it: that laugh. A voice, his voice, deep and distinct calls over to someone across the yard.

That's Johnny Von!

The world stops.

Tall, shirtless Johnny Von is doing yoga in silky white pajama bottoms!

Clouds part.

Johnny Von is right there.

Everything around me spins but the sight of Johnny Von …doing yoga …in silky white pajama bottoms.

I gasp. Like a school girl, like a maiden in the woods as a knight thunders past. I literally feel my chest jump, like a damsel seeing the dragon slayer on the horizon seconds before her demise.

Johnny Von.

His name, his perfect movie star name, whispers on my lips.

Then, as if he hears my bated call, although I know he can't, he turns.

Johnny Von's eyes pierce me through the distance.

Love strikes.

I don't know how long the moment lasts. I'm thrown out of the temporal stream. A split second on the clock, a frozen stare for minutes, I have no idea. But as the world returns, I zip my eyes down.

Johnny Von!

My insides are chaotic. I feel caught red-handed, abashed, a deer in the headlights. I don't know where I am. I feel the leashes fumble in my hands. I can't catch my breath.

Johnny Von.

Moochie lunges toward a stick. Rocky follows and the two tangle and tug. I bend over, trying to regain my senses, and wrestle the stick from them. I pull them forward.

I'm suddenly so flustered I'm not sure which direction is home. "Walk the dogs," I hear myself say. "Just walk forward." I can't tell you my name or what I'm doing here. I have only one thought pounding through my body.

Johnny Von.

I steady myself in the walking, I hear words repeating in my head that I do not immediately recognize, calling me:

And thy lovely leaves among,

There is love: I hear his tongue.

It repeats over and over as I regain myself and walk the dogs down Valley Glen Drive, like a heartbeat coming back to rest, to its right timing. I hear the words of William Blake like a steady drum beat marching me forward whether I'm willing or not:

And thy lovely leaves among,

There is love: I hear his tongue.

By the end of Valley Glen Drive, by the tree where the leaves rustled and the hawk burst forth, an inexplicable calm comes over me. All at once the colors of the houses and the trees on the street become vibrant. The air feels tingly and exquisite on my skin. My body is light and alive. The day is ... glorious.

I don't know how or why. I don't know what or when. I only know this…I have a mission — an Everest of a mission for my shy heart.

"Will you go to church with me this Sunday?"

I think about telling Mandy Kane about seeing Johnny Von as we start our walk up Runyon Canyon, but I'm torn. Of all the people I know in L.A., Mandy would have the most things to say about it. I know she would have information, leads, and ideas of approach. But for the same reason, I don't want to tell her.

"I didn't know you were Catholic?" I say, surprised by the question.

Mandy and I hike Runyon Canyon every day around 5:30. She takes the current rescue dog she's fostering -- today it's a white pit bull with half its left ear missing -- and I have my last client, Emily, a Rhodesian ridgeback.

"You know, I don't really go to church anymore," I say to her with sincerity. "I don't really believe in the whole Mass thing. I haven't resolved inside the seemingly celebration of the crucifixion that I perceive with the church. It's just something I'm working out." I'm careful not to sound judgmental. If Mandy Kane has had some kind of revelatory experience and suddenly wants to go to church, far be it for me to throw any negativity her way.

"Oh, it's not like that." She laughs and hits me like I'm teasing her. "You know how I have a crush on Mark Wahlberg?" Mandy's voice is excited as she tucks the long tresses of her blond hair extensions behind her ear.

You and I, as civilians, would never know her long blond hair came from the heads of Swedish nuns somewhere far, far away. Even outside in the wind, it looks like a shimmering golden wheat field, luminous and photo-ready, never a clip at her scalp to be seen. That she pulls it off so well is impressive. But what also impresses me is that there are nuns somewhere growing their blond hair really long and straight and then selling it exclusively to salons in Beverly Hills. True or not, that's good marketing — the implied purity. Hair that didn't get out much, it's higher grade. No teasing or hot curling in a convent. Mandy told me Swedish nun hair is the best you can get, and it's the kind of thing Mandy would know.

I think of these alleged nuns as I nod. Unsure of where this is going, I tuck my unruly brown, curly hair into the hat I wear everyday, a blue bucket hat that says "Woof Woof," embroidered on the front. I made it myself.

"Well, I found out he goes to Christ the Redeemer Church in Beverly Hills and I wanted to see if you'd go with me, so I would know when to kneel and stand and everything."

"Oh." I pause, staying friendly and non-reactive, something I've learned to do in L.A.

With what you know so far, you might be quick to "profile" Mandy Kane, as was I when we first met. Blond, spray tan, moderately big boobs, color contacts, bleached teeth, frosty lip-gloss, Louis Vuitton sunglasses, a black Cadillac Escalade -- an L.A. girl. In fact the first day at the dog park, I couldn't have picked her out from any of the other girls conscientiously discussing the decisions Linsay Lohan is making in her life.

"... my friend Stacy was at a photo shoot the other day ... she said her butt is really bigger even that it looks ... they had to, like, discuss angles to hide it ... I heard she's out every night wasted ... Did you see that picture in US

magazine with that girl ... I'm so worried about her ..." A
gaggle of L.A. girls, defined by the trendy and the superficial,
the too-cool-for-school attitude, all pretending to be
something they are not; all a show, all fake. But this is where
you would begin to be wrong about Mandy Kane. Mandy
Kane is pretending nothing.

She may look nothing remotely like the girl who arrived
here from Minnesota eight years ago; she may look like an
L.A. girl, but she is not hiding a thing. She is unfettered by
hesitation when she says, "I just really like being the center
of attention, when everyone is looking at me and wanting
to have what I have." She says it the same way Mother
Teresa would say, "I just really like helping the poor." In her
universe these pursuits are equal. But even that's not true, in
her universe Mother Teresa would have wanted to be a rich
flawless celebrity — if she could have been. While a typical
L.A. girl might pretend that she considers other points of
view or holds your best interests, Mandy Kane pretends
nothing of the sort. She came to Hollywood to be an
actress, or a model, or a recording artist, with no particular
preference. No excuses, no reservations.

"You know how it's hard to pay attention to people when
what they are saying has nothing to do with you ..." is
something she said just a few days ago, a sincere observation.
Hiding, posing, scheming behind your back, Mandy Kane
is not. She is posing, self-serving and scheming right out
in front. She would scoff at anyone pretending they were
otherwise, if it ever occurred to her to consider anyone

otherwise. Unlike an L.A. girl, Mandy has integrity. It's an unconventional use of the word maybe, but integrity still the same. You know where she stands.

"I can't find anyone else to go with me," she says to me as we hit the top of Runyon Canyon.

Although I know better, I'm still slightly offended by the fact that I'm Mandy's last resort for a partner in this ploy. Sure, we hike together everyday, and occasionally Mandy does include me in select social activities, but I know the score. Other than wanting someone to hike with everyday, there are two reasons Mandy hangs out with me. One, I'm attractive but, admittedly, appear disheveled and out of fashion for L.A., so I'm okay to be seen with without being a threat. And two -- and this is the big one -- I dated an international playboy. Although I no longer talk to him or have any connection to his jet-set life in London, it provides the kind of credentials Mandy looks for in the people she surrounds herself with.

Mandy pulls her white pit bull off of a tree it's mauling after seeing a squirrel scurry past, and we head down the back of the canyon.

To be honest, I find Mandy's plan both ridiculous and perfectly sensible. My entire Catholic career was spent in church, lusting. And while that was high school and Mark Wahlberg is not in anybody's chemistry class, I am not surprised by the idea. Mandy Kane has many stories of celebrity encounters and feats of daring. Like the time she made out with Matthew McConaughey by way of interviewing to be his assistant … the time she hooked up with a young Johnny Depp by becoming a regular at his favorite coffee shop on Mulholland … the time she called Joaquin Phoenix's press agent and said she was writing an article for *Redbook* magazine and needed to schedule a meeting.

She continues, as the dogs charge another squirrel racing up a palm tree and we both lunge forward, "I bought this new dress, it's sort of sheer but, like, covers your breasts here." She points to her chest without missing a beat. "My tits look great in it. I think it will be perfect for church."

This is why I don't want to tell Mandy Kane about Johnny Von. What happened felt pure, it felt meaningful. If I tell Mandy Kane, if I speak his name after nodding along with her plans for her breasts in church, it will just…cheapen the whole thing.

That night, I stand in the small cubicle that is my bathroom brushing my teeth, in the studio apartment that is my home since I moved to L.A., bewitched with thoughts of Johnny Von. I oscillate between feeling elated and feeling dispirited. As I pace and brush, which is my habit if something is bothering me, I begin to wonder if I should just drop it. I'm terrible at this kind of thing. I get shy and panicked; I've never been successful in pursuing guys I like; much less, a movie star. After all, the International Playboy picked me out. I didn't even know who he was until after we'd started.

I look in the mirror, I'm me and he's a big celebrity—
dispirited. Then again, I can't reason the rush of good
feeling, how his eyes felt like being struck by lightening,
good lightening—elation.

Unable to stop the back and forth, I shift to the
practicalities. Again, I am me, a dog walker having
nothing to do with Hollywood or the movies or anything
related to him; i.e. we are not going to meet through his
work. And, he is him, a celebrity who probably doesn't just
stroll around his neighborhood in the afternoons striking
up conversations with dog walkers; i.e. we are probably
not going to meet through my work. No mutual friends
to happen us together at a random dinner party. My
thoughts whittle it down to this: unless we are stuck in
an elevator together, or taken hostage in a robbery at the
seven-eleven and locked in the drink cooler until the police
show up…how could this happen, really?

Mandy Kane pops into mind.

And I immediately try to reassure myself that I am
not Mandy Kane. There must be a way for me to meet
Johnny Von, a way to gain his interest, without plotting
and scheming, without selling my soul or dyeing my hair.
Only I have no idea what that way would be. I circle back
to the beginning,

I should drop it.

My brushing stops.

On my bedside table I have an empty can of LuBeLu's

Steel Cut Oat Meal. It's been with me since I can remember, at least since college. I like the navy and light blue stripes on the label. On the front of the label is a woman in a light blue dress with white polka dots, spooning oats to her family around a table. It's a picture of a perfect happy family. It looks clean and sharp. It's there because it's the perfect size for holding my glasses, hair clips and my pens. It's a catch-all. It's something I have because it's always been sitting around somewhere, and I liked it once. On the back of the LuBeLu's Steel Cut Oat Meal can, which I see every night before I go to sleep, is a poem, a poem by William Blake. I guess it was a promotional series at the time. It's what popped into my head today, these words that I've never really read, but know by heart from time and proximity; the words that beat like a drum inside me at the sight of Johnny Von. The last two stanzas roll out of my mouth through the toothpaste:

And thy lovely leaves among,
There is love: I hear his tongue.

There his charming nest doth lay,
There he sleeps the night away;
There he sports along the day,
And doth among our branches play.

"You can't get more of a sign that that." I say to Moochie as I return the can to the table and continue brushing. "And look, 'there his charming nest doth lay'," right there, on my dog route." I beam a toothpaste smile at Moochie and head to the sink to rinse.

Moochie wags.

I push Moochie into his kennel by my bed and slip between the clean white sheets. Moochie likes his kennel now, a little room of his own. He nods off quickly from all the excitement of the day. I click off the lights. I do not nod off quickly.

It was a sign, most definitely, with the hawk. I'm not like Mandy. I didn't come to L.A. seeking fame, fortune or celebrity. I didn't come to be seen.

Not that I'm above fame and fortune; although fame scares me. But who doesn't like fortune, really? Unless it starts to weigh you down, becomes overly important, or creates a distance with people. No, I think as I fluff my pillow on the day-bed I have situated in the breakfast nook to give my studio the illusion of space—good looks, fame and fortune are not drawbacks.

As I stare at the ceiling in the dark, I endeavor to think of some organic way to bring about the meeting of Johnny Von, an un-Mandy way. Not conniving, just something to help this gift of providence along; do my part to bring about some kind of synchronistic event.

I start with a neutral premise having nothing to do with Johnny Von.

I need to make friends. This I can state as a truth.

Yes, my days are filled with endless canine affection and I have Moochie to love and look after now, but I lack human-to-human contact. The lack of human-to-human contact is not good. I need people. I need stimulating conversation.

I like the line of thinking, so I continue.

My lack of human-to-human contact, even for L.A., is a bona fide problem. It's a problem that should be addressed. Regardless of Johnny Von who lives in a big beautiful white stucco Spanish house on Valley Glen Drive, I do have to come up with something to remedy things around this personal life challenge. I have to think outside the box. Think, think, think. That's when it hits me, the just-talk-to-people-along-the-way initiative.

A shyness surges through me — it will require talking to strangers. I have a life long process of conquering shyness. It rarely wells up in me, nowadays I've trained myself to be friendly and outgoing, but the thought of talking to Johnny Von suddenly sends a bolt of terror through my body.

I have an internal pep talk.

I'll just go easy. No pressure. I'll just talk to the people I see on the walks. It's just being friendly, and I can do that. And most important, being friendly is not scheming. I'm just talking to the people I encounter on the path that is my life. And if one of those people happens to be Johnny Von or someone connected to Johnny Von, and we become friends and then I start hanging out with Johnny Von or someone connected to Johnny Von, so be it. He's irrelevant. I'm interested in self-growth.

Relieved by the thought of a higher pursuit, the un-Mandy-ness of it, I drop off and sleep like a baby.

The very next day, I'm walking on Valley Glen Drive without a soul in sight. The hour is almost up, the dogs are almost done, and there has been no one to talk-to-along-the-way. I begin to feel embarrassed about the whole thing. The whole initiative seems ridiculous, people in the Hollywood Hills are never outside their houses. For the most part there is never anyone home during the day, which come to think about it, is how I make a living. I begin to think that I'm a fool to think I could ever meet Johnny Von like this.

The next thing I know, I'm on the top of the hill, bending over to clean up after Moochie, blue doggie bag in hand, when a yellow taxi swings around the corner. I stand and pull the dogs off the street, encourage them to the curb so the taxi has the whole street. From the back of the taxi, I see someone waving to me. A big goofy wave. I can't see who it is, and I wonder if it's someone mistaking me for someone else. I lift my hand, still holding the blue plastic bag ready for dog pick-up duty, and wave back. As the taxi moves forward the waver turns to look out the back. He's wearing gold, 70's Elvis-Kung-Fu-phase sunglasses. He's smiling and still waving as they move down the road, and I wonder for a split second, due to the enthusiasm of the gesture, if it's someone making fun of me.

My pleasant on-the-street-friendly-smile drops.

Johnny Von just waved to me.

Johnny Von just waved to me with the exuberance
of a child! I feel the need to shake my head, to pinch
myself. Did that just happen? Why did Johnny Von wave
to me? Was he being sarcastic? Did he think I was cute?
Maybe he is just neighborly like that? But, it wasn't an
acknowledgement wave. It was a fervent wave! Was he
waving at someone else? Even though I know there is no
one else on the street, I double check up and down. Nope.
No one here to wave at…but me; me and the dogs. I look
around again. What's going on!

"Do you have any extra work in the house I can do?"
Three weeks into the initiative, these unplanned words pop
out of my mouth while chatting on Valley Glen Drive with
the Johnny Von Contractor.

During the first week of my just-talk-to-people-along-
the-way campaign, I meet three Hispanic gardeners, two
housekeepers, another dog-walker, and one Johnny Von
neighbor, Trudie Reed. Old-Hollywood, retired widow,
two cats, no dog. She compares the deer in her yard that
wander from Griffith Park to giant lawn rats that should all
be shot.

"That puppy of yours sure is fat." She smiles and looks to
me. "But you're a healthy size too aren't you. Not a skinny
one like all the girls today."

I find this Trudie Reed a bit insulting. I can't get a bead
on her. She seems like a sweet little lady all powdered and

perfumed, her hair soft and done for the day. But the things she is says would definitely fall under the insult category if you read them in a transcript.

She looks me up and down. "I haven't seen you around the neighborhood?" She says to me, sweet as pie, after her deer tirade.

"I walk dogs for the Sheppard's, the green house up the hill."

"Are you married, dear?"

I smile and shake my head no.

"Boyfriend?"

"Nope."

Trudie Reed looks confused. "Girlfriend?"

"No. I'm not...I like boys, I'm just not with anyone at the moment."

"Get out!" Trudie Reed suddenly yells at the corner of her lawn, her old lady voice more a high pitch call than a volume increase kind of yell. She clicks the hose to a single blast and lasers it at the fence. "Damn neighbor cat! The little rodent's been watching my bird feeder for weeks. I was married 3 times, my last marriage lasted for 32 years."

I smile, nod approvingly and try to move on, but Trudie Reed moves her bubbly round old lady body in front of us and keeps talking.

"Hold this." She says to me and hands me the hose spray, "try to get that part by the house." She talks on while I water her lawn, hose in one hand, Moochie's leash in the other. Trudie Reed then stands next to me telling me about living in Hollywood and how much fun she and her husband had in the fifties, about buying this house. I try to find a way to gracefully exit from watering her lawn and move on. "I'm seventy-nine you know."

This I find astounding. She looks late forties at the most.

Trudie tucks at the curls of her soft blond hairdo. "My Howard passed four years ago."

"Oh, I'm sorry." I offer.

"It all passes." She smiles softly at me. "We all go, don't we sweetheart." She pats my shoulder as if I'm the one who has lost someone. "Howard gave me my first job at Paramount, I was a seamstress you know, worked for all the big studios. You should get married." She winks her twinkly blue eyes. "Best way to keep in shape." She gives me a devilish nudge, then takes off her garden gloves, and pats Moochie, telling him what a fine dog he is. She then disappears into her garage.

Old people, I think to myself as I watch her, it's hard when they're crazy. I don't know how to tell her I'm not here to water her lawn. I don't want to be rude, and it's not like I have to be anywhere. I look over at her puttering in her garage; maybe she's forgotten me here.

A good ten minutes later, Trudie returns to my side, takes back the hose, smiles and says. "I bet your good with that dog," she says, "you have nice eyes."

That is nice, I think. I reassess my earlier conclusions on Trudie Reed's abrupt disclosures and outspoken insults. Maybe she's not an old bat after all.

And then she zings me, "maybe get your hair done." She looks me up and down in my dog walking clothes, "put a little more effort in."

The second week the universe kicks in and I meet the Johnny Von Assistant, who I note to be a very nice girl, not an L.A. girl at all. She stops every few days to pick up Moochie and play with him. She's a dog lover. Johnny Von has a dog lover as his right hand person. This is a good sign. I also meet the Johnny Von Contractor who is just starting the remodel on the house. I studied architecture for a few years in college, I like construction, so we have lots to chat about. Of course neither of them say anything about who they work for, but I'm on the street everyday and I can't help but see the coming and going of people—so I know, but the name, the perfect name of Johnny Von goes unsaid. Still, I feel good. I feel clean and un-Mandy about chatting with both of them. We're talking about dogs or construction. It couldn't be more organic!

"Sure." The Johnny Von Contractor says as friendly as Mayberry. "I'm sure I can find some work for you."

By week three, we'd been chatting everyday. His errands coincided with my walks and he would stop at least once to admire the dogs and inquire about Moochie's progress in puppy-hood. I'd comment on the progress of the scaffolding going up or the workers coming and going from the house.

"Why don't you come by on Tuesday afternoon?" he says as he waves good-bye.

As he drives away, all I can think is: Campaign success! I'm now very close. I talked to the people and the universe took care of the rest.

At this point, you would be correct to assume that I am very, very excited as I think about being in the house of Johnny Von four days from today. I am excited as a single woman who'd noticed Johnny Von in movies and in the press before the first day the hawk led me to him. A single woman who had registered the words "sex" and "appeal" next to the name Johnny and Von. A woman who, when she spied him at the top of Valley Glen Drive in silky white pajama bottoms, was rendered breathless by the view.

Now. All that being said, sign or no sign, breathless or not, providence or random events, you should also know this: I am not 14. I am not naïve. I am a 33 year old woman who dated an international playboy, for Christ's sake. And in the three years I've been in Hollywood, I have seen my fair share of crazy. I have rubbed elbows with psychotic industry people at parties or as dog-walking clients and been appalled. I've seen great feats of rudeness. I have gone out with friends only to watch them weird-out because the famous were among us. I've listened to more Mandy Kane celebrity stories than I care to remember, all more than once. Please know, I am seasoned.

In real life, Johnny Von may be crazy. He could be an arrogant jackass. He could be a drunk. He could be gay.

He could be all the things you don't want in a boyfriend. For all I know, he could be secretly married to a blond Swedish ex-nun with a very cropped hair cut. I know this. So you should know, that as I think of being in the house of Johnny Von in the four days leading up to Tuesday, I'm holding a healthy reserve inside.

But, you should also know that I am only human and it's no secret that Johnny Von is the perfect swirl of movie star manhood. He has the sultry, dark, soulful eyes of a young Marlon Brando; the same broad shoulders, the same edge of nice-guy-but-not-if-he-needs-to-be-hard appeal. Mix that with a kind of Americana, a John Wayne appeal. Johnny Von carries himself with that certain sense of fairness. You could see him gifted with the ability to shake a man's hand correctly. Take those two and finish the swirl with the boyish, happy, playful charisma of Paul Newman. The twinkle and toys that surround him, an easy-going and amused take on the world. Now, as if that were not enough to stop a girls' heart, top that swirl with a warm coating of Jimmy Stewart. The sincere, the reliable, the heartfelt--a salt of the earth good man. Then give this force of nature the perfect sounding name, just two words put together side by side, something that feels obvious and satisfying when you say it: Johnny. Von.

So, given the recent turn of events, I have to admit, it does all feel very synchronistic. Yes, I'd been the one to initiate the upcoming "being in the house," but still, it is as if the universe is throwing me a bone placing me here on the quiet street of Valley Glen Drive. Lining up moments, meeting the

Johnny Von Assistant and then the Johnny Von Contractor. Both are open and friendly and nice. Johnny Von could be open and friendly and nice.

When I call her on Monday, Jackie Sheppard is thrilled with the idea that Moochie wants a play date with Rocky and Theodore on Tuesday afternoon. Rocky is still a puppy and she thinks the idea of letting them socialize for the afternoon is great. She thinks the three dogs will be fine in the kitchen and tells Rosa, her housekeeper, that I will be leaving Moochie with them after the walks. So on Tuesday afternoon, free of any canine companions, I make my way up the driveway of Johnny Von.

I suppose I should tell you what I decided to wear. What I thought was a good choice when I was dressing this morning, knowing I would be working in the house of Johnny Von. I'm wearing my cut-off blue jean shorts. They are tattered with natural peek-a-boo holes everywhere. They are my most comfortable favorites, although I usually don't wear them anywhere else besides walking dogs under the summer sun. This is because they are tattered with peek-a-boo holes everywhere. They are not obscene, but I imagine them to be quite enticing. The dogs don't care; they just want me to be comfortable. As I follow the scaffolding that is going up around the back of the house, I am hoping the cut-offs will reveal that I am "relaxed and easy going." I am also hoping they will reveal the idea, "nice legs." For my top, I chose a recently purchased white t-shirt with blue trim that says "Bootylicious," airbrushed across the front. It's retro. It's a little hard to read because the t-shirt is a little tight, and the word "Bootylicious" stretches over my chest awkwardly. If you want to know what it says, you have to make an effort to study my boobs. Besides the obvious, I am hoping it will be a subliminal affirmation of my appeal. It's bold, declaring that I am indeed "Bootylicious." Of course this is construction work, so I'm wearing sturdy running shoes with clean thick gym socks.

It strikes me, as I make my way through the open back door and the painter points to the hall, that I was obviously very confident when I was dressing this morning. I have a slight moment of concern, as I make my way past the bathroom and all the tile guys turn my way, about advertising the fact that I am "Bootylicious." But then again, I think the t-shirt is funny, and I am hoping the real Johnny Von is funny.

"Hi, I'm glad you're here." The Johnny Von Contractor lights up at the sight of me. He shakes my hand and excuses himself from the guys hanging drywall. "Let me show you through the house first and then we'll get started."

We survey the freshly painted walls and newly stained floors. And then, although most of the house looks like a construction site, with all personal items safely tucked under thick layers of plastic, we pass several framed photos in the dining room bookcase. We see Johnny Von backstage somewhere having fun with friends, Johnny Von at work on a set talking intensely to someone, Johnny Von laughing with family at someone's birthday party, smiling and happy with his arms around old, normal-looking people. My eyes flash on the pictures for only seconds, but the Johnny Von Contractor catches me.

The feigning of indifference begins.

Even before I met Mandy Kane, before there were dog clients, I learned quickly when I moved to L.A.: never let on that you are the least bit interested in Hollywood-connected people. Never. It is the fast lane to being frozen out of any conversation or any invitation to anything. No matter how innocent or sincere your intentions, always feign indifference. Always. I learned this standing in the dog park one day just a few weeks after my move, when Sandra Bullock walked into the park with her dog.

I turned to the gate just as she was walking in and became very excited. I like Sandra Bullock, and this was my first celebrity sighting. So I turned to the L.A. girl on my left, before I knew about L.A. girls, and said, "Hey look, there's Sandra Bullock!"

I didn't scream it. I didn't freak out and foam at the mouth. I didn't prepare to rush at her. I am not a Sandra Bullock aficionado, although I was impressed with how pretty she is in real life.

"Did you see? That's Sandra Bullock over there," I said.

The girl on my left shrinks down, doesn't look directly at me and whispers, "Oh, yeah," then bends over and acts like she is checking something very important on her dog's collar.

I didn't really get it at the time, so I turn to the other girl on my right and again try to share the excitement. "Sandra Bullock is over there!"

The second girl doesn't even bother with the fake dog checking, she just looks straight through me. Thinking back, it is almost impressive, her ability to look directly at someone and completely, utterly ignore them.

I don't press it. I think, maybe I have something on my face, a little snot dangling out my nose? I sniff briskly and look away.

No one says another word, only smiles, Stepford Wife-like. And then, when Sandra Bullock leaves the park, the first girl says, "I can't believe she'd wear those jeans." And the second girl says, "She's not even that pretty." They then go on to talk about Sandra Bullock for the next 40 minutes, telling everyone who walks up how she'd put on weight.

That's when I started learning about L.A. girls. That's also about the time my challenges with human-to-human contact began.

I'll be honest, I don't like feigning indifference. I'm not good at it. It's hard enough for me to figure out my real feelings. But as the Johnny Von Contractor scans me for reactions to the photos, the feigning kicks in automatically.

As we move through the house, I am perfectly not overly interested as I look at the stacks of Johnny Von furniture under the plastic tarps. Nonchalance drips off me at the sight of the disheveled couch and the Xbox set up in the T.V. room off the hallway. The stack of scripts, his scribbled notes, are irrelevant to me as we pass through the study. And finally, I am blasé in my notice of the shiny silver orange press in the kitchen of Johnny Von, just like the one I have at my house! I muse, but only briefly, over the thought of Johnny Von coming downstairs to his kitchen, all bleary-eyed in the morning, deciding if he'll make some orange juice or just go for a bowl of cereal. Possibly, he'd be wearing those white silky pajama bottoms. As we end the tour, however, what is noticeably not in the house of Johnny Von is Johnny Von.

The cell phone rings on the clip of his belt and the Johnny Von Contractor excuses himself to take the call. He begins to stress out. He calls out orders to some of the crew. "That was Johnny on the phone," he says in a panic. "He's due back from his trip by 8:00 tonight. In only a few hours this house has to go from construction site to perfection!"

He looks at me and says, "You're in charge of Johnny's bedroom."

The words still dance in my head.

"Sure. Wherever." We're both still feigning away.

The Johnny Von Contractor walks me upstairs and directs me to take up all the floor protection. Then I am to un-tarp the bed and all the contents of the room that are stacked there. I have to get all the bedding out of the bathroom and finish up by making the bed, sheets and all. He then leaves me, alone, with the door closed because of the dust in the hall.

I'll be honest: It feels a little wrong. Me, alone in Johnny Von's bedroom looking at all of his stuff. Plus, I momentarily consider the fact that if I go slowly, I might still be here at 8:00 p.m. At the thought, I'm struck down with guilt. I'm sent swirling into an ethical dilemma. It wouldn't be right, purposely slowing down and not doing my best. What would my dad think? It wouldn't be fair to the Johnny Von Contractor who hired me on good faith. I can't do it! I want to linger around but I can't.

And if you are wondering -- as my friend Shelby Braxton asked me when I told her about it later -- no, I did not bury my face in one of the white pillows as I was making the bed and inhale deeply. I did not sniff anything, clean or dirty. Nor did I roll around on the bed. My "What if I go slow?" thoughts were guilt-inflicting enough.

I survey the room for a moment before I start to work. It seems like the room of a nice enough guy, not too big and fancy, not too small — all just right. There is nothing weird to be seen. A couple of old baby pictures with his parents are out on the dresser. I think that's nice. I take a breath. Alone in the quiet as I begin to work, it still feels a bit forbidden to be here. But soon enough my mind begins to drift away from the worries of the right and wrong of things, and my body relaxes. Then I do what I am here to do in the bedroom of Johnny Von. I get down on my hands and knees and start to work my way around the edge of the floor, pulling up blue tape and peeling back the protection with my un-calloused and tender hands. And this is how I find myself crawling forward, released to my imagination, in the bedroom of Johnny Von.

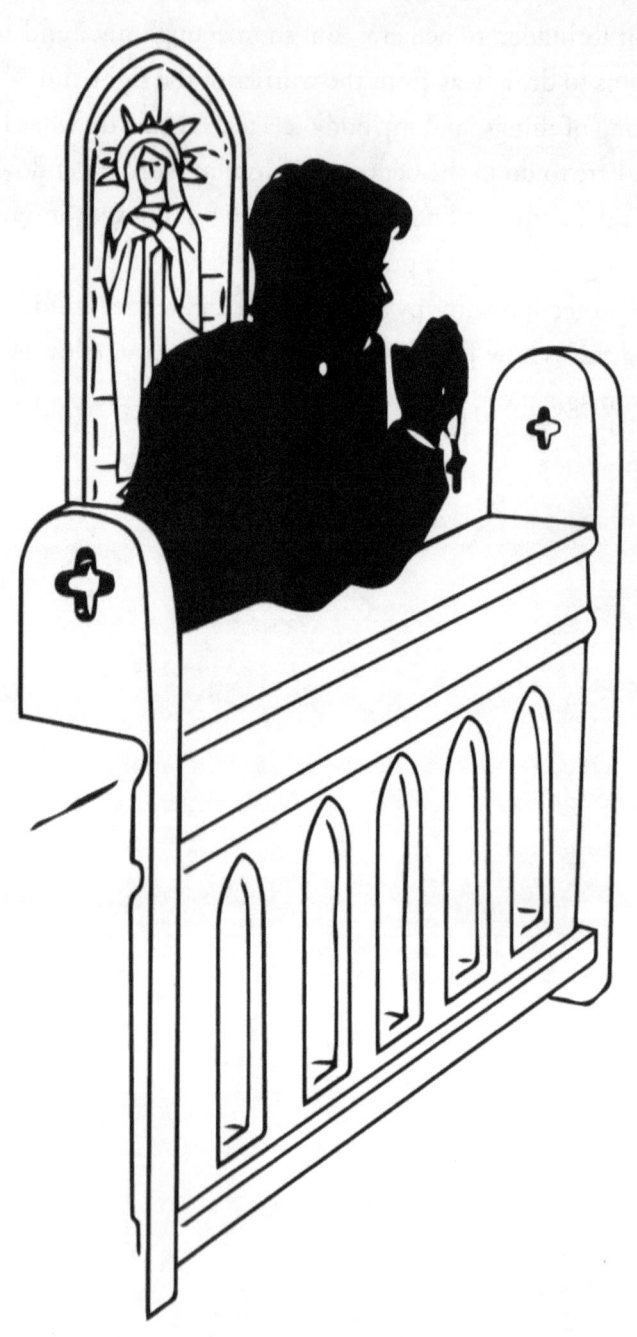

1574

Johnny Von the Priest

The wood of the confessional creaks as Johnny Von the Priest takes to his knees. In the empty church, even the smallest of movements echo loud into the endless star-filled night. He bows his head. He knows Estella will be the only other soul in this house of God tonight.

Alone behind the purple velvet curtain, he clenches his large hands, breathes in as deep as possible, tries to steady his mind, but only smells the sweet incense burning at the altar. He imagines the smell of Estella. He puts his lips to his knuckles and whispers, "Father, can my flesh be so evil? My thoughts, Father," A sweat breaks on his forehead, and he begins to gently rock, "my thoughts would cast me out if known. In the eyes of the Church, my thoughts are most impure. But what of Your eyes! How do You look down at me, my Lord? You made me a man." Before Estella, he would never have been so bold with God.

She will come, on her hands and knees, as she does

every night since the nuns took her in, an innocent girl of
16. Only now she has become a woman, unlike any other.
Now her body is the shape of a woman's as she moves
across the church. He sees her in his mind, as he has seen
her many times while trying not to look, wiping her brow
with the back of her hand, moving away strands of hair
that have come loose. Her hair, which he never sees, he
imagines long and curly. He will hear her over his prayers,
scrubbing the stone floor, plunging her brush in and out of
the warm soapy water. Working her way up, she will rub
oil on the dark mahogany wood until it squeaks with shine
under her clenched rag. Without stopping, she will make
her way to the altar and then to him. Always here in the
night, talking sincerely to God, Johnny Von the Priest sits
in the first pew on the right side of the altar.

They talk in whispers. Her words are effortless and
sincere. They whisper words, laughter, ideas that open
his mind and his heart like no scripture ever has. No one
has ever talked to Johnny Von the Priest with such an
eloquence and determination about God, the heart of man
and humanity's place under the stars.

They didn't start out so connected. Estella was sent to
Johnny Von the Priest. Her family was under Church
persecution, hunted for their name. The whole clan was
labeled heretics by association to the one who wouldn't
abide, would not concede, all of them paying for the one
who would not give in simply because they shared a name.
Estella barely knew her relative who offended the church
so, but it did not matter. Her father knew it was deadly

serious. Not knowing what else to do, he had written to Johnny Von the Priest in secret. He begged him to hide her within the walls of the very Church that was hunting him down. With a heavy heart for both his beloved friend and the actions of his Church, Johnny Von the Priest took Estella in.

He said to her that first day at the gate, "The times are very serious and I am in your favor here, but we must keep a confidence." In a low commanding voice he said with a strict tone, "You must not tell anyone who you are. You must not tell anyone your name. Forevermore, you must silence your name inside you."

Of all the losses she would have to bear, losing her name would turn out to be the hardest. How a word, a name can be so essential to the spirit of a person, Estella could not have imagined. But every time the nuns called her by a name that was hollow and fake, every time Johnny Von the Priest hesitated, didn't say any name when addressing her, she felt the hidden part of herself. She felt his silence. The hiding was a pressure always building, always reminding her that she was misplaced, that she had a secret that could cause her harm. And that the secret so threatening was her true self.

It was during one of their first meetings here in the night, that the world of Johnny Von the Priest began its destined unraveling. She was telling him about an incident earlier in the day, talking, as she often did, about Black Thomas the rooster, the terror of the coop. On this day, Mother

Superior had been making her rounds and noticed Estella talking to Black Thomas.

"You are a feeble girl," she said as she heard Estella's compliments, her cooing, trying to win over the angry bird. "You need to snap that one's neck. That bird is foul!"

Estella ignored Mother Superior and continued to lavish praise on the bird, now perched on a post between them. Estella usually tried to ignore Mother Superior, because in her mind Mother Superior shared the same temperament as Black Thomas. But today this ignoring did not sit well.

"Estella, did you hear me?"

"Yes, Mother."

"Then what do you have to say to me?"

Estella felt the corner she was being backed into.

"Well, he is fowl. That is true." Estella was taught to read and write before her family sent her to the convent. It was rare, and no one but Johnny Von the Priest knew this. They decided this would also be kept from the nuns, afraid it would cause trouble for her. But saying the word fowl, the pun of it, made Estella laugh. Which, of course, was the wrong thing to do.

"Are you laughing at me, child?" Mother Superior's face began to turn crimson and her hand went for the gate of the coop. But before she could reach Estella to strike her, Black Thomas started flapping and squawking. He hopped off the post, claws first, aiming at Mother Superior and hit the ground ready to peck the life out of her. He began chasing her in circles, up and down, in front of the coop. To which Mother Superior began yelling to the Lord for saving and then yelling to Estella to get Black Thomas away from her.

Johnny Von the Priest is charmed when Estella then says to him, "So if you have been wondering about Mother Superior today, that explains her foul mood." Which makes them both laugh. Seeing her laughter, her smile, the sound of it mixed with his own laughter, Johnny Von the Priest is struck by a new feeling: joy. A tangible happiness envelops him. It is spontaneous and easy. It feels like an opening inside.

But it is what she says next that strikes him so deeply. In the laughter between them, Estella looks to the altar, to the anguished crucifix, and says, "Which do you think pleases God more, our laughter or our penance?"

Maybe because the question comes at such a moment, or because it catches him off guard, he feels the answer instantly and it surprises him. He knows, as a priest, he should say it is our penance that God favors because He wants us saved, our souls washed clean so we can share eternity with Him. He knows he should explain that God wants our work, our self-conquering.

But in this moment, in the company of Estella so joy-filled and alive, he knows the answer is laughter. He knows it without reason, regardless. Our laughter must please God more than our suffering; how could it not? With her question, he knows something more real than he has ever read or been told, for the first time he knows beyond hope or faith something true about God. God wants our laughter.

By this night, which finds Johnny Von the Priest in the throes of deep despair, they have shared many talks in the night, and she has given vision to all of his original aspirations as a priest. His faith waning, she restored him. In the passing years, each musing they have shared, her presence, her light, has cracked the foundation he's stood upon, here in the flickering candlelight, in the quiet of the night of his church.

But along with the opening of his mind and his heart, she has awakened his body. On his knees, he is terrified. In this confessional, he is a grown man suffering the anguish of an adolescent, joined with the eternal fires of damnation threatening to give way.

"Father," he beseeches, "how can you give me such sweet desire and ask me to bind myself?" He sighs and tries to reason, "I can tie my hands. I can turn my eyes. I can walk the other way, but I cannot stop the burning. I cannot stop the desire. I cannot withhold myself." He pauses alone in the dark closet, whispers his sins, and opens the curtain. His long black robes billow behind him as he makes his way to where she will find him. In his hands, black beads click under his prayers as he waits.

Late in the night, her chores ended, Estella makes
the sign of the cross, kneels next to him, and closes her
eyes. Sitting in the pew, seeing only her back as she prays,
Johnny Von the Priest lets his eyes stray from the rosary in
his hands to her hair. A strand of hair, loose from the cap
she wears to cover her head while cleaning, consumes him.
This hair falls over her shoulders, wild and free, curling at
the skin of her neck. His eyes stop and rest here: the nape
of her neck, where he wants so badly to tilt his head, feel
her fragile collarbone on his cheek and rest his whole being.
Estella stretches her head ever so slowly from side to side,
exposing more skin. She rubs the tension at her shoulders.
Johnny Von the Priest shifts. He blushes and adjusts his
robes. He crosses his legs and looks back to his rosary.

Estella crosses herself again and sits back next to Johnny
Von the Priest. Moments of silence pass between them.
They have never been inappropriate. This is their routine.
Quiet. Then words, questions, laughter, all spaced in
between the stillness.

She notices the tremble in his fingers as he moves the
beads in his hands. "You feel so serious. What has your
thoughts this evening?"

"I am thinking about desire, Estella," Johnny Von the
Priest says without moving, without turning to her, which
is his usual way. With these words he holds his gaze to the
altar in front of them, the candles flickering.

Estella feels blood rush to her skin. She has not heard her name spoken in many years. She feels her heartbeat and her breath quicken. So many nights, alone in her bed, she imagined his voice saying her name. She does not move.

"Desire?" The word escapes past her lips. She tries to calm her breathing. He is too close to her not to notice the change, the increased rhythm of her chest.

"We know what the Church teaches about the sins of the flesh," he says sternly.

Estella worries he has somehow found out her secret. Somehow she has betrayed herself, and he knows the carnal thoughts she has played in her mind. She fears he is scolding her, that he will tell the nuns and they will lash her back until pain replaces lustful affection.

"But I cannot reconcile," he continues, "what I feel inside me, with what they would have me believe, what they would have me teach, have me be."

Estella, stunned, now fearing she is about to be sent away, banished from their meetings, says too quickly, "Are you asking me…"

Johnny Von the Priest interrupts her, his voice dominant and commanding. "I can not be an authentic man, the man of the cloth that I have vowed to be, with this conflict inside me."

Both still staring forward to the flickering lights, Estella's eyes well with tears. They sit. She whispers, "You are the only person left in the world who knows me, knows my name." She turns her head to him. "Please, don't ask me to leave?"

Johnny Von the Priest melts. He turns to Estella. He pets her cheek with the back of his hand. "No, Estella." He unbuttons the top of his black robe. "I can only be the man I am" -- he pulls off the white band at his collar -- "the man I want to be ..." in the silence, he puts the collar down on the wood. He kneels, but not to the altar.

Johnny Von the Priest kneels at Estella's lap, puts his hands timidly on her thighs. Slowly, he moves them up the stiff cloth bodice tightly cinched at her waist. He gently unties the cording at her chest and then forcefully pulls off the white cap. Her long curly hair falls to her shoulders. He pulls her into him and rests his head on the warm skin of her chest. Johnny Von the Priest in this moment forsakes any earthly vow that would hold him from the experience of her radiance. "I can only be the man I want to be, if I can be with you."

Relief rushes through Estella's body. With a force she cannot repress, she leans down and begins to unbutton him. Each button, of the never-ending line of buttons are more excruciating than the last in its delay of seeing his skin, feeling the warmth of his chest, finally knowing his embrace. Estella wraps her long legs around his back, tangled in the black fabric of his open robes.

Johnny Von the Priest picks her up, pulls her into him as he returns himself to the bench they are sharing. Leaning back on the hard wood of the pew he looks into her eyes and eternity stretches out; he takes hold of her body. Estella, completely gone to some unknown place, kisses Johnny Von the Priest. One, deeply wanted, whole-hearted, unabashed kiss and eternity is changed. There, in front of God and all things holy, in this kiss they reveal the only parts of each other still unknown. They lose themselves. Their bodies and hearts are lit afire with the power of this moment.

Why? This night could have been like any other night, they could have remained safe as they were; this was not the first time either Johnny Von the Priest or Estella had thought to say something, to do something. And for the most part, they had each other, in company, in mind and spirit. It came from outside of their free will, this moment. It came from a force bigger than the both of them, from God or the Universe, from their future selves that need this kiss to be the beginning.

In this moment, in this kiss, love finds its right place. Love begins its part in the evolution of this man and this woman. In this kiss, unlike any other, the universe changes nature and physics and time. The track of their souls, all that will ever unfold, alters here.

Johnny Von the Priest kisses Estella with such depth, with such perfect, fully conscious, all consuming love, that hundreds of candles throughout the church flicker wildly at the meeting of their lips, the wooden chandeliers begin to rattle overhead, the old wood creaks throughout, and the winds begin to blow a fury outside.

The large wooden doors of the church fly open and bang the stonewalls. The crash shatters the stained glass suffering Jesus on the right and Virgin Mary to the left. Any resistance still within them explodes into a million tiny pieces of pleasure and bursts to the surface of their skin. All the candles go dark. Leaves blow in and rustle through the air. Night is everywhere except the altar, still gold and gleaming.

In the silence, and the breathing now restoring itself, Estella looks to Johnny Von the Priest. Fear strikes her heart. How can she stay in the church? Her soul, already burdened with too much disguise, has no more room for secrets. She cannot hide this. "What will happen? Where will I go? Who am I now?"

Johnny Von the Priest looks to her, "Now you are always Estella. You are my Estella."

In saying it, now a floodgate of fear opens in him. He is suddenly the one lost, cut free and floating, unsure of his course. The Church, his only place, which has been slipping away, left his heart for good the moment he spoke her name into the air.

"I am Estella, I am yours," she says bold and sure, feeling her heart claimed, her name returned "And you are mine, then. By your side, I belong in the world again."

He feels her perfect lips under his fingertips. "I'll make us a way together." He says, feeling the confidence, the correctness of his words in her eyes. "We'll leave tonight."

Johnny Von the Priest stands. In the darkness he shuffles his robes back together. With great care and softness he laces up, loosely, Estella's bodice. He takes from her hands the white cloth hat that has hidden her hair from him for too long and throws it on the ground, next to the white collar he will never put back on. His purpose now clear in the light of her radiance, he reaches out for her hand, the two a dark silhouette in front of the shining altar. "Estella my love, let's go home." Johnny Von the Priest walks Estella out of the church and into the night.

Chapter 2

"The tree which moves some to tears
of joy, is in the Eyes of others only a
Green thing that stands in the way."
~ *William Blake*

I didn't see him that day in the house. He didn't get
home early, and I didn't dilly-dally in my work. By
8:00 p.m. I'm soaking my sore knees in a hot bath,
proud of how well I'd done in the bedroom of Johnny Von.
Thinking of how it didn't look like there was a woman
sharing that bedroom and entertaining thoughts about
how easily I could fit on the left side of that bed.

I soap up the rag in my hands and prop up my foot
on the spout of the tub. I have long legs myself; a bed

like that is really perfect because it's big enough for both someone like me and someone like him to sleep together comfortably. I take the razor and shave a strip up my leg, cutting a path in the soap.

The cabinet knobs on his bedside tables are little longhorns. How cute is that? I don't need to shave my legs, I just shaved them yesterday, but I continue anyway. Little longhorn handles, a playful touch to an otherwise masculine, guys' guy kind of room.

Thoughts of the Johnny Von house run delightfully through my head. Me and Johnny Von hanging out at the sink in his bathroom, brushing our teeth, talking about tomorrow. Me and Johnny Von, maybe he's in his white pajama bottoms at the counter, while I'm in his big tub having a bubble bath. We're chatting and he is flossing, or looking in the mirror at his hairline, or, oh, I don't know, trying to see some bump on his back, right below his shoulder blade, a little bug bite or a zit, maybe a little scratch.

"Baby, what's this?" I imagine him leaning over me in the tub to show me his back.

"What? Where? I don't see anything."

"Here." He sits on the side of the bathtub, his big ol' back facing me, and reaches around his body, smoothes his index finger over a tiny red bump.

"It looks like a little bite, maybe a little spider or a mosquito or something. Look in my bag," I'd say. "I've got some hydrocortisone anti-itch stuff. It's in a clear tube."

I imagine Johnny Von reaching across his bathroom and rustling through my make-up bag.

"This?"

"Yeah. That's the one. Give it to me and I'll put some cream on it."

He sits down again and hands me the lotion over his shoulder.

"There." I dab the spot and put the cap back on. I give a sweet little kiss to the middle of his back.

"Thanks, baby," he says, taking the tube from me, going back to the mirror and throwing the cream into my bag.

Man! I really want to meet Johnny Von.

I finish shaving and let the water out of my bath. I rinse and stand with a tinge of disappointment that today was not the day. But there is still good news, the Johnny Von Contractor asked me to come back.

The garage was full of small packing boxes filled with the contents of the study that had to be hauled upstairs and put back on the shelves. The finish on the cabinets needed a couple of days to set, so he says, "Can you come back and help on Friday?"

And I say, after thinking about it for the appropriate amount of time, so as not to seem eager, "I have to walk the dogs until about 11:00." I say this, knowing full well that I would call in sick in a heartbeat, to everyone of my clients, should my real work impede my working in the house of Johnny Von.

He says, "About 11:30 then?"

"Sure," I say. "I'll see you Friday."

"Oh my God, you're so cute." This is Shelby Braxton's first response when I tell her the whole story about working in the house of Johnny Von. She pauses, smiling at me for a moment, and then says, "So what do you think, are you going to hook up with him? I think you should knock on his door and tell him you want to walk his 'big dog.' Tell him you want to put a collar on him." She laughs. "Tell Mr. Von you need to get your groove back."

I'm a bit thrown by Shelby's sudden burst of innuendos. It's not like her. Yes, she holds my love life up to more scrutiny than I'd like at times. She asks me more than she needs to if I'm *okay* with not having a boyfriend since I moved to L.A. And she does keep asking me if I *think* I should get out more. But I always write it off as her way of being supportive. And she's funny. Shelby can keep everyone laughing.

If Mandy Kane is the North Pole, Shelby Braxton is the South Pole.

Shelby Braxton reads *The Wall Street Journal* everyday. She's in therapy three times a week, for goodness's sake. She's nothing if not all about consideration and support. When I had my wisdom teeth pulled, Shelby was there with strawberry protein shakes, a stack of my favorite DVDs and ice-packs. She did my laundry for two weeks and changed my sheets while I napped on the sofa. Shelby Braxton is the person you call when your car gets towed, or you have to have your eyes dilated at LensCrafters and you need someone to drive you home.

"I can see it now." Her tone begins to change. "You and Johnny Von, the talk of Hollywood." It begins to feel unpleasant. "I'll have to fight off the paparazzi in front of the building." Suddenly, it doesn't strike me as funny. "Oh, dear! Maybe you should just use him for sex and toss him. You better pack condoms in, like, your work over-alls next time you're there. Just in case, right. He's a player, you know."

I've never seen this side of her.

"Maybe you'll have to sleep your way up to him. Start like with the yard crew, move up to the painters, maybe the contractor." Her tone, still trying to be funny banter, no longer feels funny or supportive. Actually, it feels angry.

"And listen," she says, her voice now spilling over with mocking, "if you need back up with him, a little two on one action, you can call me."

Of everyone I know, I always think of Shelby as the person least affected by the celebrity swirl. She came to L.A. eight years ago after graduating from Brown to work for a bank downtown. She and her husband of eight years, Larry Anderson, a tax attorney, live in a big two-bedroom apartment across the hall from me. I've known them since the day I moved in. Their place is straight from the pages of the Pottery Barn catalog. And just like the people in the Pottery Barn catalog, they're always having wine parties.

What can I say? I had to tell someone. We were visiting Wednesday night, Larry's karate class night, like we do all the time, and I thought she was the safest person to tell. I wanted reassurance. I wanted someone to cheer me on, validate the possibility that even though Johnny Von might be a long shot, he was still a viable reality. As I watch the charade of teasing, listen to one unfunny demeaning remark after another pour out of her, moving me more and more away from my confidence, I realize I was wrong.

"You have my cell, right? I'll keep it on Friday. Call me when it goes down and we can double-team him."

Shelby takes a sip of wine and surfaces from her rant.

"I'm so just joking with you!" She must see the horrified look on my face. "You know I'm joking." She laughs a social laugh as she squeezes my arm.

I laugh along, because I'm Southern and I'm trained to be nice to people and to never make anyone uncomfortable, no matter what, but I'm inwardly appalled. Inwardly, I'm aghast. My feelings are hurt. And even more, I don't like the way she is talking about Johnny Von. Sure, I don't know Johnny Von any more than she does, but somehow now I feel protective.

Shelby tries to clear the awkward cloud between us. "No, really, I think it's great that you have a crush on someone. It's been a really long time for you. And look, just remember you're a pretty girl." She says it like she's my coach in the Special Olympics.

Shelby has never been without a boyfriend or a career track since she was 17. Since I've had neither since we've known each other, I don't make sense to her. I know this. But I've always thought of it as a kind of light observation between us. What's going down right now is not light.

"Josh still asks me about you. He thought you were really cute. You should go out with him?"

Josh is a tax attorney; older, divorced, three teenage kids, balding. He corrects people's grammar at the wine parties and argues about the origins of certain cheeses long after he should have let it go.

"He's so secure." This is Shelby's tag-line for Josh. It's how she tried to sell him to me in the first place. "And he's such a smart guy. And even more, he likes you." That last bit, again, said with a sort of beggars-can't-be-choosers idea behind it.

"He's secure." She says it again. I think it's how she sold herself on Larry, because I've yet to see the spark that binds them otherwise.

Maybe it's just the sting of the present conversation, but it strikes me that all this time, Shelby just wants me to be with someone, anyone — anyone equal or below Larry in stature. It is as if this idea of my entertaining thoughts of being with Johnny Von has sent her over the edge. Supportive Shelby has cracked open and she wants to scream, "Who cares about you or what you want! If I have to settle, then you have to settle. You don't just get what you want! I don't get a guy like that, you surely don't get a guy like that. Reality check." which all feels a bit extreme, given the fact that I have not even met Johnny Von yet.

And look, to be fair, I admit there are times when I see the logic of her reasoning, when I really just want a partner. When I see Larry cooking dinner because she's tired, or when I drag myself to take out the trash, because if I don't nobody else will, I feel almost envious. Sure, I want someone to surprise me with trips to the tropics. I want to know that I'll have a date on Valentine's Day. Or even just to have someone other than Moochie expecting me home would be nice. But then again, I'm not that envious.

I could never be with someone to ease life's logistics, someone to insure that I am not alone on public holidays; I can't be with someone just because it's time to be with someone.

That way of thinking and the Shelby Braxtons of the world are not new to me. I come from a whole race of Shelby Braxtons. In fact, in a roundabout way, they're the reason I'm here.

I moved to L.A. from London, post-break up, post-work dissatisfaction, post-my 29th birthday. I could tell you I came for the good weather, I came for the beach and because my brother lived in Glendale. That would all be true. I could say I came because I was free like the wind and could go anywhere I wanted to go. But really, I came because I wasn't going back to the bayou and I couldn't decide where else to go. I left the backwoods of Devil's Swamp, Louisiana running.

Of course it wasn't called Devil's Swamp on the sign at the entry of our neighborhood. When they drained it and subdivided it, it was renamed Acadia Woods. But there are still maps that call it by its real name, even though the swamp and the surrounding sugarcane fields are long gone.

I was in the second grade when we moved. I can remember my father with his jet-black hair and broad shoulders, a young engineer, proudly cutting down the trees with the workmen to clear the lot for our house. I can remember my mother tying ribbons around the trees they were hoping to save. I remember them walking through the house when it was being framed, saying, "Your room will be here, the kitchen will be here, and the laundry room is here. And come see, a cabinet will be here where you can put your books after school."

I remember them happy and young and filled with the future, their dreams fresh.

The neighborhood was nice. And the trees were big and beautiful, it's true. The snakes, however, were a problem. The size of the rattlesnakes in the newly-carved neighborhood was prehistoric. In those first years, before the neighborhood filled in, the rattlesnakes would move out when they cut the adjacent sugarcane fields.

I remember the men in the neighborhood coming to kill a big snake in front of our house, the crowd of neighbors all gathered out front. And although I am southern, and therefore tend toward exaggeration by birthright, this is factual: the snake stretched from one side of the road to the other. I know it has not grown bigger in my mind over time because my brother also remembers the snake that stretched from one side of the road to the other. The one that was so thick around no kid in the neighborhood could have put his hands around it.

The men killed it with machetes.

This I did not see. Or if I did, I've blocked it out of my memory. They chopped it clean through in two places. I know this because I remember the three pieces.

Do you know the kind of nightmares that ensue when you're in the second grade and you see a giant snake, chopped in pieces, still writhing out in front of your house? Come on! Don't tell me it didn't scare the hell out of everyone, grown-ups and kids alike. It's not like we were The Wilderness Family. My dad didn't even hunt. He worked in an office and my mom taught kindergarten. We didn't even go camping. It was the Seventies and this was supposed to be something like the beginning of suburbia.

Oh, the horrible, scary snakes! I could tell you more. But in the end, it wasn't the snakes that sent me running.

The snakes died out in a few years as more people moved in. The snakes I remember with more fascination, tinged with horror. They make a good story. No, I left because of something scarier.

I left running because at the end, the same house where my parents dreamed a bright future and imagined a cabinet where I could throw my books after school, was now dark with the anger and sadness of their divorce. I left running because half my girl friends saw high school graduation as the end of the good times in life and promptly looked around for the best guy to marry. I left running because although I'd escaped the first round of marriage-as-the-only-thing-to-do, I was in a sorority at L.S.U., where your value is determined by the fraternity of your boyfriend. And where being pretty and skinny is more important than all else — more important than school, or what you want to do, or being happy. Where buying things, the right Coach handbag, the right BMW convertible, the right clothes at the mall, is the only way the world would rank you. If you did it right, you'd marry that frat boyfriend. Your husband would be good-looking; a lawyer, doctor or accountant. You could also be a lawyer, doctor or accountant — but on the side, because that way your income was doubled and you'd have something to fall back on if you divorced. But mostly, you'd decorate his office, shop for antiques and join the junior league. He'd wear khakis and boxers. You'd cheer for the Tigers each football season and the liquor cabinet would always be full. He would introduce the two of you, forevermore, like this: "Billy Jacobs, I was a Kappa Sig. My wife was Tri-Delt."

If that is not scarier than prehistoric-sized rattlesnakes, I don't know what is! It was obvious from the beginning: I was different, and different was not good.

So in college, when the psychiatrist I was seeing three days a week kept wanting to review this "fear of snakes," not buying that it was indeed a true fear of the actual reptile given my growing-up atmosphere, when he was sure that he'd uncovered the Freudian reason for my single-hood and thus all my woes, when he kept saying, "Do you think there is something here you need to look at?" I decided it was time to leave this place. That's when I met the International Playboy.

"Brie?" Shelby gets up from the couch. "I've got Gouda in the fridge as well."

She walks into the kitchen to get a plate of cheese and crackers. I leaf through the stack of *Vanity Fair* magazines on the coffee table and think about the International Playboy. I put him next to Johnny Von in my mind as I flip through the glossy pages of fashion and celebrity reports. They may both be rich, good-looking and jet-set, but from what I've seen so far, Johnny Von seems nothing like the International Playboy.

I have a theory about first impressions. For me, at least, there is a kind of burst of information that runs through my brain in the initial moment of meeting someone, something I can't articulate. It's just an immediate feeling when you look in someone's eyes, and the closest I can come in words is "yes or no." Only I don't really know the question the "yes or no" is answering. It only lasts for a few seconds and then the curtains draw closed, and I can't get back to that pure idea of someone. After those first few seconds, it's unclear. Then it's all about hormones or image or what I should think about the other person, then the personalities and insecurities swoop in and take the relationship wherever it's going to go. I realize that this theory might sound odd, and that someone like Shelby Braxton would not understand it at all. But it's not odd, it's just a kind of intuition that strikes and stays with you only if you pay close attention to the moment of it. It's simple, like a feeling when you meet a new co-worker or neighbor for the first time and you know you're going to get along with them. It's just something about them, something in their eyes.

My first impulse of Johnny Von across the distance was yes, a very strong yes. I can't tell you my true first impression of the International Playboy. It happened before I had a theory. It happened before I was paying attention.

The Spring Charity Benefit at the home of Mimi Laflore is a New Orleans tradition. And for as long as anyone can remember, the Kappa Kappa Delta girls have dressed as French maids and tended bar at the event. That is why I'm here with a ridiculously big, black bow in my hair and net stockings with black high heels that make my legs look freakishly long. It's something I would never do of my own accord. Supposedly, the costumes are "fun" and give an air of Mardi Gras for all of the out of town guests.

"Sisters," Mimi Laflore corrals us into the entryway, "I'm so happy you're here." She lines us up in front of the grand staircase to inspect the costumes.

Mimi Leflore was a Kappa Kappa Delta at L.S.U., many, many, many years before I, as was her daughter and someday her daughter's daughter. She is old, in time and in money. Her home on St.Charles Avenue has been in her family for four generations and she has the antiques to prove it. It is a beautiful monster of a house with endless balcony's that stretch around the entire three stories.

The Leflore fortune goes back to cotton and cane at the turn of the century; modern day revenue flows from oil and politics. Of course this is never discussed. It is just one of those things that is known.

Mimi, as she tells us in her opening address, is a giver, a philanthropist. She invites the Kappa Kappa Delta girls to serve cocktails here every year so the out-skirt society girls, girls like me, can be introduced "into the fold." A chance to meet and greet, a chance to network and make connections with the right kind of people.

"Girls," Mimi's voice is raspy from years of cigarettes and

charity events, "I know you will conduct yourselves as the smart beautiful women you are this evening." She paces in front of us like a drill sergeant with a cigarette in one hand and a drink in the other. "That you will keep in mind the idea of public and private." As she passes me and sips her drink, I'm overcome with the smell of hairspray, make-up, orange juice and vodka. "No one is telling you what to do, or what not to do, just remember the difference between appropriate public displays of affection, and gestures best kept behind closed doors." She primps her short, very blond hairdo, which moves as one unit when she touches it. "Have a good time, and I trust you will govern yourselves accordingly with my guests." She smiles and winks.

I begin to wonder what exactly is going to happen here tonight.

Mimi Laflore then waves her arms in the air and everyone is given a tray and directed to the various bars set up around the house.

As the guests arrive, one wealthy older man in a tuxedo holding a cigar and a highball after another, I begin to get the impact of the earlier speech. I see that Mimi is indeed a giver—providing all these pretty young things for all the men of society to "socialize" with. It hits me, as one such well-connected man with a lusty look in his eye calls me over for a drink while he still has a full one in hand, that I'm in Sugar-Daddy central wearing a French maid's outfit.

I head to the back of the bar and stand between the wall and a large ficus plant. I'm only two hours in, the bus to the hotel won't be here until 1:30 a.m. and I certainly can't hide in the bathroom for the next five hours. I wonder how long the plant will hide me before one of my tipsy sorority sisters finds me and pulls me out to join the fun.

"You must be bored off your tits here." I hear a deep voice with an English accent. I peek through the green leaves and see a red swizzle stick dancing between very young, attractive lips. I make out broad shoulders.

He reaches in and separates the branches. "Do you want to join me for a cigarette outside?"

He is a tall, dirty-blond, ex-rugby player with blue eyes and a wicked smile. He's independently wealthy at 25, due to several very good investments in property and the market. This is what I learn as we stand on the side of the house smoking cigarettes like kids. He also drives Formula One race cars as a hobby. Of course I think he is probably lying about all of it, but I don't care. He's attractive and I have someone to talk to away from the Sugar-Daddy Fest inside.

Apparently, this year he donated a very large sum of money to a children's charity that Mimi Leflore chairs. That is why he is here. He was flown in and treated to a week in New Orleans, Leflore style. He does not know Mimi Laflore, nor has he ever met anyone like Mimi Laflore, which makes him completely irreverent to the whole social order of things. This quality makes him most attractive to me. There is a kind of recognition between us, an instant familiarity. We are two fish out of water.

We decide to make the best of our situation. We resolve

to go inside and make fun of as many people as we can. We vow to stick together and talk to everyone.

For some unknown reason, of all the French maids at the Spring Charity Benefit, the International Playboy, who is now the life of the party, who Mimi refers to as, "that rascal," who has every sorority girl buzzing with interest, shines a light only on me. And maybe because I think I'll never see him again, or that he is of no consequence to me in the bigger picture of things, or that the whole thing is just too ridiculous to be real, I take the spotlight he's giving and I flirt with abandon, I radiate — without a trace of shyness. It was a fluke.

By the end of the evening, the International Playboy is singing show tunes with Mimi, who's donned a feather boa and sprawled her little old lady self across the top of the black baby grand piano, while I commandeer the dance floor with Lloyd Northrup.

Lloyd, who I learn is a lawyer from downtown in his late 40s, keeps his drink in his hand while we dance. Mimi breaks into "New York, New York," a tune familiar to the International Playboy. Lloyd tells me more than once, as I high kick to "New York, New York," that he has a suite at the Fairmont. At the close of the song, I call this information out to the International Playboy.

"Lloyd Northrup has invited everyone to the Fairmont for the real party in his room," he announces to the scruffy and liquored-up crowd still on the dance floor. The entire party decides the suite at the Fairmont is a great place to continue the fun, and files out the front. The International Playboy grabs me. We ditch the crowd, head to the corner and wave down a cab. We walk and talk and laugh. We listen to live jazz in all the late night bars of the French Quarter and make out through the streets until dawn. He then walks me back to my hotel, sees me safely to my room and makes me promise to send the pictures.

It was one of the best nights I've ever had. I thought I'd never see him again. A flurry of postcards, faxes, phone calls followed. And then I thought, "Finally, my ship has come in!"

Within months, I had my bags packed and a one-way ticket to London in hand. And that's how we started.

"So what do you think …?" Afraid she's shown too much of herself, Shelby Braxton clicks back into support mode.

"Think?" I say curiously, but I know where she's going. It's time for therapy.

"About liking Johnny Von?" Her voice is sensitive, almost gentle.

"What do you mean?" I take a sip of my wine. Shelby as therapist drives me crazy. I shuffle through the stack of CDs on her coffee table.

It always starts with a leading question, "What do you think you learned from that? …Why do you think that happened? ...How did that make you feel ... ?" All said with that tone — that tone that is overflowing with the fact that she has an absolute opinion on the answer, but in her wisdom she wants me to search for it first. She doesn't listen to my response, she waits through it. And then, regardless of what I say, she gives the opinion she had in the first place. All with a put-upon air of self-discovery.

Today's leading question is, (reminiscent of the snake obsessed therapist of my youth) "Do you think there is something here you need to look at?"

Annoyed by her earlier rant, I decide not to play therapy today, and say matter-of-factly, "No. No, I don't."

Shelby smiles and rolls her eyes a bit. But she can't help herself, she has to say it. "You don't think you like him because he's just a bit unavailable to you?"

We both sip the white wine.

I shrug and smile.

I think about storming out and never talking to Shelby Braxton again. But she's my most solid friend in L.A.; besides, she lives across the hall and keeps my spare keys. I don't want to make a rash decision. I don't want to pass her in the hall every day from now on and think, *we used to be good friends until that time I liked Johnny Von and she thought I wasn't good enough for him.* It didn't feel right, especially at this point.

"I had my first poetry class on Saturday." I offer an olive branch.

"Oh my God, you're so cute. I forgot you were doing that. That so great, how you can just do that kind of thing, take a class for no reason, and you don't have to worry about work. God, I love how your life is so simple."

The subject is successfully diverted, even with the condescending tone it's better than therapy. I make a mental note: Don't talk to Shelby Braxton about Johnny Von.

Poetry class was the second different thing that happened, after that first day when the hawk did what hawks normally don't do. Realizing it was a William Blake poem on the back of the LuBeLu's Steel Cut Oatmeal can that had popped into my head on that first day when I saw Johnny Von, I went to Borders Bookstore and purchased every book I could find on William Blake. It was all confusing and dry and it didn't mean anything to me, so I looked for a class. I flipped through the UCLA extension catalog: Saturdays, 10:00 a.m. -- Introduction to Poetry. The teacher's bio read: "Andrew Banks has taught poetry for the last 25 years. His thesis and focus are the work of William Blake." I took it as a sign and called immediately.

I should tell you why it seemed important, some key to all of this. You see, I know something about William Blake. I know about him not just from the LuBeLu's

Steel Cut Oatmeal can, although I hadn't put it together until I walked into class and read the poem Andrew Banks handed us at the doorway. That's when I remembered it.

William Blake was married in a little church in Battersea on the Thames River. He had a love. And from the penthouse home of the International Playboy in Chelsea Harbor, you can see this church perfectly across the river.

Saint Mary's Church stands out like a little island of the past. For well over 1,000 years people have stopped there to talk to God; to ask him things, to mark big events, good and bad, in their lives — that one little spot of earth. It's not a fancy church. You won't go there on a tour, what with Westminster and Big Ben to see while you're visiting London. It's just small. From across the river, it looks as if someone plucked it from a miniature train set and placed it just so on the edge of the Thames. At night the steeple lights up and glows, a tiny flicker on the water with London sharp and bright, all grown up around it.

On my own, I made the trip over the Wandsworth Bridge more than once to find out about Saint Mary's and take the very short tour. This church, the image of it at night, I remember with more detail than the fine furniture and silk drapes in the penthouse surrounding me. More than the yachts docking at the harbor in from the south of France, more than Michael Caine's trendy, ultra-interior-designed restaurant where people eat on special occasions; where we ate, simply out of convenience, like it was our own private kitchen. Many nights on my own, while the

International Playboy traveled and traveled, as international playboys do, I gazed out across the water to St. Mary's Church, dreamy and hopeful. Imagined it, as I shouldn't have, filled with white flowers, smelling of jasmine and roses on a crisp spring day. Imagined myself, as I shouldn't have, walking down the aisle to the International Playboy, his eyes happy and eager for me to be beside him.

But that's the thing about international playboys: by definition they don't usually marry, at least not while they're young. And mine was young. Maybe I was being naïve, or I didn't want to see it, or I thought I'd be the exception; that I could love him until he was ready. I guess, going into it, I just didn't get the whole international playboy-ness of it all.

There was a time when I loved St. Mary's Church, loved to imagine it. And then there came a time when the sight of it pained me. When every time it crossed my mind, my heart hurt. Same place, same pictures in my head, very different feeling in my heart.

So, when I entered the poetry class, and read this William Blake poem on the cover sheet, waiting for everyone to file into class, I knew something was up. The dynamic of feelings Blake was talking about splashed me cold in the face as images of St. Mary's Church rushed back to me. Not because it was about a chapel, and not that I can really articulate it well, but something about loving with a reverence or a sweetness someone or something or somewhere, and then having the same place turn dark and painful, having some outside force binding you. I know that feeling. This was the poem:

The Garden of Love

I went to the Garden of Love
And saw what I never had seen:
A Chapel was built in the midst,
Where I used to play on the green

And the gates of the Chapel were shut,
And "Thou shalt not" writ over the door;
So I turn'd to the Garden of Love
That so many sweet flowers bore;

And saw it filled with graves,
And tomb-stones where flowers should be;
And Priest in black gowns were walking their rounds,
And binding with briars my joys and desires.

On a sunny Friday at 11:30 a.m., I now find myself walking up to the house of Johnny Von a second time. This is round two. I'll tell you again what I decided to wear. I'm wearing my everyday dog-walking t-shirt. It's navy blue with the logo of my service, The Woof Woof Walking Club, in bright yellow. While it is less of an overt statement than "Bootylicious," I wore it because this is what I wear everyday on the street and I thought it might work toward future recognition. Branding is a science, you know.

The subconscious and the primal self are always working; looking for patterns, identifying one's place in the discernable world. That's science, provable facts. It's something I've been thinking about a lot lately while walking dogs on Valley Glen Drive, thinking about my poetry class and wondering about Johnny Von. Things like images, the experience of recognition and the forces inside you that seem to be leading you places. How poetry uses images, words, names, and sometimes you understand it even though you don't know why. How much of what we do comes from the primal, the subconscious leading the way. How much about love is about recognition, from the superficial surface to the soul? Is it all about sifting through the sands of men until the recognition hits me? And do I have the patience and what it takes to trust that part of me? I've thought intensely about these ideas ... and about what I should wear.

I went with nondescript khaki shorts. I decided they were bland enough not to scream "look at me" but short enough to again put across, "nice legs." The strategy was this: you've seen me borderline racy, and now I'm everyday play clothes. Which says, I'm hoping, "Hi, I'm versatile. I'm flexible. I'm more than just one thing." Since I didn't see Johnny Von the last time I was here, I'm not sure to whom I'm saying this. But what you wear is really about your attitude and setting a tone with yourself anyway.

The Johnny Von Contractor meets me at the garage. On one side of the garage is a large stack of boxes. On the other side of the garage is a black Trans Am.

Johnny Von drives a Trans Am.

I find this exciting. I've seen him in it on the street. And I don't care who sold me what brand image about it, or what it reminds me of from my past or why I like it, but I like it. I'm not a car girl. I don't know what year or what engine it is. It's not a vintage Trans Am. It doesn't have the T-top or the flaming phoenix on the hood like Burt Reynolds in *Smokey and the Bandit*. What I do know is that it's not a tinted-windows black Mercedes or Jaguar, like most of the Hollywood newly rich who suddenly need to be incognito. It's not a Toyota Prius, to show the world he's politically correct, except for the jet fuel when flying privately. No, it's not a look-at-me/don't-stare-at-me Hummer, or an I'm-cool-and-street Cadillac Escalade. It's not even an expensive, trendy classic car. Nope. Johnny Von drives a Pontiac Trans Am.

Look, I just know this, when I'm walking on the street and he gets in the car and revs the engine, I can feel it rumble from the top of Valley Glen Drive. And if I have my iPod on and he comes up the street behind me, I can feel the thunder of the engine before I see it or hear it. It's hot. And like I said, I'm not a car person. I don't know, maybe we are back talking about primal things — girls and fast cars.

The Johnny Von Contractor explains that I need to unpack all the boxes, sort through the books and CDs and get everything looking nice and organized. Today I'll be in the study. He introduces me to a few people: the Johnny

Von Assistant, whom I've already met on the street, the other guys on the crew today, and Johnny Von's sister, who is organizing the work on the house. They are all warm and friendly people. And I'm not just saying that to be nice or because they are real people and it might get back to them. I want to paint a picture for you and I am sincere when I say, everyone is normal and nice. I don't know if Johnny Von is in the house, and no one is saying anything to indicate one way or the other.

The Johnny Von Contractor leaves.

The cast of Johnny Von people mill in and out of the room, but mostly, it's just me in the study, deciding if I should break the CDs into genres and then put them into alphabetical order, or put the whole collection into alphabetical order.

I wonder what Johnny Von wants. Should they go on the middle shelf for easy access, or just the ones that are most used go in the middle, and the others are on the bottom shelf? But then how would I know what is everyday music and what is every now and then music?

I start pulling out the CDs.

Eminem? What's this doing here? I'm sure Johnny Von doesn't listen to Eminem. Wait. Okay, the label's not broken. Must have been a gift or something. I'll put it on the bottom shelf.

Country music.

I vote a resounding "Yes." I love country music! The older the better. He's got a lot of great stuff. I imagined he'd also have some classic rock, maybe some current stuff, maybe some Counting Crows from the 90s, possibly some hard rock. All of that's here.

Sarah MacLachlan? That's surprising. Maybe Johnny Von unwinds to a little Sarah MacLachlan in the background?

The first box is now empty and the CDs are stacked in front of me. I have to decide how to arrange them. By genre, then alphabetically seems most right. I'll put them on the side shelves, but in the middle. I begin to wonder if this will seem overly enthusiastic. I'm thinking a normal worker would just unpack them and stack them neatly on the shelf. I want to seem like a normal worker, but I also want to do a noticeably good job. I start to feel pressure building. Ultimately, I just want to be myself.

That's what people always say, isn't it? To people like me, who tend toward shyness. "Just be yourself."

Thanks.

What a revelation.

At this moment, if I could stop the soon-to-burst flood of self-monitoring thoughts, if I could find any touchstone whatsoever to the real me, don't you think I would grab it like a branch before the edge of Niagara Falls? I need more than "Just be yourself" at times like this. It's a circular thought and I end up in the same place, except now I have the added heavy feeling that you're trying to help and I can't even take the good advice. And why can't I just be myself …

"HEY!"

Johnny Von calls out to his assistant.

Johnny Von is in the house!

I hear him move downstairs at the bottom of the steps, and then out in the hall. Johnny Von is in the next room over. The Johnny Von Assistant calls back. She is working in and out of the office, coming and going, and he is calling out to her talking about this and that. He wants to know if the last three pages from his agent's office have come in over the fax.

I'm shocked at how steady I am inside at this realization. Happy and excited, but steady. I figure it can only lead to a natural "bump into" and possible chat. I think, "How great is this? A perfectly natural way to talk to him has just fallen in my lap." So I proceed with the task at hand. I'm happily sorting CDs. I opt for "by genre" but not in any order, other than putting all the different albums by the same artists together.

Time passes.

I begin to notice everyone is a little more uptight today. The Johnny Von Contractor, the other guys, the Johnny Von Assistant working in the office, I don't know, maybe it's me. Or maybe the paint isn't drying right or there is something up that I have no idea of. Regardless, it starts to cook inside me. I start thinking maybe it is me. I'm out of place here.

A couple of hours go by. I don't see or bump into

Johnny Von. I only hear him. He never comes into the office.

"Should I take these out to the pool house?" I start to volunteer myself for tasks that would take me through the house, cover more area.

"No. I'll do it," the Johnny Von Contractor says flatly.

"Do you want this taken down to the trash?" I say a few minutes later.

"That's okay. Give it to Bill, he can take it."

By now, I'm still mostly steady inside. But I do start to have this little thought that maybe the Johnny Von Contractor does not want me to bump into Johnny Von.

Hmm. I begin to think I'm getting a vibe from the Johnny Von Contractor that Johnny Von is not to be bothered by me.

And then, although I've not hit full-blown neurotic yet, I start to think, what if Johnny Von actually said to him, "That girl freaks me out. She stares at me on the street, and I don't really want her in my house." And what if the Johnny Von Contractor asked me here because he likes me, thinking Johnny Von wouldn't be here, and now he has to hide me in the study! The pressure inside me leaps to full blown internal stress, the likes of which I haven't felt since high school.

"That's ridiculous!" I try to talk myself back from the ledge. "Why wouldn't Johnny Von like me? What have I done to make him not like me? I haven't done anything wrong here. I haven't done anything out of place. I'm not some kind of monster!"

"I mean, I'm nice and genuine, I know I am, and I'm pleasant enough to look at. For goodness sake, I just like him because I like his work. I think he is funny and I'm attracted to him. That's perfectly normal! Besides, all the people around his house have been nice to me."

My internal pep talk is failing.

I begin to feel myself start to spin out of control. I have visions of Catholic schoolgirls with straight blond hair, leaning over me in plaid skirts and white shirts, a modern day Greek chorus, haunting me from behind. "Why is she here ... Who asked that girl ..." they smirk in unison. "Doesn't she know he doesn't like her ... Didn't she see Shelby's face when she told her ... Take a hint ... I'm so embarrassed for her." They begin to chant, "He's so out of her league."

Before it all gets too out of hand, before I have to excuse myself for a little cry in the bathroom, I have this thought: "Maybe it's just the Johnny Von Contractor."

I straighten up a little.

"Maybe it's his whole weird thing. Maybe Johnny Von hasn't decided that I am a freak after all, and this is just a twisted vibe thrown at me by the weird Johnny Von Contractor guy."

The next thought to hit me is this: "Hey! Fuck the Johnny Von Contractor. And anybody else that has something to say about it! That's not nice." My despair switches to the life-giving energy of anger. "Making me feel like I'm the second servant in the house, that I shouldn't pester the Lord of the Manor!"

I square off my shoulders.

"What a jackass! I'm not going to let somebody make me feel like I'm below anybody. Who do these people think they are!"

1901

Johnny Von the Boss Man

"We work a hard day, Ma'am." Johnny Von the Boss Man stands in the entry foyer of Hollyway Plantation.

The morning air is turning from cool to hot as noon approaches. The fans turn slowly, high overhead. Estella sits at her father's large desk, swallowed behind the dark oak wood. In the open windows that stretch from the 14-foot ceilings to the wooden plank floor, sheer panels of curtains move, just barely, with the slight breeze.

"My men are skilled." He holds his hat in his hands. Bought new two seasons ago, it's filthy now. Smudged with grime from the earth, from laboring in the fields as the Boss Man of this gang of migrant workers. His hands are worn and calloused. His fingernails are rounded and dirty. They look rough and sore as he moves them back and forth gently at the brim of his hat.

"It's not my custom to hire a crew I don't know." Estella,

her pale skin brushed with only a dab of rouge powder, is too young to be running this plantation.

She was born here. Hollyway has been in her family for four generations. It has known hard times like any plantation, but never like this. Last season, she lost her mother, father and younger brother to the cough. She nursed them all with diligence, care and the help of the staff, but she lost everyone in just a few months. She lost everyone. Last year this house was full of life, bustling with rosy cheeks, health and prosperity. In just one turn of the leaves, she has been left abruptly alone. The whole plantation is on her shoulders. Wearing a delicate black dress, her hair braided and twisted into a neat bun at the nape of her neck, she is a girl forced to become a woman before her time.

"I understand that, Ma'am, but let me assure you, I am in control of my men." Johnny Von the Boss Man does not cast his eyes down, does not dip his head like the others. He looks at her straight and tall.

Isolated here on the plantation with only her small staff, she knows she needs Johnny Von the Boss Man, but she also knows she has to present a strong resolve. She is just a girl; he and his men could, if they decided, completely overtake her land. She knows she can't show any signs of weakness, of fear, of need.

"Do you have men of a criminal past with you, sir?" She tries to ask the question as if she knows how to hire a crew, as if she has asked this question a hundred times.

He smiles, but not condescendingly. "Yes, Ma'am.
Some of the men have worked the chain gangs, but I'll
vouch for them. You won't have any trouble with us.
We'll set up in the bunk house and bring in the harvest on
time, for price."

"I pay wage and I don't cook." Estella puts a sternness in
her voice, bracing for the bartering she has seen between
her father and the bosses in the past. Instead she receives
the opposite.

"That'll be just fine, Ma'am. We'll move in today and
start the fields tomorrow."

Unsure of what to do next, Estella adds, "I have suitors."

"Ma'am?"

"I have many suitors. That is to say, there are many men
that come to call here at Hollyway."

As soon as this comes out of Estella's mouth, she realizes
the awkwardness. In her mind she thought a statement
of this kind would put the idea in his head that she is
not alone, not vulnerable. Instead it makes her terribly
uncomfortable. Not just because she is lying, but because
Johnny Von the Boss Man has no response. He only
stands there, staring at her, as if he does not know the
answer to a question she is asking him.

"I'm sure to be married to someone prominent very
soon." She cannot stop what is stumbling out of her.

"Of course, Ma'am." Johnny Von the Boss Man stands
still in front of Estella, unsure of what to do next.

"I don't allow drinking on Sundays!" Estella remarks with sharpness, trying to regain her composure. "And if you are going to work for me, call me Miss Estella. That is what the staff calls me. That would be fine. Miss Estella. That would be appropriate."

Johnny Von the Boss Man nods in agreement and puts his hat back on his head. "I'll go move the boys into the bunkhouse then," he smiles, "Miss Estella."

Johnny Von the Boss Man runs his crew with equal care and strictness. Alone at night, the doors of her balcony open to relieve the unbearable heat, she has heard them down at the bunkhouse laughing, drinking and kicking it up. She has also heard him severe. She knows he ran off Luke, one of the workers who certainly had a criminal past. And in her heart she was happy about it. She didn't like the way Luke stared at her. She didn't like the way his eyes felt on her.

She heard the fight that night, the yelling. She was told the next day by the staff how Luke exploded at Johnny Von the Boss Man, rushed him with a machete. Unflinching, Johnny Von the Boss Man took him down with one blow.

"Had the boys take him to the river and put him on the ferry one way," Martha told her with great excitement as she came into her bedroom that morning to open the drapes. Martha is older than Estella. She's laid down with men before. The staff was prone to gossip even before her parents passed, so Estella knew. But since Estella's become the only one running the house, Martha is much more indiscreet with her ways and her language. She talks a lot more about men, about who she would be with and who she wouldn't be with, if given the opportunity. "He stitched the cut on his arm himself, without a wince, as if he was darning a sock," she says with a tone in her voice that makes Estella uncomfortable.

The thought of Johnny Von the Boss Man in a violent brawl with one of the workers and then tending to the wound that protecting her house had inflicted, causes a rush of emotion in Estella. Something new to her. He is not like other bosses she's been around in the past.

Wanting to separate herself from Martha, not wanting to hear the way she would talk about him, she grabs her mother's pale blue shawl, which she keeps with her at night, and wraps it around her shoulders as she steps out to the veranda. She sees him in the field in the morning light, directing the workers. He is forceful and strong with the men, like the other bosses. But as she continues to watch him across the distance, she sees him whistle to one of the new pups playing on the side of the dirt rows. He seems gentle. He has a way about him that suggests a kindness. But Estella is all alone, here on the land, in the house that she may lose, the only one left after four generations, and she is unsure. Unsure if this quality is just something she wants to see, something she needs to see in him. She pulls her mother's shawl tight around her. She has no one to ask about this.

He came to the house that evening and stood just a few feet off the veranda steps.

"Miss Estella, we had an incident at the bunkhouse last night." He holds his worn hat, smoothing the brim with his rough hands, just as he had on the day they met. "Before it comes to you through someone else, I've come to tell you that I've taken care of everything."

Estella, not wanting to let him know that her staff has been expanding on the story all day long, nods with a querying look. "Oh? What happened? Is there something I should know?"

"No, Ma'am. It's business that need not concern you. I just want you to know that everything is fine." Normally, the business of the bunkhouse is never discussed with anyone on the outside, much less the main house. But since she is young and doing her best to run this land on her own, Johnny Von the Boss Man doesn't want her to hear stories and then start to worry. Knowing that she is inexperienced and wanting to act as an advisor of sorts, he justifies this visit by telling himself that he doesn't want the rumors of the brawl to foster a fear of the workers in her. But his true concern, if it were to be known, in coming to the main house to tell her about last night, is that he doesn't want her to hear the stories and then fear him.

"Do I need to send word to the sheriff?" Estella knows there is an internal justice among bunkhouse workers, but she wants to come across strong and resolved. She wants to verbalize some authority. "Is this something that needs to be reported in town?"

"No," he says calmly, with a smile so gentle she feels the warmth of it cross the distance of the steps between them. "No need for that. Just had to send one of the workers away. Just a disagreement that had to be handled. Only wanted to let you know that what needed to be done was done." He pauses. "You put your trust in me."

Maybe it is her trying so hard to seem strong, or the way that her being afraid all the time has worn on her, that makes him want to say something else, something more. That he sees this in her and she doesn't have to worry. It's safe. He's here now. Johnny Von the Boss Man is drawn out of his normal ways to try to express something he is feeling. He struggles with the impulse as he stands there, looking up to her on the veranda, the main house big and intimidating behind her. He is a man with few words. His vernacular is confined to the slang of bunkhouses, the talk of men, or the language of the fields. He does not know how to communicate to Estella that he knows she is frightened and that she needn't be because he is here for her.

"Everything is all right." He looks to her eyes to convey what he cannot say, "Miss Estella."

Estella has a sudden urge to rush down the veranda steps and wrap her arms around Johnny Von the Boss Man. It startles her as she sees it playing out in her head. That she would even have such thoughts for a man like him is unacceptable. It ruffles her composure. She smoothes at her white apron and tucks at her hair. Returning to her authority voice she says, "I rely on your judgment." Her voice then softens more than she wants it to. "Thank you, for letting me know."

As she watches him nod and walk off, she hears Martha next to her on the veranda. "Sure is good to have a man like that running things. I thought he was too young to run things right, but I sure do feel safe with him at the bunkhouse. Seems like a good man to have...as a boss man." Estella does not turn to Martha. She keeps her eyes on Johnny Von the Boss Man making his way back to the bunkhouse.

It was true, as the fields came up, as she saw him, leading the plow, cracking his whip in the air, moving that great black ox forward, she was becoming safer. She was calming down. She was lingering longer at the balcony, watching him, wondering if the burlap sack of crop seed chafed, as he placed its weight so easily on the bare skin of his sweat-drenched neck. Moving with ease, as the impossibly heavy sack rests high on his shoulder, he points out directions and shows one of the younger men how to balance the weight perfectly. Estella can't take her eyes off the experience and efficiency of his body, the way the tan skin of his back glistens in the heat.

This observing, this growing awareness of another was not one-way. Johnny Von the Boss Man had noticed Estella. In his line of work, it was not likely he would take a wife. He knew this. He was always moving. He was gruff and

unrefined. He had no idea how to live in a main house. The
bunkhouse was all he had ever known, and because of this
knowing, he'd never let himself look to a woman in that way,
a heartfelt way. Johnny Von the Boss Man had resigned
himself to the life in front of him. Only distraction and
disappointment could come from such imaginings, only
remind him of things out of reach.

But still he noticed. He saw her riding the black stallion at
the edge of the fields as her father had done, hoping to make
her presence, as the master of the plantation, known.

"Planting the back field today?" she'd call out. Or, "Those
rows are coming up nicely at the bend, aren't they?" she'd say.
Sometimes, if she couldn't think of anything else, she'd say,
"What do you think the weather will do?" when there wasn't a
cloud for miles. It tickled him.

He'd call back and tell her just a little more than he'd
normally say to anyone else. He'd call her over to show her
some little something about how the crop was coming in,
what to look for on the leaves, and what to expect from the
soil here and there. He talked to her in a tone that implied,
of course, that she knew these things. That he was only
consulting with her as part of his job as the Boss Man.

It was early on, one day in her little vegetable garden,
which was looking tattered and beaten, when she became
aware of this. She was hard at work, her hands in the soil
pulling weeds, when he walked up. He stood quietly, there
at the edge of the garden, with a pail in his hand, waiting for
her to look up.

"I'm sure you'll want these." He lifts the bucket filled with old dried eggshells.

Estella smiles, having no idea what she would want to do with them. "Of course." She politely takes the bucket from him. "Thank you." She sets it down next to her and returns to her weeding, hoping he will move on.

Instead, he spies her more closely. "I see you're pulling up the seedlings that have fallen from the plants before. They sprout up quick, don't they?"

Estella looks at the pile of what she assumed were weeds.

"That's a good idea," he says. "Take the little ones and move them out. I could fill some boxes with soil for you if you wanted." He pauses.

"Yes," Estella says slowly. "That would be nice." She tries to fill the quiet. "I could put them on the boards by the side of the house, keep a better eye on them." She looks back at him, seeing if he will offer more.

"Until they're stronger," Johnny Von the Boss Man offers.

"Yes," Estella agrees. "And the eggshells," she begins, "they will be good."

"Slugs are always a bother this time of year." Johnny Von the Boss Man says. "I know you didn't have enough eggshells to crush up and spread around, what with it just being you and Martha and a few others in the main house." He adjusts his hat. "Besides, the boys eat more then those hens can keep up with."

Estella smiles. "I'm glad to have them," she says as they both begin to ease into the conversation.

"I see the bluebirds haven't discovered your little patch yet?" Johnny Von the Boss Man says, stepping in closer, looking to some of the insect holes in the leaves, touching a leaf and flipping it over so she can see him study it.

"Can't say that I've seen any bluebirds around," Estella replies.

"We'll build them a house, then. They must be holding out, waiting for you to call them here with a few little houses that are just the right size, ready and waiting. They'll be all over this garden, eating their fill of bugs here."

Johnny Von the Boss Man nods. Estella smiles. He tips his hat and walks away.

And this is how it began between them, this way of communication; an understanding between them. His quiet nod. She would know the importance of what he was saying. Her returned smile. He would know she understood. With each passing day Estella grew to value, rely and trust, more and more, this unspoken understanding of how he would teach her.

He began to value their exchanges as well. They brought him closer, more aware of how a woman could be more that just one thing. He saw, with the appreciation of a man who understood nature, her little garden begin to flourish.

A few months later, he was walking past that garden, checking up on things when she wasn't around, seeing if there was anything she should know, when he noticed a white lace ribbon caught on a vine trellis. It was blowing in the wind. He untangled it, wound it carefully around his hand, and put it in his pocket with the intention to leave it with Martha, or give it back to Miss Estella when he saw her next. But it smelled of lavender and fresh scented soap and he kept it. Some nights, he would take the lace out, not often because he did not want to dirty it, and he would gently breathe it in, touch it to his cheek. It was the smell of her hair. It brought out a tenderness in him that had never been.

She was the perfect mix of strong and soft, smart and innocent, and if he were to think of such things, of the touch of soft skin or his hands on the curve of a woman's waist, she would come up in his mind. He would always stop himself. Remind himself, this is not real. She is not his in that way.

Before they both knew it, the sowing and reaping came and went. True to his word, Johnny Von the Boss Man brought in the harvest, on time, at price. On the day he sent his crew away, she was a mix of relief and anguish. Soon he would be up to the house to settle with her.

She had run the plantation through one full season, the books would show a profit, and never would she have a first time again. She was proud. But this also meant Johnny

Von the Boss Man would be moving on. The circumstances of Estella's life had forced her to know loneliness, but thinking of the bunkhouse empty of sound, the fields without his gleaming skin under the hot sun, the plow without his strong hands, was almost unbearable. She wished time would stop, that she would not hear him on the veranda, and that she would not have to say, in her authority voice, "Goodbye."

Knowing he would come to the house alone, she sent Martha to town to visit her sister, and then sent Billy and Jess to the feed store in Granville. She didn't know what exactly this would do, she had no plan, no practiced words for him, but she found herself clearing the house anyway. She wanted to be alone with Johnny Von the Boss Man. She picked out her favorite dress and took extra time to braid her hair just so. It was not like he was coming to call, but still, she found herself excited and hopeful. Hopeful for what, she could not settle on in her mind.

Hearing boots on the steps of the large plantation veranda, Estella quickly pours two glasses of the lemonade she'd made fresh that morning. She hurries out the back screen door, hoping to get them on the table before he rounds the corner, but as she turns out of the doorway, it is not Johnny Von the Boss Man she sees. Startled by the dark figure, she screams and drops the tray. The lemonade glasses crash at her feet.

It's Luke, his eyes wild and angry, a large knife in his hand. He saw the boys in town and knew Johnny Von the

Boss Man would be on his own at the bunkhouse tonight. He's come to settle the score.

"Don't you look pretty?" His teeth are black, his hair matted and he smells like piss and sour milk.

Before she can run inside, he grabs her arm and jerks her close to him. "I know he likes you. Maybe I'll just start right here." Luke slithers his tongue down Estella's cheek and then cackles.

She tries to run, to fight, but he is overpowering. He pushes her down, pins her to the wood floor with one knee, puts his knife down and rips the back of her dress down the middle. Her pale smooth skin is exposed down past the curve of her waist.

Taking his time, watching the sun go down, the sky turn to dusk, Johnny Von the Boss Man ponders what he could say to Miss Estella this evening. He thinks this might be his last chance. But he can think of nothing, no combination of words that would bring her to him, that could make who he is any different. He lets himself imagine her anyway. Knowing this is his last night, and that his time as her Boss Man has ended, he lets his mind go as he washes his hands at the pump. Taking an extra moment to scrub his fingernails clean under the spout.

He imagines her laughing and smiling and chatting with him as they did in the fields each day, only in his head they are in a house, sharing a name and a bed. In his head he can wake in the night, feel her warm skin next to his, the scent of her hair always on the pillows; have her, again and again, in the moonlight. In his head there are rosy-cheeked children everywhere and lush green fields always in bloom out the windows.

He walks slowly to his horse, adjusts the reins, and is suddenly shaken from his reverie as he hears Estella's scream in the distance. With a fury he's never possessed, he pulls his shotgun from the saddle and is in full gallop to the house, knowing it's Luke and knowing what he will do. He'll kill him.

He sees them just as Estella's dress is ripped down her back. Riding full force, he cocks his shotgun.

"Luke!" He shouts and takes aim.

Luke reaches over Estella to grab his knife. As he turns to see Johnny Von the Boss Man straight on, the blade of his knife slashes Estella's back from her shoulder to her hip. She screams in pain.

As this unbearable sound touches the ears of Johnny Von the Boss Man, the trigger of his shotgun is already squeezed. The last thing Estella sees is Luke hitting the floor before she passes out.

Estella wakes on her side, still in the dress she had chosen for her rendezvous with Johnny Von the Boss Man.

The room is lit only by the kerosene lamps at her bedside and a candle on the bureau.

"It's not bad at all," he whispers.

She feels his hands on her bare back, at her naked waist. They are not rough, as she had imagined. They are like worn leather, soft and warm on her. She does not move or turn her head to his voice. She does not want to give reason for his hands to leave her.

"It's just a surface cut, Miss Estella. But," he pauses, "we need to wrap it. Where is Martha?"

"She is at her sister's 'til morning." Estella turns slightly and feels the sting of her back.

"Okay, then," he says. She can feel the nervousness pulse through his hands as he pulls them away.

Johnny Von the Boss Man takes the clean white cloth from the table next to the water and the blood stained rags he has already used. Gently, he takes Estella under her knees and at her arm and sits her at the edge of the bed. She quickly catches her dress at her chest as it falls away from her shoulders. They both stop.

"I know I probably shouldn't be …" Johnny Von the Boss Man tries to offer words to ease the self-conscious hesitation they both feel, but falters.

Estella looks to him and says what she wanted to say to him over lemonade, but knew she never could: "I need you with me."

Johnny Von the Boss Man casts his eyes down, as if to say thank you, as if Estella is offering him token words to protect his feelings.

He offers the white bandage and Estella stands. Johnny Von the Boss Man starts to wind the cloth at her back. As he moves his large hands softly over the wound, around her waist, her side, Estella holds her elbows as high as she can, until he can go no further. She lets go and her dress slips to the floor.

Johnny Von the Boss Man pauses, and then continues smoothing the bandage around her, touching her stomach through the thin gauze, pulling the fabric with great care over her bare chest. He holds her there, over her soft bosom to join the fabric at her back.

Neither move.

He continues to wind the ribbon of cloth around her. From top to bottom he circles and pauses. He slides her petticoat down, exposing her hip bones. He circles the fabric in front of her one more time and then tucks the end of the bandage right below her hips past the small of her back.

Before he can take his hands away, before he can leave her, she grabs them there. "I want you to be here." She turns to face him kneeling on the floor in front of her.

"Miss Estella, I'm not good at ... I'm not the kind of man who ..." Johnny Von the Boss Man hesitates, feels himself trapped behind words he can not find, can not put together.

He looks away from her eyes, afraid she will see a weakness that men like Johnny Von the Boss Man are not allowed. "I'll stay the night, here, of course, Miss Estella, 'till Martha returns in the morning."

"No." She pulls him up to her. "I want you to stay. You're the only one I want here." His broad shoulders are true and sure in front of her. "I don't care how it is. Or what people will say, or what is right or wrong. I want you in this house, my room, sharing this bed."

Johnny Von the Boss Man stays in her embrace, but remains tense and uneasy.

Estella is struck by the contrast between the sureness in his hands and apprehension in his eyes. "Tell me you'll stay." She leans into him. "Tell me you'll stay with me, not as the Boss Man ..." she says slowly, "as my man." Staring into his eyes, she does not know how to tell him that she knows he is unsure and that he needn't be. That she is here for him.

Estella kisses Johnny Von the Boss Man for the first time, but it to her, in her heart, she has known this kiss forever.

Johnny Von the Boss Man feels his body rush. With this kiss he feels what he never feels: he feels afraid. But even bigger than the fear that has sparked inside of him, Johnny Von the Boss Man feels alive. He feels belonging to this girl in front of him. Only she's not a girl, she's a woman, and he trusts this woman. His heart is safe in her gaze.

He then does what he never does: Johnny Von the Boss Man lets go.

His entire being relaxes as he holds her gaze and nods.

This nod, slight and soft, here in his arms, is more assuring to Estella than all the words he could have ever put together. It is the understanding between them. This nod is the only thing Estella needs.

Chapter 3

"The essentials to happiness are
something to love, something to do,
and something to hope for."
~ *William Blake*

I open another box in the study. Tammy Wynette, Buck
Owens, Patsy Cline, Dwight Yoakam. I feel better just
seeing them. I don't know if it's the repetitiveness of the
task, stacking the CDs, or my affection for country music,
but I start to feel better. I start to unwind from my earlier
train of thought that the Johnny Von Contractor has callous
and selfish plans to hold me hostage in the study.

Johnny Von hollers up the stairs as the day moves to late
afternoon, "Hey, have you seen Blood from a Stone?"

I bite my tongue and look down into yet another CD-filled box.

Blood from a Stone is one of Johnny Von's first dramatic roles. It's in my top five all time movies. Johnny Von has the chops to do funny, and I guess that's what people know him for, but I noticed him in Blood from a Stone; young, strong, beautiful and new. He played Billy Byrde McIlhenny, a man on the run from himself; a self serving mercenary soldier; the charming bad boy, who looks after number one and only number one. Through his arrogance, egotism and drunken judgment, a young soldier in his unit is taken prisoner. Given orders to move out and abandon the kid, Billie Byrde unexpectedly goes AWOL on an impossible mission to save his unlikely friend.

"Hey." Johnny Von calls out to his assistant again, excitement in his voice, "Have you seen Blood from a Stone?" The Johnny Von Assistant is standing not two feet away from me. She and I are the only two people in the office.

I want so badly to peek out of the doorway and say, "I saw it! I saw it the very first night I drove into L.A." I want to crawl out from where I am on the floor sorting CDs and make eye contact with Johnny Von, who is standing at the bottom of the stairs, and say, "I saw it and you were amazing, amazing, amazing." I want to talk about his character, Billy Byrde, and my favorite lines and the location of the shoot.

I want to tell him how I cried when Billie Byrde walks in the prison cell and sees the kid, bruised and battered in the squalor of that third world torture camp, hysterical from fear and panic, and the kid blurts out, "I woundn't have done it, Billie Byrde." Head in his hands, "I woundn't have come for you…" He breaks down, in a sudden shadow of guilt, through tears and slobbering, "I would have never come back for you, never come back to such a Godless place to save you."

And then Billie Byrde reaches out, "I didn't come for you." For the first time in his life, Billie Byrde stops running.

The young soldier is losing it, breaking down all over the place and Billie Byrde puts his big hand on his shoulder and says, "I didn't come for you, I came for me. You know what I mean?"

The kid goes quiet in his delirium and says in a moment of clarity, "I know, Billy Byrde. I know. I told them, they said you wouldn't, but I told them you'd come…" he breaks down again, "I knew you'd come for me. I knew you'd come for me, even if you didn't know."

The faith of the kid, the redemption of Billie Byrde — the power of all that innocence leading the way for a hardened Billie Byrde to reclaim himself; to be the man he has in his heart to be; risking all to dire and unknown consequences!

Damn, I love that story.

And I love big Johnny Von coming to the rescue. Reaching to the heart of the matter and pulling you up with the brawn of his shoulders. Knowing, without knowing why, that he has the strength to do it—to do whatever needs to be done. That he is the kind of man that has a kind of strength inside him that a woman, even the strongest woman, can never have.

I want to say all that to Johnny Von.

But I can't, so I focus. Patsy Cline comes after Johnny Cash in the country genre stack. I decided to go with alphabetical order by genre after all.

Of course I can't say anything like that! I can't holler out. And not because it would blow my cover, not that I even want a cover. In fact, I'm almost sure, at this point, that if my attraction doesn't soon become uncovered I may implode into a pile of rubble on the newly polished wood floors.

In a flash of seconds, I reason that I cannot call out because it would not be appropriate. Or it would be out of place for what I'm doing here. Or it would paint me as some groupie, some hanger-on. I am not a hanger-on. But even those aren't the real reasons. The real reason I can't call out is this: despite the entire insane internal Johnny Von dance that I am doing, I am just a girl with a crush. This simple, seemingly innocuous truth, benign—even cute to others, hits me like a death sentence. It doesn't matter that he's who he is, this is who I am! I haven't felt this kind of terrorized shyness in years. I cannot call out, now or ever, and remain cool, and I know it.

I cannot call out casually and say, "Hey, nice to meet you, I'm helping in the house today, blah, blah, normal talking tone, blah …" because I have a crush, a situation that never ends well for me, that chokes me, even now, at 33. It's recalled a kind of Grand Canyon of shyness in me, utterly impassable in all directions. I mean, I'm not completely paralyzed, I can still move my limbs and form words, but I feel it.

I then realize, I must be here, in the office of Johnny Von, sorting through his stuff, among his CDs, his movie keepsakes, the pictures he keeps out on his desk, by some sheer force of nature, some mystical design, because as the freakishly bashful person I intimately feel myself to be at this moment, I could have never figured out how to be here of my own accord, deciding if Elvis should be his own genre.

The Johnny Von Assistant calls out, "Yeah, I saw it. It's on the kitchen table by the other DVD's I put out for you."

"Thanks." He calls back.

Thank god I didn't say anything!

"What'd you think of it?" He continues, "I just talked to the director. He's talking about another project …"

Okay, now I could say something, if I could say something.

"Yeah," she says distracted by the calls she needs to get to and the notes on the desk that she is sorting. "I thought it was good." She continues shuffling through papers and picks up the phone to call someone.

Good. It's excruciating. She thought it was "good."

If he just walks into the office, I could handle it. I could say at least something, even a little something on the topic. I could force my way through. I could smile and talk in a low-key tone, I'm sure I could. I could handle that. I calculate in my head that it would not be inappropriate now, to say something if he walks into the office. I pray. I really focus, envision him walking into the office.

I hear Johnny Von move around downstairs. The Johnny Von Assistant gets on with her phone call. He doesn't walk into the office. The moment is over.

Damn it! Why didn't I call out? I may never get a chance again! What the hell is going on here? All day and still I have seen no Johnny Von. No casual "bump-into," no natural conversation chattiness. I might have just missed the only chance I'm going to get!

"You'll have many chances …" says Andrew Banks, my new poetry teacher as he checks off everyone's name and gets our first class under way. He closes his roll book, takes out a large stack of poetry books and file folders, "…to read your work." He says, looking up at everyone.

He is a big older man, awkward in his dress and movements but confident in his gaze as he peers from behind his reading glasses. He looks like an older John Lithgow combined with Papa Christmas. As he takes names and talks about the class, he's bold and authoritative with his subject matter, while at the same time soothing in his tone when he interacts with the students. There are only seven of us. He carries an air of excitement for our discovery of the beloved poets he's taught for the last 25 years. I like him.

What I don't like, what catches me off guard is this "reading your work" comment. I signed up for a beginning poetry writing class, not a learn-to-read-your-writing-out loud-to-other-people class! I'm here to learn about William Blake. I'm not here to perform, to stand up in front of people, to be seen and judged!

As if he's read my mind, Andrew Banks then says this. "Before we start today, I would like to talk about reading your poetry. You should know that I will not call on anyone to read; it is strictly volunteer-only." He pauses, studying the room. "And you should know that some students never read their material, they just sit quietly, only taking it all in, keeping their words to themselves." He begins to walk around the circle of desks. "Perhaps there is a place for that in poetry writing. I'm sure Emily Dickinson would think so." He smiles, amused with himself. "Other students come with their work in hand each week, and still they do not ever read." He weaves slowly in and out of the desks as he talks. "They sweat and fumble with the pages, and I watch them try to raise their hands. Certainly, there is a place for that in the life of every great poet." He smiles and pats the shoulder of a very awkward, slightly overweight young girl who is balled-up over her notebook, scratching the cover with her black ink pen. He does it in a way that does not draw attention, but seems to relax the whole room.

I'll never be able to do this, I think, surprised by how much resistance and panic is welling up inside me as he talks. I don't know what it is; it's not like I'm worried about these seven strangers. I don't even know these people. I scan the circle of desks. A motley crew of three old ladies that should be in the second level knitting class across the hall, the awkward girl, a skinny Gothic rocker with dyed black hair and tattoos up one arm (also in the fetal position over his desk) are sitting across from me. On my right is a Hispanic man, middle aged with a green work shirt that says Carlos on the stained badge at his chest. On my left is an older man who keeps pulling Halls cough drops out of his plaid shirt pocket. This is a UCLA extension class. There are no grades. What do I care what these people think?

Andrew Banks continues. "But I know you will all be different." He smiles. I imagine him taking out a pipe, but instead he sits himself down at the top of the circle in front of the blackboard. "You will be brave and bold. 'Do not go gentle into that good night,' said the poet Dylan Thomas. You've come to learn poetry, by reading it and writing it. To know that a poet's heart cannot keep hidden from the world the life he or she is living on the inside. They must distill it in language and tell it outward. We will take his sage advice and 'Rage, rage against the dying of the light.'" With that, he slaps his knees and opens the large text in front of him.

Here on the floor in the study of Johnny Von as the day is winding down, in the despair that I have an impassable distance of shyness to cross before I could ever do something like call out, or introduce myself, or talk in a normal talking tone to Johnny Von, this is what I feel most intensely: the dying of the light.

All day, back and forth, thinking I'm either on a metaphysical brink to some cool, dream-come-true scenario, some happy surreal event, where what you want to happen actually happens. That, or I'm in the midst of some very dark and twisted joke of the gods. I've tripped into some nightmarish portal where Johnny Von stays three seconds out of my eye line and one thin-walled room away. I get to be around everything that is his as much as I want, get to know everyone that knows him, but I never get to him. Johnny Von remains forever just a flash out of reach.

How can the universe, the gods of hook-up, the dealers of fate, do this to me? Don't they know I've had no dream-come-true moments yet! No grade school leading parts in plays, no won spelling bees. All those years of sore toes, and no principal ballet parts. There were no successful high school cheerleading tryouts, no homecoming dances with oh-my-God dates, no college moments! No "I'm an adult," look-at-my-career moments!

I don't mean to be ungrateful. And I am not denying that I have had good times, including that night with the International Playboy and the other good times we had in the beginning. I know I have been exceedingly fortunate in many, many, many ways.

But I'm 33, for God's sake! I can't have any more false starts.

All this time I've been thinking the gods must be saving up something really good for me, because I haven't really caught a break yet. And they know it!

The daylight begins its fading into dusk through the white sheer curtains in the office. The Johnny Von Assistant says goodbye and makes her way downstairs to leave for the day. The Johnny Von Contractor comes into the office as the sun is turning that pink shade on the walls. We finish up the study together, putting the sofa cushions back on the couch. We chat. The Johnny Von Contractor is a good enough guy. I'm covinced he has no maniacal plan for the demise of my potential happiness.

The only thing remaining to bring the room to perfection (his word, not mine) is to take two empty beer mugs and a dirty ashtray downstairs.

"Here, you take these down to the kitchen. I'll meet you out front and we'll settle up for the day." He hands me the mugs.

I'm actually glad it's almost over. I have to say that not only am I physically exhausted from hauling boxes and sorting through stuff, even though it was Johnny Von's stuff, but my nervous system is shot. The mental roller coaster of insecurities and imagined scenarios has taken its toll. At this point, I'm resigned that I have no idea when or if I will ever see Johnny Von. Or even if there really is a Johnny Von at all. Whatever. I'm too tired to think of any of it anymore.

I load up the mugs in one hand, the heavy glass ashtray in the other, and make my way down the steps. The downstairs is empty and the late evening sun is streaking its last yellow on the walls. I make my way across the foyer, past the living room around the dining table, and I hear him. I hear Johnny Von on the phone.

I know it's the kitchen phone.

I keep the same pace. I am normal, normal, normal. I've got a hold of my confidence. I am steady. I turn into the hall heading into the kitchen and there he is, Johnny Von, standing in all his tallness. Johnny Von is talking on the phone, staring right at me, head on. Just Johnny Von at one end of the hall, and me, walking toward him, from the other. Johnny Von, standing there, six feet of air between us, he's talking and looking straight at me.

Suddenly everything about the hall is a blur and all I can see are his eyes. His deep brown eyes are like tractor beams. It's like some kind of Superman force field energy is beaming out of them. I smile at him, because that is all I can do. That, and tell myself right foot, left foot.

If I were the Superman, his stare would have been the most powerful kryptonite in the entire universe. The beer mugs and ashtray would have turned to lead and dropped to the floor. In his stare I would have crumbled down the hall in slow motion until I was slumped at his feet, transfixed by his eyes.

I am a couple of steps, smiley steps, into the hall, which have taken an eon of time in my head, when I hear a "clink" and a "bump." It is a huge clink and bump in my head. Johnny Von probably doesn't hear or notice it, but I lose my inner cool completely.

I'm mortified. I've just scraped the beer mugs against the newly-painted walls. I don't look down at it. I tense up. I'm stuck in his stare and make an "oh-no" grimace on my face. I think I ruined the paint job. I throw out an "uh-oh, I'm-so-sorry" expression.

Johnny Von nods at me from his phone conversation, gives me an "it's okay" look and waves me forward. I scurry past him with a nervous laugh, murmuring something like "sorry I'm in your way" under my breath.

I walk in fast forward motion past him to the sink, where I grab a hold of myself. I concentrate on being in the kitchen doing what I came here to do, which is to wash out these beer mugs and clean this ashtray.

I assess things.

I am now in the kitchen with my back to Johnny Von, who is standing four feet behind me talking on the phone. We are the only two people in the kitchen. I inhale, exhale, and turn on the water. I'm freaked out, but rationally, probably, no harm has been done. Perhaps no outward displays of my inner Lucille Ball have been seen. This could be it. This could be where it all starts.

I'm okay. I'm just here in the kitchen with Johnny Von and I cannot turn around. I want to. I want to turn around really quick and see if he is checking me out. I want to turn around and catch him, and then give him a wink and a laugh. Maybe toss my hair, but I don't. I am frozen. I decide, by default and self-survival, to ignore him.

I clean the glasses thoroughly and put them in the dishwasher. I clean out the ashtray and wash it as no ashtray has ever been washed. I relax a little. I check around the cabinets for a towel or a paper towel, like I belong in this kitchen, like I'm at home in this kitchen, like I am not even really aware that there is anyone else in this kitchen.

As I relax, I begin to hope that at any second he will hang up the phone. And then I'll turn around and we'll chat. He'll say something and I'll say something and then we'll be off, off into friendship, off into chatty friendship-land, me and Johnny Von.

So pleased with that thought, I decide to wash the two other ashtrays sitting on the counter. I'm drawing out the time, giving him a chance to exit his phone conversation. At the very least, I think maybe he'll get some imprint of me that I am a considerate and conscientious person—she saw two dirty ashtrays that needed cleaning and cleaned them, even though it wasn't her job. She must be nice. That's good girlfriend material.

I take as long a time as would be appropriate to clean, conscientiously, two ashtrays, dry them, then dry the counter around them and search for the trash to throw away the paper towels.

I now cannot stay a second longer without seeming like I am lingering. So, I abruptly turn, head up, and look straight at him. He is chatting away, aware that I am looking at him but not turning in my direction. I walk out of the kitchen, not looking at him long enough to constitute "a look," not longer than I would have looked at any other person that was in the kitchen talking on the phone. It is a normal look.

I meet the Johnny Von Contractor out front. He thanks me and pays me. I walk to my car and look up to the sky. I'm dog-tired. The evening pink is now blue gray dusk turning to night. I don't know if I feel excited because of what just happened, or kind of like I want to cry. I realize I am going to need a miracle, a big one. I need a miracle that will totally take me out of the equation, totally override me, because I don't think I can do it. The sky is empty except for a few streaks of white lines that cut through the fading blue. I feel like that -- streaks of sadness in me.

If I didn't know better, I would swear Shelby Braxton is listening for me to walk down the hall Friday Night. Her door flies open as she hears Moochie and I arrive home and fumble with the keys at my door.

"Well? I thought about you all day. How did it go? Did you see him? What happened?"

I'm fragile. I cannot hold up to Shelby at the moment. I cannot counter whatever this whole Johnny Von thing has called up in her and brought to the table of our friendship. I try to calculate some response that would defuse the whole situation. I muster what energy I can. I turn to face her and I begin lying.

"Yeah, I met him, he was there today. In fact, he hung out all day while I worked in his office, talking to everybody, you know, he's a nice guy. But I don't know. I don't think he's my kind of guy. I'm not really into all that party Hollywood scene."

"Oh." I see a dash of relief flash in her eyes and then she says, "Well, of course, the minute it looks like you could be with someone you like, you shut down."

I'm confused. I don't know what direction she is going now.

"Don't you think now, that he's a real person to you, you don't like him because of your intimacy issues? Don't you see how you did the same thing with Josh?"

The only thing I see is that no matter what I say, Shelby is going to find some way to twist it into some reflection of my defunct emotional life, and then bring in the idea that I'm flawed for not wanting Josh, a.k.a. her husband Larry's twin.

Before I can respond, Moochie saves me. He starts bucking and jumping and flinging his body into the air. He eats dinner as soon as we get in every day. We're home and it's now time to get the eating underway. He's a Lab. He doesn't have time to chat at the doorway when there's food to be served. He gives a little happy bark and continues to wag himself into a frenzy. He starts bucking around like a little bronco bear. Besides saving me from the moment, it also makes me laugh.

"Look at my dog! Shelby, I've got to feed The Moots before he faints. I'm around this weekend, we'll talk later." I close the door on Shelby and make another mental note: Don't talk to Shelby about anything relationship-related ever again!

I hit the button on my answer machine and pull out Moochie's bag of kibble.

"So there's a service at 7:00 am, but I don't think Mark Wahlberg would be at Mass that early." Mandy's voice is first. "There's one at 10:00 and then 11:30. I don't think we should go to both on the same Sunday. Maybe 10:00 this Sunday and 11:30 next week. Call me."

Mom's next. "Sweetie, I'm just calling to say hello, see how the new class is going. Call me when you get in, baby." Followed, ironically, by my dad. My parents haven't said a word to each other in the 12 years they've been divorced, but they always seem to call back to back. "It's me. Just calling to see how you're doing. How's work? How's your car holding up these days? My plane is in Sunday,

I'm staying with your brother before I leave for overseas Thursday. Call me and we'll make plans, I'm around this weekend."

As I watch Moochie gobble up the dry dog food, I decide not to return anyone's call, and head straight for a bath and bed. It's only 7:30 p.m., but I'm a nester. I gravitate to my bed when I'm stressed.

I spread out all my new poetry books on my comforter. I set a cup of hot tea next to my bed, open my new clean notebook complete with my new five-dollar ink pen, and try to relax. I don't want to show up to poetry class with nothing, even if I don't read anything, I'd like to have something. I look at the picture I was given. Andrew Banks gave everyone a picture on the way out the door last week, for inspiration, in case we couldn't think of anything to write a poem about. My picture is a single tree on a hill in the middle of a wheat field in autumn. The leaves are bursting with color against the blue sky.

It's beautiful — but so what?

Yes, only God can make a tree. Fine. Gorgeous. We all know that. I ponder. I contemplate. What kind of poem can I write about this picture that is not going to sound stupid? What rhymes with leaf other than beef.

I can't think of a poem. I can't think of anything except Johnny Von.

Moochie bounds into my breakfast nook/bedroom area from the bathroom. He's excavated a red plastic Dixie cup from the trash and he is thrilled with himself. He's come to show it off. Dixie cups are his favorite. He'll toss it around, flirt with it, and bounce it off the linoleum, impressed with the noise he is making. And then, when he's satisfied with that, he'll stare it down for a few seconds and then pounce on it, in a surprise attack! He'll then proceed to shred it into a million tiny pieces of plastic; like a lion or a wild wildebeest.

I scoop him up and cradle him like a baby. He's almost too big to hold like this.

"Be the baby," I say to him as he wiggles. This is our new game. He hates it.

"Woof." He gives a little bark and squirms. I love to tease my dog.

"Be the baby!" I say louder and squeeze him.

He settles for a second, looks me in the eye and then, "Woof, woof!" He gives his big-dog bark, as if to say, I'm not the baby. "Woof!" Did you see what I can do to a Dixie cup? Lady, I'm ferocious!

I know he's just a dog, but I can feel my heart when I look at him. I love him, whether he knows it or not. So what if it's all just about food and attention, as science would tell me. That my attachment, my feelings of affection are all my creation, projected onto Moochie, who is just instincts and symbiotic survival. What does science know about feelings from the heart? I think Moochie loves me, when he wags at the sight of me, when he brings me a Dixie cup to play with; and even if he doesn't love in the way that I love, if science is right and I'm wrong, it still feels good. It's like a free gift to me to feel love for him, an energy that flows out of me, effortlessly, and it makes me happy about life. I kiss his little head and let him get back to work on the cup before he has to go into his kennel for the night.

A poem. I need a poem, about a tree alone in the middle of a wheat field in autumn, a tree bursting with color without a soul around to see its majesty, a beautiful thing with no one to appreciate it.

I've got nothing. Nothing but thinking I'm too shy to ever talk to Johnny Von for real. It makes me want to cry. And not because I'm worried I'm like Mandy Kane, not because of what Shelby Braxton thinks, but because I know it's what I want most. I want to break inside at how much I want to be someone who could look in Johnny Von's eyes and be seen. I could drown in the wanting and the worry that it won't come. That the people I want to see me, won't. That eyes, like Johnny Von's eyes, which fill me with desire, won't say yes to me. The thought that the love I feel inside me won't find a person to flow to overwhelms me, and the idea that I'll have to stifle the parts in me that want shine in love until I'm given that yes…it strikes panic in me. It's my darkest place. I can't talk about it.

I need to write a poem. I decide to scan other poems for inspiration. I flip the pages, William Carlos Williams, e.e. cummings, Robert Hayden, Gwendolyn Brooks, Wallace Stevens, Maya Angelou. Their pictures, so ordinary, stop me even more than their words. As if you could pass them all on the street without notice, unless they looked you in the eye. It's in their eyes, the something else beyond the plain everydayness of them. All of them, looking out from the black and white photos, knowing something essential and obvious that the rest of us are missing; looking at me from the pages, with their lives behind them, like they know what I want most, like they've sailed the seas and come back to tell the tales; each poem a map through the impassable inside me. I am starving for their answers, but their poems, their words silent on the page are all cryptic and none of them rhyme.

I move to the two little books on William Blake, the poet that started all this. His poems and prints, his Songs of Innocence and Experience. His Marriage of Heaven and Hell. Again, it's the pictures that pull me in. The soft colors and sumptuous tree lines. I have no idea what he's talking about any more than the others, but I know they all have something I don't. I hate them. None of them are afraid of what they want most. They could all talk to Johnny Von. They all have the words for everything inside that wants to get out but doesn't know how.

I give up. It's only the second class tomorrow, what does he expect? I'm new to poetry. I gather up all the little shards of plastic Dixie cup and herd Moochie into his kennel. I dump all the poetry books onto the floor, click off the lights and pull the down comforter up to my neck.

I feel the streaks of sadness.

He did see me in the hallway. I try an internal pep talk. We did make eye contact. Johnny Von's endless brown eyes. It was mostly a good day. Johnny Von did smile and nod, wave me forward. Nothing bad happened. I start to feel better. What was the guy going to do, drop the phone, grab me and declare love at the kitchen sink? Nothing bad happened today. I shouldn't feel this sad. I still have a chance.

He was wearing a yellow shirt and his hair was scruffy.

It could all turn around for me.

He's really tall in real life, with nice big hands. And his eyes, his eyes are beautiful.

It's a long shot, sure, but that's no reason to give up now.

Yep, Johnny Von has beautiful eyes.

I think it's going to be okay.

1943

Johnny Von the Fly Boy

"It's going to be a cold day in hell, boys." Johnny Von the Fly Boy jumps down from the wing of the P-40 Warhawk he's just landed. As his big black boots hit the dewy morning grass, he dips under the wing, kisses the palm of his hand and slaps the metal backside of his girl. The long-legged pin-up beauty smiles back, as she always does, with her hands in her long brown hair and her red high heels kicked up in the air. He painted her on the nose of his plane from an image in his mind, no one in particular, just his idea of a beautiful woman. He named her Trixie Valaine, after a showgirl he'd heard of in Chicago. He just liked the sound of it. She was the kind of girl he wanted to know, a girl he thought the opposite of the girls back home in Ohio. He wrote her name in script, Trixie Valaine, in bright blue letters underneath her. She has been with him since his first time. She's taken hits, lots of hits, but she always brings him down safely.

Johnny Von the Fly Boy drops his pack, takes a moment

and whispers to her. What he whispers each time he lands, nobody knows. "It's between the two of us," he says when they press him. "And I'd never kiss and tell." He winks. "Got my girl's modesty to protect."

In from a pre-dawn mission over France, Johnny Von the Fly Boy leads the ranks in one on one air combat. Eamon, his wingman, Peter and Jon head in from the field along-side him, the only remaining members of the original group that came over in '39 under a special arrangement with the U.K. They could fly for the R.A.F., defend democracy in Europe, and still retain their U.S. citizenship. Answering the call of adventure, they came over together, sure of themselves. They originally flew with No. 609. In '40 they saw action in the Battle of Britain, in the sky with seven other Americans. Holding their own, they flew Hawkers and Spitfires, and were part of the Eagle Squadron until the U.S. joined in '41. Today, they're dogfight specialists, saved for the most important, sent into the most dangerous, and they thrive on it. They thrive not out of glory or lust for aggression, they thrive because they are the best and they know it. They have earned the label not through ambition or ego; they have earned it by staying alive. Today, as they head in from the field rag tag and tired, they are still here to defend democracy, but survival now holds a higher place in them than adventure.

Johnny Von the Fly Boy unzips his leather jacket and fumbles for the half smoked cigar he keeps in his front left pocket. The night before every mission he smokes a cigar

walking alone by the line of planes under the open starry
night. This is the only time he is not with his buddies.
Alone on his walks, he carefully puts the cigar out at the
half way mark and vows to re-light it the next time his feet
hit the ground. He is like this. Johnny Von the Fly Boy
has his certain ways, his patterns. His way of making order
out of the uncontrollable world he has found himself in.

"They're sending the dame pilots." Peter sits down on the
hard wooden bench in the mess hall next to Johnny Von the
Fly Boy.

He laughs and slaps Peter's shoulder. "Sure they are,
buddy." He looks over at Jon and Eamon, "And I'm getting
laid tonight. The Rockettes are shipping out right now to
meet me in the showers."

Nobody laughs, nobody smiles, they usually don't, but
today nobody looks away.

"What the hell are you guys talking about, they're not
sending them overseas?" Just then, four women walk into
the other end of the mess hall; all dressed in jumps suits,
lugging parachute packs behind them.

"We don't have barracks set up for you girls. To tell you
the truth," Colonel Meyers says without reserve, "I didn't
want you here. I don't think you belong here, and I don't
think there is anyone here that believes any differently. You

can bunk in Hangar 16. We've put out cots and designated latrine time, because I'm under orders to accommodate you. But you want to play war, you want to act like men, then you'll get what they get." His craggily John Wayne voice escalates. "And know this, you put my men in danger with your hysterical nature and I will put an end to this program, orders or no orders." He leaves them and walks past the boys, satisfied with his display. "I don't think you'll be here very long, anyway. Incompetence has a hefty price out here, girls."

"They're civilians." Peter tells the whole story to a horrified and surly Johnny Von the Fly Boy as they walk to the tower. "The war effort has them here on a special mission to ferry planes."

"I don't care who has them here, or why. Women can't pilot planes! It's wrong!" he yells across the office of Colonel Meyers. "You're going to put a woman in a plane when she can't even scrub a hospital floor clean or put a hot meal on the table for her husband without flapping around like a chicken! Come on! They can't do it!"

The Colonel lets Johnny Von the Fly Boy whip himself up into a frenzy, hoping the boys will work it out in their own way. "My hands are tied." His chair creaks as he leans back.

"Well, mine aren't!" Johnny Von the Fly Boy throws his

wooden folding chair to the ground, storms out of the office and heads straight to Hangar 16, grumbling expletives the whole way.

Estella is alone when she hears the ranting at the door. The other girls decided to brave the mess hall, but Estella stayed behind to soak her foot. As she dips her foot in the almost boiling water, she hopes the color will return to her toes. Two toenails are black and she worries about losing them to frostbite from her last flight. The girls can be given long ferry routes that have them battling hypothermia. That they are more expendable than men, than real pilots, is no secret. Estella doesn't blink at the sting that rushes up her leg from the bucket. She's been flying for the Air Transport Auxiliary for six months and she has never felt more right inside.

She could hardly stand it when Roberta, who practically raised her, left Ohio at the end of '41 to fly with the A.T.A., leaving her behind. It took her two years, and the unfortunate news of her family, to convince Roberta to help her lie about her age. Although Roberta was flying ferry routes in the north, she pushed the paper work through for Estella to be stationed in the south. They added two years. Two toes is nothing. Estella would give anything to fly. It is her one and only thing, it is her reason. It is what her heart beats for.

"Just a minute!" she calls out.

Sent as a child to her uncle's wheat farm in Ohio, she started flying at the age of 13. The first time he took her up, the lift off thrusting her body back in to the seat, the first time she felt the air of the sky filling her chest looking down at the quilt work pattern of the hills, as she put her hand out to touch the clouds they cut through, she knew she'd never get over it.

Uncle Teddy Jay was supportive and he did show her a thing or two over the years, especially as she became good. But it was Roberta who taught her to fly.

Roberta, a broad woman with wild sandy hair, was an early barnstormer, a woman with her own mind who followed her heart beyond the convention of the day. She lived three fields down and kept a red bi-plane in her barn, along with Teddy Jay's two planes. The airstrip they all used was on her land.

Of course flying would have been unacceptable to Estella's parents back in Chicago, had they known. It was between her and her Uncle Teddy Jay, their secret that Roberta was teaching her. He had no children of his own and his wife was frail, often housebound, which is why Estella had been sent to live with them. Estella was to help around the farm, but every weekend or free day she found, she was at Roberta's.

Roberta taught her everything she knew. And she knew a lot. She alone knew what Estella was capable of, and for reasons no one could have foreseen, both Roberta, and then Teddy Jay, taught her to be an ace.

"Open the door!" Johnny Von the Fly Boy shouts and kicks the door with his boot.

Back in Ohio her life was laid out; she would have to eventually leave the farm and go back to Chicago. There would be a husband, a home to tend to, children to raise. There would be no more flying, no more of that feeling. The one place she felt fully -- fully herself, fully alive -- would be denied, cut off to her.

It was all rushing towards her that year and then the letter came from the A.T.A. Her parents were shocked, emphatic, but she could not help herself. She had to go. She was more sure of what she had to do than she'd ever known herself to be, more than a woman is expected to be. With the war, everything for Estella changed, in the best and the worst way. No matter what happened next, she left heading in a direction that would never let her return, victory or no victory.

"Calm down!" Estella pulls her foot out of the water, "I'm coming. Calm down!" she shouts at the frail metal door rattling on its hinges with each hit.

"Open up, lady! You want your hands on a stick? Well I've got a stick for you. And it's the only one you're going to touch around here, lady. Open the Goddamned door!"

After all she went through to get herself here, after six months of war, of unrepeatable sights and sounds, that she offends the social order of things is nothing to her now. Estella knows how to handle herself. She shoves her foot into her boot and tightens the cotton scarf around her head. She is tough. Matching fire with fire, she starts yelling to equal the volume of Johnny Von the Fly Boy -- "Who do you think you are?" -- and flings open the door.

As the two meet eye to eye, each cursing up a storm, they are both suddenly stunned by the sight of the other.

Johnny Von the Fly Boy stops in his tracks, profanity caught in his throat as he looks at the living replica of Trixie Valaine standing in front of him. His pin-up came from his imagination; it was an ideal, not a real person. And Estella is not in red heels with her long hair flowing. But still, standing there in front of him, there she is, Trixie Valaine. He is struck dumb.

"Stay out of my way!" he yells.

Of all the things he planned to say while walking to Hangar 16, this is all he can get out. "You just, better stay out of my way!" he blurts again. He is shocked by her resemblance to the image of a woman he has emblazoned inside his heart and mind. The woman he whispers to, while his hands still tremble, each time he lands.

At the very same moment, Estella is also struck dumb. But not by Johnny Von the Fly Boy's resemblance to another. Estella is shocked because she knows him. Not from the war, not by his reputation as an ace pilot. Estella knows him from Ohio, from her Uncle Teddy Jay's farm.

She's been looking for him.

He doesn't recognize her.

But Estella doesn't miss a beat. "Fly Boy, you think I care about you?" She's done this more than he has. "You think I'm going to lose sleep over what you have to say about it?" It's not the right time. "Newsflash, honey, not only can I fly circles around you, but I don't take orders from you. Look at me! Take a good hard look, up and down, right now. Because if you see me in the sky, you won't get a second look." She just needed to see him. "You think you're the first man to come by and bully poor little ol' me?" She was never sure what she would say if she found him. How she would tell him. "Sweetheart, I have men like you for breakfast. So get out of the kitchen because trust me, a little man like you can't take the heat."

Johnny Von the Fly Boy is thrown completely off balance. Women don't talk to him this way.

Estella reaches across the doorway and pokes him, "Look again, get it all in right here and now. I can cook it and clean it. I can serve it up and bed it down. And I can put a Warhawk on a dime in the dark. Farm boy, my skills with a joystick would leave you crawling for the door. So you," she pokes him one more time, "just better stay out of MY way!" She slams the door before he can say another word. She hears him walk off muttering in the night.

She takes a moment there, at the door, to calm the trembling in her knees. The trembling is not from the shouting match, nor is it from keeping from him who she is. Her tremors are from relief: she's finally found him, and he's okay.

On the mantle in the living room there is a picture of a young Johnny Von the Fly Boy and Teddy Jay standing in front of her uncle's favorite barnstorming plane. A blue bi-plane, a plane Estella flew many times after Johnny Von the Fly Boy was no longer around.

"Born to fly planes, that one." T.J. would point at the picture as Estella studied it. And then say nothing more. Never talking about how he left. Never talking about where he went. But Estella felt his sadness.

One day when she was fixing breakfast, a rare day when Mary Alice was up and around, she told her how T.J. came back to the farm alone after WWI. She told Estella how she was amazed that he never uttered a single word about what happened. Not one word, ever, about what he saw. Of the morning he carried his baby brother for as long as he could, the life gone from his body. About how he had no choice but to leave him, there on the cold ground, so far away from home. He never spoke one word about the things that still had him walking around the house in the still of the night 25 years later. What he did say was that the U.S. had no business in Europe.

The only time T.J. ever did talk about Johnny Von the Fly Boy was when he was teaching Estella. He'd go on about their times over the golden barley fields of Ohio.

The air shows and fairs, and how natural his young student was in the clouds. Why they fell out, why they never heard from him, her uncle would not say. Estella was still just a girl then, she didn't understand, and it was not something anyone would talk about. But still, he used him as an example in every lesson, every comparison of how to be good up there.

Estella sits down at her cot, the bucket of water turning cold. Estella looked at his picture many times over the years. The first time she saw him she was 13, that first summer at the farm. He soared through the air above Roberta's corn field, landed like he was sliding into home plate, and jumped down from T.J.'s blue biplane with a confidence only God-given talent affords. She thought he was the most handsome thing she'd ever seen.

"Boots." That's what he called her those six months before he left, when she was out in the field, or standing by Roberta while she worked on her plane, or when she'd grab his pack as he walked into the barn.

"I'm leaning to fly," she'd said.

"Okay, Boots," he'd say, patting her head and smiling.

She didn't have any work boots she could fly in, so Roberta gave her an old pair of hers. They were too big and she had to wear as many socks as she could to keep them on her feet. She loved them. Wore them all day long around the planes. She had that image of him, smiling at her and saying, "Boots," memorized. So many times she thought of it, ran the memory of it in her mind that it would sometimes blur and fade and she couldn't see it. And then she'd relax and find it again in her head.

But as those five years passed without a word of him, she'd also look at the picture on the mantle and feel the missing piece, the way he seemed to lurk around and haunt the one thing she loved. She didn't like it. She knew she would find him one day, that she had to, so she could make sure he was safe. But never did she imagine it would be like this.

Neither Estella nor Johnny Von the Fly Boy told anyone about their exchange. And the hazing progressed just as Colonel Myers had hoped it would. The fly-bys, the latrines left dirty, the constant catcalls and remarks, an ongoing barrage of disrespect and innuendos. It was mostly from the lower ranking guys, but Johnny Von the Fly Boy and his buddies all played their part. Condoned it with their silence and smirks. When there were words, it was usually between Estella and Johnny Von the Fly Boy, and it usually ended in shouting.

She was going to tell him. Or, maybe she wouldn't. Maybe it was enough just to know he was okay. It was never the right time, the right circumstance. As the weeks passed, Estella could not put together the two worlds of Johnny Von the Fly Boy and the young man she remembered. The young man of 22 who had called her "Boots." The young man T.J. loved and missed so much. The man she'd crossed the world to make sure was safe. She was growing convinced that she hated him.

Johnny Von the Fly Boy was sure he hated her. He thought she was uppity and brash. He was constantly pushing out any thoughts that she resembled Trixie Valaine, and couldn't imagine she was anything close to competent as a pilot. His opinion was unwavering. He was sure of it, the utter wrongness of it all. Sure, until a Thursday afternoon five weeks after their first encounter.

On a special air route delivery, ferrying a Hawker Hurricane to a neighboring airfield above Dover, Estella overhears the radio call from Johnny Von the Fly Boy. Eamon is down. Jon and Peter are engaged in enemy fire just off the shore. He is hit but still up with a Gerry closing in fast. She knows the coordinates they are calling out and knows she can get to them in time. She also knows that if she breaks from her route, if she sees any combat, she will be terminated. But the fact that she's been given an armed plane to ferry, which is against A.T.A. regulations to begin with, that she heard the call, that she is on this ferry route that is so far off her normal route, Estella knows it is all too much to ignore. She doesn't think twice about what to do. It's why she's here.

Without asking, without calling in, Estella breaks. Within minutes she is coming in from the sun, in the middle of the dogfight. With a blink she dives, circles, zeroes in and blasts the Gerry on the tail of Johnny Von the Fly Boy.

Wild-eyed he tries to look back, see what has happened, see who has saved him, but only catches sight of the call letters on the Hawker Hurricane out of the corner of his eye. His rudder catching and sputtering, he heads back and makes it to the airstrip just in time. He lands Trixie smoking, but still in one piece. It is the closest death has come to him. It's a bad sign. He blames the dames.

The next morning no one knew of a British air mission, nor could anyone account for who had been up there. And then he heard the boys outside talking.

"She brought a Hawker over yesterday, it's a three or four hour drive." They were deciding who would go out to pick up Estella. Johnny Von the Fly Boy was on the road before anyone could ask him why.

"If you discharge a gun by mistake again, I'll have no choice but to ground you indefinitely." Estella nods to the British Sergeant as she sees Johnny Von the Fly Boy walk into the room. "I'm recommending you be taken off duty for a few weeks. Take it as your first and last warning."

"Sir, I can explain," Johnny Von the Fly Boy is about to tell the tale when Estella interrupts him.

"Explain ... explain why he is here! This is my ride." Estella grabs her papers, "I'm sure you've heard of Johnny Von the Fly Boy. He's got to get back, of course. Is there anything else, I'm sure he's in a hurry." She pushes him out the door before the British officer can say another word.

"What the hell are you doing!" Estella starts in as soon as they get outside. "If he finds out that I was in that dogfight, he'll ship me back stateside before I can tie my shoes."

"What the hell are YOU doing!" Johnny Von the Fly Boy counters back. "You want to tell me about stealing fighters and jumping into combat without telling anyone?"

"I didn't steal anything! I saved your life!"

"Maybe."

"Maybe!" Estella squawks.

"This is exactly why women should not be up there. You don't go off by yourself, in a plane, into battle. What are you, some kind of crazy?"

"I know what I'm doing up there as much as you do! You're going to look me in the eye and tell me that I should have heard the call and let you burn?"

"This is the army. This is war, Estella! This is not an at-will, do what you want, when you want, game. You follow orders!"

"I know damn well this is war! And I know how to follow orders. But I'll never be given any orders! Women don't fly planes in combat, remember! I'm a civilian, an ace-pilot civilian that can never do anything but ferry planes back and forth, what the hell good is that? I'm discarded. My talent, the only damn thing I want to do in the world, is discarded because I'm a woman!"

Johnny Von the Fly Boy is struck by the frustration in her voice.

"I flew yesterday, just as good as any man! Better, even! I proved myself and you know it."

He does know it. In fact, he has never seen anyone fly like that, anyone but Teddy Jay. He does know she saved his life and that he is damn happy she broke rank. But he hates that he knows it.

"God damn it, woman! We'll keep it between us. But never again!"

"Yeah. We'll keep it between us," Estella adds, "so no one finds out a girl saved ace pilot Johnny Von the Fly Boy's skin."

And with that, Johnny Von the Fly Boy feels his heart jump, "Enough!" He's in love with her and he knows it. "No more talking!" And he hates that he knows it.

Two hours pass, winding the backcountry roads west of Dover before another word is spoken.

"Where did you learn to fly like that, anyway?"

Estella, still miffed that she has not been thanked for saving the life of such an arrogant bastard, imagining that she'd stayed on course, picturing his crashing plane with a tinge of delight, fires back before she has thought it through. "I'm Teddy Jay's niece. That's how I know I'm better than you. He told me."

Johnny Von the Fly Boy slams on the brakes and they both jolt forward.

"What did you say?"

Estella, immediately regretting her words, suddenly doesn't have anything to say.

"You're T.J.'s niece!" He looks over to her and a sudden wave of recognition washes over him. The image of Trixie Valaine flashes into his mind. He sits stunned for a moment. "Boots?" He's confused. He looks around and then rubs his forehead with exasperation, "I know he doesn't know you're here!"

Johnny Von the Fly Boy starts up the jeep and begins driving. "So you know who I am, you knew this whole time."

"I know that you're an ungrateful bastard and that T.J. didn't deserve what you did. Leaving him high and dry like that. Never a word, never a letter, nothing."

"Is that what you think, that I just left?"

"Well?"

Johnny Von the Fly Boy slams on the brakes, again they jolt forward. "T.J. kicked me out. Told me if I signed up overseas, if I left to fight, then I was never to come back again, that I was dead to him. He's the one who left me, doll! How do you like that, the only kind of family I ever had. Found my bags in the yard! Wouldn't even talk to me, wouldn't even let me on the Goddamned porch!"

Estella had only known that T.J. took Johnny Von the Fly Boy under his wing when he was young, that his real parents hadn't been good to him and that T.J. raised him like a son from the time he was nine or ten. He'd let him work the farm and live out in the house on the backfield. That, and that T.J. taught him to fly. And that he flew like no one anyone had ever seen.

It's dusk, and the light is fading, but Estella is sure she sees Johnny Von the Fly Boy tear up. Sitting here, stopped on the road with him, Estella starts to put all the pieces together. She is struck by the moment. After all the death, all the loss, all the utterly unthinkable things he has seen, that this memory of T.J. wells up emotion in Johnny Von the Fly Boy catches Estella off guard.

"You're damn right I didn't go back. Go back like some dog, begging for bones."

Estella is all at once moved by the wall of pride and pain in his voice, the loneliness of Johnny Von the Fly Boy. She'd only ever seen him in the context of his buddies, in the light of Teddy Jay's affection for him, or with the crush of a schoolgirl. Here with him now, she sees him as a man, as he is, and she softens.

Johnny Von the Fly Boy starts up the jeep again. The rest of the winding road is silent.

That night after everyone is down, except for a few card games she can hear in the mess hall, she sees the light of Johnny Von the Fly Boy's cigar far out in the field, in front of Trixie Valaine.

"I've got nothing to go back to either," she says, coming up behind him in the dark as he stands looking at the image of Trixie Valaine.

Her arms are still folded, but her voice is offering, not accusing. Johnny Von the Fly Boy looks to Estella and holds her gaze here in the dark of the English countryside, the two of them lit by a moon so bright it casts shadows on the ground. "Flying is the only thing I've got, the only thing that has kept me alive, even before this damn war. It is the only thing that I have wanted in my life no matter what." Her voice is soft with the truth of it.

She continues on, trying to get all the truth out. "I had to know. I had to know that you were all right. That's why I lied about my age, why I didn't tell you when I first saw you. I came because my heart needed to know you were okay."

Johnny Von the Fly Boy takes a drag of his cigar and the red embers glow. His eyes are soft and tired, his beard scruffy. He puts it out with great care, slowly and deliberately.

"Estella." He reaches out in the darkness and pulls apart Estella's crossed arms. For a moment they stand there, staring at the other, breathing. And then, as if lightning strikes life into them both, Johnny Von the Fly Boy pulls Estella in and kisses her, open and deep, wanting to taste all of her. Estella melts in the embrace and the whole world disappears, the airfield, the planes, the war drops away, the wounded past and the blurry threatening future, all gone.

Time shifts and she cannot tell if it happens fast or slow, the moving, the undressing. The dropping to his knees, how he lays her down in the grass under the plane is all one thing, broken free from time. Estella is only conscious of sensations, the tingle of her skin, the taste of his neck, his warm hands finding her through her clothes, being touched and sucked and stroked. Her awareness weaves from moments lost to the pleasure and then back to him. He feels better than she'd ever imagined, his gorgeous deep moan at her ear as she draws her hands down him, her body to his, the hollow of her hip bones to his, the softness of her inner thighs against him. Sex is not new for Estella, a woman out in the world as she is, a woman raised by the likes of Roberta, but making love is. Estella feels him embrace her completely skin to unending skin. Johnny Von the Fly Boy holds himself right here.

"Estella." He whispers her name to her as if everything up until now has been a bad dream and he has come to call her back, gently kissing her forehead, brushing her cheek with his fingers. "Estella," he says, checking in with her one last time before he lets go, wanting to know that she is okay, that they are okay, "Estella," he whispers, wanting to see her eyes before he makes another move.

Her only thought, her only hold still to this world, is the unstoppable desire. She pauses in his eyes and then kisses him entirely. Her body rises to meet his chest, to get her heart as close to his as possible. She wraps her legs around his back and his mix of force and tenderness unleashes.

Johnny Von the Fly Boy is enraptured, taken over by the feel of her soft body moving under him in this rhythm of ecstasy. He lets the intensity take its own course, his heart stripped fragile and open, his body is hard and strong.

In the world they are here, two bodies, together on the cold night ground, but inside they are up in a warm blue sky, flying through sunlight, lost together in the rapture of a quiet, sun-sparkled ground below, bathed in the feeling of endless freedom. Voyeurs to God's earth, green and gold, safe underneath them as they make their way falling and lifting through air. The sun breaks the clouds and pleasure strikes through them, intense and sharp, bringing them back into their bodies in a flash of the light. Tingling and floating to the ground, Estella hears once again the breathing, his soul, now resting tenderly on her chest, is home.

Johnny Von the Fly Boy lays in the grass under Trixie Valaine, clothes disheveled, Estella wrapped in his jacket safe and warm. He looks to the sky in this moment and then to Estella, perfect in his arms. He remembers the look in T.J.'s eyes the day he announced he was going to fly in Europe. The day T.J. stood on the porch not saying a word to him. Understanding it now, by having one clear, irrepressible thought, "I can't let her fly."

Now, for all different reasons, Johnny Von the Fly Boy cannot stand the thought of Estella in a plane. He pushes the idea out of his mind, knowing she's grounded for a few weeks. Thinking maybe he can figure out a way in that time to tell her he loves her too much to see her in a war-filled sky.

"We've got to win this thing and go home," he says to her. "We'll get a place like old T.J.'s. Hell, with my war money we can buy T.J.'s place. Get him out of debt and run it ourselves, build a little house behind him. Take the ol' bastard up in that two-seater over the fields when he gets too grumpy to do it himself." Johnny Von the Fly Boy pulls Estella closer, lost in his imaginings he turns to her in the night. "Maybe run a little flight school, together, a whole family of Ace Pilots." He laughs. "What do you think about that?"

Estella is shaken out of the blissful afterglow with his words. "There's something I need to tell you. Something I should have said." She leans up on her elbow, "T.J., you know he loved you like you were his boy. Goodness sakes, he talked about nothing but you when he was teaching me to fly. So much that I thought you must have been made of gold. But Teddy Jay ..." she fumbles for the right way, her eyes filled with worry.

"I know. I know why he did what he did." He cuts in. "It will be all right now, I understand."

"No." She looks him in the eye. "Teddy Jay ...You were right. He doesn't know I'm here. T.J. died two months before I came over. Mary Alice passed and then he just faded, not six months and he was gone."

Johnny Von the Fly Boy does not move. He only lies in the grass looking up, saying nothing, pulling Estella in as close as he can.

It was a clear day when Estella's plane caught fire, when she looked out to see her left wing smoking, realizing the flames were moving fast. She wasn't afraid for herself, about dying, she only thought of Johnny Von the Fly Boy. Of how he would be standing on the airstrip waiting for her, as he did now every time she was due to return. Always waiting to see her come back safely. As she called in her coordinates and ejected from the plane only two miles from him, she imagined him standing outside of Teddy Jay's collecting his bags that day, looking lost and alone. She thought only of making it back home to the fields of Ohio with him, of flying over the golden barley fields, when her head struck the popped windshield and she lost consciousness.

It was Johnny Von the Fly Boy who found her crumpled on the ground, carried her to the jeep and held her body close, crazed with panic at her shallow breath.

It was Johnny Von the Fly Boy's eyes she looked into when she said, fading, "I'm not going to fly again, am I?" His eyes she saw look at her twisted legs and begin to cry. It was Johnny Von the Fly Boy who heard her whispered words before passing out again: "It's all right, I have something else now. I've got something else that I want, no matter what."

After the medics and the surgeons and the nurses had their way with her, he finds himself again at her side under the white gauzy tent. His panic is inconsolable as he sits next to her. "Estella," he says, brushing her cheek with his fingers. "Estella," he says, trying to call her back. "Estella," he says, unable to move, searching desperately for her eyes.

At the last moment, when he is sure he cannot bear not having her, she blinks ever so faintly. Johnny Von the Fly Boy draws close to Estella. He puts his trembling hands on her, feels her soft warm body under the white blanket, and begins to whisper. What he whispers, only Estella knows.

Chapter 4

> "I must create a system or be enslaved
> by another man's; I will not reason and
> compare: my business is to create."
> ~ *William Blake*

After that second day working in the house, Johnny Von and I begin what I like to call our "waving relationship." Up Valley Glen Drive, down Valley Glen Drive, from the Trans Am, from the passenger side of his assistant's Explorer, occasionally from the backseat of a shiny black limousine, Johnny Von throws out a neighborly wave to me whenever he passes. I happily return it. Granted, it's not the friendly friendship-land that I was hoping for, but I take it as a definite positive. I feel it is heading in the right direction.

Two weeks into our waving relationship, Johnny Von's sister stops me, mid-Valley Glen Drive. She rolls down her window as nice as anything. I say that because, while for the rest of the United States this is normal niceness, for L.A. it's substantial niceness.

"My friend and I are putting together a country music night at this club The King King. It's this band that we know and the guys are great."

She hands me a small printed postcard with the date and the event. "You should come, and tell all your friends." She doesn't know that most of my current friends are canine in species, and while they might like country music, they really don't do well at clubs. She also does not know that I could be Three Finger Brown and still count my L.A. friends on one hand. But it's not really the time to go into that.

"We're trying to make it an ongoing event, so we need a good turnout."

I smile and tell her I'd love to and thank her for inviting me.

"It's this Sunday." She waves good-bye to us, me and Moochie and Rocky, and rolls away.

I look at the little postcard.

I look at it like Charlie, in *Willy Wonka and the Chocolate Factory* — the Gene Wilder version — when that little nappy-headed Charlie unwraps the last of the golden tickets, the way that kid stares at the gold paper like it's holy. That's what I look like, there on the street, as I read each little word, burning it into my mind.

"Do you know Johnny Von?" I say to Mandy as we start our trek up Runyon Canyon. Mandy and I are on our evening walk. I've been back and forth about telling her all day, especially after my earlier decision not to tell her, and Shelby's reaction to the whole thing, but I don't have many options. If I want to go to the King King on Sunday night, I can't go by myself.

"Yeah," she nods. "My friend Jessica used to date his roommate when they were making *"Kings of Vegas."*

While Mandy Kane seems like the worst choice, she really is my only choice. I need an ally, a wingman.

"His sister asked me to this party, it's not a private thing or anything, it's just this country music night. It's this Sunday."

"I can totally see you two together!" Mandy says this before I tell her about any of it, her voice fresh with excitement. She means it and it shocks me. For all her physical façade, Mandy would say straight out what she thinks, nice or not nice. "He's way too tall for me, but I think he's really cool. You guys would make a great couple."

"I don't know." Gun-shy from Shelby Braxton's reaction, I'm afraid to show any cards, but Mandy has me down cold.

"Really. I think you guys would be good together. I'm totally into going with you. What are you going to wear?"

I don't know if it's the relief that Mandy finally has some guy-related conversation to have with me, or that she feels a new bond between us, but she hasn't been this animated in a long time. The last time I saw her like this was the day I told her about having my eyebrows shaped at Anna St. Clair's Salon. She was floored that I got an appointment with Anna St. Clair herself. Julia Roberts to Oprah, Anna St. Clair does everybody's eyebrows; you name a big one, she's plucked them. More than once, the day before I was scheduled, she asked me if I was sure it wasn't an assistant I was seeing, an underling at the salon.

"You don't understand. Nobody gets to see Anna St. Clair." Mandy was very impressed.

It was a glitch in the system, a fluke in scheduling. I got the number from a dog client and I didn't even know who Anna St. Clair was when I called, but I never told that to Mandy. I didn't tell her that everyone stared at me like I didn't belong there. I didn't tell her that when they realized I didn't have anything to do with the industry or anyone connected to the industry, they glazed over. I didn't tell her how, while Anna St. Clair herself was quite polite, everyone else chatted over and around me in the private salon area while I waited for my turn on the table. I didn't want to spoil it for her.

"I think you should wear that halter top, the purple one with the spaghetti straps," she offers enthusiastically.

In Mandy's mind, we now share a common goal: to partner with someone famous. I cringe at the thought, but then reason, *so what?* So what if Mandy thinks it's all about his celebrity? I know it's not. I know that it's about his eyes, how they stopped the rotation of the planets when he looked at me. I know it's not about his Hollywood status, and besides, I need her. Of course this means I'll be going to church with her now, and not to pray, but I figure it's a small price. We talk back and forth the whole hike, a new record for us. We usually only find common ground on topics that concern dogs; then it's just Mandy talking about Mandy. But not today! Today we talk about Johnny Von, about clothes and hair and make-up, and about our love for The Drybar. We talk about guys and shoes and low-carb foods.

"Angela, that was beautiful."

I'm weeks into my poetry class. Angela, the slightly overweight girl, and Tim, the Gothic rocker, have started dating. They haven't said anything, but I saw them holding hands walking to the parking lot last week. Love is blooming. I take it as a good sign. So far, I'm the only person who hasn't volunteered to read yet. Until today, Carlos hadn't read, and before last week there were three of us still holding out. Tim and Angela both have knocked it out of the park, reading not just okay poems, but really good stuff since day one.

"Anyone else?"

The grannies have all read their work, mostly rhyming stuff about harvests and rainbows and a few wild horses running free. Lillian writes a lot of things about her grandkids, Turning one/What fun/You are the sun etc.

"Is anyone else reading today?"

I look down. The whole room is stiff with the knowledge that it's me he's talking about. I'm the 'anyone.' Everyone looks around and avoids my eyes, except the Grannies. They look over at me and smile that unnerving Grandma smile. That patronizing sweet don't-be-scared-we-read-and-the-sky-didn't-fall smile. Damn grannies! Mocking me with their unconditional support. I don't have a full poem. I did try, but it's just parts and it's not readable. It doesn't mean anything and it doesn't rhyme. It just feels lifeless. It feels like it's trying to be a poem. Trying too hard and coming off contrived. I'm not reading it. I'd rather bare the shame of silence than the public humiliation.

Mr. Banks continues, "Angela's work is, dare I say, very Blake-ian."

"Finally." I think. "Finally, we'll get to this William Blake and see why the universe has me on this trail, because I'm sure I'm not here to be a poet.

He stands and uses his hands as he talks. "I say this because the poet" — he looks to Angela with fatherly pride — "seems to start with the reality of things, and then switches to showing us an imagined world. The poem then ends implying more value to this imagined existence." He looks around to see everyone nod along. I agree with him although I'm sure I don't know what he's talking about, and I'd wager that the grannies, at least, don't either.

"You see, William Blake believed in the power of the imagination over all outside authorities." He reaches for a stack of handouts. "Which gives me the perfect segue."

He flicks down the lights and clicks on the projector. "William Blake!" He begins his lecture with drama.

I like this about Andrew Banks: mild-mannered, slightly frumpy, dull older gentleman on the street, who turns Technicolor and passionate when he speaks about poetry, especially William Blake's poetry.

"Was he a genius? A mystic? More poet, more artist?" He flips through the slides quickly, flashing the colors and images of Blake's artwork on the white screen.

The grannies ooh and ahh in unison.

"Many people believe Blake was crazy, in more than an artist way; a certifiable way. His visions started when he was young and his parents kept him home from school — he was different." Andrew Banks winks at the Gothic rocker, whose heavy blue eyeliner is slightly smeared. "Others claim he was part of an underworld of pseudo-religious ritual sex cults of the late 18th century." He shakes his head and slightly laughs, as if the words are absurd to hear aloud. "They read into his work, a man on a mission to justify free love." He then looks over and winks to the grannies. They blush and smile like teenagers. I'm surprised by it. But then I realize the grannies ushered in the '60s with the likes of Andrew Banks.

"Lillian, have you been telling tales out of school again." Ruthie, the leader of the pack whispers loudly.

Great, now the grannies are interrupting my Blake lecture with their grandstanding.

"Only the good parts, Ruthie." Her friend answers over the clicking of the slides, as the class laughs. "When and where you bared your bottom on the grounds of this very campus, oh so many years past, causing us all to be arrested, is safe with me." She winks back to her friend through the light of the projector.

Ruthie zings back, "Painting a peace sign on our buttocks, which is the only reason we were singled out, was Joanne's idea, not mine, and I will stand by that until the day I die."

"I wasn't there." Joanne counters as the whole class cuts up with laughter.

"Joanne Grace Jacobs, no matter what you tell your grandchildren, you know you were with us, and I have the picture still to prove it. How the school newspaper knew our names, now that is still a mystery." The four break into silly laughter, an unabashed laughter of old friends, and then Florence, the most reserved of the group, says, "Skinny dipping by the light of the moon is the only way to see my bare buttocks now." All four grannies break into hysterical laughter while they agree and amen the comment.

Thoroughly amused Mr. Banks says to them, "Is there more you ladies need to share?"

They laugh and smile and nod no.

For a moment I picture all of them young, in the summer of love, long hair and beads, at Woodstock. Intertwined maybe, like Blake's lovers on the screen, with soft, plump baby skin. I smile to think of them this way, wild and free. I love these damn grannies.

"If I may..." Mr. Banks gives them a wicked smirk. The grannies nod and Mr. Banks returns to his lecture.

"Blake believed our imagination is what links us to our soul, and from the soul's imagination blooms love, blooms energy, blooms life force. This dialog with one's own imagination, one's soul, is what compels the poet to speak."

Mr. Banks clicks through slides in rapid progression. "To Blake, it is through the senses that we come to know desire. And it is this desire that gives birth to the imagination."

He clicks the next slide, "What do you desire?"

Artwork from Blake's etched plates from the *Marriage of Heaven and Hell* fill the room. My eyes take in the blowing tree, the girl reaching up to the hand of her lover from the heavens...languishing nudes at the bottom edge. I feel my skin tingle and my face flush. All I can think of the Johnny Von.

"Start there." He leans over to the grannies, "And I don't just mean desires of the flesh, ladies, I mean all desires. It can be for anything or anyone ...what ever pulls this feeling out of you. Take the raw energy of it—beyond the object that calls this energy from you, and fashion it. Follow the desires inside you."

Mr. Banks flips to some of Blake's more known artwork, drawing his lecture to a close. "For Blake, this is the only true religious experience."

He flips the slide to *The Ancient of Days*, Blake's watercolor of God beaming down creation from the heavens. "'Desire is infinite,' quotes Blake, and it is in this idea of the infinite that we are at one with our creator."

I don't know if I know what he is talking about, if I understand how I could get any of this from reading his poems or looking at the etchings, but I do know that I like it. Andrew Banks ends his lecture with the same drama he began, "Thus William Blake proclaimed: the squelching of desire... the rejection of the 'Energies,' as he coined it, — is the only real tragedy for man."

On Wednesday night, my brother and my dad come over to spend time with me. They're single. So is my mom. Come to think of it, everyone in my family, extended and otherwise, is without a significant other. There is not a relationship in the bunch right now.

My parents divorced after 25 years of marriage. At the end there were no dark secrets revealed, no addictions or adulterous affairs to point at, there was just the North Pole and the South Pole. A bird and a fish, very upset that the other wouldn't change. Very upset that the idea they had for a family and a happily-ever-after, was not working out because of the other one.

Perhaps it's the preconceived idea of others that get in the way love. I don't know, maybe we all hold images of the other, or of ourselves — the way we want it all to look... and when it turns out differently we either revise the plan or get out. Or maybe it's just rare to genuinely see another person at the outset. To let them be lacking. Or more even, to feel lacking in ourselves and not ask the other person to fill the void.

I don't know. I do know that at the end of the day, you can't revise yourself. A bird can't be a fish and a fish can't be a bird. Even the most perfect fish or the most beautiful bird, setting out with sincere love, can't stay companions. They have different places to go. But really, on the other hand, 25 years seems like a long time to be with someone and then not be able to talk to them ever again. The silence, the stalemate between them, is so loud.

My dad, brother and I decide to stay in, make tuna sandwiches and rent a movie. I'm happy about it. Whenever my dad and I go out to eat, he ends up adding and re-adding the bill, flabbergasted. Then everything we talk about from there out winds back to the cost of living in California. The two-dollar bacon strips at the Highway Café on the corner of Franklin is a topic we revisit often.

As we walk the aisles of Blockbuster, I reach out and grab a DVD, a Johnny Von movie, *The Time of the Owl.*

"What about this? I've already seen it, but it's pretty good." I say casually. My dad scans the back. It's a comedy, but he thinks it's a spy movie.

"Sure, kid."

About 15 minutes in, he grabs the paper and starts scanning the front page of the sports section. About 20 minutes in he says, "What do you think, kid, how about some ice cream?"

He putters around the kitchen and then offers, "This isn't any good, and you've seen it. What about putting on the movie your brother picked out?" He reaches for a copy of *Clear and Present Danger* with Harrison Ford.

"Yeah that's cool." I punch out the DVD. "I just wanted to see it again because that's the guy I was talking about, that actor that I like, the one where I walk the dogs."

"Oh come on! Not that bozo." My dad drops the paper and looks out over his reading glasses. "That's the guy you like? You're kidding. He's not even good-looking."

So much for a confidence boost coming from this direction.

"No, I just like him. I think he's nice, and talented, and funny."

"He doesn't look so talented to me. Do you know this actor?" He turns to my brother.

My brother nods. "Yeah. That's Johnny Von." He shrugs his shoulders and continues to play with Moochie, tugging a chew rope on the floor. My brother is a man of few words.

"What do you think of him?" My dad reaches over to hit him with his newspaper, trying to get his attention.

My brother ducks, his reflexes quick from years of practice. "He's all right. I don't know, for some reason girls just really go for him." My brother's interest level is about a negative one on the topic as he continues to play with Moochie.

"Come on, put in that other movie and let's watch it." He hands me the Harrison Ford DVD. I click it on and return to the chair next to the sofa.

"Kid, you've got a dog now, and a business to look after, you have car payments, don't go chasing that bozo." He clips me on the arm with the newspaper now.

"What? I'm not chasing anybody. I just said I like him, and I worked in his house a couple of times."

"Humph. You're not chasing? Okay; well, just remember you have bills and responsibilities, and you don't have time to run around after some guy. You got it?" He tags me with the newspaper again before I can duck, which makes me laugh even though I don't want to, "You weren't chasing after that bozo in London, either, and look what happened." My laughter abruptly stops. That last bit pisses me off. I try to share with these people, and look where it gets me.

"I'm not chasing anybody. He just seems nice, is all. I just think he might be nice to get to know. What's wrong with that? Wanting to get to know someone is not chasing."

My father is a practical man. Often this comes across as callous, and often I have to remind myself of this. He is old school, a guy's guy, an engineer where only end results count. There is no middle value, no true love conquering, no sweetness on the way to be savored even if it didn't all work out. Life is work and car payments and saving for a rainy day. I like him, my dad, don't get me wrong. I like his company ... but no wonder I can't come up with any poetry, look what raised me! Poetry, smoetry.

"I just said I like him is all." I say, and close the subject before I get emotional. Before anyone can see it's important to me. My father doesn't notice.

"And that reminds me, I checked your air filter and it's filthy."

Love, poetry, tall Johnny Von, or auto maintenance. Which is more important?

"We're going to Auto Zone first thing tomorrow, so I can make sure you change the damn air filter, and we're going to change the oil while we're there. You got it?" He starts to whip himself up in the importance of it, and my lack of interest. "You have to take care of your stuff. I want *you* to take care of yourself. You don't need some bozo. You can look after you."

"Alright, alright already. I know."

"Well then take care of your car. They open at 9:00. Are you listening to me kid?"

"Okay. Whatever."

"Not 'whatever.' I want you to pay attention and take care of your car!"

"Fine!" I laugh. "Okay!"

"Now stop talking," he swings the rolled up newspaper at both my brother and I, but can't get a direct hit anywhere, which makes us all laugh. As Harrison Ford bursts onto the screen, my father says, "Stop moving and be quiet, I want to watch the damn movie!"

"I know I can't wear the same thing twice, but it's too bad, because my tits look really great in this." Sunday 10:00 Mass goes by faster than I expected. Before I know it, I am traveling down Sunset on the passenger side of Mandy's Cadillac Escalade, watching people watching us, peering in Mandy's tinted windows, thinking she must be someone. Sadly, Mark Wahlberg was not at Mass. "I'll just have to find something else to wear next Sunday." Mandy is deep in strategy mode. "I think my pink dress from Lisa Kline next week, and the new Jimmy Choo sandals."

It's a skill I struggle with — fashion for social profit. I only manage, but Mandy is like a good cook who can scan the cupboard and come up a gourmet meal from just a few bits and pieces. "I wasn't sure," she continues, "but I saw a lot of people in high heels today."

Mandy Kane did a national commercial for Pizza Hut the first month she arrived in L.A. It has afforded quite a lifestyle, although I sense some of her cash flow is revolving credit. But that is purely speculation on my part; I'm not in the industry. From what little I know, a national Pizza Hut gig, even just one, is a pretty big payday.

"You're wearing the purple halter tonight, right?" Mandy asks this question with the intensity of a medic on the battle field. We've already talked about this extensively. I liked all the girl talk at first, but now it's just making me nervous.

"And the faux snake shoes?"

Again I nod.

"Ohh. I love this song." Mandy jacks up the radio.

While Mandy sings along to some really hard rap song about ho's and pimps, I think again about preconceived ideas. About how much time is invested in crafting ourselves, in creating a desired image to show the world. And I start to think about tonight and Johnny Von and how much time he must have to spend crafting his image. About how impossible it is, even in normal everyday life, to see someone clearly, see someone through all the preconceived ideas, much less someone whose entire life's career is heavily, heavily, tied up in image -- attended to by teams of people who make their living doing it well! The whole idea of trying to get to know Johnny Von, even if I wasn't scared to death of talking to him, seems impossible. Even if I was the coolest girl in the world, some kind of socializing ninja, some modern day Betty Crocker mannered, supermodel bodied, on the list of every party in town woman, social savant…with the skills of the best stripper in all the land to boot, as a hobby…who always knows exactly what to say, even then, I'd still have to make it through the distance of him, to the real Johnny Von behind all that image. No wonder celebrities have trouble with relationships.

"I'll come over early, about 7:00, and we can dress," she says as I climb down out of the car.

I haven't dressed with anyone since prom. The band doesn't start until almost midnight. I wave and smile, a bit concerned about Mandy and tonight. What is going to take four hours?

I scan my closet when I get home. I have a lot of nice things, I just don't have the opportunity to wear them. I don't take the time each day, just for the dogs. This is something that has been brought to my attention now more than once by Trudie Reed whenever she hijacks me on Valley Glen Drive to help her water her lawn. It's become quite a routine; Friday's conversation went a little like this:

"You're a fine boy, aren't you?" First there is a dog biscuit for Moochie, which stops our forward progression. Pat, pat to his little brown head. Then she says, with a pat on my arm now, "Honey, can you move that hose behind the roses there." Now she has me.

"You must like being a working girl, having your own money." As I tie Moochie to the mailbox and begin to pull the green garden hose around the corner of the house Trudie Reed starts her musings on my life, "Before I met Gerald, my first husband, I worked at Saks Fifth Avenue. A proper kind of job for a young lady."

"You should get proper gardener Miss Reed." I offer hoping the conversation will not veer off in the direction of observations on my marital status, which it usually does. "The Sheppard's gardeners are great, I could ask for you."

"Nonsense. I don't want anyone else fooling with my yard. The joy of it is all mine. Well don't put that sprinkler there, that's terrible, that will kill the bushes!" Trudie Reed directs me around her yard, looking for the right spot for her sprinkler.

"Katharine Hepburn, Lauren Bacall, Elizabeth Taylor, the studios would send over all the big stars back then, and I would dress them to the nines. Not there, don't put the sprinkler like that, move it behind the tree. I tell you what, I had a sharp eye, better than all the other girls, and I was a bit of a knock out myself so they sent me everybody."

She tells me how her job was the precursor to what stylists do today—the store liaison to all the big Hollywood people, dressing all the movie stars in the forties and fifties, and about how she picked out a tie for Cary Grant, for which he sent her a handwritten thank you note.

"Men had manners back then, they knew how to treat a lady correctly."

I can't deny that it is interesting, hearing about all of it, but I am paying for it by hauling bags of dirt from the garage.

After 20 minutes of the decline in fashion standards, the problems with shop girls today, the tragic endings of movies stars of yester-year and lessons in lawn care, I make my way back to my reason for being on the street and begin untying Moochie.

Trudie Reed then says, "Such a shame people don't dress like they used to, don't take the pride in their appearance." She sighs, "Look at you, you're a pretty girl, but you're no clothes horse are you, honey."

I don't want to be any kind of horse Trudie Reed!

I don't say that to her. I want to, but of course I don't. I just smile and tug Moochie forward. Actually, she it sort of makes me laugh. She just says it so matter-of-factly I can't be offended. In fact, to be honest, in light of all the image contemplation, the preconceived ideas, the feigning of indifference, the Mandy Kanes and Shelby Braxtons, the heightening concern I'm having over Johnny Von, I am beginning to find Trudie Reed refreshing. Like a splash of cold water to the face.

Old people can just call it as they see it, the same way small children can. Pass 70 and you return to that same clemency for rudeness. It's no-holds-barred on saying what you think. No self-censoring. I like it. A four-year-old kid, fresh off Sesame Street, looks at Aunt May and says proudly, "You're the biggest." Her mother scolds her. And she says, in equal love for all of them, not yet knowing what image is judged the best, "But it's true. You're big, Nana's bigger, and she's the biggest." It's abrupt at first, sure. But it's also kind of nice.

But let's get off the topic of "biggest" and get back to what I'll be wearing to The King King. Tonight, I'll be in my skinny jeans. This, in and of itself, is celebratory. I feel a tinge of pride as I lay the jeans out on my bed. I've been on a perpetual diet since I was 12. God made me curvy and curly. I want thin and straight. We've been pushing back and forth on this issue since I can remember.

When I was living in London, I had a friend from Israel, Timor, an earthy, natural-beauty girl. We were walking to yoga one day and I was going on about wanting to have a longer body, so I would have a waist, and telling her that the yoga could probably stretch out my spine to do this. Currently, I'm long legs and no waist. She looked at me like I was a Martian and said, "That's like saying I'm going to change the color of my eyes. This is your body, this is who you are."

So I said to Timor as we unrolled our mats, "We change eye color all the time in the States. It's called color contacts." Which in the moment, sounded absurd and made us both laugh.

Timor was a good friend. Someone that sees straight to you, sees your value in places you miss. She gave me the heart shaped stone that is rumbling around the bottom of the LuBeLu's Steel Cut Oatmeal can.

Timor never said a negative word about the International Playboy, but I knew she thought he was silly. I knew she was somewhat unimpressed, that she thought I could do better — which would then cause me to look at *her* like a Martian.

She was there the first night I witnessed the phenomenon that I would come to term "When Girls Attack." My first social outing in London with the International Playboy.

"Shags!" Flicka Gerson calls out from across the room. She throws her arms up, halfway falling out of her Arabian belly-dancer costume. "I'm so happy to see you, darling." She wraps her arms around the neck of the International Playboy and plants a big kiss really close to his mouth. He drops my hand and kisses her hello. She pulls back, and all I can think is cleavage. And I'm a girl, it's not usually where my eyes go. She squeezes his arm and leans into him, "I was just telling David about the time we all striped naked in Hyde Park!" She laughs, "The night you were with Ann and Elizabeth both!"

Flicka went to school with the International Playboy, or should I say university — they were together at university, Oxford. Flicka then went into banking and has done well. So well she now has her own consulting firm and lives in a state of semi-retirement at 26. When he described her, I pictured a small demure English girl, plain, brainy, something like a homely Alice in Wonderland. But standing in front of me is someone tall, tan, booby and loud.

This Arabian Nights Costume party is for her charity. She has her own charity. It's something for sick kids and hospital equipment in under-developed countries. The kind of thing you really can't find any fault with, even if her breasts are popping out of her costume and she is hanging a bit too long on your date.

I stand smiling, trying to make eye contact. Tonight's gala is in a large warehouse off the M5 that has been transformed with endless elaborate colored tents, silk cushions, dark rugs, twinkly candles, silver goblets and robe clad waiters—a sheik's paradise. I patiently wait for the introduction moment, while spying a live camel being led through the crowd by a man in a red fez hat with a monkey on his shoulder. Flicka has gone all out. The International Playboy takes my hand again and introduces us.

Flicka scans me, turning only her eyes, not her body to greet me. At first she looks at me as if looking at something alien she can't interpret, like I'm a specimen of some kind, perhaps amusing but mostly irrelevant.

Flicka then smiles.

She smiles like Cruella De Vil smiling at the soft plump puppies. She looks back to the International Playboy. "Your little American friend!" She reaches out and squeezes my forearm, but keeps her eyes on the International Playboy. "Shags, you rascal, come with me. She reaches for him. "Imogene is here, and my sister, you must say hello." She steps between us, pulling apart our hands. She then grabs the first man to walk by, Walter Pickens. Firmly gripping my arm, Flicka pushes me into Mr. Pickens. "This is Shags' new American friend." Before I've put out my hand and announced my name, she's halfway across the room with the International Playboy in tow.

Granted, I probably should have gone on alarm when she screamed out his university nickname, "Shags," from across the room, but I'm not the jealous type. I don't look for those kinds of things. I thought, these are his old friends and it's just, you know, camaraderie. She's just being social, and helping me into the fold by introducing me to their mutual friends, their "crowd." I'm not that comfortable in big social settings so I think, it's just me, being insecure.

Mr. Pickens says nothing. He seems too old to have gone to university with them. He looks at me for a while and then says dryly, "You Americans are certainly fit, aren't you?" I grab a champagne goblet from the passing Omar Sharif waiter. I smile and make the effort.

"How do you know Flicka and the gang?"

Mr. Pickens smiles, revealing his crooked, tobacco-stained teeth, and says with his clenched-jaw English accent, sounding like Thurston Howell III from "Gilligan's Island," "I work for Her Majesty's Council to Paraguay, Solicitor General for the Committee to foreign aid and sanctions." He takes a swig of the large red wine in his hand, then slurs out, "Flicka's father and I yacht frequently from a fabulous little island off of Portugal." Walter Pickens laughs excitedly, revealing more teeth. "Quite a sailor, that good man!"

I crane my neck, looking for the International Playboy, and excuse myself. I search through the crowd and see him boisterously telling stories in the middle of a group of men. I politely circle the crowd, hoping he'll see me. It's awkward, standing alone, lurking on the side. I start thinking: I could stand here all night like this. A circle of three or four women on my left look at me, whisper and then point to the International Playboy. I reach out through the crowd and touch his arm. He turns like he's surprised and happy to see me at the party.

He pulls me toward the dance floor, but before we can get there, he's sideswiped by a boozed-up redhead. A redhead built like a super-model. She's tanked. Her Cleopatra eyeliner and mascara are smeared around her eyes. She throws herself around him. "Flicka told me you were here! I'm such a big fan. I saw you test drive for Renault in Monaco. I was at the party after the race with Jacques De Luc."

He smiles and unwraps her from around his body
— and then I don't think I imagine this — he checks
her out as she steadies herself. Not blatantly, but still.
He smiles as she babbles in a high excited pitch about
watching his last Formula One race. It is a smile that
masterfully stays on the edge of just being polite. A
smile that could legally go either way. To her it could be
interpreted as a "yes" smile, to me it could be argued as
an I'm-a-gentleman smile. The redhead looks to me only
briefly, her bloodshot eyes trying to focus, giving me the
what-are-you-still-doing-standing-here look. He sends
her on her way in one smooth move, and reaches to pull
me on.

We get to the dance floor, where two more girls bound
up at once. They screech and giggle and pull him toward
their table, saying something about the time they all met
in Ibiza. He smiles and recognition sweeps across his
face. Waving no, he hugs them and gets back to me on
the dance floor.

This sort of thing happens all through Boy George's
"I'll Tumble For You," the first of the '80s medley the
DJ is spinning. Girl after girl leaps towards him, waves
and winks across the dance floor, cuts in between us as
we dance. I notice that I feel the urge to look down at
my body and check that I am still here. I have to keep
reminding myself that the International Playboy is my
date here tonight. My legitimate date; we didn't just
bump into each other at the entrance and decide to hang

out. For the last couple of months since I arrived in London, we've been inseparable.

As the DJ cuts in the Bangles' "Walk Like an Egyptian," I notice that in my discomfort I begin to evaluate every woman that hurls herself into the International Playboy. Without wanting to, I calculate a quick comparison to what I look like and what they look like, and I catalog how he returns their advances.

"Let's get a drink, baby," he calls into my ear.

The International Playboy maneuvers his way through the crowd to the bar. I watch from the edge as he waits for the drinks. Three girls at the table to the right of the bar buzz and point and whisper, the bold one jumps up, pushes her way through the crowd and squeezes up to my dates back. I watch in disbelief as she rubs up against him and grabs his ass, and then swooshes her long, bleached-blond hair and smiles as he turns to see her. The International Playboy blushes, nods and chats. I notice, again, that he neither accepts nor refuses. The International Playboy is gregarious, he talks to the world, he flirts with everyone, he's the center of the room, I like this about him. Only tonight, it feels different. He's flirting with everyone and no one, but that includes me.

As I watch him move away from the ass-grabber with our drinks, instead of being upset toward him, or these women, I begin to feel this lack in me. It's not like he's not paying attention to me, I reason. Every time it happens, every time he gets pulled away, I just tap him or grab his hand, and he turns looking genuinely thrilled to see me. I feel confused. I'm over thinking all of this. I'm making more of it than it is. Is it me? Am I not being fun enough, engaging enough? Maybe I'm not saying enough?

"Let's go look at the monkey and camel!" See, that's fun. That's the International Playboy I like. But even at the monkey and the camel, even as the International Playboy dons the red fez and pulls me in for a picture, I begin to feel the <u>need</u> to get his attention. The monkey's great, but what about me? I begin to want him to see me, pay attention to <u>me</u>.

It's about this time that Timor walks up. We'd met the week I arrived, through his friends, when I was looking for a yoga class. It was then, in the reflection in her eyes as she looked at me as a genuine friend looks at you, that I thought: maybe the International Playboy doesn't really see me at all. The thought was only a flash. It didn't feel good and I pushed it out of my mind.

I call Mandy and suggest we meet at The Drybar then go to my house and finish getting ready. Four hours of primping had me worried and nothing relaxes me like a trip up Sunset to The Drybar. She declines, but I book a blow out anyway and tell her I'll meet her at nine.

I have good hair. It's undeniable. The thing is, I can't manage it. I'm not good at 'fixing' it. I'm 33 and admittedly,

I still can't 'do' my hair very well. The one beauty asset in my corner, and it is still hard for me to maximize it's potential. It is one of those things that would have really paid off had I lived in my Grandmother's era.

My Southern Maw Maw never missed her Wednesday beauty parlor appointment. And for most all Wednesdays in high school, it was on me to drop Maw Maw at Josie's after school let out. I never really paid attention to it then. It was a chore on my list of things to get done so I could have free time to meet up with friends.

Every Wednesday Josie Price set Maw Maw's hair in a black chair sandwiched between her best friends, Tess Walker and Miss Ann. Women in curlers and vinyl, flower-print capes, ladies talking without agendas, worn magazines on laps but never looked at, it was friends unfolding their lives in real time. They didn't have to text or have a girls-night-out to make sure they were still in each other's lives. Rain or shine they showed up in the little house with linoleum floors that smelled like perm and rosewater back behind Josie's driveway.

I'd walk in with Maw Maw some days and say hello.

"Estella!" They'd say. "Your getting so big now, don't you look beautiful. So nice to see you, baby." Stepping inside from the humid unbearable hot of the Louisiana sun, that had my hair in a permanently thick, frizzed-out mess, into that little mirrored room and being hit with the ice cold of the air conditioning was glorious. And then Josie, who was on her own since her husband died, would say, "Take a Coke from the cooler, Boo," her accent thick and Cajun.

I'd smile, say, "Thank you Miss Josie." Pull the ice-cold bottle of coke through the metal rails of the cooler and rush out. Rushing never to be like that, to be older, to be stuck in some beauty parlor in the middle of no where, having my hair be the important thing in my life.

But now, I wish I'd stayed longer, listened more, and witnessed the undercurrent of real friendship entwined with the dance of the perfect hair-do. I wish I had people that knew me, even though back then it was stifling and everything I didn't want. As I think back on it now, I'm so envious I could spit.

Over the noise of the big plastic dryers and the whirl of the glorious freezing cold air pumping out of the wall, all the life and death, the bankruptcy and family dramas, the loves and losses, were shared, were unfolded. Spoken or unspoken, it all came and went with friends who abide. It was all eased with pretty hair.

I know there is power and there is solace in pretty hair. From here I can see what it was about. I know, taken in the right way, in the shared humanity of being a woman, kind of way, I understand the value of the beauty parlor. Putting time and money and attention there, in someone standing over you, caring that your hair looks good before you stand up and go back out, alone, into the world.

It's not something Mandy gets, or maybe she does. Maybe that's why she does it all to such an extreme extent, she is reaching for that value thing too. I don't know. To Mandy, it seems, it's not beauty for her sake; it seems like beauty for what others think, for fashion, for men, for currency sake. I don't know.

All I know, is that The Drybar is the closest I can come to Miss Josie's Beauty Parlor in Los Angeles. When it opened on Sunset, I knew it was for me, for my kind. With it's white marble counters and crisp yellow accents, it's unpretentious and friendly and clean. It's much fancier than Miss Josie's, but the principles are the same. Pretty hair can make things better.

At the Drybar they just wash and blow out your hair. A job that would take me the better part of two hours without promised results, they can do in 45 minutes to a stunning effect. For a reasonable price that this dog walker can afford, I can get a block of blow-outs and go every couple of weeks!

Maw Maw would be proud.

Even if I don't have the friends beside me like I want to right now, the ritual itself, the thought of Miss Josie's, sitting with someone else scrubbing by head does something to relax me on a primal level. Here in the cool of the Drybar, safe from the cars and ads and crazy LA-ness of Sunset Blvd, I can let someone else care how I look and watch a movie where the girl gets the guy, or talk to the lady next to me that just had a baby and is worried about all the hair that she is losing. I can remember something about how we are all the same, sitting here looking into the mirror, beginning as wet cats and leaving like Angelina Jolie. I can look in the mirror at the end of the hour and stand up and own my part in beauty, in wanting beauty for myself, in wanting something shared about being a woman. I can leave the Drybar every two weeks, grab a cookie on the way out and think, "Yes. I can do this." Somebody like Johnny Von could definitely be into me. I see it's a good thing.

As Mandy arrives and begins to spread her make-up over the entire bathroom counter. I think about Timor, and what she would think of all of this. What I loved about Timor was that it was beyond her, why I would want to be other than I am. She was a far cry from magazine pretty, but had every guy in yoga falling all over themselves. And she didn't shave her armpits. Shocking. But she loved her look, and it made her vibe sexy. There was nothing in her fighting herself, and as she looked out at people, that was what they saw. She just shined as herself, with whatever clothes, make-up, jewelry or hair that she liked. It was always attractive.

Watching her at yoga it dawned on me for the first time that the concept of beauty and what is sexy might be more than I was trying to fit myself into, more than what the International Playboy and his friends designated as sexy. That it might be about what's going on inside the girl.

I don't know. I still battle inside with all of it. I want to totally embrace the curves and curls of my being. I want to shine and feel pretty and adorn myself with clothes that I love, I want to remember the things that I think are pretty about me, and not obsess about what doesn't match fashion standards. I want to believe that I will find my "other" by just being that. But it's tough. Nobody's really selling me that story.

So tonight, I'm putting on my skinny jeans. I haven't had a carbohydrate in months and my hair is straight and shiny. I feel victorious. But if I'm honest, I do feel that it's all off a little. The internal discord to get into the skinny jeans can't be right. I look at Mandy Kane and all the effort and I know something is off. Using looks as currency in trade for attention and romantic connection can't be right. I'm not talking about giving up shaving, wearing a burlap sack, and letting myself go, but I know something in me is still missing a mark, on an existential level. I just can't find it yet.

Sunday night, 11:30 sharp, after lengthy make-up and hair and clothes discourse, as well as unsolicited flirting-with-celebrity tips: "Don't talk about their projects unless they talk about their projects, definitely don't ask them what their working on now, but absolutely tell them how much you love their work. Call the directors they've worked with by name, and tell them how great they look now; and last but not least, dominate the conversation. Talk down to them just a bit, like you would a yard man or like you know way more famous Hollywood power players than they ever will."

It was all absurd and just made me more wound up as Mandy and I now make our way into The King King.

And yes, I'm wearing the purple silk halter-top with little purple straps. It's sexy and backless and has a little line of beaded trim at the bottom front that moves nicely. I'm also wearing the faux snakeskin shoes; my favorites because the faux snake is quality faux and they are out of the norm.

I'll be honest, I'm nervous. After all, I'm walking into The King King knowing Johnny Von is hanging out with his friends inside and that this is it. That's valid, I think, to be nervous over that. That's normal. Okay, I don't know for sure if Johnny Von is inside, but I feel 99.9% sure there would be a Johnny Von inside, if he were in town. He seems like the kind of guy that would go to his sister's event.

It's not a big club. It's not crowded. The bar is centered in the room. Mandy and I step up, order drinks and out of the corner of my eye across the way I see Johnny Von see me. I think I see a slight happy recognition wash over him, but I can't really trust myself with the idea. It's in my peripheral vision.

My plan is the universal plan when you like someone and you see them out, which is: ignore them. I haven't altered the universal plan because Johnny Von is the target.

Look, it's not my plan. If I was in a war-room of strategic planning somewhere and The General called out, "What's the plan, Sergeant?"

I'd say, "Well, the best plan if you like someone and you see them out, is to go up and talk to them."

Apparently, The General would fire back, "Wrong! Are you trying to get everyone killed? It's too obvious. The other side won't know what to do with such direct attention. A foot soldier would know better. You get in there and you pretend like you don't see them at first. And then, whatever you do, you wait until they come up to you."

It's the universal plan. Maybe it's just the universal plan for shy people and most all the guys I know, I don't know. But the General and his war room have gotten me through every social setting I can remember. He's how I cope. I'd never get out of my room without his yelling orders to me all the way. Besides, Mandy seems to believe very much in this plan.

We stay stationary at the bar and I begin to drink and chat. I decide to focus and engage in conversation to divert my attention and my growing feelings of anxiety.

Of course everything I am saying, everyone I am talking to, is only occupying .02% of my attention. The location of Johnny Von in the club is taking up the other 99.98%. I'm good at splitting my attention, and he's tall in the crowd, so it's going well. Plus my friend knows the score, so she is carrying a lot of the interaction.

A good 45 minutes into the night, I'm chatting with a girl next to me about my poetry class. I say chatting.

When you talk in clubs you really yell at people. You really talk directly at their ear, loudly, in short clips. This is why I am not good in clubs. Here I am trying to talk about my newfound interest in poetry with some person I don't even know. Confessing that I've not been able to write anything so far, and the class is half over. Admitting to this stranger that the thought of reading something aloud terrifies me.

I'm just not good with hip little conversations, buzzwords, and short flirty phrases. I can't come up with something short and witty to yell under the gun, to get your attention.

So I'm saying all of this into the ear of this girl, and I feel someone standing next to me, a presence stopped next to me. Without looking away from the ear I am shouting into, I realize it's Johnny Von. Johnny Von is standing next to me! And then I realize he is waiting for me to finish. All I can feel is my heart jump into my throat.

Before I turn, I grab myself inside and shake. I hear The General: "Grab a hold of yourself and calm down, soldier! You turn around and you talk to Johnny Von. You talk to him like the friendly personable girl that you are." I politely excuse myself from the ear of the girl next to me. The General continues, "Cut the shit! You get in there and you do this! You do it for God and Country! You do it for all those times you liked someone and you choked at the moment of truth. Do you hear me, soldier?"

"Hi," I turn and lean into Johnny Von. "I worked in your house the other day."

Johnny Von smiles at me. He puts his hand on my arm and moves to my ear.

A rush of warm sparkly affection washes over me!

I want to stop right here. I want to tell you what this feels like, what Johnny Von looking at me feels like. It's delicate and quiet, even with all the club noise. It's the feeling that something special and big is happening, but with a familiar-ness that floods comfortable everywhere.

"I see you walking in the afternoon all the time," he says to my ear. "Do you live in the neighborhood?"

And this is how I begin talking to Johnny Von, out at The King King. We cover dog-walking, what I do, who lives where on the street, and the weird lady across the way. I ask about the work in the house, how that is all going, who's who in his house, etc. We cover the basic "out" exchange and then there is the pause. The natural lull. But in our lull, a girl rushes him.

"When Girls Attack" rushes through my head.

"Heeeeyyyy!" She tackles Johnny Von in front of me. He greets her and hugs her, but keeps his eyes on me. This is different. This is good.

I'm okay, I think. I'm still talking to Johnny Von. She then starts talking at breakneck speed to him. And he turns to her. I begin to free-fall. What do I do? Is that it? Was that it? Is that all the Johnny Von conversation I'm going to get? Did I blow the audition? I can't tell how it was going. Do I stand here and wait? What do I do? I start to panic.

I hear The General: "Incoming! Incoming! Quick, turn your back. Turn your back on him before he looks back at you. Basic maneuvering, turn you back right now! Do it!"

So that is what I do. I turn and start talking to my friends again. The band starts. I'm unsure about what's next. I don't know the success or failure of the status of things. I remain calm. I feel this is the most important thing. Don't freak out. Don't draw conclusions. It's too early to determine anything. Just remain calm.

In a few minutes, I feel a bump. I turn. Johnny Von just came up beside me and did The Bump. You know, The Bump, the dance from the 70's. I'm startled, but I smile. This is unlike the International Playboy. The International Playboy never comes back around to you. You always have to seek him out. But Johnny Von just came back around and did…The Bump.

Johnny Von then looks at me, he laughs and says, "Don't mind me, I'm just walkin' the dog." And then he does a little imitation of me walking the dogs as he moves away in the crowd. This makes me laugh. Keeping his eyes on me as someone pulls at his arm to shout in his ear, he smiles.

There and then, it hits me. As glasses clink, and cigarettes light, as people shout and mill around closer and closer, as the band starts to crank and the lights get darker, it strikes me like a bolt of lightening right here in the crowd at The King King—Johnny Von is <u>flirting</u> with me!

1592

Johnny Von the Silk Trader

Large sheets of bright yellow silk billow in the breeze as Johnny Von the Silk Trader steps out onto the balcony. On the lines that stretch across the courtyard, past the large vats of bubbling dye that line the stone walls, the copious squares hang in a carnival of colors. Today the court is filled with a yellow so vibrant the sun itself is envious, but on any given day the atmosphere could be alive with azure, saturated with indigo or sage, soaked in buttermilk, accrue or honey. Tomorrow this same courtyard may be drenched in a rich chocolate brown.

Johnny Von the Silk Trader calls down to his setaioli to inquire about the progress of the fabric. He notes in the tablet that is always with him, the numbers his servant calls up. This afternoon he will meet with the most powerful merchants in Venice and he wants his inventory full. He is always prepared. He has built a fortune; sculpted himself into a razor sharp trader who knows his rank at the top of this commerce. He didn't start out this way, here at the top.

"The boat is at the steps, sir." His housemaid steps out to the courtyard balcony.

"Thank you, Adriana." Johnny Von the Silk Trader scribbles more notes, "Tell the boatman I will be down in a few minutes."

His golds, blues, and greens take market value, no different than any other trading house in Venice. This is not what sets Johnny Von the Silk Trader apart from the others. These ordinary colors did not build the empire he now surveys from the balcony. It is not the common colors that made him the man he is today. It's the violet. His dark livid violet brings a king's ransom. It brings a never-ending river of gold ducets to his door. The royalty of the world, the wealthy and the famous come to Johnny Von the Silk Trader for violet.

To find the right hue of purple, to grind the kermes and immerse the raw silk threads the three and four times needed insures a shine and quality that is unmatched and justifies a high price. But any good silk trader with integrity and practice can do these extras. The magic that created this unrivaled violet comes from the beginning, from his love of the world of color.

"A note from Alberini, sir." His first attendant hands him a small wax sealed envelope.

"Thank you, Fausto." He opens the note, like the many notes he will be handed today, and reads it. Fausto waits by his side.

"Alberini has a guest who will visit late this afternoon. If I am not back, please show her in and give her full access to the inventory. He's covered her completely. Anything she wants."

Fausto, a man of few words, nods without question. "Of course, sir." It is rare he would grant anyone this favor. He puts the note back into the leather portfolio that is always at his side and returns inside.

Before there was commerce, there was this love of the sensuous pleasures of color. To Johnny Von the Silk Trader each hue is a feeling, an emotion, a symphony of its own, calling out and filling him with a delight and wonder that permeates to his very soul. As a boy he realized this hold color had over him was not shared by all, but he relished it anyway. It drew him into an early apprenticeship in his boyhood. It led him to learn the recipes, the craft of taking every imaginable color nature could feed him and turn it into fabric. He created textiles to adorn a body, dress a salon, outfit the great stallion of a kings' knight into battle. The craft of color enthralled him. On the edge of his manhood, he found silk and never looked back to wool again.

"The shipment from the fields outside of Rome has arrived. Should we send Petrach to the docks this morning?" Fausto steps on the balcony once again.

"No. Petrach haggled too long with the dock manager and I don't want him to cause any more lost or damaged shipments. His wisdom may be great, but his wit is too sharp for the likes of dock hands." Both men chuckle at the thought. "I'm leaving in a few minutes and I'm early this morning. I will stop on my way to the Grand Canal."

Johnny Von the Silk Trader stands tall and powerful surveying the giant silk sheets with the care of a farmer looking over a bountiful crop one last time. This is his normal morning routine. But Fausto notices something this morning he has not seen in his master all these years. It is new to his eyes, this flash, especially while looking out to the silk. It is a slight almost undetectable look of indifference or sadness. So small is the change that Fausto cannot yet discern which it is.

Fausto calls him from this flash in his eyes. "The boat is waiting, sir."

While still an apprentice, the first yards of silk he ever purchased were in Venice. With all the little money he had, he brought home to his mother four yards of sky blue silk. It was the most beautiful thing he'd ever seen. Alone and ill by that time, she would never make a dress out of it, as he hoped for her. But still, they marveled at its feel as he sat on her bedside. Only a few days later, he wrapped her in that silk and laid her to rest in the earth.

After he returned to her little box of a house to collect what she had remaining in the world and realized there was nothing to collect, he walked out of the house he was born in for the last time.

He didn't return to the city directly. For two days he walked the lavender fields she'd worked in all of her life, deciding on what his life would be. The lavender field that she loved, even though it worked her too hard and made her old before she needed to be old.

"These are violets, my favorite."

When she was young and he was small they would walk the fields admiring every color God made. Taking his hand in hers, she would bend next to him and point to the delicate flowers that edged the lane. A long line of wild violets popped with brilliance next to the greens and pale lavender. "Don't pick them," she would say. "They'll die. We'll have to come here if we want to see them."

He'd pick them anyway, with the mischief of a boy out playing in the fields, and bring them home to her. He would make up a new story with each wild bouquet, how it had not been he who'd pick the violets, it was some other unruly child or a poor beggar passing through, or he'd simply found them plucked from the earth this way. He couldn't resist seeing her eyes smile and shine on him. Of course they wilted and faded, and seeing the end of them gave him a certain hesitation, but he was a boy and he did not notice endings as much as she did. For a boy there are always more beginnings than endings.

Now in this field, he is not a boy. And this ending changes the way he sees things. Changes the way he feels about violet. Now violet he feels more than anything.

He returned to the city and spoke to no one until he'd created a color familiar to God, but new to the silk trade; a breathtaking violet which would never fade or wilt or die.

On that day his apprenticeship ended and he began. He's built his overflowing fortune on the depth of this feeling of violet. That is why no other can reproduce it. It is not a recipe or process, it is made by the poetry, the feeling inside of him.

Johnny Von the Silk Trader returns to his house just as the servants are lighting the candles at the landing. Dusk is rushing into night and he is more tired than he can ever recall feeling. The entire day was talking, negotiating, haggling and not backing down. It was a day of black cloaks, black stockings, and black hats; hard wooden chairs and cold marble tables. This day without color, of cajoling, refusing and then flattering at just the right moments, has taken its toll.

Which is why he is caught completely off guard as he crosses the courtyard and hears a man's laughter coming from the inventory storeroom. He cannot, for the life of him, recognize the voices and is momentarily alarmed. He swings open the large wooden door as the sun shoots its last rays of the day onto the walls from the large windows that look out to the water.

"Fausto?" He opens the door to find Fausto in a deep and hearty moment of abandon, laughing. In all the years they have been together, the always composed and highly professional Fausto has never broken his composure.

Johnny Von the Silk Trader walks into the room passing the stacks of fabrics. "What's going on in here?"

Fausto, shocked that he's been caught off his guard,

grabs his leather portfolio quickly and motions across the room to stop.

"Who's here …?" Johnny Von the Silk Trader turns the corner of the racks of hanging silk to see two of his house-men wrapped in togas of green and pink silk, one with a woman's hat, its plume dancing as he reaches for a bolt of heather gray high overhead, the other with cheeks of rouge; both looking punched drunk happy. Not able to comprehend the sight of these large men in his employ running around the storeroom like children, he looks back to Fausto.

"What the …?" Just then he hears the voice of a woman chirping merrily down an aisle.

"Now this is just beautiful! Fausto you're next, off with that cape, I must see you wrapped in this sky blue. I'm sure you'll be a dream…"

He turns back to Fausto, who is now blushing.

"Have you felt this silk, dear Fausto? It's absolutely unbelievable. Take off your shirt. You have to feel this against your chest. And to think, it is all up to you to oversee all of this beauty …"

Her joyous banter stops abruptly at the end the aisle. "Oh, my," she whispers as she sees Johnny Von the Silk Trader staring at Fausto like a rooster about to scold the chicks.

"Don Johnny Von the Silk Trader, may I introduce Estella Corsuccio," Fausto says, returning to his stature as the head secretary of this house and hoping to take Johnny Von the Silk Trader's eyes off of him and onto Estella.

He turns. In the failing light of the day he is momentarily confused as to what he is looking at, the loose curls of her long hair, the plump curves, her pale smooth skin, the softness of her dress, the colors surrounding her, the light that is radiating off of her, the shine in her eyes; some light-filled angelic girl, mother, woman of a creature. What is it?

"Estella is Alberini's ..." Fausto seldom at a loss for words, trails off.

Estella erupts with laughter, "Fausto, we are too friendly now to be so shy! I've seen you in your stocking feet."

Johnny Von the Silk Trader looks down to see Fausto's large black stocking feet on the stone and his shoes off to the side. Before he can imagine why, Estella walks with her head high to him. "I am Alberini's lover. He is one of the men I keep in my company. I am here because I was told of such beauty and luxury that would make my head swim. Your faithful servants have shown me no less. It is a pleasure to make the acquaintance of such an artist." Estella takes the hand of Johnny Von the Silk Trader, who is now confused, flattered and shocked, all at once.

"I've found so many things I want here today, so many beautiful colors I want to wear, but now with the light fading, I'm afraid I'll have to return tomorrow." Estella smoothes her hands over the sky-blue silk as she puts it down on the table with the other fabrics. "Certainly the night lets us feel what our eyes cannot take in, but I want to see all that you have." She turns back to Johnny Von the Silk Trader. "I want to see your silks in the proper light."

As she speaks straight to him, he instantly feels warm inside, completely eased by her eyes, as if he is the only man in the world worth looking at. This is her trade, the talent she was given. Johnny Von the Silk Trader feels suddenly manly, virile even, in her gaze. He resumes his role as master of the house.

"That will be all, Fausto. I'll show Estella through the rest of the rooms, unless you've already given her the tour."

Fausto nods, motions for the men to un-toga themselves, and puts his shoes back on. "The cook has saved dinner for you, sir, he is at your service whenever you please. Good night sir."

Johnny Von the Silk Trader turns away from Estella and back to Fausto. "Thank you and good night, dear Fausto. Sleep well, after all you will need to be well rested for all the beauty you'll have to oversee tomorrow." The sarcasm is not lost on his faithful servant. Fausto scurries the two men out of the door.

Johnny Von the Silk Trader returns to Estella's eyes.

"It is not my practice to let anyone into the inventory, please excuse our fumbling manners. I'd hope to return before your arrival to show you through."

"Not at all. I won't have a bad word spoken, your house has been nothing but delightful." She tilts her head and smiles. "And Basco looks stunning in pink."

Her voice is light and her words flow with a humor that is open and inviting. The softness is entrancing. Johnny Von the Silk Trader returns her smile, extends his arm and leads Estella into the main hall. The curls of her hair move and brush her bare neck. It is mesmerizing.

To be honest, Johnny Von the Silk Trader knows of Estella Corsuccio. Her fame precedes her. And this morning when he read the note from Alberini, he was excited by the idea of meeting her. Being more of a businessman than a society hound, what socializing he does only serves as a necessary means to an end. And she is a courtesan of such celebrity that, had this chance occurrence not come to him, he would have never had this opportunity to meet her.

He is not under the false belief that invitations are extended to him for any other reason than his money and the power he wields at the top of this food chain. While there is some company outside of his house that he trusts and enjoys, he has not fooled himself with the mirage that the world of society offers the naive. He knows its fickle nature. So although he wondered about her, just like all the men in Venice, imagined her from the passion-filled stories he'd heard whispered, Estella is someone he would have never come into contact with. She keeps the company she wants to keep, sees whom she wants to see. For a woman in Venice, without a name or a husband, for a courtesan, this is unheard of, but her reputation has granted her this kind of freedom. Estella is the one who advances.

Johnny Von the Silk Trader stops and turns to Estella in the archway of the South Hall. "Alberini and I have done business together for many years and I would not deny him a single request."

"And what of his courtesan? Do you honor such a request to a courtesan you've never done business with?"

Her eyes are so open to him, her presence so sure and easy, so comfortable in her own skin, that his thoughts spark with images of her lips, the feel of her tongue on his, her hair falling on his collarbone and running his hands through her long tresses.

"Perhaps," he says, "it is only that we have not done business yet?" He imagines her moving down his body.

"Perhaps," she says, her smile laced with such a delicious mischievous expression that he is overtaken with thoughts of her skin on the white sheets of his feather bed, losing themselves behind the red silk curtains of his bedchamber. Johnny Von the Silk Trader feels the surge of attraction run through his body.

"Any friend of Alberini's is a friend of mine. I, of course, extend this gesture. Any request, I am yours."

"I was hoping as much, for I am famished." Estella strokes his arm with amusement, "Let's feast upon your trade tomorrow when I return and give the rest of our evening to the care of your kitchen."

Food is not the direction Johnny Von the Silk Trader was hoping this conversation would turn. Venice is a pleasure-seeking city, and while never one to seek the company of courtesans, he is a man of the city. And she is <u>the</u> Estella Corsuccio, here, bathing him in desire with just her eyes, casting her spell the minute he turned to her.

"Sweet mistress," Johnny Von the Silk Trader offers, "I've not prepared for the company of such a lady. There are no servants other than my cook and housemaid to attend to us. It would disgrace my staff to entertain someone such as yourself in such a meager way. And not kind of you to make such a request, when tomorrow I could have my house prepare a banquet in your honor." He looks to her with confidence and smiles. "Perhaps there are other appetites I can attend to?"

Estella buzzes with laughter, "Don Johnny Von the Silk Trader, how you delight me. Such formality. Let's not give pretense a place between us, for there is nothing I admire more than a man who has risen," she lingers in her words, "from meager beginnings." She looks at him now, with confidence and smiles, "It reminds me of my favorite story, that of my own." She pauses, looks him up and down, admiring him as if considering his offer. "There are so few of us." Estella pats his head with the tip of her fan. "You have a silver tongue that serves you well, I am sure. But now is not the time for your tongue. If you were at the Grand Canal today, as Fausto said you were, I am sure a man such as yourself must have a tired tongue from so much circling talk."

It is the work of a great courtesan to turn the conversation to whatever direction she desires. Estella possesses this skill in spades. But her skill rises to art with her ability to have this turn so pleasing to her acquaintance that he'd wish it no other way.

"So please," she squeezes his arm with affection, "let's take to the kitchen, relish warm ale, whatever stew is bubbling and I will hear your real stories. And then if you are lucky and have charmed me enough, I will regale you with mine. And that is how we shall become friends, you and I."

Johnny Von the Silk Trader is delightfully taken aback at such candid and direct talk from a woman, the likes of which he's not heard since the fields back home, and never from a woman so articulate and beautiful as the one on his arm right now. He can think of nothing he would rather do. He feels a genuineness for this woman, an odd recognition that surprises him. His carnal drive takes its correct place and steps back behind his heart.

"You are rare and lovely, aren't you, Estella?"

They sit at the square, humble table next to the stove. The cook puts two bowls in front of them and two large pints of ale. They talk like old friends, laughing and chatting and filling the room with all of themselves. As the candles descend and the moon crosses the night sky, they leave nothing back behind the personas they must wear in the society of Venice everyday.

Estella feels so familiar to Johnny Von the Silk Trader he forgets himself and says, "Such a shame that a woman such as yourself would be forced into the life of a …" He catches himself, seeing her tighten up, before he says anything else.

Estella sees his discomfort and rushes to ease. She says to him in a soft voice, "We all sell something."

He nods in agreement. But she can see it is just a polite acknowledgement and feels a loss at the posturing it brings back to them.

"I was never forced. In fact, although I did not have a society name, I did have a dowry that would have found me in a modest house. But I knew myself from a very young age, and I would have wilted and died in such a cage. I'm judged because people think it is my body that I sell, but I've never offered up myself to anyone I didn't enjoy and want to know in that way. Men, all different shapes and sizes, young and old, can be wonderful. I've never given myself to the company of a man whom I didn't want to know in many ways. What wife can know this side of men? Where in society can she make choices and know what different experiences feel like, whether they be experiences of a sensual nature or an intellectual nature? My life opened to me full libraries and discourse about politics, poetry, science and economics. I share my bed with men that live the edge of great thoughts, and yes, sometimes delicious forbidden thoughts, all of which they speak to me. What wife gets this? I am allowed everything."

Her honesty inspires his. He says with a gentle curiosity, "And do you not think it unnatural, out of order, to lay down with more than one man? Are we not made to be man and wife, one given only to the other?"

"Who determines this other, a name, the size of a dowry, a father, a mother, social circles determining the appropriate candidate? How can this be natural? Nature has given us so many other options to feel our way to each other, and they are shunned and shamed before we can even taste them. We think of our bodies as limited, our carnal drive overly precious, when it is always renewing. It can never spoil or ruin or run out or whatever it is that everyone is afraid of. We do not betray each other by following our bodies."

Johnny Von the Silk Trader has never viewed a woman this way, never heard the thoughts of a woman not imbued with societal perspectives or held in check by the dictates of the Church.

"Chastity is not the same thing as loyalty," she says with a tone that does not push against one way or necessarily promote another. She seems to speak from a place of tolerance, which he finds incredibly freeing. As if she has come to a clarity and then gauged her life by it.

"I will tell you this: there were 27 offers for my virginity. The bidding held the attention of Venice for months. I took the highest offer ever put on the table for such, but I'll tell you now, virginity is a novelty. It is a conquest perhaps, but the depth of carnal pleasure is not in virginity. And

I have been with enough virgins to know this from both sides of the bed."

She laughs and pauses.

"Give yourself to one other because you want to, not because you are bound to by law. Promise all of yourself now, instead of part of yourself always. And if one continues to hold, then so be it, have only that one."

"But you sell your bed. You are not promising yourself in part or whole."

Had this come for anyone else, Estella would have been offended, but somehow his voice is soothing, his tone filled with a compassionate humanity.

"What I sell is my company, and my sensual nature is part of that company."

"And you never pretend, you are never other than you would like to be? Forgive my directness, but I find that questionable at best. I pretend less than most of the women I know, less than most of the wives of the elite class of Venice. I would have lived a life of lies had I done anything else. At the Grand Canal today were you not other than you would like to be at times? Do you never pretend in your dealings, your alliances, in your needed relationships? I find that questionable."

"That is trade, that is commerce."

"Show me a marriage that is not bound by commerce. A union not serving some lack in the other."

"Yes, perhaps, at first; perhaps most even: but a heart needs a place it can rest without need of trade, without the threat of negotiations." He says this as if he is reconfirming it within himself. "A man needs eyes that smile and shine on him, that he knows are without bargain." He says this with a certainty that is from a deep place inside of him, confirmed by just saying the words out loud. He looks to Estella. "It must be the same for a woman, for you."

Estella feels herself soften more than she lets herself soften. It catches her off guard and startles her. Men of Johnny Von the Silk Trader's stature do not think such things, do not consider such perspectives. They do not equate a woman to a man in any way. His candor throws her off balance. She is usually the one to control the room with straightforward honesty.

She drinks the last of her ale. "It is late. I should take to the canals before the moonlight gives way to the day."

Johnny Von the Silk Trader, so enjoying this talk, is jolted by the sudden turn. He stands as she stands. "I can ... my boat will take you home, I will send Basco and Thomas to escort you." He takes her arm to lead her through the torch-lit hall to the entrance. "I -- I have enjoyed this evening very much, I hope I've not..."

Estella cuts him off. "I have also enjoyed myself here with you."

"Please come tomorrow." He takes her cloak from Thomas as she puts on her gloves.

"I will have my staff prepare ..."

"Not a banquet," she counters. "There is not business between you and I. We are friends now."

He smiles. "Then as a friend, I will not tell my staff how you took advantage of my soft nature and raided my kitchen like a heathen."

"Oh, thank you for that!" She smiles back. "And I will not tell Venice the scandalous news that Don Johnny Von the Silk Trader feasts most nights on his favorite mash-and-mutton stew, chased down with a most common ale."

"We will have a proper lunch then," he offers

"A modest lunch," she returns.

He wraps her cape at her shoulders and she raises the hood before they exit. Hiding her face to the streets is a habit she no longer notices.

She turns to him one last time as he holds her hand onto the water. She asks with a sincerity, a curiosity, that is extremely touching for such a worldly- wise woman, "What you said, at the table, is that how your wife looks to you?"

His reply is just as surprising.

"I do not have a wife."

Estella woke with the dawn, sending her entire household out to the streets to find out everything they could about Johnny Von the Silk Trader. How is it that a man of his wealth and power had gone mostly unknown to her? Moreover, how could such a man move through society and rise to power without a wife or a scandal to his reputation?

By the time Fausto took her hand at the landing on a particularly crisp, cool, and clear day in Venice, Estella knew this about Johnny Von the Silk Trader: half of Venice was under the impression he had a wife on the mainland, at his large country estate, who never came to Venice due to her frail health. A quarter of Venice knew of a few affairs, some with notable ladies of court, some with common chambermaids; there were a few rumors of a dalliance with the wealthy and beautiful widow Marchesa Leona Medici. Why they had not come to pass, no one could tell Estella one way or another. The rest of Venice had either not noticed, thought he preferred the company of men, or attributed his lack of matrimony to a medical inadequacy.

As she makes her way up the steps of his house, one thing is clear to Estella. Whatever it is, Johnny Von the Silk Trader had somehow managed to stay under the swirl of gossip. For a man in Venice, with a fortune such as his, with a business so intimately involved with society, this is unheard of, but somehow he has managed this kind of freedom.

"You are expected in the south hall," Fausto says cheerily to Estella as he takes her cloak and closes the doors to the outside behind them. Just as Fausto had noticed a flash of dullness in his master's eyes the previous morning, today he'd noticed a glint of happiness, a freshness he'd never seen before. He knew she was the cause. "Lunch will be served on the west balcony at two o'clock, overlooking the harbor."

"Thank you, Fausto." Estella winks at him as she takes his arm.

Fausto blushes.

The large wooden door of the south hall opens to find Johnny Von the Silk Trader laying out the most beautiful, delicate silks in his collection. Behind him are endless rows of silk. Racks from the ceiling to the floor of hanging colors, like the book stacks in a library, only instead of books it is a secret maze of luxurious fabric after luxurious fabric.

He lights at seeing her entrance. He takes her hand, looks her up and down, studying her dress. "Perfect. I was hoping you'd be wearing something like this."

Estella has no idea what he means by this. She'd taken extra time this morning to put together her dress. She is wearing her tightest corset, which pushes her breasts especially high and full, with a pale yellow bodice that laces in the back and a full deep yellow skirt. Her outfit is topped with a jacket of long panels of light blue fabric fitted at her shoulders. It brings the whole dress together and clips in the front at the center.

"It's nice to see you," she says as she passes her hand over the rainbow of impossible colors.

"I've only pulled a few. I thought you'd like to walk through." For two people who'd talked so easily the previous night, they both find themselves a bit awkward. It is not something either is accustomed to. They are professionals that live on their ability to talk, charm and put at ease. Oddly enough, they both like the newness of the sensation.

So they begin, just the two of them, walking the labyrinth of fabric, pointing and pulling down color after color of silks, velvet weaves, elaborate brocade pieces that dazzle the senses. They spend the entire morning navigating through the textiles, collecting colors, both easing themselves into the gaze of the other.

"Let's take off your jacket," Johnny Von the Silk Trader smiles.

"Please don't tell me we are taking off our clothes so soon in the day. We've not gotten to lunch yet," she teases him.

"You do like your food, don't you? Food, food, food. That is all we ever hear from you," he teases back. "Madame, I am a professional. I merely want to see the colors next to your skin. So as a professional, I am removing your jacket."

"How refreshing. I'm usually the one to say such things."

He holds a dark red fabric over her shoulders and studies.

"Absolutely," he says. He adds it to the stack they are collecting. They both begin to hold fabrics up to each other and nod approvingly.

As they weave their way through, their conversation follows this maze, light and playful at first, and then more pointed, more authentic, the further they go into the colors.

Johnny Von the Silk Trader stops. "I suppose Alberini will appreciate the silks he is so generous to supply." He doesn't know why he says it, it just pops out of him.

Estella, jolted from the light fun she is having, stops.

"I apologize. I didn't mean it like that. I don't ..." Johnny Von the Silk Trader tries to back up.

"Alberini won't be paying for these silks. I am buying these silks," she says with a stubborn determination. She turns to him, but can't help herself from softening. "I will think of no one but you when I wear them."

"You are not buying these silks," he says in a stern voice back to her, "I won't have it. I want these for you. I will not let you or anyone pay me."

"That's very bad business," she smiles. "Nice, but not very clever to give away your goods." She takes a more serious tone. "I do not want to be owing. I want to pay you."

"Well," he says, understanding her dilemma, "I won't take your money, so I guess you will have to stay here and work off your debt." He turns to the fabric and continues to walk. "You can start in the spinning room. If you're good I might move you up to a loom, but," he turns, takes her hands and studies them, "I won't hope for too much.

You have to be good with your hands, nimble, and I don't know…"

She playfully hits him and laughs. "My hands are fine. My hands are very good. Ask any man in Venice, I'm good with my hands." They both laugh and continue on further into the colors, talking and laughing and talking more. Easy soulful conversation flows, until at last they find themselves in the center, standing in front of the violet; the violet that is only his.

Estella gasps, feels the tightness of her corset and is suddenly dizzy by the brilliance.

Johnny Von the Silk Trader then does something that is odd. Instead of moving to it, pulling it down and draping it over her, as he has done with all the other beautiful pieces, he hesitates. Estella watches as he moves away from it, avoids it with his eyes, and gestures toward a green brocade on the opposite wall.

"What's this?" She reaches to the violet, she doesn't look to the fabric but to his eyes. She sees it in his eyes, what happens to them, as they turn to her and then to the dazzling color.

A moment of clarity overtakes her. She looks to the violet and then to Johnny Von the Silk Trader and then back to the silk.

"I see now," she whispers.

"See what?"

"Johnny Von the Silk Trader, there is not a man known to me that I have not been able to see plainly from the moment of meeting him. I can find someone inside; that is how I do it. Not by the way I look, or dress, or the sharp wit of my banter. I can look into the eyes of a man and then find him on the inside, know what it is about him, his character, his circumstances, his humanity or lack of it. I ply my trade on what I find. It is a skill, a gift, that I have made my fortune with. It has kept me safe, given me power, allowed me to write my own way in the world. Only last night" -- she turns from the violet silk to Johnny Von the Silk Trader -- "I went home and I tossed and turned, trying to find you."

She moves closer to him in the stacks. "And I couldn't."

Johnny Von the Silk Trader wants to move towards her but instead backs up.

"This morning I sent out my entire household to find every word about you, why a man like you, powerful, wealthy, a man of heart, did not have a wife in his bed chamber and why the most famous courtesan in Venice," she smiles coyly, but not too coyly, "why I did not have you in my bed chamber."

Johnny Von the Silk Trader shifts. Feels something turning inside him, something about to break. He wants to grab her and kiss her before she says another word. As if she is about to reveal a mystery, unraveling a secret by each next spoken word, something he is afraid to know out loud.

"And now, as we have been talking, I could feel it coming to me, this something about you unlike anyone I've known. It started whispering to me." Estella looks deep into his eyes, studying them, reading them. "There is nothing in you lacking."

He doesn't move, he looks uncomfortable, but she keeps going.

"But while this is rare, there are men who achieve all they want to achieve, money, power, satisfaction from every direction; all their earthly desires met. These men normally do not entertain my company, they are most likely to have a wife that satisfies the life they have define for themselves."

Estella turns to the violet fabric and draws her hand over it. "But you do not have a wife." She closes her eyes, brushes the violet gently to her cheek, "and now I see why. It's in the violet."

"What is?" He feels his heart pounding.

"Eyes that smile and shine without bargain," she whispers to herself.

Estella opens her eyes bright but sad, lost in the violet, "No one knows the feel of genuine love more than a courtesan. The contrast teaches it, carves the absence of it into the soul."

Entranced by the silk, she breaks and looks at the man standing next to her, as if seeing something new to the world. "You know what love feels like, don't you."

Johnny Von the Silk Trader grabs his chest and inhales deeply, fighting the water welling up in his eyes, the lump in his throat.

"That is what you are waiting for ..." she says looking straight to him.

He is shocked to hear it spoken. The truth of him.

Johnny Von the Silk Trader looks to the silk, moves his hand over the large roll of hanging fabric in front of them. He reaches his hands out to the ends and begins to pull, whipping the silk up, stretching out a large sheet of it as he steps back to pop it in the air. He looks to it moving. He studies it with a poignancy that fills the room.

Violet swirls and billows.

"And I cannot buy it." He whispers with a sadness, "I cannot craft it."

Estella lifts her hands like a little girl to feel the silk cloud falling in the air. "And I," she whispers, "with all the beauty to behold, all the men, all the choices and freedom, for as much as I try, I cannot convince or compel it to my bed." She sighs, "I cannot craft it either."

Johnny Von the Silk Trader breaks from the lonesomeness that grips him, he looks over to Estella, "And yet here you are."

As he says it he lets go of the silk and moves into her eyes. It is her eyes that his heart recognizes. The way they lock on to him, see all of him. A stillness strikes them both. The moment is held static, as if eternity has been waiting patiently for their embrace and has now stopped time to savor it. His hands release the silk and find her waist. The violet hovers and floats around them. As the fabric swirls to the ground, he kisses her with a passion that moves them both out of time and space, out of past and future. A kiss that is completely and only violet.

In the kiss Estella feels herself rushing out, giving all of herself completely for the first time, here in Johnny Von the Silk Trader's arms. This is Estella's virginity, this is her innocence offered. In the kiss she knows it will be this one man, a love not bound, not bargained, but simply recognized.

"Here we are," she says pulling back to gaze into his eyes, and then again returning the depth and passion of his kiss, as only Estella ever can.

Chapter 5

"Children of the future Age
Reading this indignant page
Know that in a former time
Love! sweet Love! was thought a Crime."
~ *William Blake*

The band breaks after a long first set and Johnny Von finds me again at the back of the crowd. By now, I'm loose. By now, most of the crowd, which has thinned out considerably, is loose. Drinks and music have been flowing for a couple of hours. Johnny Von has served up the attention. It's now my time to step up and volley it back.

Johnny Von clinks my glass cheers and reaches for a cigarette in his pocket. I ask him for one.

This is how I started smoking. At 16, bumming a cigarette is an easy way to strike up a conversation with some guy. It provides a structure for standing around and talking, an excuse to engage. Then the nicotine momentarily relaxes me enough to say something. It's my second line of social coping behind the General. It has worked very well for me through the years. Too well. It's horrible really. Smoking. I'm the worst kind of smoker because I don't smoke all the time. So I can't quit cold turkey. I could go for months without one, but then I love a good cigarette. I know it is a killer, and it smells bad, and it's bad for my skin, and it makes my breath horrible. And even if I am smoking sporadically, I can't run for my workout. My lungs can't handle it. I know, from the wise words of an older Merle Haggard, "I have to put that tobacco down." For good. But it ain't goin' be tonight.

I keep thinking there will be a line, there will be a time when I'm in a solid kind of relationship, and not only do I start eating better, and working out consistently, but I don't smoke at all, not even if I'm out having a drink. It will be a time when I have someone to make plans with about the future. My health in the future will be important to someone, hopefully even a few little someones. I imagine it a time when I don't get nervous about guys or what's going to happen or socializing. When I was 16, I thought this time would have happened much earlier in my life. Much earlier.

I know. It's off the mark. I know this is not really the right way to think about things. I know that it is too much to put on someone else, on a relationship to change things. For a relationship to make me feel real in the world. I know that I should be taking this kind of care of myself now. But look, I can't do everything at once, and right now, all I am trying to do is talk to Johnny Von.

"Where are you from?" Johnny Von strikes up the talking. We cover my New Orleans, which he's been to, and his Chicago.

"What do your parents do?" Johnny Von leads off again. I like it. No one in my history of "out yelling-chatting" has ever asked me this question. We cover my parents, their divorce when I was 19, what they do for a living, and where they're from. And then his parents, what they do; his grandfather on a farm in Ohio; the origin of his affinity for country music. His grandfather wanted more for his family, wanted to get them off the farm to a better life.

And then Dwight Yoakam strolls up. For real. The real Dwight Yoakam walks up. He is here to play a couple of songs in support of the country-night event. I have to tell you, I know every Dwight Yoakam song, ever. I might even be so bold as to claim myself a Dwight Yoakam aficionado. When I learned of Johnny Von's enthusiasm for Dwight Yoakam, I took it as a selling point for his character. I think the quality of his voice and what he does on his guitar is beautiful, soulful and creative. He's friendly with Johnny Von and they exchange a brief buddy greeting.

If this were a movie, Dwight Yoakam would be appearing through a fog, the divine messenger, the mystical catalyst. He would be playing the part of the guitar-slinging charmer who's come to whisper in my ear, "Now it's time to see why your here." Johnny Von introduces us, they decide to talk later, and Dwight moves off into the crowd.

The Dwight Yoakam magic takes effect. I feel good. I feel my game. I lead off. "Johnny," I say with a coy smile. "Can I tell you something personal?"

Johnny Von stares, takes a slow drag of his cigarette, looks me straight in the eye and says, "Darlin', It'd be a crime if you didn't."

This makes me laugh. I bat my eyes and say to Johnny Von, "You have two of my all-time favorite books in your study."

Johnny Von looks a little nervous. "I probably haven't read them. I don't know what I have in there. But go ahead, hit me."

"*Where the Sidewalk Ends* and *The Giving Tree* by..."

"Shel Silverstein," Johnny Von cuts in, smiling.

And then -- I don't think I imagined this, even though I'd had a few drinks and it was still loud -- Johnny Von leans into my ear and rattles off a few Shel Silverstein lines.

"Sarah Cynthia Sylvia Stout/Would not take the garbage out!" or was it "Little Peggy Ann McKay/Said, I can not go to school today." Or maybe it was "Jimmy Jet and his TV Set."

I can't remember now, I know it wasn't "Ickle Me, Pickle Me, Tickle Me Too," because I would have remembered that, even after a few glasses of wine. Whichever Shel Silverstein poem it was that Johnny Von rattled off the top of his head in rapid manner, in a smoke-filled club that night at The King King, it was impressive. Very impressive. So impressive, had I not brought it up first, I would have thought it was some kind of pick-up line, part of his shtick.

Johnny Von had very few books in his study, so these stood out. But they stood out to me like blaring giant flashing signs from my past. I'm the baby of my family and I don't have kids around me in my life, so the last time I thought about where in the hell "Ickle Me, Pickle Me, and Tickle Me Too" flew off to in that shoe, or how much that Giving Tree loved that little boy, I was in the second grade.

The second grade sucks. I don't know about you, but if someone told me I had to choose between re-living the second grade or standing in a red ant pile, I'd take my chances with the red ants. I went to Catholic school and I can remember clear as day walking up the concrete steps. I was carrying the book bag my mom and I made, with the Yogi Bear & Boo Boo iron-on decals, up to Sister Grace's classroom at my new school. I can remember looking at the steps, at the black shoes of the girl in front of me in line and praying my life was a movie. That at any moment I might flash forward from here to my life as a grown up, a jump cut in time. That I might suddenly be to a point in the future and I wouldn't have to live out the excruciating days, the years ahead of me in this hellhole called grammar school.

Let's be honest, the nun had it out for me from day one. I don't know why. Maybe she had something to prove, she was new; wanted to be known as a strict disciplinarian, didn't like my hair, who the hell knows. I just know that's when the worry stomachaches started.

It's the first part of the school year, just a few weeks in. I don't know what day of the week it is or what's on the lesson plan for the day, what I do know is this: I am in a new class and I have a bunch of new kids to get to know. So far, I've made two tentative friends, Janice and Carla, and I know just about everyone's name. There is only one other new girl, Catherine Whittler, but her cousin is in the class so she has an instant "in."

Anyway, I was a finicky eater and on this day Sister Grace gets a bee in her bonnet that I am going to eat my lunch, which Carla informed me in line was pig butt. Of course it wasn't "pig butt" exactly. It was brown and greasy and runny, yes, but it was some kind of pork stew meat-by-product type of something. Quietly opposing Sister Grace's decision, I was firm in the belief that I was not now, nor would I ever be eating the lunches here.

She circles at first, she treads lightly requesting I "taste something." Time passes. As the lunch period ticks away, she stands stationary behind me, waiting, tapping the yardstick she carries everywhere on the linoleum tile floor. She begins to remind me frequently that I will indeed be eating something before the end of lunch. More time passes. Looking up to the clock, with three minutes left to lunch, seeing my untouched pig butt, Sister Grace blows a fuse. The vein in her forehead starts popping, the yelling begins. The focus of the whole class, along with most of the lunchroom, turns to us.

I stay quiet and resolute, gripping the chair and staring at the plate. Sister Grace is incensed by my not only not eating, but not responding to her either. She tackles me. I try to fight her off. There is kicking and hitting as best I can, but she grips me in a headlock. She is huge, a big nun with girth on her side, and I am just a little girl, the odds are not mine, even with my feisty nature. She pinches my jaw in one hand, scoops up a large helping of pig butt with the other and wedges the spoon into my mouth. She throws the spoon on the table, shuts and covers my mouth with her hand, and screams at me to chew and swallow.

By this time, I've got smeared pig butt and tears rolling down my face and the whole school staring at me. A moment of silence passes. Sister Grace begins to look happy about the whole situation. She takes her hand away from my mouth to which I respond by immediately projectile vomiting.

And not just a spoonful of pig butt. I spew vomit all over myself, all over her arm, and half way across the table. I don't know what I had for breakfast that morning but I hurled it in chunky volume. And now, in a silence so quiet you can hear a pin drop, vomit is dripping in oatmeal-like clumps from the table to the linoleum tile floor.

The only way I can best describe to you the look on everyone's face, including Sister Grace, is this: Shock and Awe. My new fellow classmates look at me with such a blend of fear and disgust that I feel sorry for them. The look on their worried faces is so serious that I, being the caring little person that I am, smile at them. I want to convey that I'm all right, I am not The Exorcist. I don't want them to be scared on account of me and what they have just seen.

Needless to say, the 'I'm okay' smile is not taken by Sister Grace as such. If you thought she'd blown a gasket before, she is now ready to act out Revelations.

"Look at her, she's laughing!" she says in exasperated disbelief. "Is that what you want, you want attention? You think this is a joke? Well, I'm going to give you attention."

She yanks my chair out from the table and slides me across the lunchroom, streaking the vomit across the floor. She plants me at the exit. She then throws a stack of brown paper towels at me and says, "You can clean yourself up. How do you like that? You think this is funny? Then you can just sit here and clean it up yourself, because I'm not helping you."

I'm in the second grade. I can barely brush my own hair.

She rinses her hands in the sink and yells, "Let's go."
She marches my class out the door in front of me.

Everybody stares, but nobody really says anything as they
pass. A couple of girls hold their nose, maybe some of the
boys say something like "gross," I can't remember. Carla
and Janice look the other way as they pass. After that, I
don't make eye contact. I'm just trying to clean up the
vomit with these non-absorbent brown paper towels and
making it all worse.

Sister Grace redirects the other teachers, then files the
whole lunchroom through the same exit. I don't look up at
any of them as they pass in front of me. I stay quiet. I go
away inside. I make myself invisible.

Johnny Von smiles after riffing his few lines of Shel
Silverstein and says, almost bashful, "You know, when
something touches you as a kid, you kind of remember it
more."

"Yeah," I nod in agreement.

Many a day in the second grade I lost myself in the pen
and ink drawings of Shel Silverstein. Many a lonely recess,
I wished I had a tree like that Giving Tree to play with. I
took solace there. Only I'd never be like that boy when
he grew up. I wouldn't leave the tree lonely like that, even
though the tree was always happy for him. I wouldn't ignore

him, even though the tree always took him back. The boy turned into a grown-up and chopped it all up. Typical. I knew then and there what kind of grown-up I would be: the opposite of jackass Sister Grace, and nothing like her minions from hell, the kids in my class.

I look Johnny Von in the eye, "I know what you mean," and say no more. The second grade stays put.

Fucking second grade. The social recovery on projectile vomiting and subsequent public humiliation took years. It broke my heart. Only when you're a kid, they don't say, "That second grader has a broken heart," while talking in caring whispers. They don't ask you if you want a chamomile tea, or if you need a vacation to take your mind off things. If they say anything, it's something like, "She got her feelings hurt at school today." Maybe Mom makes your favorite dinner. Maybe Dad tucks you in and rubs your head and tells you not to worry about it. They try to comfort. But then, they send you back in the next day, because what else can they do— school is school, and this is the only one in town.

They say things like, "Well, just try to go to school today," or "What's the worst that can happen? They are not going to line you up at the chalkboard and shoot you." And you're a kid and you have to go to school. They take time and explain the situation to you. "This is the way the world is."

The band starts the second set.

I look at Johnny Von standing next to me in the dark light. Tall Johnny Von. I know he's polished and smooth now, I've been watching him all night, he has it down, his version of the international playboy. But there is something else, something different behind it.

I try to imagine him as a boy, before all of this, before anyone knew his name. I try to imagine what he looked like in his second grade photo. If his hair was rumpled from the playground, if his grin was unpracticed and unabashed, if he stood in line cutting-up with his friends and then beamed for the camera when it was his turn, with no distance between his heart and the world. And then, I wonder when and where his heart broke for the first time.

I don't know why Shel Silverstein sits on his shelf, I don't know him and I don't know his stories. But here in the shadows, I know he has them. As the room swirls with drinks and smoke, as I catch his glance in the colored lights of the stage, I recognize it in his eyes. And as out of place as it sounds, I want to tell him not to worry about it, I want to tell him, "Don't go away inside. Don't make yourself invisible, just to be a movie star."

Dwight Yoakam takes the stage, his eyes hidden under his cowboy hat. The bright spotlights bounce off of his white cowboy hat and pearl-button shirt, radiating a halo around his body. He counts out the beat over the crowd noise and then takes over the place with his voice. He positions his guitar up on his heart and plays that thing like only Dwight Yoakam can, in a way that you can't not feel it inside you.

"Here." Johnny Von hands over a cold beer from the rounds that his buddies are passing through the crowd. He talks and jokes with his friends as people start to fill in at the stage around us. Johnny Von winks at me and clinks the bottleneck of my beer with his across the crowd between us.

I take a swing and wink back. Of course, we're not kids anymore, we are adults in a bar in Hollywood. My lunchroom trauma is long, long over and forgotten. I managed my resulting shyness. I tackled it, not so differently from the way Sister Grace tackled me that day. I locked it down and I reconfigured myself to be cool. By the time I was in high school, I went with the popular kids to parties at the lake. I played and dated and ran around with the right people in college. I wore the right clothes, and joined the right sorority and dated frat guys. I built up enough layers to look the part and seem like everyone else, but I never once felt like myself, right in myself. I locked it down though, and I did it as long as I had to.

Maybe that is what I recognize in Johnny Von. The layers, the way he's managed himself, configured himself. Acting. What better way to hide, than in plain sight…than the life of celebrity? A life that brings the in-crowd to you, money enough to buffer things, a required, methodically-crafted image that keeps a safe distance between you and the world.

I've seen it before. The way a person can hide behind themselves, behind the successful life they've created.

When I met the International Playboy, he was the shiniest thing I'd ever seen. Like no one I'd ever met in the South, electric and engaging. At the time it felt like I'd found someone who made me visible to the world again. Without a second thought, I positioned myself on the arm of that wealthy International Playboy, the perpetual center of the room, who dripped with charisma and made everybody laugh. From there out I was living the life! Good food, great sex and big money. I'd beaten it. I ran off to London without considering the layers people put on and what might be underneath. I'd found some place exciting and better, and far, far away from Devil's Swamp. And I never looked back to visit the world of Shel Silverstein again.

"Bella!" Nichola, a large older Italian man, calls out to me as I walk into his deli on the Kings Road in London. I'm meeting the International Playboy here, this is "our little place." He discovered it one day when he was waiting for me to get off work. To keep busy while he travels, which he does often — in fact, more than half of the two years I've been here, he's been off in other places — I have a day job in an art gallery.

"You want I make the one hot chocolate?" Nichola calls over to me as I take one of the small tables in the back. We meet up here often because it has the hot chocolate we love.

"No. Just a cup of tea. I'll wait till he gets here." I wave to the girls behind the counter, his three daughters, and loosen one of the two wool scarves I'm wearing. I'm always cold. I just can't seem to acclimate to the perpetual gray, cold moisture — the misty rain that never turns into a real downpour. I miss the Louisiana rain, something I never thought I would say. But at least it has a beginning, a middle and an end. At least it thunders and rages and says something. And then it rolls on and the sky clears and the sun comes out. Here it's just one ongoing, uncomfortable thing.

One of the bus boys puts a tea in front of me, and I nod thank you.

I rushed here from the bookstore, and I'm surprised that I'm the first to arrive. I'm a little excited. The International Playboy and I have had a great couple of days. We always have fun. That's sort of what is good about us, we never fight or have drama. We are light. But the past couple of days have been different, closer; maybe because he's been traveling so much, I don't know. Last night we fell asleep in front of the fire. It was fantastic. That's the only saving grace of the constant cold overcast, it's good snuggle weather.

I take out the book I just bought for him and scratch the price off. The International Playboy is not much of a present guy. On one of his first trips without me, he brought me back a t-shirt. It didn't fit. But I'm not the kind of girl that needs that kind of thing anyway, so it works out. And it's not lost on me that he pays all the bills, so I always try to have a little something for him. I can't compare financially by any means, but I try to always get things that show I know him, that I'm not just taking without considering him.

"The lasagna's fresh, just made right now," Nichola calls over to me.

I smile, but shake my head no.

"You take some home." He throws his hands in the air. "I'll wrap some to go."

Nichola's lasagna is the International Playboy's favorite food. That's another reason we come here a lot. Sometimes, on my lunch break, I run in, get a plate to go, and bring it to him as a surprise. It takes my whole lunch hour to get to the penthouse and then back to my desk, but I love what he looks like when I show up unexpected with a gift. Maybe it's my Southern background, or maybe it's one of those primal things, but I love to watch a man eat his favorite food; especially if I put it on the table in front of him.

I fumble through my bag for my good ink pen and practice how I will sign the inside cover a few times on the back of my check register, double-check the spelling of "ashram." The International Playboy is between trips right now, in from Monaco, on his way to India tonight. We weren't supposed to meet up, he's flying out of Heathrow at nine, but he called me at work to have a quick chocolate and chat.

I sign and date the front cover. This is Deepak Chopra's latest book. Conrad, the International Playboy's best friend, has turned suddenly very spiritual and yoga-oriented. The International Playboy sort of looks up to Conrad, and they've planned this big trip to India. All things New Age, of the East, all things Deepak, he is bonkers about. You can't talk to either one of them anymore about anything but India and Ashrams. But I think it's good for him, time to outgrow his party life-style. I know he wanted this book, so I rushed to pick it up for his flight after he called. But the book is not why I'm sort of tickled about this gift.

I pull from my purse a photo strip of me. In the photos I'm tan. I took it in the train station in Nice while he was buying tickets to Paris. One of our first trips.

"Roger, you dog, why didn't you tell me you were in Monte Carlo last week?" I can hear the International Playboy on his cell phone as he enters the front of the shop.

In the first frame of the photo strip, I'm fixing my hair. In the second frame, I'm making a goofy face.

The International Playboy waves to Nichola as he talks. He winks at the girls as he moves through the crowd lined up at the counter. He points to the cigarettes and motions for a new pack of Silk Cuts while still on his cell. "Yeah, yeah, we all met up at the Royal-Riviera for drinks....no, I had a suite at Le Metropole. John Bowler and I hit the casino on Thursday."

I wanted to write something on the back of the photo, but he's here already. I look at it quickly and smile. In the third frame, I'm giving myself rabbit ears while holding a card that reads, "I," written with a fat tipped Sharpie I had in my bag to mark my luggage.

"Did you hear what happened to Simon?" The International Playboy reaches over the crowd to grab the cigarettes over the counter.

In the last frame, I'm smiling holding up a card with a scribbled heart and the letter "U." I guess it doesn't need to say anything else. I date it, write the city quickly on the back and tuck it into the cover of the book. I put the book in the gift bag under my chair.

The International Playboy pecks me on the cheek and sits down. I point to the menu and whisper a query for the hot chocolates. He nods yes, and keeps talking.

"No, it was a whole bloody yacht of super-models. Some big fashion thing was in town." He roars with laughter. "He didn't show up for two days. He said he woke up in his socks and had to borrow clothes from one of the galley men." He throws his head back laughing again. "Yes, he did. He turned up at my hotel suite in a friggin' chef's coat and trousers."

I smile as I watch him laugh. I kept the photo strip because I felt shy right after I did it. I never felt like the time was right before.

The International Playboy looks to me. An odd expression

flashes through his eyes, "Look, Roger, I've got to go, I've just turned up at a coffee shop to meet a friend."

Friend? I know Roger. That's odd.

"Thank you for meeting me here." He flips his phone closed. He sounds strange. *Thank you for meeting me? Since when does he thank me for meeting him?*

Nichola puts two hot chocolates down in front of us and banters back and forth for a minute with the International Playboy. They begin joking and waving their hands, the International Playboy drops his weird formality and clicks back to his old self. Nichola pats him on the back, winks at me, says something in Italian and walks off. The International Playboy turns back to me. I see his eyes change. They're flat and distant.

For reasons I haven't consciously registered yet, I kick into high gear chatting about anything and everything. Even though he's been back for days, I buzz out a litany of questions about his trip to Monaco. Who was there, how was the hotel, did he go to that place we'd been that time when we went to the beach? I chat about my job, how the men came to fix the water heater in the second bedroom, about the great skirt I picked up at Marks and Spencer's. I talk like I've never talked before, I'm witty and funny and doing everything I can to change his eyes back.

"Before I forget" -- I clap my hands and snap my fingers -- "I got you something for your trip ..." I fumble for the gift bag through my coat and scarves under the chair. Before I grab it, he stops me.

"Look, you and I, it's not ..." He stops mid-sentence, looks down and unwraps a new pack of Silk Cuts.

I'm hot. I can't breathe. Our little place is closing in around me, moving quickly from comfy to claustrophobic.

"It's not working for me," he says, talking through his cigarette as he strikes a match and lights up.

My chest tightens. I can't have heard him correctly. I don't know what he means. He can't be breaking up with me, here, like this. There's nothing wrong. We're best friends. We never fight. He has everything. He has all the freedom a man could have, and me.

"I don't understand? What ..." My words are in slow motion. I am trying to stay calm and logical. That's what he likes about me, no drama. But the busboy behind me is crashing plates and cups into his plastic bin and yelling in Italian to the back, the fluorescent lights at the kitchen and the deli display are stark and flickering, the couple at the table next to us is too close, and I can't think. I can't find a reason. "What happened?" I struggle to get my voice out, to speak loud enough to be heard.. "Is there someone else?"

"No. This is not about anyone else. There is no one. I'm just ..." The International Playboy takes a drag. His voice is so loud. It's louder than the crashing plates, the yelling Italians, the couple crowded next to us. He feels louder than the people ordering at the deli or Nichola and his daughters, louder than the street noise beyond, the taxis and cars and people on the King's Road, louder than the whole city.

"I want to just be friends," he says, stubbing out his smoke. "I think we should be mates." He takes a sip of his chocolate.

"We are friends." I smile, trying to win his eyes back, even though I feel the tears starting to well up in mine.

"Darling," he doesn't smile back. "I mean just friends, and that's it."

I feel a few tears start to spill out against my will, I look over and see Nichola and his daughters looking over and then turning away.

"Look." His voice sounds almost angry at my slight show of emotion. "I'm really trying to be more honest in my life now, more spiritual. Like Conrad, you know, I'm trying to be more conscious and in the moment." He looks at me and then looks down at the table. "So I'm just going to say it…"

He looks me in the eye. "I'm not attracted to you."

I feel a lump in my throat.

Then he says it again, emboldened by hearing it aloud. "I'm not attracted to you." As if I've challenged his statement, he puts his hands up in a "what can you do" way, and then he says it again. "I am not physically attracted to you."

Each time he says it, it's lashes on my back, cutting my tender flesh. What about all the sex we have, the last two years? When did he stop being attracted to me? We snuggled in front of the fire last night?

I look down. We still feel the same to me. I can't look at him. We still feel close, to me. All I can see is the film forming on top of my hot chocolate, the square ceramic of pale multi-colored sugar packets, the white vase and fake red carnation on the metal cafe table. There is nothing I can say. There is nothing I can do about not being attractive enough for him.

I would have lost it right there, and started really crying at the table, which he would have hated, but then the International Playboy says this: "I don't think I was *ever* really that attracted to you."

Everything inside me stops. I feel the breaking inside. I have no tears, no words, nothing but a weak smile.

I make myself disappear. I go away inside and become invisible.

And then I think about that damn photo strip, how stupid I am. As I see him sitting in front of me, pulling another Silk Cut from the pack, all I can think about is how I can get that photo strip out of the book without him seeing it.

"Bloody hell." Relief washes over the International Playboy as he takes a long first drag of his cigarette. He sighs and rubs his chest, he almost smiles, as if I am not even at the table, as if this is some practice conversation he is having with one of his buddies. "I'm so proud of myself for getting that out. I've really been clearing out a lot lately, working on myself. It's just time in my life, you know, I want to find my soul-mate."

I'm trapped at our little table in the back, cornered in the bustle and swirl around me as he continues telling me that we'll find me a super little flat and that we'll still hang out as much as ever. That now, we can be even closer friends because he won't feel pressure. It will be just the same, but we won't sleep together.

And all I can think about is whether I should give him the book now or not. Of course I'll give him the book, it would be childish not to. It would be petty. I'll just take the book out of the gift bag myself, that way I can pull out the photo and leave it in the bag. I just can't feel anything about it here, I can't break down here. I think, *if I can just hold on inside until he leaves.*

Oblivious to anything going on inside me, the International Playboy looks at me, as if I should share in his victory of honesty, his marked self-growth, as if I should be proud of him as well.

But I can only I look across the table, confused and bewildered. I feel like a loyal and sweet barn dog that has just been shot by the farmer, who is now standing over me as I bleed out. I look across at him and think *why, why would you do it like this, I love you.*

I cried and I packed my bags. What was I going to do? This is the way the world is. And then I cried some more. *This is the way the world is,* I'd heard it before. Twenty years of tackling myself, 20 years of reconfiguring to be cool, only to feel as humiliated and powerless as I did in the second grade. That's when my heart broke a second time.

The evening at The King King is winding down. Dwight plays all his songs and I know every word. It's like a private Dwight concert. Johnny Von is standing next to me drinking and laughing and talking with everyone. And I can't believe it. I'm here at practically my own personal Dwight Yoakam concert, in Hollywood, at a club where you have to go around the back to get in, in the wee hours of a Sunday night, looking good, drinking, smoking and talking with Johnny Von. It can't get any better.

"Let's dance!" Johnny Von grabs my drink, puts it on a table next to us and pulls me into the crowd by the stage. I'm crunched and elbowed in the ribs by everyone else dancing in the crowd as he swings me around but I don't care, I'm out of my wits happy.

The band winds down, finishes the last song, and Dwight takes his bow. Johnny Von has his arm around my neck as we clap and cheer. He gives me a squeeze before letting go to find us a cigarette, and it hits me: THIS IS THE MOMENT!

This is the moment in my life I wanted to be flash-forwarded to when I was in the second grade. There is no other place on the face of the earth where I would rather be, no time in the imagined future that is better than now, no setting that I have to put myself away inside for and bear the time until it gets here.

It's here. Now. This is it.

ONLY I CAN'T CROSS THE BRIDGE! As the energy in the room begins to wind down, I feel myself start to struggle again. I can't blend myself into the scene. I'm at the threshold where I can see everything in front of me that I've always wanted, but I can't walk through the door. I should be living it up! But I can't.

As I stand waiting for Johnny Von to return with smokes, it dawns on me: it's the part of me I abandoned. It's the part I left behind in the lunchroom that day, the part I continued to abandon at that little café table in London. It's the genuine me... before coolness, before international playboy boyfriends, before sorority socials and high school parties at the lake. She's come to call, to collect her due. She wants to be seen. The genuine me wants out to play with Johnny Von.

Johnny Von? Johnny Von, of all people, is evoking the genuine me left behind decades ago?

I look out, at where I am, at a bar in Hollywood at the end of the night, with girls circling all around Johnny Von, and I know with all my reasoning that I should click into international playboy mode. I should have clicked into socializing-with-an-international-playboy mode at the first moment of feeling my game early this evening and not looked back. I'm no babe in the woods. I might be currently experiencing some kind of Dwight Yoakam induced existential crisis, I might battle with paralyzing shyness in the face of someone I have a crush on in the stark light of day, but...I know how to handle myself in bars! I know how to handle international playboys. I'm seasoned in all this now, and I know how to handle these types of situations…only…I don't want to *handle* the situation.

It hits me that this is an irony that could only happen under the Hollywood sign.

The genuine me wants out to play with Johnny Von!

Johnny Von? A guy who is the embodiment of the coolest kid in town, the guys' guy with a flair for Xbox and a thing for drinking and country music?! Johnny Von, the celebrity, whose reputation always precedes him. Guys want to be him, girls want to be with him. *He* is evoking the genuine me?

Johnny Von returns with a lit cigarette to share. His eyes happy I'm still standing here. Maybe that's what it is, the something in his eyes that is calling out from underneath those layers that I find so compelling. That I find different. Maybe there is something in him behind it all that is genuine, that wants out to play as well.

Only I can't. I can't be the genuine me, I don't know that girl and I don't know what she might do.

I watch him watch me pulling back, receding back into my shyness, drowning in the moment with nothing to say, barely able to make eye contact, right in front of him. I feel the nice vibe between us slipping through my fingers, turning uncomfortable, but I can't do anything about it.

I'm overcome with the feeling of being trapped. I can feel the pre-lunchroom, genuine me trapped behind a thick, green soundproof glass. I see the real me, there, silently yelling to let her out. And even though she's jumping around like a demented little mime, hitting the clear surface until her fists are bloody—yelling to be let out with the yearning of 20 years of build-up—I can't. I'm losing the moment with Johnny Von and it's killing me, but I just can't get her out.

I don't know how.

1968

Johnny Von the Crook

Johnny Von the Crook pulls at his black onyx cuff links, perfects the wide knot of his dark red silk tie, licks his fingers and smoothes his long side burns.

"Don't fuck this up." He turns from the mirror to his three stone-faced partners. He adjusts the holster of his Colt .45 Automatic. "This is the Cote d'Azur, this is not some pawn shop on the south side of Chicago." He takes his Foster Grants from their soft leather case and puts them on just so, turning back to the mirror. "We do this right and we all walk away."

In tan slacks and matching tan platform shoes, he towers over the three men. "Manny sent us for one reason and one reason alone." He takes out his gun, pulls at the slide and checks the round in the chamber. "These fucking frogs think they can cut Manny out of the deal," he flips the gun, "and we're going to explain otherwise." He clicks the release, checks the full magazine and then slams it back.

"I don't plan to be subtle about it." He rubs his thumb over the pearl inlay bearing his initials, JV, smoothing the surface so it gleams. He looks to the three men he's been teamed with, a crew he doesn't know. "Manny told me to shoot anybody that can't handle the job." Johnny Von the Crook dips his nose. He looks out over the top of his Foster Grants, "And I don't have a problem with that." He returns the .45 to the holster under his arm, throws on his hounds tooth jacket with suede patches at the elbows and they head out the hotel room.

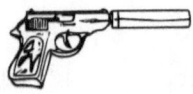

Estella sits at her vanity table adorned with crystal perfume bottles and Max Factor powder puffs. She takes a bobby pin and secures a powder blue pillbox hat perfectly on her up twist hairdo.

"Don't fuck this up." Her husband, Rorey von Burlington, grabs her arm above her elbow, just at the cuff of her three-quarter length white glove. He jerks her hard. He's still drunk from the night before.

Estella tenses and looks down at the table.

"I want everything right tonight." He squeezes her arm. "These clients are a big deal. I don't want your socialite bitch behavior turning them cold." He releases her with a jolt. "Turning everything cold. It's what you're good at, isn't it?"

Estella ignores him.

"Isn't it!" he yells, knocks her with a force that throws her from the chair, and walks into the back room of their hotel suite.

Estella pulls herself up, looks into the mirror and tries to breathe. She never wanted to marry Rorey von Burlington, but her father had made the deal. The family needed the money and the alliance to his business, and that was that. She was sold to the highest bidder, a beautiful bargaining chip.

"You're going to Jacques Pierre's this morning. I bought something yesterday." He calls out to her from the other room. "I want you wearing that fucking rock at the table tonight. If last night is how it's going to be now, like fucking an empty fucking hole in the wall, then you better be good for something." He walks back into the room and stares at her putting on her makeup. "Sad fucking shame, nobody gets a hard-on once they know you, do they?" He takes a swig of the highball in his hand. "If I have to call a whore every time I want to get off, then you'd better be good for something." He steps in closer and Estella braces herself. "You get that ring and you wear that fucking thing in front of those rich cocksuckers tonight, your kind of people. You hear me?" He stands back, behind her in the mirror. "Hurry up and get out. I've got a girl coming at 10:00."

Estella looks down at the vanity table in front of her. She takes the pearls her mother gave her before she died, out of the black case she keeps them in. "A woman's burden."

That phrase is all she can remember of the speech her mother gave her as she handed her the case at her bedside. She imagines her mother would tell her to stay away from him when he drinks. She would tell her not to upset him. Not to cause his anger.

She remembers that phrase, "a woman's burden," and the sorrow in her mother's eyes. A sadness like the eyes of a wild mustang that has been broken and then beaten too many times, long after submitting. It was a speech about finding beauty where you can, in small doses, to savor later. Something about a man's world, not always kind to women.

She puts the choker around her neck, and clicks the tiny gold clasp. She can't think of a way out, away from him. He'd never stand for it. He'd find her. Her hand stays on her neck. A razor blade could do it, there at her neck or wrists, but she's too afraid he would get to her before she was gone. She wasn't always like this, not wanting anything but to die.

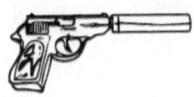

Estella notices Johnny Von the Crook immediately as she sits at the glass display counter in Jacques Pierre's. Waiting for her salesman to return, the diamonds glittering under the glass, he is the only other person in the store. Estella tries to ignore him. His interaction with the salesgirl at the counter is loud and obvious. She turns away to look out the storefront window. She stares out at the beach and the sails. She feels her stomach knot.

In the south of France, the people behind the counter are even more beautiful than the clientele. Johnny Von the Crook has zeroed in on a blond French clerk standing behind the Rolexes. The girl is tan and thin, wearing a white knit dress with no bra. She's standing next to him, brushing up against him as she leans over to open the display. It's vulgar. The woman knows her nipples show through her dress, she flaunts it. Has them on display as if they are jewels to be shown with the rest of the merchandise. Johnny Von the Crook touches her blond hair at her neck. Brushes it back to smell her perfume. It repulses Estella that men want that, that he wants her. Again she turns her back to them, tries to disregard them in her mind. She focuses again on the harbor, the boats that her husband sells, all lined up, neat and clean. But Estella does feel a wave of envy cut through her disgust when she hears the woman peal with laughter.

"I can dig it." Johnny Von the Crook taps the glass counter with his knuckles. "I'll just sit here while you find out."

"We'll probably have to open the vault in the back," the blond says in her sultry French accent, "but I'm sure my manager will approve it. As long as you don't mind him watching us."

Johnny Von the Crook winks. "I know you French chicks like to play it kinky." She laughs and turns. "Far out," he says as he looks her up and down. She leaves them the only two patrons in the front.

As soon as they are alone, Estella feels his demeanor change. He looks at his watch, sits down and unfolds a newspaper in front of him. Estella feels her face flush. She is suddenly nervous. She pulls at the hem of her powder blue skirt, covering her crossed knees.

"You American?" he says to her from behind his paper.

"I'm Mrs. von Burlington." Estella pulls her alligator handbag close to her stomach. "My husband is here on business. He sells yachts, most of the ones you see in the harbor, he sold. Perhaps you know him?"

Johnny Von the Crook flips his paper down. He looks at Estella, stares at her. "I don't know him." He flips the paper back up, "He must be a strong man though." He says from behind the paper. "That's quite an impressive mark you've got." He flips down the paper again.

He stares at the bruise on her arm and then at her, straight at her eyes.

"Must not know his own strength."

Estella pulls up at her white glove, and down at the sleeve of her powder blue Jackie O. jacket. Before she can say another word, her salesman returns with her diamond ring, ready to fit.

It is a ridiculously large pink diamond surrounded by two small rows of brilliant diamonds. The ring looks harsh, larger than life, on her un-calloused and tender hands. This is the first time Estella sees the ring.

Johnny Von the Crook peeks over at the ring as he stands. The manager walks into the room. He smiles, reaches out his hand to greet Johnny Von the Crook with his security guard on his right and the blond French sales girl at his left.

Although she is distracted by the discussion of her new ring with the young man helping her, Estella is sure she feels Johnny Von the Crook brush her back with his finger, lean into her and mumble, "Time to Hokey Pokey."

But before she can turn around, before she can check the reality of it, Johnny Von the Crook pulls out his gun. He takes the outstretched hand of the manager with his left hand instead of his right, pulls the small French man into him and zips a bullet through his chest. He throws him to the ground in one smooth move. Then, "zip, zip" his silencer dampens the sound as two more bullets cut into the head of the security guard, and the belly of the tan, thin, sultry voiced French girl.

Estella cannot take her eyes off the red stain blooming on the white knit dress as the girl lies on the ground in front of her. It doesn't feel horrifying to her. She is rattled only by a feeling inside her that the images seem matter-of-fact, almost satisfying. Estella, numb and lost in her life, feels only an odd gratitude that something extreme has happened, at least something, even if she's next to fall.

The first two moves, the bloodstain, happen faster than she can take in, but then the whole scene switches to slow motion.

Johnny Von the Crook swings his arm over Estella's pillbox hat, zips another bullet into the young sales clerk still holding an empty ring box in his hand. She is the only one left in the room.

"Get down," he says, business-like, in a whisper.

He walks to the middle of the display floor. He looks up to the security camera, "Manny sends his love," he says loudly to the top corner of the room.

He starts at twelve o'clock in front of him. He fires a bullet into the first display case and glass explodes everywhere. He stays still and centered there. He begins firing bullets into each display case clockwise around the room.

Estella feels each blast of the raining glass.

"One o'clock! Two o'clock! Three o'clock!" he calls out as he shoots.

Estella crouches down on her knees as small as she can.

Three men in rubber masks and black suits bolt from the back of the store.

Johnny Von the Crook looks at his Colt .45. "Seven plus one," he says to no one in particular. With the grace of a samurai, he empties the used magazine. He takes a clip from the left side of his belt, loads the slide with a single bullet, drops the magazine, returns it to his belt, and then unclips another. He jams a fresh seven into the grip.

"Vault's open," a man calls out from behind his mask, pulling down the shades and locking the front door. The other two frantically grab at the rings and necklaces in the shattered displays.

Johnny Von the Crook begins again, "Four o'clock. Five o'clock." He calls out each shot like a circus ringleader calling out the amusements.

Glass is flying everywhere while Estella huddles on all fours. Her eyes are transfixed on the pink diamond on her hand. Millions of colors shimmer off its perfection. Her husband flashes in her mind, then the pain of his grip this morning. Then suddenly, as if hypnotized by the jewel, the perpetual knot in her stomach switches from fear to calm. Estella looks up.

"Six o'clock. Seven o'clock. Eight little piggies!" Johnny Von the Crook, pleased with himself, is still shooting his way around the room.

Estella stands up. She stands as if she is bulletproof, out of her body. She feels not fear but exhilaration at the sights and sounds of the destruction crashing all around her.

"Nine o'clock. Ten o'clock. Eleven!" he calls out. "Ladies and Gentleman, that's seven plus one again," he says in a low voice, mechanical now in his theatrics.

Out of display cases, Johnny Von the Crook looks at Estella now standing across the room from him, her up-twist hair falling from its tight pins. No witnesses, other than the camera that the cops will never see, that's the deal. He reloads.

As his hands move with the same graceful choreography of clips and bullets, he looks her in the eye, stares at her, as he had before, stopping time with his eyes.

Estella holds his gaze.

Johnny Von the Crook feels his heart beat. He then looks up at the chandelier, centered on the ceiling between them. His eyes twinkle.

"How 'bout a baker's dozen?" he says, as if this was all for her, as if they are the only two people in the room, as if he is waiting for her reply.

Estella will never know if she nods her approval or if Johnny Von the Crook just sees the yes in her eyes. He nods yes, answers his own question in agreement with her, and unloads the remaining bullets at the ceiling.

The huge chandelier dangles. Hangs for a moment, like a great trapeze artist about to jump from his ledge, waving to the crowd, and then pops its cable. The perfection of the priceless fixture, static in one moment then released to an unalterable course the next, is breathtaking. Estella watches with fascination, as it is set into motion, alive, falling through the air and then slamming into the ground. It crashes down, bursting on the terrazzo floor into a million pieces of flying, glittering spectrums of light. Destroyed into a million unrecognizable pieces at their feet.

What it does to Estella to witness this is unexplainable. The beauty of the explosion is indescribable, the breathtaking beautiful violence of it.

Johnny Von the Crook pauses looking across the room over the devastation he has just orchestrated and locks in, once again, on Estella's eyes. He clicks out his empty magazine and grabs a fresh round.

Estella knows the next bullet must be hers, but she doesn't move or run. She doesn't even tense her body. She can't find any fear, any terror inside. She can only stand in her powder blue pumps, oblivious to the many tiny cuts the shattering glass has caused all over her legs, acutely aware of everything else outside of her. Every color, sound, and movement, every bit of sparkling glass at her feet, the shining silver of his gun, the sharp red of his tie, and the way his brown eyes are endless when he looks at her.

Johnny Von the Crook jams the handle of his .45 and points the gun at her, he looks at her one last time, then to the boys scurrying around the room stuffing the jewels into sacks, and then back to Estella. Instead of firing, he calls to the boys, "Back into the vault. We've got three minutes left." He signals to Estella, still pointing the gun at her, "Come over here."

"No," she hears herself say, in a tone that is new to her voice.

Johnny Von the Crook, shocked, smiles at Estella. He walks in his tan platform shoes through the puddles of broken glass, around the broken display cases, counter clockwise, around the lifeless chandelier, pointing his gun the whole way. When he gets to her, she braces herself, as she has many times in her marriage. But Johnny Von the Crook does not strike her. Instead, he stands behind her, slides the cold metal of the gun under her jacket and blouse, and stops it below the center of her shoulder blades.

"Mrs. von Burlington, let's walk to the vault."

Things happen in the vault too fast for Estella to remember with any accuracy. Where the front room was more vivid to her than she'd ever experienced, the vault is all a blur.

"What's she doing here?"

"I'm taking her."

"He said no witnesses!"

"I'm running this job and I'm taking her."

"Manny said no witnesses! If you're not going to do it, I will…"

Estella sees the barrel of a Thompson submachine gun lift to her eye level. She then hears Johnny Von the Crook fire. Bullets spray off to the side of her as the first masked man goes down, the barrel of the machine gun falling away.

The second masked man turns from the stepladder he is on, pulling down boxes from the top of the vault. He drops the loot. Looks to his gun on the table, while the other masked man, standing close to Estella, swings his Tommy gun up to fire.

As if he knows their moves before they do, Johnny Von the Crook fires two shots into the masked man next to Estella. The man jolts backwards, bullets spraying into the air. The gun kicks back and hits Estella hard in the head before it drops to the floor. The second masked man is down.

Johnny Von the Crook unloads three more bullets just as the final masked man gets to his gun at the table.

Estella feels the pounding at her temples, looks down on the floor at the three men, the blood spilling everywhere, looks to Johnny Von the Crook, blurring in her vision. He walks across the room. He steps on the outstretched hand of the final man down, only inches from the Tommy gun on the table. "Look at it!" he flashes his gun, his initials gleaming. "That's a Colt .45, motherfucker."

Estella hears the sirens outside. She sees the panic flash through the eyes of Johnny Von the Crook. They can't go out the front. He scrambles around the large room of the vault, looking for a way out, looking up to the ceiling, around the stacks.

Estella, through her haze, sees the thick green sound-proof window in the back of the room. They did deals from the vault. They'll be a back door to the alley on the other side.

Estella's had enough. Enough of it all. From a place inside her she thought she lost long ago, she crosses the vault. She going to walk out of this place. She's going to

have a different life even if she has to shoot her way out
-- or die trying. She staggers, bends, and pries loose the
submachine gun from the hands of the first masked man
down.

Johnny Von the Crook turns at the sound of Estella
firing bullets at the thick green glass. The gun kicks up and
half the first round of bullets sprays up the wall.

"It's bulletproof!" he says, shocked by what he is seeing.
"We can't get out that way!"

She holds the gun, pulling down as she fires again. She
empties the gun. The glass starts to crack. She looks
over at him as he becomes more out of focus, "Nothing's
bulletproof forever."

She drops the empty gun and picks up the Tommy gun
on the table.

She uses everything she has left to riddle the glass with
bullets. A white spider web of cracks begin to fill the
green glass. She says in a dizzy slur, "That's a submachine
gun, motherfucker." Estella drops the gun, stumbling
backwards.

He gets to her as she falls, giving in to the thumping of
her head. He catches her in one arm, then fires one bullet,
dead center into the thick glass with his .45. The final
bullet breaks it wide open. As Estella passes out, Johnny
Von the Crook throws her over his shoulder and heads out
the back.

"The first package is on its way." Johnny Von the Crook
stands in his black socks and garters talking into the heavy
beige handset of the phone. He looks at himself in the
mirror of his darkened hotel room as he talks. "The guys
got out of hand! Yeah. Yeah. What can I say, Manny, we
lost a few lambs. It's nothing to worry about. I did what I
had to."

Wearing nothing but tight shiny maroon briefs and
a gold chain, he adjusts himself, licks his fingers and
smoothes his sideburns. "Look…look! The shepherd's got
the flock, baby. I've already dropped the first case, I just
got back." He's quiet on the line as he listens to Manny.
"Yeah. I've got the second package with me now." Johnny
Von the Crook looks over to an orange Samsonite suitcase,
then back to himself in the mirror. "This is it. Just like we
said. I deliver to the boat and then I walk." He takes his
brown paisley, polyester-blend shirt that is draped around
the back of the chair. "It's all there, Manny. When have I
ever screwed you over?" He swings his arms into the long
sleeves of the silky shirt and leaves it unbuttoned. It flows
behind him as he reaches through the lamplight, across
the desk to grab a pen. "Manny! The second package, the
boat and then I walk." Johnny Von the Crook flares up.
"I'll be there, you prick!" He yells into the phone, "I don't
care who she is! She's outside of the deal. I don't care who
the fuck her husband is."

Manny reproaches Johnny Von the Crook. He knows about Estella, her husband is looking for her. Rorey von Burlington made a dirty deal for the stolen ring and he's pissed off. But Manny knows Johnny Von the Crook, knows how to handle him, how to play him, the master to a junkyard dog. He's careful not to wind him up too much. Johnny Von the Crook still has half the diamonds.

Calming down, he scribbles the time and location, throws down the pen and grabs his onyx cuff links. He knits them through the buttonholes at his wrists as he listens to the other end of the line. He starts to laugh, "Yeah. Yeah. Manny, I know. I'm going to take care of it. Everything is fine, mother fucker." His eyes shift in the mirror, from himself, to the bed behind him, and then to the pink diamond ring on the table. "And Manny," he spins the ring on the table, then says without a trace of asking in his tone, daring the receiver to question him, "I'm keeping the ring. We'll call it a souvenir."

Johnny Von the Crook puts down the phone, turns to the bed and hears Estella begin to stir. He's worked for Manny close to 15 years now, since he got out of reform. He secures the ties at her wrist and the knots at each bedpost. He checks that there is enough slack for some movement, but has still strapped her tight enough not to get loose.

Johnny Von the Crook does not know a lot about life, the normal life that people live. But he knows about his life. He knows about looking good and looking the part.

He knows about hiding and getting through, about back rooms and short-term leases. He knows about Manny and about bringing in a job. And he knows that Manny is never going to let him go. He knows it, no matter what is said between them.

He looks at Estella, not yet back, and passes his hand lightly at the bump on her head, then at her smooth pale cheeks. He touches his finger just barely at her lips. He feels longing in his chest as he touches her chest. He caresses her breasts through her blouse and the thick textured lace of the Cross Your Heart Bra Estella wears. He draws his hands down.

The longing has always been with Johnny Von the Crook. Until just a few days ago, he thought the longing was for beautiful things. Until just a few days ago, he set out to accrue enough beautiful things to assure himself he was not the boy with nothing. He was not the boy in the back of the state-run school whose parents didn't want him because he was ugly and dirty, because he was nothing, as he had been told every time they hit him.

Houses, high-class hookers, cars, and cash, he'd had it all. He did what he set out to do, he learned what the best of everything was and he took it. What he realized, just a few days ago, was that the longing was still there, even with all the things. Still, he has to put distance between him and that boy. But the something that will do it escapes him.

He saw it in her eyes too, the need for something. A need that would understand destroying everything to get to it. A need that would justify killing. A need so intense, so deep, death was irrelevant in the face of it. It's why he took her. Not because she was another beautiful object he wanted, but because he recognized the need in her eyes.

Johnny Von the Crook adjusts his shiny maroon briefs as he feels himself starting to get hard, his head filled with thoughts of Estella looking at him, the way she looked at him in that flash during the robbery. The way she said no to him. Maybe she knows what it is, this something he can't figure out.

He sits on the side of the bed next to her and puts his big hands at her knees. He reaches up her powder blue skirt and unclips the garters at each thigh. Careful to be gentle over the small cuts on her legs, he pulls down the shredded stockings, leaving them rumpled at the ropes tied to her ankles.

Estella wakes at the sting of the alcohol-soaked cotton balls Johnny Von the Crook is pressing into each tiny cut on her legs. She says nothing, only moans at the ache from her head. Johnny Von the Crook tips the alcohol bottle again; now seeing she is awake, he presses the cotton ball at the next tiny cut, lifts it, and then blows.

As the shadowy room comes into focus, Estella feels the warmth of his hand under her knee, a sharp sting, and then cool relief. Up and down her legs, the rhythm, the quick pain and then release by his whispered blowing.

"What am I doing here?" She stares at the ceiling, hiding

her fear, accusing in her tone as her head pounds. Johnny
Von the Crook doesn't answer. He just keeps at the cotton
ball, the gentle blowing, moving up her legs, the inside of
her knees. As she comes to, Estella realizes that he is not
dressed, that she is tied up, and that he has plans that go
farther than nursemaid.

"Whatever you're thinking, you pervert, you're wrong."
She pulls at the ropes. "You should have killed me in the
vault." Estella feels the anger rise inside of her as he moves
her skirt to get to a cut inside her thigh. "I don't know
what you think, I'm not some…" her mind races, enraged
at how out of control and turned on she is becoming as he
handles her legs, as she feels his sideburns touch the skin of
her thighs when he blows, "…some sex crazed hippie."

She jerks at the ropes again, thinks about how it was
only this morning that she was contemplating ways to kill
herself, and then goes lifeless.

"Ask my husband, you're barking up the wrong tree.
Whoever the fuck you are, you're going to be sorry. I'm
frigid. You might as well jerk off in the corner, because
whatever you think is going to happen, isn't. I don't care
what you do." Her eyes flat, she looks at nothing and says
as if she's been here before, "I don't care what you do to
me."

Johnny Von the Crook doesn't stop, doesn't pay
attention to a single thing Estella says, doesn't pull back as
he feels her disconnect from her body. He finishes each
small cut, each little mark of pain, taking his time, putting

his lips together to blow, up and down her legs. He then kisses a patch of smooth skin on the top of her thigh.

"Ask me to set you free." He pulls back from her bedside, sits in a chair not three feet from the bed, and stares at her, the same endless stare.

Estella stares at the ceiling.

He leans in, and says again, "Ask me to set you free and I will."

Estella looks at him, confused by her own silence.

Johnny Von the Crook takes off his garters and socks. He stands and clicks off all the lights. He crawls on the bed, straddles Estella, but not heavy, he's careful with his weight.

He opens her blouse in the silence, one button at a time.

He slips his fingers under the wide white straps of her bra at her left shoulder. Draws his fingers down to the clasp at her chest. He grips the strap and the clasp in his hands and then in a burst, rips it open. He doesn't expose her, only breaks the garment. He does the same to the other side, a slow draw down from her shoulder then a quick grip, popping the fabric loose. He leans down, his gold chain dangles, his lips close enough to kiss her, but he doesn't. He reaches his arm around her back.

Estella's body arches, makes way for him as he unhooks her. He slips the white Cross Your Heart Bra off her body and onto the floor.

Johnny Von the Crook slides his body down Estella.

She smells the blend of clean soap with a hint of Old Spice.

Ever so slowly, he inhales her, kissing her neck. In the kiss, he shifts off to her side, moves his hand from her breast to her stomach and puts his head softly on her chest. He cuddles into Estella.

"We're dropping the diamonds in two days." Without another word, he slowly drifts off to sleep.

Estella lies still, noticing the rapid course of her breath starting to recede as she hears the rain starting outside. She feels his warm breathing on her bare chest and cannot explain the familiarity she feels for him. She is utterly unable to make sense why she feels the way she feels, somehow right, with a killer coiled in next to her.

Estella wakes, hours later, in the dark night of the hotel room, to find herself kissing Johnny Von the Crook. She is unsure if the rainstorm now thundering outside wakes her, or if it's the surprising feel of kissing him, with full consent, that calls her back.

Without opening her eyes, she feels him push her skirt up to her waist and move her silk underwear to touch her. There in the dark and the movement, she cannot identify herself. Shocked by how excited she is at his touch, she pulls at her legs and wrists and feels the bindings. She feels like someone she does not know. Her body, she does not know. She does not open her eyes. She pulls again at the bindings, the wanting to get away and not wanting to get away, battling inside her. She cannot tell the good or bad of it, if it's pleasure or torture, she can only feel the intensity, the inescapability.

Johnny Von the Crook is relentless in his focus. This is the quality unlike any other time, unlike her husband, whose intensity is all self-serving, all consumed with her as a means to serve his own satisfaction. But Johnny Von the Crook's attention is not like that. It doesn't let up, doesn't move away from her. He stays aware of only her and her body.

He moves the sucking from her bare chest down between her legs. A wave of pleasure wells up so forcefully inside Estella that she scrambles to suppress it, jerks her legs and tries to move him off her. In one motion he grabs her thighs and grips each leg not hard enough to bruise, but firm enough to pin her still.

Johnny Von the Crook has developed skills between a woman's legs. The experience, the texture, the pleasure of it, is not new to him, but the taste of Estella sends a charge through Johnny Von the Crook like no other. It races through his body like a shot of heroin. Like something he's never had. He does not do drugs, doesn't like the idea of being out of control. But now, as his kiss meets her here, this taste is the closest to a drug experience he imagines. Not because he loses his focus of her, but because it overtakes him. Causes sensations and impulses not premeditated in him. This is not an experience he would choose, to be in unknown areas of himself. But like a drug, it is too late, he's swallowed.

Maybe it is being bound, or maybe because she is in another world, maybe because it is dark and he is the way he is, maybe it is because just this morning she had no other thought but how she could go about ending herself, she doesn't know why, she doesn't care why, Estella feels something unexpectedly break free. And it is not the ropes.

He moves quickly, keeps his body on hers, pulls his shiny maroon briefs off. He reaches to the drawer of the bedside table. He jerks it open and grabs a large buck knife as she squirms and moves under him.

She moves against the bindings and under him not in an attempt to get away, she moves in a desperate attempt to get somewhere she's never been, to follow the unalterable course of her body.

With the buck knife in one hand, supporting his embrace of her with the other, Johnny Von the Crook says again, "Ask me to set you free and I will."

She nods frantically, hears herself whisper, "Yes."

He reaches down her right leg and cuts the ropes.

"Ask me!" he says forcefully.

"Yes," she says again, her voice more audible, more present to the question. He twists again and cuts the ropes at her left leg. In a rush, he cuts the stiff fabric of her underwear and garter belt. The skirt, he rips at the seam and flings to the floor. He drops down on her naked body.

Wrapping her legs firmly around his back, she begs him with her body, to move.

He says it without question, while hard but unmoving, "Ask me to set you free."

Estella's eyes lock into his. She is Alice through the looking glass, up is down and everything is opposite. And for some uncontrollable, unexpected reason, she smiles. The question, his request, the ropes, the robbery! The intense physical pleasure she feels for the first time in her life, it is all too absurd. She tries to ignore him, to move, to rock, but he keeps still. Johnny Von the Crook repeats the question.

"Ask me. Ask me to set you free, Mrs. von Burlington."

A wave of unstoppable laughter breaks out of her.

"Estella," she calls out. "My name is Estella." She feels him break with laughter as well. Her body frantic with pleasure, her mind lost to the waves of laughter. She is on the other side of the glass, with this crook, and she is never going back.

In that thought, she is free. She is free, here, tied to the bed, here with a man holding a buck knife, a cold-blooded killer, torturing her with a sweetness she has never known, a man that doesn't know her name.

"Yes, set me free," she says coming down from the laughter. "Yes, whoever the fuck you are," she says releasing the last few waves of laughter, "set me free."

Johnny Von the Crook smiles and starts to rock her body with his. He puts the buck knife at the rope on her right wrist.

He starts the rhythmic back and forth of his body.

"Johnny." He cuts the rope, kissing her neck.

She wraps her arm around his back.

"Von," he says and jerks the blade of the knife through the final rope, drops it to the floor, and frees Estella from the last of her bindings.

Estella's body explodes with motion. She grips his back, inhales the smell of him, no longer soap and Old Spice, only sex and sweat. She is lost to the sound of their bodies moving, the slamming of the headboard at the wall, the feel of his tongue. She scrambles to join all the sensations, blend with them and then pour them all back on Johnny Von the Crook.

In a flurry, in a fevered passionate madness, Johnny Von the Crook feels Estella's whole body contract, sucking him in completely, consuming all of him. He hears her call out his name and sees something that he will forever add to his list of beautiful things. He sees the wave of pleasure wash across her body, her face, and her eyes looking into his. He then hears his own moan of ecstasy; as if she has been the one this whole time seducing him. As if she is the one reaching deep inside and pulling out the something he has never had but always wanted.

In the flash, in feeling himself burst, Johnny Von the Crook leaves his life, up until this moment, behind him. Inside of him a line is drawn, everything that went before this, and everything that will come after this.

Holding Estella, both out of breath but electric with life, he erases everything that went before. He removes it from himself. He will finish this with Manny, and her husband if needed, whatever it takes. And then he will have only this side of the line.

Estella moves in, cuddles into him now. She sees the Colt .45 on the bedside table. "You'll have to show me how to shoot," she says as if joining the world for the first time, waking up and propping herself up on her elbows, her hair falling free and wild. On this side of the looking glass, in the power of this freedom, which he has seduced out of her, there will be no bruises to hide and no burden to bear.

Wearing a multi-colored print silk scarf on her head, a green mini-dress *sans* bra, in her bare feet with her toes painted red, Estella stands on the lacquer wood deck at the front of the speedboat, her Tommy gun strapped to her, still smoking.

Johnny Von the Crook steps over the body of Manny, and two of his boys. He takes the orange Samsonite suitcase and throws it from the 30-foot yacht to the back of the speedboat.

"Pull the boat around to the other side, baby," he calls out to Estella from behind his Foster Grants. "There's something else I want before we go."

He dips under the large sail, scurries down the side of the boat to the bench at the back. He props up Rory von Burlington on the yellow cushions and rifles through his jacket, avoiding the bloodstain at the wide lapel. He feels for the pink diamond ring, grabs it from an inside pocket and turns his back to the lifeless body. He takes a few steps. He takes a purple silk handkerchief out of his own pocket, wrapping the ring to surprise her with it after they're away.

Pop! Pop! Bam!

Johnny Von the Crook jumps, startled by the loud crack of the shots.

He turns, his heart pounding.

Rorey von Burlington is sprawled out on the floor of the boat directly behind him, small pistol in hand, now dead with out a doubt.

Relief rushes through Johnny Von the Crook's body.

"I told you not to forget the small one strapped to his leg," Estella says from the back of the speedboat, holding the smoking .45, the initials JV gleaming in the sun.

Johnny Von the Crook smiles. He pulls the ropes and jumps from the yacht to the speedboat.

"I guess I have to save your neck every time," Estella says as he takes her place behind the wheel.

"Yeah, well, what did you use, baby?" he says as he shifts the boat into gear.

"What?"

"At the moment of truth," he smiles and comes in close to her as the boat pulls away. "Say it. Not that submachine gun. What did you reach for when you needed the real deal? What? Say it, baby."

Estella grins, clicks the safety on, reaches across his body and puts the gun back into the holster hanging at the side of his chair.

"That's a Colt .45, motherfucker," she says and laughs as Johnny Von the Crook nods yes behind his Foster Grants.

The speedboat cuts the water, sprays an arc of white foam as the engine revs and tears away. Estella and Johnny Von the Crook disappear into the sun.

Chapter 6

"The eye altering, alters all."
~ *William Blake*

In a last burst of effort to recover some connection, I lean over to Johnny Von, "I heard you guys are going to London."

His assistant and I were chatting on the road a few days earlier about her trip with him to shoot in the U.K. for a few weeks. We cover his upcoming trip, my having lived there and his never having been there. The band starts clearing the stage.

"I have a list for her of places to go. Don't let her forget to call me," I say.

Johnny leans in. "Why don't you come by on Tuesday and drop it off?"

"I'll have the dogs, I don't want to bother you guys if you're working."

"It's no bother, bring the dogs with you," he says as the bar room lights click on. "I've got some stuff in the morning but I should be done in the afternoon," Johnny Von says as he hits his buddy's arm. "You ready to go?"

Ever polite, Johnny Von shakes my hand, pecks me on the cheek and says good night; a perfect gentleman.

As soon as Johnny Von is out the bar, Mandy zooms up to me. "It's so on for you." She whispers in my ear. "Come with me." I'm light-headed from the whole event, so I'm a little startled by her sudden instructions. She says we should wait a bit, go to the bathroom, so that we don't leave right on his heels and run into him in the parking lot. We don't want it to look like we're out of here just because he's gone. I look around and see the bar is closing. The bartenders are walking around and asking people to leave. I don't think he'd really think that we are leaving just because he is leaving, but I agree with her anyway. Mandy has been outstanding this evening.

As we stand in front of the mirror and Mandy reapplies her lip-gloss and powder, it starts to register with me just how remarkable Mandy has been tonight. Without seeming obvious, or even needing to be asked, she deftly became "the goalie" after the first girl rushed Johnny Von in a when-girls-attack type manner. She stood just enough away from Johnny Von and me not to seem there, but close enough to see other girls en route to him. With skill that would put David Beckham to the test, she would, at the right moment, step into their path. She'd compliment them about their hair or their handbag, ask them where they bought those great boots. If the compliment did not slow them down, she would aim for an insecurity, politely tell them their lipstick was smeared or they had something in their teeth. If it looked like a serious case, she'd pull out all the stops and whisper, in a sisterly way, that maybe they started their period or sat in something, sending them to the ladies room to check it out. Mandy was good. Not only did she goal-tend like a professional, but she also displayed excellent peel-away technique. If Johnny Von had a buddy next to him, she'd talk and engage and get him to the bar with her, circling the two of us like a skilled sheepdog, separating away the other guys, increasing the ease for my singular attention from Mr. Von. So smooth was Mandy Kane this evening that I felt, upon reflection, suddenly at the feet of a guru.

"Of course, you know you can't go over Tuesday," she says, turning away from herself in the mirror, after I tell her every detail of what was said by whom. The glow around Mandy Kane abruptly blinks off.

"What?"

"You absolutely can't show up at his house. In fact, I think you should stop walking in front of his house altogether. This is a crucial time and you need to be really unavailable."

"No, but he seemed really genuine when he said it. Besides, it's where I work anyway. I guess I could walk a different way, but I don't think I should. I mean, he really did seem like a genuine regular guy to me."

"Yeah. Johnny Von seemed genuine. He's an actor. He's an actor who has been drinking all evening." She laughs a bit. "Look, you don't understand what you're dealing with here. Johnny Von is the kind of guy who is only going to go for you if he feels like he can't have you. He's only going to chase you if he feels like you're a little out of his reach. If he thinks you're on the fence and he has to play you to get you."

"I don't know. He didn't seem like that kind of guy."

"He's Johnny Von! And listen, while **I** don't think he's a big deal, trust me, he thinks he's a big deal. You have to play him, you have to play him better than he plays you, otherwise I guarantee you will not get him."

"But maybe he just wants someone he can talk to? Maybe he wants to get to know me? Besides, how will he find me if I don't walk by his house? Won't he think it's rude that I said I'd go over and I don't show up?"

Mandy Kane looks at me like maybe I'm too big a

project for her. Maybe her hope that I would be an ally, a Robin to her Batman in pursuit of celebrity boyfriends, was only wishful thinking.

"He grabbed my ass, you know," she says with a tinge of hostility in her voice.

"What?!"

"While you were at the bar. Whatever, it's not like he meant anything. And I totally gave him a look like what-the-hell, dude. And I'm only telling you so that you understand how it is."

This is the other side of Mandy Kane. This is what Mandy Kane can do if you're on the opposing team. True or not true, the idea of Johnny Von reaching out for Mandy Kane's butt is stinging at best. She softens. "I'm on your side, and he's probably attracted to you. So look, whatever you do, don't go over there tomorrow."

I suddenly feel the different planets Mandy and I are on. But she's thrown down the gauntlet. She put in her time tonight, and now has a vested interest. This is serious celebrity dating — she is the authority and I'm the neophyte. I know that if I say one more thing about why I think I should go over, she'll go off on me. She'll tell me seven ways to Sunday why I will never be with Johnny Von, or anyone like Johnny Von, and right now I'm so pleased with the night that I just can't hear anything more that might spoil it.

"Yeah. I guess you're right." I take the lip-gloss she

hands me, touch up my lips and think, I'm going over to Johnny Von's house come hell or high water. And then I make a mental note: Don't ever talk to Mandy Kane about Johnny Von — ever, ever again.

I am now walking up to the house of Johnny Von a third time. This time I'm expected. This time, dogs in hand, I am having a very serious talk with myself.

"I will not pass out. This is just some guy. This is nothing. I'll be fine. I'm invited. He invited me. He said, "Stop by tomorrow afternoon." Those words came out of his mouth, while directly addressing me. I know I didn't imagine it. I was casual, easy even. I was fine Sunday night. I can be myself, my genuine self. I will not throw up. I will not pass out."

I walk the hill of his driveway, trying to breathe. I ring the bell.

No one answers.

"This is stupid. He was drunk. He doesn't remember. He won't know who I am." I start sliding down, "He talks with a zillion flirting girls a day. What the hell am I doing? He won't remember me. I'm about to make a fool of myself." My fingers slip the rock face of this cliff I am scaling. "I'm an idiot. I'm about to incite an awkwardness that will most likely end in restraining orders!"

I think about turning and running away, but I've got the damn dogs and someone might see. And then I'd be that girl who walked up to Johnny Von's house, rang the bell and then ran away. I'm not that girl. I'm not. The real me is in here somewhere, I know it. I can do this, I know it. I catch myself, the rope jerking me as I dangle on the side of this mountain.

"Walk around! Go to the back! Call out hello!" I now have The General and my pre-lunchroom second-grade-self strong-arming me. I walk. I call. I see Johnny Von appear at the second story window. He waves his big paw hand, smiles and disappears again.

My heart thumps wildly through my whole body. I can't hear or see clearly. I'm sort of tunnel-visioned, like what happens to you in an emergency.

I wait.

I can't track time. It seems like forever or maybe like no time at all. And then, there in the light of day, is Johnny Von. Majestic at the top of the steps, in a black concert T-shirt, jeans, bare feet and rumpled hair.

"Who do we have here?" He is warm, as he was at the King King, warm and laced with awkwardness.

My favorite.

I melt. I take a deep breath and introduce my friends Rocky and Moochie. He walks down to where we are and pats them on the head.

A nervous flutter re-launches inside me and I start

talking. I hand him the map of London and the places-to-see list, which I'd put together for his assistant. I have a reason to be here. I hear myself chattering, unsure of what words are coming out. I see him nodding along. I surface from my monologue. I switch to Q & A, get him talking. "What's your schedule? How long are you guys staying? Have you been to London? Do you know your hotel?"

Johnny Von is now sitting on the steps. He is looking forward to London. He is there for three weeks filming. He'll be working mostly, but his assistant will like this list. "Thank you, that was sweet ..."

I feel a shyness come over him. Johnny Von in a blush of shyness.

Wonderful.

Without thinking, I say something funny and he laughs.

Johnny Von in a little laugh-burst!

Wonderful, wonderful.

I don't know what I said. I don't remember what made him laugh; it popped out from inside me, as if from someone else. I just remember the feeling of seeing Johnny Von laugh.

Wonderful, wonderful, wonderful.

(Actually, that's a lie. I do remember what I said, but I don't want to tell you. In all the world, it's just me who knows what I said that made Johnny Von laugh. It's forever mine. It feels sweeter if it stays that way.)

I then ask Johnny Von if he wants to invite me inside for a tall cool drink of water. He nods yes and I tie up the dogs. We head up the stone steps.

I lead, he follows.

Midway to the top, Johnny Von trips on the steps behind me. He stumbles and recovers and plays it off like it didn't happen, talking over the tripping.

This little trip sets me free.

I spend the next 40 minutes talking and hanging out by the pool with Johnny Von—Johnny, more comfortable inside than I can remember being in ages.

We talk about this and that, London, the International Playboy. We talk about Johnny Von's friends, about Dwight Yoakam, about the movie he's about to shoot. It's the biggest project he's done so far. He doesn't say it in a boastful way, but more in an excited kid kind of way. He talks about acting and why he loves it and how fortunate he feels about everything he's done so far.

It the most spontaneous, easy conversation I can remember having with someone in a long, long time.

But I should tell you, it's not so much what was said that I remember. It's not the topics of conversation that have stayed with me all this time. As good as I can ever be at words and ideas, they're never really the thing anyway. What has stayed crystal clear in my mind is the feel of him, the pauses, the beats of meandering conversation. Mostly his eyes — and the way he laughs.

Johnny stands to say good-bye; his agent is on the phone.
He leans over and hugs and kisses me on the cheek. He
feels to me awkward in the moment and unsure with
his body, like this is the social protocol, crossed with the
feeling of "You're a nice pretty girl whom I don't know
what to do with."

He says something about my being a "great girl."

I say something about "I know."

He deadpans, "Don't yell at me."

I return, "You don't yell at me," which makes us laugh.

"I'll see you when I get back," he says.

I wave and go to untie the dogs as he goes inside.

He'll be back in three weeks.

1919

Johnny Von the Clerk

"Three more positions opened up today for returning soldiers." Johnny Von the Clerk sits at his big wooden desk on the second floor of the Anderson Brothers Mercantile Company. His buddy Albert calls over from the desk facing his. "A manager and two assistants."

When the Great War started, Johnny Von the Clerk went to sign up. Was hopeful that this would be a turning point for him. That he would be trained and then fight in famous battles, maybe save someone's life, but after the physical his papers were declined. He was a big overgrown man, but he was born with his right foot turned completely inward. And even though he'd worked his whole life to compensate, to walk straight and tall, the doctor at the exam told him the army wouldn't take him.

"You're just not soldier material," the doctor said to him while scribbling on his clipboard.

"I, I, I ca-can do anything you want. I, I can run fa-fa-faster than you thi-thi-think."

Seeing the disappointment in his face, hearing the stutter in his voice, as sometimes happens to Johnny Von the Clerk when he gets upset, or nervous, or talks about something important to him, the elderly man with his stethoscope and white coat says to him, "You'll have to stay here, son, and look after your wife and family." He pats him on the back out the door, not knowing Johnny Von the Clerk has no wife, no kids, and says, "You will serve your country and this community well by continuing to work here in Chicago. Going to your job, keeping the economy running." The doctor doesn't realize that Johnny Von the Clerk is just a clerk.

When the others left for the war, Johnny Von the Clerk was given a desk by a large picture window that looks down on Michigan Avenue. Until then, for the 12 years he'd been with the Anderson Brothers Mercantile Company, which occupies seven of the ten floors of the Baker Building, including the basement, he'd been on the second floor, his desk in a dark corner on the north end. But since he'd been told he was not soldier material, he's been watching the city from behind this glass. And now he can't remember a time when he wasn't sitting here watching things. Watching horse-drawn carriages turn to motorcars, watching the women parade for causes and organizing in the streets, watching the crowds gather around the newspaper boy to read about things like electricity, the shame of Shoeless Joe and the troubles over on 29th Street between the coloreds and the whites. And in the last few months he has watched the soldiers return, slowly filling the streets with their uniforms and their stories.

"We'll never move up now, will we, Mac?" Albert is hard-of-hearing in his left ear, so the army had turned him down as well. He was given the desk across from Johnny Von the Clerk there by the window, but even in the daylight, he was always looking at the dark side of things. Always talking about how they would never move up, never have things like the other people did. It wore on Johnny Von the Clerk, because he didn't have anyone else to balance out the reasoning. Albert had a wife who was always ignoring his dark side, countering his view of the world. But Johnny Von the Clerk didn't go home to anyone but his mother and she didn't say much good about the future. But Albert is talkative, and maybe he is like a dog that barks a little too much, a mutt that bounds up, slobbers all over you and then runs away, but he is loyal. So he guesses Albert is his best friend, not that they'd ever said it. Not that they did anything too much outside of the floor of the Anderson Brothers Mercantile Company. They did go to ball games sometimes, when they could afford the tickets. But then Albert talked constantly about the price of the ticket, and the price of the beer, and that sort of spoiled things.

After lunch the three new employees came around to each desk, led by Peter Anderson, the Anderson Brothers nephew that had gone to college and was now the head of accounting. He was a man of small stature, but friendly enough.

"These boys have done a great service for our country and I'm sure they are going to do great things here at Anderson Brothers. I'm sure you'll hear all about their heroic tales as you get to know each other." Johnny Von the Clerk shakes each hand very politely. And that is all.

Johnny Von the Clerk doesn't have stories. He is a clerk, no more, no less. Here at Anderson Brothers he addresses mail, he stamps files, and on occasion he tallies inventory. He sits here behind the window, looking out. And at 4:30, he takes off his work smock, puts on his jacket and his hat and walks home alone, through the streets of a changing Chicago, wondering how it can be that nothing changes for him.

"You should get a place of your own. You should get married." This is what his mother says as they sit at the big dining table, places set in only two of the ten chairs. "My sister Rosa can move in, she can shop for me." She puts a plate of bread in front of her favorite son.

Johnny Von the Clerk has three sisters and two younger brothers, all married and out raising families. He still lives in the house where they grew up, looking after his mother, although she doesn't really need much looking after. Really he just shops, visits the grocer for her, but he figures he'd be doing that anyway if he was in a place of his own.

"Ask that nice girl at the greengrocer's on the corner."

She hands him a napkin for his collar and pats his balding head.

"Ma, she's married. Married a soldier right before the war. Remember? Uncle Howard told you about the wedding his brother's cousin gave them." She puts a plate of pasta down in front of him and spoons in a rich beautiful sauce.

"Oh, yes. Never mind. What about the sister, the one who works around the way in the printer's shop?"

Johnny Von blows on the pasta and sauce that he twirls around his fork and grimaces at the thought of Mary Ann, the sister that works in the printer's shop.

He'd put on his best suit the day he walked into the printer's shop. He'd been thinking of Mary Ann for a long time, and when the occasion to run an errand there came up, he savored the thought of it. He took his time thinking about what he would say. He practiced so he wouldn't stutter. He thought how she would be different, surely, from the other girls he met. Other girls didn't know of him, didn't know his family. Mary Ann knew his family, it wouldn't be like a stranger. She would be perfect. She was not too pretty and she seemed smart. She worked at a printers shop after all.

"I'm busy," was what she said when he first suggested it. Not being familiar to asking girls out, Johnny Von the Clerk took her at her word and asked for the next night and the next weekend. It took him four 'Sorry, I'm busy' replies

before he realized. Before he noticed the guys at the press
smirking or the girl at the register laughing behind her hand.

"No Ma. I don't think I'd like that Mary Ann."

Estella calls out from her bedroom upstairs, in the home
she shares with her mother and father. "No, Mother, I won't
be late. I'll be right home tonight." Estella is always right
home, unless she stops at a concert to hear her father. But
her mother knows this. It is the same tone she uses when she
says, "Do you have any plans on the weekend?" while sipping
carrot soup, the three of them searching for conversation each
evening. There is always a hopefulness in her mother's voice,
a put-upon nonchalance that Estella does not know what to
do with. It feels like weights in her swimming costume at the
shore, when she is not a good swimmer anyway. When she is
doing everything she can, not to drown in the shallow surf, in
front of everybody.

"Good, dear." Estella's mother sits at the kitchen table in
their brownstone on LaSalle Avenue sipping coffee. Estella's
grandfather on her father's side came to Chicago in the early
1800s with only his violin and made out well in the new
world. He was from a good family in Croatia. He married
a girl he met through the orchestra, the daughter of a senior
cello player, Estella's grandmother, and they had two sons,
Bernard and Linus, Estella's father. Both carried on in the
family business, becoming musicians. But the line of music

stopped there. Estella was an only child that came along late. It didn't occur to anyone to teach her.

"The Henderson's are coming over for dinner and I'll need you to bring home a few nice turnips for the stew." Estella's mother rustles the newspaper she is reading. "Your father has rehearsal until 7:30, so we'll be eating late, dear. Do you have lunch? Have you made your lunch?"

"It's fine, Mother. I'll be home right after work." Estella kisses her mother in the kitchen and her father behind his pipe and paper on her way through the front room.

More than not, she wakes a cheerful type of girl, although "girl" would be a word to hesitate on now. She is 25, and she guesses now that most people would say "lady;" that "lady who works in the music shop."

It is not until she gets down to the street, walks in crowds of people whose nights, she imagines, are filled with others, that her cheerfulness begins to wane. A young man she passes on Randolph Street she sees with a night full of love-making to a beautiful new bride. As she makes her way down State Street, she sees a mother stepping into Twine's Haberdashery. She envisions a night filled with the calls of babies, and nuzzled kisses on little heads. She sees an old man shuffling across Jackson Street and imagines him in his kitchen in the middle of the night getting water and then quietly getting back into bed, so as not to wake his wife. And as she finishes her walk up Wabash Street, she sees a group of older women for the Organization of the National League of American Prosperity pass her, and she imagines the large one in the red hat staring at her husband's snoring, wondering if she will get any rest before her big day. None of them are waiting. None of them are worried. None of them are lonely in the night.

When she arrives at her uncle's store, Munka's Sheet Music and Orchestral Supply, she catches her reflection in the window and fights the impulse to cry. Is it so bad? Surely the space between her teeth or the shape of her nose, the thickness of her waist can't be what will keep her from those kinds of nights. Maybe her skin is not fair and maybe her face, her dress style, not like the pictures in magazines, but certainly that cannot be all there is? Marriages happen every day. What has she missed that others understood? She reads it in *Good Housekeeping* every month; women all over the city are pouring their hearts and souls into the homes of their families.

"Morning, Little Mouse." The white hair of Uncle Bernie tips just above his desk in the back of the store. Bernie Munka and his wife did not have any children, so Estella is theirs as well. Of all the family, Uncle Bernie has no idea of Estella's struggle, he thinks she is beautiful. He has always worn very thick glasses. But it is not that. In the store he sees her smiling and hears her laughter, knows her wit that shines when no one is around. And he knows her secret love of jazz. He catches her in the listening booth when the store is slow, when she thinks he is dozing in the back. He keeps it to himself.

"Hello, Papa Bee," she calls out to him with a wave while pulling up the front window blinds. She puts on her apron and opens the till to set the register up for the day.

Maybe she was wrong. Maybe she should have let the marriages her mother and father tried to arrange go through, but how could she? How could she go against herself and join with men she didn't care for in her heart? Men that always looked around her and not at her, men that never talked to her about anything interesting, men that felt they were doing her a favor by the offer. Estella is angry just thinking about it. And secretly in her heart, she feels resentful of God, mostly because she can't see anyone else to blame.

The front bell rings.

"I have it, Papa Bee. It's Leonard with the mail." Estella rushes to the door. It's new jazz records, Wilbur Sweatman's Original Jazz Band. She'd been waiting for them for weeks. Jazz is frowned upon in the family, and she ordered the phonographs without telling Uncle Bee. The decision was that the store would not promote or sell jazz; after all, they'd stretched enough adding the sheet music of military bands to their inventory. So Estella would have to wait until Uncle Bee was out on errands or she was closing on her own before she could listen to them.

Estella steps out to a windy sidewalk and closes the shop door behind her. "Thank you, Leonard." She quickly takes the packages and turns to go.

"Hold on, Estella. I've got another package for you." As he takes out a stack of sheet music, Estella blushes at the site of the label. A new Negro publishing house out of New York, the Pace and Handy label is there in plain view for Leonard and Uncle Bernie and the whole world to see. She quickly takes the package and tries to tear away the top of the brown paper on her way inside, but the wind picks up and the stack of pages gets away from her. All at once sheet music is swirling in the air.

Holding his hat from the wind and looking down as he walks, Johnny Von the Clerk doesn't notice her dancing around the sidewalk, chasing papers in the crowd in front of him. It is only when he is hit in the face with the title page 'Down by the Chattahoochee River' that Johnny Von the Clerk stops abruptly. Momentarily blinded by the yellow page, he hears laughter. This is his first impression of her, hearing her laughter. It is light, sweet and contagious. He pulls the paper away and looks down at his feet. Estella is circling around him like a little girl giggling, playing hide and seek with the sheet music, catching the last of the strays in the wind. When she finally settles in front of him, grasping the disheveled stack of papers, she is still smiling. He doesn't see anything but that.

"I think that's mine." She points to the paper in his hand.

"Of course." Johnny Von the Clerk comes back to the sidewalk, to himself standing here in front of Munka's Sheet Music and Orchestral Supply. He hands Estella the title page to 'Down by the Chattahoochee River.'

Uncharacteristically, he starts talking. "Don't want to lose this one." He glances at the title, "Down by the Chattahoochee River," studies the music notes, "I don't think I know this song."

"Oh, it's a…well it's new…it's out of New York…" Estella folds the pages into her arms and turns to go.

"An-An-And can I buy a copy here?" Johnny Von the Clerk doesn't play the piano and he doesn't know why he says this. He doesn't play any musical instrument.

"No!" Horrified that he might come into the store, ask Uncle Bernie for the Pace and Handy song he saw in her hands, Estella answers sharply rushing back to the door. "No. No, you can't, this is special order."

"I can't get 'Down by the Chattahoochee River' from you?" Johnny Von the Clerk feels crushed. She must have noticed my foot, he thinks. He feels an ache.

Estella turns back, in a sort of double take and notices Johnny Von the Clerk standing still in a crowd of dark suits and hats moving around him. It looks odd, like a single mackerel in a school of fish that has suddenly stopped and decided he might like to swim in a different direction. She notices how tall he is, how he seems like a quiet pause in the noise of the street. She notices how he is looking right at her and how he seems hopeful of something. She wants to look around her, look side to side, to see what he is hopeful about.

"Well, we have books of other sheet music that I'm sure you would like." She steps towards him. "We have Arthur

Fields, Campbell and Burr, Bert Williams, and we even have 'Since Katy the Waitress became an Aviatress,' Fred van Eps' new song. That's just in. Come here, look in the window." She steps towards him and points to the window.

Johnny Von the Clerk looks in at the titled pages with much interest. Estella, feeling it important to divert him from the Pace and Handy title, is talking more than she usually would to anyone. "And we have phonographs here as well. We are the only store on this side of town with listening booths. I'm sure you could come in and find something else that you like."

Johnny Von the Clerk is suddenly lifted. "I will come in." He steps forward, taking her invitation very personally.

"Oh? Now then?" she says, stepping back.

"No." He steps back, "No, I've got to go. I'm on my way to work now."

Estella pulls the door to the shop open, "You must come by another time." She waves good-bye.

"Yes. I must," he says boldly, more boldly than he has ever said anything in his life. Johnny Von the Clerk turns up LaSalle Avenue, the bitter wind suddenly feels refreshing. He steps lightly, looking up, making his way to his window on Michigan Avenue.

"Like America itself, we are readjusting things here at Anderson Brothers." Peter Anderson steps into the

middle of the open floor while Johnny Von the Clerk
and Albert are hanging their coats. It is very out of
the ordinary. "As you all know we are opening our
doors to returning soldiers, and I'm sure you feel the
pride I feel, the thanks and admiration for these fine
men." He gestures to five men in suits standing on the
floor next to him, and everyone on the floor applauds.
"Just as President Wilson is helping to carve new lines
on the maps of Europe, we here at Anderson Brothers
are reorganizing, and re-mapping the clerical and
administration assignments. We are leaping into the age
of modern office technology."

He turns and gestures to a large new office machine at the
back corner of the room. It is just like the picture Johnny
Von the Clerk saw in *Modern Inventor* a few weeks ago. An
avid fan of the magazine, *Modern Inventor,* Johnny Von the
Clerk saw it in an article about scientific efficiency in the
workplace. He remembered it specifically because it was next
to an advertisement for new careers in Electricity. Electricians
they would be called.

"This sorting machine has the capability to seal, stamp and
count 250 letters a minute at a cost of 10 cents per 1,000!
It can do the work of 16 employees! It is only one of many
new office machines we are implementing today and in the
coming months."

Everyone murmurs and seems excited by this news. And
while it is shiny and very modern looking, and it is impressive
to see in real life, Johnny Von the Clerk cannot help but do

the math in his head: more workers to place and less need for workers because of modern, new, shiny machinery.

"Mrs. Laney, my secretary, has the new assignments. Please see her first this morning. And let me say on behalf of the entire Anderson Brothers Mercantile Company, we look forward to a prosperous future. We have been lucky not to be plagued with such unfortunate incidents that many companies have suffered recently. The strikes and the rising anti-Americanism will not be a part of the Anderson Brothers Mercantile Company. I'm sure you are upset, as am I, about a greedy labor force out to kill the very businesses that pay their wages. It will not be a part of the Anderson Brothers Mercantile Company." Peter Anderson stomps his foot to accent his message. Because he is a man of small stature, it comes across more child-like than authoritative. "Here, we have no use for unions or Bolshevism or any other un-American activities that are a slap in the face to these men. So I am sure you will stand with me, as I stand with you in these changes, and look to the profitability it will bring the Anderson Brothers Mercantile Company."

Everyone on the floor claps, including Johnny Von the Clerk. He is, after all, very much for America and profitability.

Two hours later, Johnny Von the Clerk sits staring at Albert across a large desk in the basement of the Baker Building. They were both promoted, due to their seniority, to the new division "Document Dispersal and Recording."

They received a wage increase and a new title. Albert thinks this is the best day he can remember in a while.

But as Johnny Von the Clerk looks around the room, filled with banks of filing cabinets and no natural light other than the small frosted basement vent windows, he can only feel tightness in his chest. The only thing he can think of to keep his entire chest from imploding is what kind of musical instrument he would play, if he could play one, and whether it is too late for him to try.

"There were three of them today," Mr. Henderson says in a low voice to Uncle Bernie and Estella's father. The men sit in the front room smoking and talking about what they would not say at the dinner table. Estella listens from the steps, while her mother, her aunt and Mrs. Henderson share coffee in the kitchen, fretting but not talking about the same thing.

"Came to my office at the theater, asked to see a list of all the hires." Mr. Henderson stands at the fire, poking the logs with the iron. "Had my secretary note nationality and immigration information next to each."

Uncle Bernie shrugs his shoulders. "I had a man in the store two days ago."

Estella's father sits up alarmed at the news.

"I didn't want to say anything," Uncle Bernie confesses. "It will all blow over anyway. Why cause trouble, why raise eyebrows around the house? And besides, we have nothing to hide."

"Bernard! This is serious, you should have told me!" Estella's father slaps his leg in frustration. "They closed Hans Mooers' laundry on Wabash, you know that. Announced he was a Red, without a doubt." Estella's father's voice escalates, infused with a mix of anger and bewilderment. "Arrested him on a Tuesday and then closed the store on Wednesday. You should have told me!"

Uncle Bernie shrugs and waves off Estella's father.

"Bernie!" Estella's father says, in a whisper. "They may deport the whole family."

Mr. Henderson stands rubbing his forehead, intently smoking his cigar as if the answer might be at the end of the embers.

"Linus, Linus." Uncle Bernie tries to soothe the air. "The Mooers' have been part of the meetings since the beginning. Hans is a bad apple. Always, I didn't like that boy. Always causing trouble. This is why I run the business and you still play the orchestra, all the dramatics." Uncle Bernie hits his cane against his younger brother's chair. "It will all blow over, Linus."

"If they close the shop, what will we do? We can't go back. And what about Estella?" He slaps his hand on his knee again in agitation. "She has no husband, no one to take care of her if something happens to us, if we lose the business. If we lose the house, or worse." Estella's father sits back in his chair. The three men say no more in the smoke-filled room.

Estella tiptoes from the steps to her room. Heavy with worry, she lies in her bed and tries to cry, but no tears come. Estella does not cry very easily. She did as a child and as a young girl. In fact, she cried at the drop of a hat, she was known for her water works. Small tragedies to large, whether it was finding a bird with a little broken wing or at her grandfathers' funeral, Estella would display emotions in great proportions. And it was not just sadness, tales of triumph and happiness also sent tears rolling. Hearing her aunt tell the story for the hundredth time about the happiness of coming through Ellis Island or about the time her father was complimented by the famous German conductor, Fredric Pretroc, the night they played Bach at the opening, tears of tenderness and heartfelt emotion spilled. But that impulse, that inner freedom had left her somewhere along the way. Only frustration and a dull sadness settle in her at bedtime now, stifling what her heart naturally wants to let go of. It is a very long night. It seems it has been weeks and months, maybe years of very long nights.

"The total comes to 16 cents." Estella rings the register and begins to wrap the sheet music in brown paper.

"I heard this song in a club on State Street," Johnny Von the Clerk says to Estella. "I think it's one of Fred Van Eps' best."

Although he has been into Munka's Sheet Music and
Orchestral Supply seven times now, sometimes on his
lunch break, which took the whole hour, and sometimes
in the evening on his way home, and although he has
purchased an assortment of sheet music titles each visit,
these are the first words Johnny Von the Clerk speaks to
Estella since their encounter on the street six weeks ago. It
is a lie.

There is a place on State Street and the musicians there
have probably played this song, but Johnny Von the Clerk
has never been there. He only knows about it because
Albert went on and on about it a few days ago.

He had to take his mother-in-law out for her birthday.
All day he talked about how it cost him way too much
money, how the band was too loud, the dance floor too
crowded and the turkey dinner too dry.

"My wife wants to go back, but I tell you what, Mac, I
think it's too overrated. Not the kind of place for guys
like us, anyway." When he said it, Johnny Von the Clerk
nodded in agreement. But in his head, he noted the place,
just in case, in some roundabout kind of way, it worked out
that he might go there some day, maybe with that girl from
the music store.

"We have the phonograph as well. Many customers
ask for it. Did you look by the wall next to the listening
booths?" Although Estella thinks he is familiar and
friendly enough, she does not recognize him from the
street. Perhaps it is the family troubles that preoccupy

her. Or maybe it is that in the store, he is on his own. The contrast of him that had impressed her, the way he looked highlighted, still and quiet that day in the sea of hats and suits on the windy Chicago street, is not there. The look of hopefulness in his expression is not there to remind her either. But she does not see it only because she does not see his eyes. So far Johnny Von the Clerk has not looked up when making his purchases; so far, he has not been able to say anything.

"I'm going, Little Mouse," Uncle Bernie calls out from the back of the store, fumbling at the wall of phonographs and scurrying back to his desk to grab his jacket. At Uncle Bernie's age he can spot a musician from miles away, and this young man is no musician. Uncle Bernie has taken notice of this new customer's frequent visits, his mix-match of musical taste in sheet music. Uncle Bernie has noticed the way this young man looks over at Estella when she is not looking, and then quickly back at the stacks of music. His glasses are thick but his heart for his niece is keen and sharp. "You'll be okay to close up then, little one?" He says smiling as he puts on his coat and hurries out the door. He pats Johnny Von the Clerk on the back as he passes behind him.

"Of course, Papa Bee." Estella, not used to having the attention of men, is completely at a loss to the signs of a man wrestling for courage of an affectionate nature. Estella looks over to Uncle Bernie wondering why he is acting odd, as she closes up all the time.

She hands Johnny Von the Clerk his neatly wrapped sheet music as the bell on the door rings at Uncle Bernie's departure. "Would you like to hear it?"

"Oh yes. I must," he says boldly, and then swallows nervously. He never says things like "I must."

Estella moves to the wall of records outside of the four small listening rooms in the back of the store. Still unaware of any specific attention towards her, she draws her hand over the shelves of phonograph records.

"Here it is." She reads the paper wrapper and pulls the pressed tar carefully out. She looks back at Johnny Von the Clerk still standing statue-like at the counter. "You have to come here, you have to be in the booth to listen." She motions with her elbow for him to open the last door at the end.

He hurries to the door, opens it like a gentleman, as if he was opening it for her to step through into a grand ballroom.

Estella walks into the little room with bare walls. There is just enough space for a phonograph on a small desk, a chair and two, maybe three, people to stand. She goes to the phonograph the way she does day in and day out, puts the record down, and begins to crank the box. She looks over to Johnny Von the Clerk still standing outside the little closet, holding the handle of the door.

"You have to come in and close the door." Estella feels a slight annoyance and begins to wonder how late she will have to stay with this customer.

"Of course," says Johnny Von the Clerk. He steps just in the doorframe and closes it at his back.

Estella bends to match the needle of the handle to the fragile edge of the black disc.

"I'm a clerk!"

She stops before the needle hits the edge and stands.

"I don't play the piano," Johnny Von the Clerk declares.

"Oh?"

"My mother does. That's who I buy the sheet music for, my mother plays the piano. Plays like an angel, really. It's my mother who plays the piano." This is another lie. Johnny Von the Clerk has no idea why he is saying it. He only knows that he feels warmer and warmer under his jacket in this little room with Estella.

"Oh." Estella bends, but then stands again. "And she likes Fred van Eps?"

Johnny Von the Clerk begins to talk and the more he talks, the faster the words seem to come. "You know my father, her husband, passed away and I have five brothers and sisters and she wants to stay young. She likes the popular music, really. She likes old music also, that is not to say that she does not like music that is more proper for her, but she likes that she can play the popular music for the children. Of course there are no children in the house. I live in the house, but I'm not really children, *per se*, I'm her child, yes, but I'm not small ..." Johnny Von the Clerk gasps for air. "My brothers and sisters are all married. I'm not married, although I think marriage is certainly something, but I'm not married. I'm the middle, three older and two younger. Three older sisters and two younger brothers. They do have children, however. My father worked as a smith on the Southside, but he did well for himself and luckily he could afford to have many children. We all miss him. There are seven nieces and six nephews all together. Wonderful kids all of them. I love kids." Johnny Von the Clerk gasps for air again. "But I take care of things, take care of her, my mother. I shop the greengrocers, you know, I do what I can. And she likes the young music, what can I say, she is a wonderful woman. So yes, I would say that she likes Fred Van Eps. I would say that she means to like the popular music, for the children and all, and that Fred Van Eps falls in to that category. I'm a clerk and that's the kind of thing I do as a professional. I think about categories and what not." As abruptly as this rambles out of Johnny Von the Clerk's mouth, it stops just as suddenly. He cannot think of one thing to say next. His mind is completely blank.

Estella looks him up and down. "That's nice." She bends again and focuses to get the needle to the record's edge this time.

They stand smiling at each other, their backs to the walls of the small listening room, as far apart from each other as possible. They hear a moment of static and then instead of Fred Van Eps' popular new favorite, jazz - a low down and dirty jazz, blasts through the phonograph. Estella turns bright red and Johnny Von the Clerk watches as she dashes and bounces the needle off the record.

"I don't know how that got in there. I must have misread the label. I didn't mean to put that on, I just looked at the paper. It was in the wrong space. I didn't read the record label. We don't sell this, I just have it."

Johnny Von the Clerk floods with relief and delight watching Estella turn three shades of maroon as she speaks.

"Wait. Let's hear it," he says, calm and collected.

"I can't, I mean … this is mine. I'm not supposed to have it in the store."

"That's okay." He pauses, then motions to the record. "Let's listen to the jazz."

Estella breaks from her fluster and starts to laugh. "You can't tell anyone," she says, and her laughter swells at the shock that just ran through her. Hearing her favorite secret blare out in front of this odd man suddenly amuses her. As she laughs and he smiles and joins in, as their backs peel away from the walls, she remembers him standing on the street. She puts the needle back to the edge and relaxes in the look of him. They listen the whole way through standing easy next to each other.

"I like that jazz," Johnny Von the Clerk says to her as easily as he would say it to his sister or to Albert or even to his mother. And he means it.

Estella nods. "I have more." She grabs his wrist and flings open the door. She climbs up the ladder to the top shelf and hands down a stack of records. Johnny Von the Clerk takes them in one hand and without hesitation holds her arm down the ladder.

For weeks, Johnny Von the Clerk meets Estella at closing time of Munka's Sheet Music and Orchestral Supply. His visits last maybe half an hour, other days longer. And while neither allows themselves to indulge in thoughts of the others' interest outside of jazz, Uncle Bernie has full view of the situation. For reasons Estella has not questioned, he has had one thing or another to do at the end of every day, prompting his early departure from the store. Johnny Von the Clerk tells no one and Estella tells no one. It is not that they have made a secret agreement or have even discussed it with each other. And it is not because they are playing jazz, low down and dirty jazz. It is merely born out of the fragile place of hope both seem to be treading inside themselves. Two orphan deer meeting in a clearing in the forest, moving out of their territory a little bit more each visit, both still tentative and unsure if they can rely on the good intentions of the other. Both ready to bolt back to a corner inside themselves at any sign of retreat from the other side.

"You sure seem somewhere else these days," Albert says to his buddy as he slams closed a wooden filing draw in the basement of the Anderson's Brothers Mercantile Company.

"It's just things," Johnny Von the Clerk says from behind his desk, which he has moved to the edge of the wall to be close to the small window vent at the back of the room.

Albert has been worried about his buddy for the past few weeks. Initially, he figured it was the move downstairs. Albert thought his buddy didn't like change, didn't want change. He thought this because over the years Johnny Von the Clerk would say things like, "Boy, the city sure is changing," Or, "Nothing's new with me." Of course Johnny Von the Clerk found the changing city exciting and the fact that nothing was new in his life depressing, but Albert misread such statements.

And for the past few weeks, to be honest, Albert is finding Johnny Von the Clerk disagreeable. No longer is he concurring with the plight of things as Albert professes them. And often now he says things like, "I think Horlick's Steak Restaurant on the corner would be a good place to take out a girl. I don't have a girl, but if I did," or, "On the new wages, does your wife want to have a family now?" It is odd.

Being his friend, Albert figured all this was about Johnny Von the Clerk not having a girl. Albert often wished he didn't have a girl, so it was like a light bulb went off in his head when he figured it out. And also being his friend, he decided the only way Johnny Von the Clerk would ever have a shot at a date would be if someone really pleaded his case to someone they knew very well, someone who owed favors that could be collected on. Someone just like Martha, his sister-in-law.

"Well, I tell you what, buddy. I made us plans after work."

"Albert, I can't. I have…"

"Plans?" Albert winks and socks his buddy in the arm.

"I noticed you've been rushing off every day, running errands for your mother, but not today. I've arranged something. We are taking off a little early, so just be ready."

Johnny Von the Clerk nods no.

"You can't say no. And all I'm going to say is, you can thank me later."

Albert throws a few fake punches in the air around Johnny Von the Clerk's back and heads out the basement to collect documents from the third floor, pleased as peaches with himself.

Had Estella not been so excited to play the new record that came in that morning, a Negro spiritual out of New Orleans by Sweet Mama Sugar Bell which had been very tricky to get, perhaps it would not have cut in and hurt her so deeply to see Johnny Von the Clerk across the street when she went to the corner store half an hour before closing. He was standing in line to get into Horlick's Steakhouse with a beautiful, blue-eyed blond girl.

The girl, chatting with the couple standing next to them, looking easy and happy with her arm tucked into his, is straight out of *Good Housekeeping.* She is petite and doll-like, wearing a blue dress that cuts her figure perfectly.

The image sears into Estella's heart. She stands still and shocked, but quickly swallows the hurt of it down. She does not make it to the store for the cold drinks she was getting for Johnny Von the Clerk to enjoy with her later. She rushes back, hearing the quick pace of her shoes on the sidewalk. She is worried she has made a scene. Worried that the break in her heart, the rush of disappointment has resounded up and down the street, loud and cataclysmic, witnessed by all. She feels stupid and ridiculous for being such a foolish girl. Estella walks to Munka's Sheet Music and Orchestral Supply smiling pleasantly to everyone she passes. She gets to the door completely numb inside, unsure if she is still breathing and in the world.

"You're right, Albert. He is a little pet." Martha rubs the tuft of hair centered on Johnny Von the Clerk's head.

As the first round of drinks hit the table, Johnny Von the Clerk is taken by the fact that a beautiful, blond blue-eyed woman is showering him with attention. And she is not just pretty 'for a guy like him.' She is objectively attractive, and he notices other men notice her. He can't deny it; it does make him feel good to have her on his arm. He always thought if someone could just get to know him, even someone as pretty as Martha, then he'd have a shot. That he could be just like the guys in the clubs, just like the others here in Horlick's Steak House socializing and telling stories, he could be part of it all. Maybe this is the blossoming of his time, this is his chance. He feels on top of the world.

As the second round of drinks hits the table, Johnny Von the Clerk begins to notice something is not right. He realizes that Martha does not talk to him in a way that progresses into conversation. He wants to think that any moment they will touch upon something that will launch interest in him. But his hope is fading. The talking feels like a drunken bird that swoops and circles but can't get to the branch. And for the first time, he realizes this lack of social savoir-faire has nothing to do with his side of things. He suddenly feels shocked to realize that Martha, in all her petit perfect beauty, talks constantly about nothing. And more than that, she doesn't comment on anything he says.

"He is cute, Albert," is all she seems to say, going again to pat his head each time she announces it at the table. Each time she says it, she giggles. And while the men at the surrounding tables seem to look over in delight, it strikes Johnny Von the Clerk as a thin imitation of laughter. He feels his heart pound. It is nothing like Estella's laugh.

By the time the third round of drinks make it to the table and Johnny Von the Clerk watches Martha throw a tantrum because the waiter has brought her the wrong drink order for the second time, he feels his whole body break out into a cold sweat.

Albert leans over to him as the girls excuse themselves to the ladies room.

"That Martha is something else. Listen Mac, she really likes you. She's been talking about wanting to settle down." Albert winks at his buddy victoriously. "Imagine if a guy like you ended up with a girl like that! Man, you sure couldn't do any better."

Johnny Von the Clerk takes out his handkerchief and pats his large forehead. All he can think about is if he leaves now, right now, he still might be able to catch Estella at the store across the street.

"Hey, listen, buddy," Albert says, "don't be nervous. I told her you were just a clerk. She knows you live at home too. See though, she still seems to like you." He socks him in the arm like they've just pulled off a great caper.

Johnny Von the Clerk looks around Horlick's Steak House as if waking up from a dream, only to find himself in a nightmare. Albert, bobbing up and down in front of him, painting pictures of a life with this woman who's turned from a beauty to a monster, the tables in the background full of people all talking, talking, and talking about nothing. Suddenly they're like jackals scrounging for meat, telling stories no one is really listening to, stopping only to laugh at the right moments, a horrible, hollow laughter. The room starts to spin.

"You okay, buddy?" is the last thing Johnny Von the Clerk remembers. The next thing he knows he is standing outside of Munka's Sheet Music and Orchestral Supply rattling the front door. All of the shades are down, but at the edge of the window he can see a light in the back listening booth through the dark store. He feels the emergency of the situation. If he doesn't see her now, he'll never make it back here and he knows it.

Of course he could have rounded the block and found the back door at the alley behind the building, but going around seemed too risky, which is why he jumps for the fire escape. It isn't hard; he is big and tall. He makes his way up the building over the roof and down the back fire escape. He would have been a good soldier, he was right. He can run as fast as anyone.

The back door is open and Johnny Von the Clerk rushes through Uncle Bernie's back office to find Estella in the quiet, sitting at the phonograph in the back listening booth. She doesn't jump up. She only smiles a pleasant smile, as if he is just another customer in the middle of the day. She is holding the Sweet Mama Sugar Bell recording on her lap.

"It's okay," she says as if addressing a customer who has just broken something in the store. She offers it before Johnny Von the Clerk even says hello, before he even has a chance to explain where he's been, and what happened to him. Before he even has a chance to tell her he is in love with her and he knows it in his bones.

"I knew you probably wouldn't be around tonight, I saw you with your friends."

Johnny Von the Clerk feels a lump in his throat.

"You have a pretty girl. Have you been with her ..." Her voice breaks its pleasant tone, cracks just barely, "... very long?"

"I-I-I do-don't ... she, she, she ..." Johnny Von the Clerk sputters and struggles to get out everything, something, anything, to return Estella to him.

"We're closing for a while," Estella says, still formal. "It's just temporary, we think, and I just wanted to let you know. But I can give you directions to a store across town. They don't carry jazz, but ..."

Johnny Von the Clerk drops to his knees to try to get to her eyes. "If-If-If they don't have jazz, then I ca-ca-can't go." He wants so badly to get back to just yesterday, just hours before.

"Th-That was Albert's sister-in-law."

"She is pretty." Estella smiles and tries to look at him kneeling right next to her. "It's okay." She breaks her composure slightly seeing him so close. "I know. I know I'm not ..."

He can't hear it. Johnny Von the Clerk cannot bear that Estella would feel less than a woman like Martha. He just wants it all not to have happened.

"Let's listen to this," he says, as he's said now many times over the past few weeks. He tries to take the record from Estella, but she holds tight.

"I can't, I mean …" She looks at him. "I'm afraid if I listen, I might just cry, and if I start crying" -- she looks so deeply into Johnny Von the Clerk's eyes that he feels it all the way down his body -- "I might not stop. I might never stop."

And when she says this, everything that was ever unsure, everything that was intimidated by others, every idea that he was not enough, or that he did not know how to be in the world leaves Johnny Von the Clerk. All at once in this little booth in the back of Munka's Sheet Music and Orchestral Supply, it leaves him in the eyes of Estella.

"That's okay." He smoothes his hand over her cheek and strokes her hair. "Let's listen to the jazz."

He takes from her hands Sweet Mama Sugar Bell's spiritual and cranks the phonograph. "Come here." He stands her up from the chair, sits down and leads her to his knee. She sits down on his lap, awkward and unsure. He puts his hand on her head and gently leads her into his shoulder. And then places the needle to the record's edge.

He puts his hand back to her head. Sweet Mama Sugar Bell calls out a deep sound of soulful angst. It is a calling, a keening, that reaches straight into them. It is a sound they both know.

As the record plays, Johnny Von the Clerk says to Estella, who is still stiff against his chest, "In Waukegan," he tucks her hair behind her ear, "we can get married without out a certificate."

Estella chokes back tears that want to burst.

"In Waukegan," he says without a stutter, rocking her just barely, "we can get married without anything."

Tears start to roll down her face.

"In Waukegan," he whispers, "we can get married for only five dollars, and I have five dollars on me right now. If we take the train tonight, we'll be back in a day."

Estella's body melts into the chest of Johnny Von the Clerk. All the tears that have been worried and waiting, all the tears she has been storing in the night flood out.

"In Waukegan?" she whispers.

"In Waukegan," he says.

Chapter 7

"Those who restrain desire,
do so because theirs is
weak enough to be restrained."

~ *William Blake*

J ohnny Von, Johnny Von, Johnny Von. It rolls off my tongue and trips off my lips, Johnny Von. Up Valley Glen Drive and down Valley Glen Drive, I'm drunk with saying it. Johnny. Von. I mark three weeks on the calendar and begin to really think about Johnny Von.

After that day beside the pool, being myself, chatting with Johnny Von, the genuine me starts to surface more and more. I find myself skipping down the street, singing along with my iPod. I have days of effortlessly writing line after line of poetry on the little notepad I now keep in my back pocket as I walk the dogs. I have countless moments each day in which I can not help myself from stopping in my tracks and exalting on how unbelievably beautiful the blue of the sky is, marveling at how endless are the myriad shades of green Mother Nature offers to the pleasure of my eyes from every plant and leafy tree that moves and breathes with life. I cannot help myself from admiring the exquisite, divine design of each little squirrel, chipmunk and woodland creature that zips around us as the dogs and I walk these hills called Hollywood. With each passing day the world comes more in focus, animates and dances around me, showing off with pride the raw pleasure of creation.

The world is alive and I am in it!

"Good Afternoon Mrs. Reed!" I call out to get Trudie Reeds attention. "The yard looks great. How are you today?" I stop and offer myself for lawn care duty before she even has the dog biscuit out for Moochie. "Should we water the roses? What about planting marigolds along the drive sometime? Why, I'd love to help you!"

"Well," Trudie Reed says a bit stunned, but crafty as ever, "I'd have to clean out the garage, clear that counter and sink if we did any planting."

"No problem, I'll come early and move the boxes."

So goes the days as I tick off my calendar, thinking about Johnny Von.

As I soak myself in all the good feelings, I also begin to notice a kind of building pressure, a blooming of sorts, with the passing of time. Only it's not the nervous shyness, like before; and it's not the intrigue of infatuation wanting attention; although I am still shy and by all means very infatuated with Johnny Von. But the feeling that is flowing through me is more than that, it's "other" than those kinds of familiar feelings. What I'm feeling is new to me.

I walk the streets for days mulling it over, trying to find words to articulate to myself what I'm experiencing. I've gone silent to everyone else about anything Johnny Von-related, so I talk to the dogs. They're all I have left, so I talk to Moochie.

I'm standing in the dog park, tennis ball in hand, mulling over this new phenomenon, when it comes to me in a single moment of understanding. As I lob the ball high in the sky and watch Moochie throw his pudgy body into the air at just the right moment before the ball hits the ground, as I catch the light in my dogs eyes the split second he leaps, I've got it.

It's desire.

Pure, unadulterated desire.

It's William Blake. It's what Andrew Banks was talking about in class, the raw energy of everything good.

Desire.

Sweet desire.

And I'm not talking about lust and sex. I mean sex is good, obviously I'm for lust and sex, but suddenly I understand, that's only one shade of desire — a common association. As this awareness unfolds, I know that it is more than all of that. This desire I feel flowing through me is unreserved. It's not even about romance necessarily, although it could be that. But still that's only one color, when desire is an infinite spectrum of colors — reaching out to you from a myriad of sources, over as many different things as there are things to dream of. I'm talking about a kind of desire that is unique because its draw is unquestioned inside you, because it gives you a life-expanding feeling.

Desire, sweet desire.

Desire that grows the trees and blooms the flowers and turns the earth. The kind of desire that finds you singing in the shower without realizing it, that has you waking up in the morning feeling excited about the day, happy for no damn good reason. The kind of desire that makes you want to write important poetry—about bumblebees. A sensation that calls from the genuine, pre-lunchroom, second-grade, shining self, part of you! I'm talking about the building blocks, the fuel, at the birthplace of art or love.

When I think about Johnny Von, this desire wells up in me in volumes.

I walk dogs, so all I have is time to think.

"To Blake, it is through the senses, which are fed by the world, that we come to know desire. What William

Blake put forth in this work is that the body is not separate from, or lower than, the spirit. He did not see the body as something that needed to be disciplined, corrected, or ignored. Through the senses comes desire, through desire comes imagination, and through imagination everything comes into being."

Andrew Banks is giving his final lecture on William Blake. I have only one class left after today, and no, I haven't read anything yet. But it's stopped being a thing in class, a silent spot. And I've turned in poems—three now, since that day at the pool, since I've been carrying around my little notepad walking dogs in utter happiness. And besides, I understand it now, why the universe sent me on this trail of William Blake—obviously to understand this sensation of desire, to name it and revel in it. To feel how open my heart is, and how blissful it is to be inspired by something beautiful like the sweet Johnny Von desire; and to be your genuine self because of it. I get it. I don't need to read my poetry, out loud, really. I'm not here to be a poet or a writer or an artist. I was my genuine self with Johnny Von. Johnny Von! That was obviously the point of all this. My reason here is done.

"Blake was prone to visions. Religious minded, definitely, but not a church man. When he made this illuminated book, *The Marriage of Heaven and Hell,* it was outrageous to suggest a union between the two -- heaven and hell -- to propose that one needed the other. To join the un-joinable was scandalous by its very suggestion! He was outcast for blasphemy and shunned by everyone around him."

Andrew Banks clicks to the first plate of this work. My eyes follow the clouds at one side and flames on the other that edge the title page, the two opposites meeting in the middle. I pause at the languishing soft lovers from each place entwined in a sweet kiss there on the page, where the two worlds meet. It's beautiful and I can't imagine anyone offended by such sublime images.

Poor William Blake, so misunderstood.

Andrew Banks continues, "To William Blake, the souls' evolution needs contrast to come to know its true nature. A decision needs the two sides to navigate between, to authentically know the self—in art, in life, in love. Heaven and Hell are both needed aspects of humanity. Simply two ends of a spectrum, one is meaningless without the other. Virtue is nothing but a mockery to Blake if it is dictated by the voices of outside authorities, by a religion or a social code.

"What about a marriage of just hell?" Lillian calls out from the shadows of the back of the classroom, "Ruthie could write a lot of poems about that. Ask her about her first husband."

The grannies start to cut up, but I don't mind. The grannies. How blessed they are to have such loyal and sweet friends to go through life with. To tease and poke and laugh with, about all of it, from the day it seemed like a good idea to streak through the world with a peace sign painted on your butt, to that 'first' bad marriage, all with a light heart. I look over at them, and even with their wrinkly skin and awkward fragile bodies, they have a satisfied strength about them. Like warriors with nothing left to prove, understanding, appreciating even, a subtle humor and irony of being alive through time. It's as if they get the punch line of a joke, and I'm standing next to them saying, "I don't get it? Why's that funny?" It annoys me about myself, because I want to be laughing too, it bothers me that I'm not in on the joke, that I don't get it. As Andrew Banks clicks the lights back on and I watch the grannies gather their bags to leave, I'm surprised to realize how much I envy the grannies. They've already navigated through the contrasts, and it's seemed to have relaxed them into themselves.

On a Tuesday morning, I cross off the day of the return of Johnny Von to the neighborhood.

And then a week passes.

And then another week passes.

And now the raw beauty of creation is being slightly displaced. My attention begins to split. I'm on the lookout. I walk up Valley Glen Drive and down Valley Glen Drive. Cars swoop by me day in and day out as I walk the dogs, but no Johnny Von. I keep thinking every day might be the day. That he will pass and stop to chat, or that I'll bump into him around the neighborhood, but so far nothing.

I am still skipping down the street. But I start to notice near misses, and I don't think I'm imagining it. I catch the taillights of his Trans Am turning a corner. Like a bad dream or a B-movie, I see the outline of him behind dark tinted windows, but no him. No flesh, blood-and-bones Johnny Von.

Before I know it, another week and two more days have gone by, still no Johnny Von. It is as if the hand of the universe that dropped me in the orbit of Johnny Von's gravitational pull has plucked me up and put me on the other side of the galaxy.

And then something unexpected hits me out of the blue.

A thought occurs to me that I'd not considered in my weeks of sheer delight, a notion which shakes me at my core. I'm walking down the street when two roads come into focus ahead of me: The absence of Johnny Von versus the sweetness of the Johnny Von desire.

My heart pounds. I don't ever want to give up the sweet desire.

"It hasn't been that long." I reassure myself. I reason that it's still legitimate to let myself stay in the Johnny Von desire. I bolster myself, from the pen of Harper Lee, as if I had a wise Atticus to ask about all of this. "It's not time to worry yet."

"So, how's the weather out there?" My mom calls me from

Salt Lake City. She's the headline speaker at a weekend sales seminar. She's given me her stories, and now it's my turn.

When I was 12, my mother went into sales. On the surface it was because she wanted something to do, something more than teaching, and the extra money to buy the things that weren't necessities. My father is a necessities kind of person, so her finding work with "unlimited income potential" allowed for things like clothes you buy just because you like them, or eating out at a nice restaurant without feeling upset about the bill, or having your hair done at the salon in the Fairmont Hotel in the French Quarter (a very fancy trip for us back then.) Looking back now, though, I think it was freedom that she wanted -- not really the things that money can buy, so much as the open road and the limitless possibilities. The circus came to town, and there was no going back.

The irony is that not only did my mother enjoy the life of a traveling salesman -- or woman, rather -- but she also had a kind of gift. It was her calling. She was a sales maven, a virtuoso. Before we all knew it, she was flying the country, on national tour.

It was at that point, I think, that it became clear she was the bird, wanting the boundless sky, and my father was the fish, content, safe and happy in the pond. Her new life crystallized the difference, and my parents' marriage was a slow downhill from there.

"It's good. It's California," I say, feeling the light air on my skin as I watch the dogs play in the park.

"And the dogs, how are the dogs these days?" My mom is being supportive.

When people ask my mother what her daughter does for a living, she says, "It's something with dogs," and leaves it at that. Sometimes, she adds that I'm very happy, and doing quite well at it.

My mother is a Southern woman. I should explain to you what I mean by this.

For the first 17 years that I knew her, she slept with rollers in her hair every night, plastic on top, pin curls in back. I never saw her out of the house without make-up and pantyhose, and I didn't know her to own a pair of jeans. When I was seven, she made me a Holly Hobbie bedspread with matching embroidered pillows. Sewing and cooking are basic Southern woman pride-skills. I was in love with Holly Hobbie, and I remember with great detail the colorful, complicated stitching on the pillows, but whenever I had a friend over, I had to say, "We can't sit on my bed."

"The dogs are good, business is smooth these days," I tell her with a little extra zip in my voice.

"Well, that's good," she offers back.

Given her Southern temperament, it's easy to see how my mother doesn't altogether understand the dog-walking business. The outside in dirty dog parks, the slobber and mess, the walking the streets all day "picking-up" after animals that are not even yours -- the attraction eludes her.

It's not that she grew up pampered; in fact, her mother could not only sew a straight line like nobody's business, but she wrung a chicken's neck from the backyard coop on a regular basis.

What flummoxes my mother is that I would choose such a line of work, when there are so many other things I could do that wouldn't ruin my skin over time. But that's the thing about Southern mothers, especially mine: the sun rises and sets around her kids, her children can do no wrong. She is fierce when it comes to her children, so she says with pride, "it's something with dogs," even though she doesn't quite get it. And then, from time to time, in a neutral tone she says to me, "Do you think, maybe, you want to do something else now? Do you think it's time for a change? What about working in sales?"

"Your voice sounds up. You sound really good these past few weeks. What else is going on?"

"Nothing really." I pick up a tennis ball and fling it across the park. Moochie and two of my other charges bound after it. "There is this guy…"

"A guy." Her tempered excitement makes me cringe a bit. "That's great." Even with her forced casual tone, I can feel her rushing out to buy her mother-of-the-bride dress this afternoon. That's why I haven't told her anything of Johnny Von yet.

"What's the story, what's he do?"

"He's an actor."

"Oh." She pauses. "It's not David, is it?"

"No. It's not David." David is a guy I briefly dated when I first moved to L.A. He came on strong and disappeared. He did daytime television. He was a soap star. Well, not a soap star -- more like a soap regular. My mother didn't like the sound of him from day one.

"You know, Mom, I don't talk to David." I haven't talked to David since he stopped returning my calls and disappeared, two years ago, but for some reason my mother still worries about it. I guess because I haven't dated anyone else in two years, and this worries her.

"Well, this is exciting. Where did you meet this new guy?"

"I met him on the street, walking dogs."

"And what's he like -- it sounds like you like this one? Have you been going out a lot together?"

"No. I just met him."

"Recently? Then he's new?"

"No, it was maybe a couple of months ago now, I guess; but, I mean, that's all — I just met him, that's the only thing that's happened. I think he's away, out of town right now. I'm not sure. I've seen his car, but..." The more I talk, the more eighth-grade it sounds. "We haven't gone out or anything. I met him once and then talked to him for a little while, is all. It's been about six and a half weeks ago."

"Oh," she pauses. "Well, I see. That sounds good, sweetheart."

I decide to tell her the whole story, so it sounds better. It sounds right. I start from the day with the hawk. My mom doesn't know Johnny Von from Fred Fawn. It's a lengthy explanation.

After I'm done she says, "So, your father saw him."

"No. It was in a movie. Dad was over and we watched a movie he was in. Anyway. It's not a big deal, Mom. Never mind."

"Well, don't be like that. I think it's great. I always liked that George Clooney. What about dating him?"

"Mom."

"What? I'm just saying, George Clooney is a nice-looking man. I'm sure this Von person is attractive. And I'm teasing, anyway. I'm saying *I* like George Clooney, even though he looks so much like your father when he was young. Anyway, never mind any of that. I think this all sounds great with this guy. I'm sure you'll meet up with him any day now."

"Mom, you don't think it's too late? You don't think it's been too long now?"

"Baby, it's never too late. Life is not like that, it's always giving you the next moment, always offering another chance for everything. Look at me, my life didn't even get going until I was 40 years old. I didn't even know who I was until then. Don't worry about time."

"Are you sure?"

"Yes. I'm sure."

For the first time in days I feel settled again.

Then my mom then gives me a motivational speech. It starts with, "Just remember, you won't get the sale, unless you believe you'll get the sale. It's that simple." Halfway in, she begins to whip herself up, "...and any boy out there would be lucky to have you. And I'm not just saying that because I'm your mother! When I think about that little, wimpy, sniveling English jack-ass, I just want to get on a plane and wring his neck. He never had it so good. And let me tell you, he never will ..."

"Okay, so I should go, Mom..."

I do like her, my mom, don't get me wrong. I like her company, and I admire that she followed her nature even though it was frowned upon in Southern women circles. But everything always goes back to sales and marketing, and sometimes — it's just tiring. As I listen to her final points on how to connect with others in order to position yourself to "close the deal," I feel like I did with my dad lecturing about car maintenance. I know it's their way to channel the love they have for me with how they see the world, but still I think, "No wonder." No wonder I struggle with the poetry. Poetry is not seven steps to financial freedom. Poetry is not a PowerPoint presentation, or a bestselling, high-profit product that lets you track your success on a graph.

I tell her I love her, that I'll keep her updated, and

pocket my phone. I round up the dogs from the park and we all head out the gate for home.

"The marigolds are looking great." I stop and chat with Trudie Reed. Truth be told, I linger now outside of Trudie Reed's, I'm lurking around Valley Glen Drive, hoping street time might line up some crossing of my path with Johnny Von's path. And god knows Trudie Reed doesn't mind.

"You planted them too close together. I told you they should have more space between."

Officially it's been two months and a six days now since chatting beside the pool and I've not seen hide nor hair of Johnny Von.

In real life that is.

I've seen him plenty at the counter in the grocery store. Johnny Von's latest movie is rapidly turning into a mega blockbuster, a box office phenomenon. It's the one he did before the project in London, the one he was resting up from when I first saw him that day in silky white pajama bottoms. The press has started tracking him. There are photos of him coming and going from all the Hollywood hotspots, and little blurbs about his life and his recent filming in London. And the question, the question, "Who's he with?" Rumors and speculations and inquiring minds all want to know. "Is there a woman in his life?" It makes my stomach hurt.

I've stopped going to the grocery store.

"I think the marigolds look good, Trudie. They look healthy."

As Trudie Reed and I debate the vitality of the marigolds, I see a big truck pass behind us and park in front of the house of Johnny Von. Hispanic workmen pile out and start to unload panels of iron bars. I excuse myself from Trudie Reed, which is not an easy thing to do, and tug Moochie forward. When we get down the street, I see what's happening. Johnny Von is putting a giant iron fence around the perimeter of his property. Giant. Every nook and cranny of it backed with green vinyl panels. Landscape people are scurrying around the edges dropping buckets of thorn bespeckled climbing ivy.

I look down at Moochie, "This is not a good sign."

The next day, as Rocky and Moochie and I pass, it's all finished. It's now impossible to see the property or the driveway or any part of the beautiful white stucco house of Johnny Von. From the top of the hill, through the bushes and the green leafy trees, no longer can you see the lush green grass of Johnny Von's back yard. The iron curtain is up, the place is secure, only a cold, impersonal metal call box on the street connects it to the outside world.

I feel my chest tighten. I feel a little panic run through me. I look to the dogs and I have no idea what to do about it. How to proceed. I don't understand what the universe is doing. I call the dogs along and think, *I have to do something!*

Had I remembered William Blake and just stayed trusting in the energy of the sweet Johnny Von desire, or not taken the bad omen of the fence so much to heart, I would not have done what I did next. But you should know that when I wake up on Friday morning, officially three months after last talking to Johnny Von, I do not know what to do with myself.

Inside, I have all this sincere energy bubbling out of me, all of this sweet Johnny Von desire, with nowhere to land, thinking *it needs a place to land!* I can feel myself off-kilter in a way that is more than just a crush not working out, more than just liking someone and never getting to hook up with them, I'm overwhelmed with an impulse of not wanting to lose something important. I guess I could go on with reasons why, but just know that it's misguided. Take heed, and don't ever do this kind of thing if you find yourself with the good fortune of stumbling into a vein of golden pure desire.

On this Friday morning, I lose all trust in myself and I decide to seek outside advice.

I start with Shelby Braxton on the phone on her way to work—then my mom, my dad, Mandy Kane on our hike, my brother as we shop at Sports Chalet — everyone. And I don't just stop with people that I've vowed to never talk to about Johnny Von, I expand the poll to people who don't know me all that well, hoping to get a more objective take on it. I consult with a woman in the locker room at the gym putting on her make-up. I converse in broken English with Maria and her daughter, who clean my apartment every two weeks. I chat with the girl at Starbucks waiting in line with me for the bathroom, and the well-dressed gay man I say hello to in the dog park every now and then. I tell them all. I tell them everything.

This is a big mistake.

What everyone thinks, without exception, boils down to this: "You have got to FORGET about Johnny Von!"

Their words stab into me, coming to kill this good thing.

They reason well with their bad advice. They should all be lawyers. They cite facts: "If he was interested in you, he would have found you ... It's been months. I think you should face the reality that he's not into you ... You spent what, 20 minutes with the guy? He's an actor ...You don't know him, how can you like him, you haven't spent any time with him ... Do you know who he's dating?! I don't mean to hurt your feelings, but I don't think you have a chance ...You need to stop hoping and get on with your life ...You have a hell-freezing-over, never-going-to-happen kind of situation here."

They look sorry for me and continue their bad advice: "You need to make friends ...take a class ... you need to get out and date ...You need to speed date ...you need to internet date ..."

"What else can you do?" Their words hit me hard, "This is the way the world is."

My stomach knots at hearing it again. In the second grade, and then with the International Playboy, and now with this.

They all say it, so with a heavy heart I think, they must be right.

So I try. I try to take all the bad advice. I try to stomp out all this sweet desire, to tackle down the feelings inside me and shove them behind soundproof glass. I try to replace all these good feelings with bad ones.

So here I am, walking up Valley Glen Drive and down Valley Glen Drive, with the dogs and no Johnny Von, feeling bad. Struggling to forget about it, because probably everyone is right. At least they all seem to agree with one another.

Only this is the thing: once pure desire is realized, articulated, it's nearly impossible to put back into the box. I can't tackle it and put it behind soundproof glass anymore …without going back, without canceling out the genuine me. And the something happy and real, the something authentic and pre-lunchroom inside me, doesn't want to go back.

I can't do it. I just can't. So I think of William Blake, and his rejection of outside authorities and I decide: "Screw'em. Screw'em all."

I write Johnny Von a poem.

A poem written while walking Valley Glen Drive, blissfully thinking of him.

And I think about sending it.

I feel a liberation inside me that has never been before! I feel a level of freedom I've never had.

The cat's out of the bag, so everyone showers more bad advice: "You're going to do what...What do you think he's going to do?! He's a CELEBRITY! ...That's like emotional assault, sending someone a poem when you don't know them ...I'm sure he'll be flattered, like, his ego will like it, but I can't imagine he'll ever talk to you again ...Don't do that, that is totally going to freak him out ..."

But I don't care. I'm free. I'm beyond their authority, their opinions. I'm slaphappy drunk in this river of creativity and pure desire. I don't care if sending this poem makes me the village idiot. William Blake was right. I just want to bath in the currents of sweet desire and see where they take me. It feels so damn good, I don't give a rip what anyone thinks. I'm so proud of myself and my poem, that for a bold moment I don't even care what Johnny Von thinks!

I put the poem in a card and I put the card in his mailbox outside the shiny new giant gate.

And look, I'm not telling you the poem, because it's personal.

It's private.

On the other hand, it is kind of crucial to the point

of the story. And you know so much already. And, you have come this far with me -- for which I'm grateful -- so I guess I should tell you the poem.

But know that it's just between me and Johnny Von— and now you, so just read it once, so you'll know, and then tear out the pages or fold them down or something. Read responsibly because, you know, I'm still shy about all this.

This is the poem:

Labrador Bliss

Moochie has never
eaten pizza,
but he is sure
he would like it.

Watching
from the paper plate
across my thighs,
the grace of motion
to my mouth-
amazing mozzarella,
precious sausage,
perfectly crunchy crust.

Moochie does not need
to have tasted pizza!

With a focused, subtle
lift of the nose,
he sniffs.

His pensive manner
breaks
to a Cheshire grin.
He pants,
shows his tongue.

Moochie has a plan.

I can not, should not-
table food gives him gas.

He stares.
He uses dignity,
no barking,
no whining,
just eyes.

I can't stop myself,
I fling
the medley
of mouth watering desire
up into the sky.

Before it leaves
my fingertips,
arcs into the air,
Moochie's eyes have lit.

He leaves the ground.

In a chomp
it is done.

Moochie looks at pizza
the way I look at you.

I'm high for days! For a week! For a week and a half.

By two weeks, I'm unsure again.

By two and a half weeks, after seeing the tip of his Trans Am at the top of the driveway everyday (the only thing you can see now from the street), so I know he's in town, I start to wobble. I start to lose the solid ground of creative purity where I'd so proudly placed my flag and staked my claim. I no longer feel bold about not caring what he thinks. My stomach starts to hurt. I'm nauseated all the time.

On Monday, three months and three weeks after talking to Johnny Von, a week and two days after sending him my poem, as I walk the streets, it starts to unravel inside me — I've mustered all the courage I could find, broken free from giving a rip about what anyone thinks, followed an impulse from my heart, and not been rewarded for it in the least! And today...today is my birthday.

I'm 34 years old.

I'm walking dogs for a living, with no plans for anything later. The day is more than halfway over and no one's called me.

I hear the rumble of the Trans Am behind me.

Maybe now ... maybe this is the moment!

He speeds by.

He doesn't wave.

Johnny Von swerves around us and doesn't even look my way.

I feel everything, all my thoughts about Johnny Von sink from my heart into the pit of my stomach. There, in the middle of Valley Glen Drive, I start to cry. I start to sob. I dip my head, so the brim of my hat covers my eyes, so nobody sees that I am crying.

I hate poetry and creativity and the torture of desire! It's all bullshit. And on top of that, I hate myself. Genuine or crafted coolness, it doesn't fucking matter. My whole life, I'm not skinny enough, I'm not pretty enough, I'm too shy and my life ... my life is going nowhere. I don't have a family or a career. I'm nothing yet, and I'm 34!

Tears are flooding out of me now. My nose is running, I can't see straight, Moochie doesn't know what's going on, and I think, perfect ... I've lost it ... I am crazy.

I'm a crazy person. I can't control myself. I can't stop crying here, out in public, on Valley Glen Drive, because of some guy! I'm shattered because of some guy who I don't even know, a celebrity at that, doesn't like me. Only it's crazier than that, because I don't even know him enough to know if he doesn't like me. I'm that small, that insignificant. I'm that invisible.

I feel my heart breaking again inside my chest. I look down to Moochie at the end of the leash. Is this going to be how it is for me the rest of my life? Alone? Forever back in situations where the story ends with: This is the way the world is. Where my feelings don't carry any weight? Where I am powerless, invisible and heartbroken?

Overcome with tears, I stop walking. I sit on the curb and I lose it.

I start to drown in the thoughts.

In the midst of losing it, I look over to Moochie at the end of the leash. At first he sits politely next to me, his puppy eyes filled with worry. He's never seen me cry. When he sees me look his way, he wags. He gets up, wiggling his body as much as he can, he bounds up to me, bumps me and wags some more. He then scurries into the ivy behind us and grabs a stick. Still wagging as much as he can, he circles and bounces around me. He shows me his best moves.

I smile.

Moochie notices the break in my crying and drops the stick. He presses his furry fat nose into my neck and starts kissing me. Licking my ear and cheek until he almost has me on the ground in the ivy.

Moochie loves me.

That's when the next thought hits me, it comes from nowhere, as if someone is whispering it into my ear: "Think a different story." It's gentle and calm, like a grandmother that you love, picking you up after scraping your knee, smoothing your hair off your forehead, and saying to you with sweet eyes, "Powerless is not your story, my baby. You are not invisible."

The idea trickles in, as I sit on the curb, wiping away the slobber and tears. Patting Moochie's belly and rubbing on his head. It forms in a way that equates to this: "You want to be seen and visible? Then think a different story about yourself, start now, and it will carve a new path."

I pick myself up, stand on the empty street and take a breath. Even with Moochie, leading me forward, it's hard. It's hard to think differently because, you know, reality is so convincing. But I reach anyway. I reach, not because I am sure of it, sure of the epiphany. I reach because I am tired of drowning. I've had enough of giving into "the way the world is."

It is only a little thing at first. It offers only the slightest feeling of relief, but it is relief all the same. This new line of thinking, this new story I will tell myself starts like this: "My feelings do carry weight…with me."

At the moment the thought crystallizes, I hear the rumble again of the Trans Am. Down the hill it rushes toward me, top down. Johnny Von is on the passenger's side, his assistant is driving. They slow at the corner where Moochie and I are walking, to veer around us.

His eyes light with recognition. Johnny Von sees me.

He turns, leaning over the back of the seat as they slow to pass us, he waves to me like a happy kid. "There she is," he says. "Hey Baby!" Looking excited to see me, his expression open and his eyes beaming, he calls out, "I love pizza!"

He read the poem! I beam back a smile and laugh. I wave and step toward the car.

And then I see the trace of shyness in him, the pull-back and reserve. All in the flash of the moment, he changes. It's almost as if he is suddenly afraid of something. The open expression snaps shut, "I'll talk to you later," he calls and they rush on.

Now, I'm really confused.

"I have told that damn UPS man a thousand times to put my packages on the back step! Can you imagine, leaving a box out here by the edge of the driveway like this, my Lord, what is wrong with him." Trudie Reed pulls out a dog biscuit from her housecoat and Moochie bolts. I'm too fragile from my emotional roadside-breakdown to hold him back. I drop the leash and let Moochie meet her half way up the drive. I'm battle worn, if it's now time to take a beating from Trudie Reed then just let her bring it and hopefully it will be quick. As I get to the two of them, I can see that Trudie Reed has noticed my puffy eyes and I brace myself for a comment about make-up and how girls today just let themselves go all natural.

"I was hoping I would see you two today. I've got something for you. Come inside." I'm confused but happy not to be insulted right off the bat. I anchor Moochie in the garage and follow Trudie Reed. I've never been inside her house before.

"Take your shoes off right there! Don't track those filthy sports shoes all over my clean floors." I pause at the door and strip my feet to my white gym socks.

Trudie Reed's house is picture perfect 1955. Her kitchen is worn but clean as the day she moved in. Her rotary telephone, a beige-mustard color, hangs by the fridge, the long coil dangling almost to the floor.

"Wait in the den, but don't sit on the couches!" I look across the kitchen, through to the den and see the light beige couches with doilies on the top. "You're backside is like a barn-hand's. Just sit by the fireplace, over on the bricks of the hearth."

"I'm fine, I'll just stand. I'm okay."

Trudie takes off to the back of the house down the hall. I walk down the steps to the sunken living room toward the fireplace and stop at the dark mahogany built-in bookcase. In the center sit two Academy Awards for screenwriting, six Emmy's, and countless plaques and honors. The shelves and surrounding walls are filled with photos. Everyone, and I mean everyone who was ever anyone in Hollywood, all the greats, are there laughing and whooping it up with Trudie and Howard. I knew she was a seamstress and that Howard worked at Paramount at some point, but I had no idea. Before me, I see the rat pack with Howard, "You saved the picture!" scrawled across the front. There's George and Gracie and Trudie laughing at an outside table somewhere, "But where's the duck?" is written at the bottom of the photo. There's one with Sophia Loren, Howard, and Marlon Brando, with his arm around Trudie giving her a teasing kiss on the cheek in some restaurant.

Bogart and Bacall and some other guys in horn-rimmed glasses are looking over a script, with "Ask Howard what to do!... All the Best, Bogie." scribbled in black ink. There's Hepburn and Hayworth and De Havilland sprinkled in the shelves. There's Newman and Redford, just boys, with Howard sitting on some set, deep in discussion. There's a small color photo with an early twenties, baby-faced Meryl Streep and an older version of Howard on a rehearsal stage somewhere in the 70's.

"There's my favorite one, right there in the middle." Trudie Reed puts down what she's carrying into the living room, walks to the case and picks out a photo right in front of me. One I hadn't noticed. It's Trudie and some other woman, taken in the late forties/early fifties. She rubs it with affection and then hands it to me.

"Now, who's this." I smile.

"Mary Sue Whitman. She was my best friend. We called her Apple, because her cheeks were always rosy. She died so young, summer of forty-nine. You remind me of her. Of course Apple would never go out of the house looking like that." Trudie Reed scans me up and down. "But she had nice, soft eyes and a friendly temperament. We were peas in a pod from the day we met. She was Howard's first wife."

"What?"

"She told me when she was near to the end, 'Trudie,' she said, 'Howard needs you. He's always been fond of you, and I know you have affection for him.' At the time, I was divorcing my second husband and Howard had just started working at the studio, not yet noticed by anyone. 'Trudie, you can tell him your stories,' she'd say. 'The two of you would be great together.' And she was right, we were good together."

"And Howard was a screenwriter?" I ask looking up at the shiny Academy Awards.

Trudie pauses for a second and looks me in the eye. And then her tone changes, she gets softer. "I loved Howard." She says in a quiet confessional way. "And don't get me wrong, I was always happy and we had a wonderful life together." She pauses again, unsure if she should go on, "but, Howard had the imagination of a wet paper bag. He wrote…but they were my stories."

Trudie Reed shakes her head and laughs. Her whole demeanor changes, like the weight of the world has been lifted from her little old lady body. Like she'd braced herself to say something really sad, but when she heard it said aloud, it amused her.

"It's not like it is today. There were only certain careers for women and I was satisfied standing by his side, and I loved him. I wanted to watch him shine in the world." She shrugs her shoulders looking at the pictures in a light-hearted kind of way.

"We worked in this very room for years and years, me telling stories, him reading back. The two of us working over lines and scenes together. It was pure happiness. It's why I haven't remodeled after all this time, why I never changed a thing. This room heard my voice, and Apple heard me before that, and that was enough. But the world, the world heard Howard." She winks at me, "And look what came."

"So, wait. I don't understand. Nobody knew you were the…talent. How could that be, I mean…" I look up at the wall of trophies.

"Well Howard did have talent. Amazing talent. He could understand people, their nature. And they loved him for it. He could talk to actors. And he could talk to people on the sets, and in the offices, and on the stage; about drama and three act plays, about behavior and emotions, about lighting and camera angles. He was a brilliant man. He should have been a director," she sighs a bit, and puts the picture back in its place, "but this town is full of things that should have been."

She turns to the pictures and scans the wall of movie stars. "Look at all of them. They loved him. They loved him because he genuinely saw them as they were. Maybe that was his greatest talent. Even when fame and fortune was brutal to them, Howard was steadfast. He didn't try to be something he was not. That's the irony. Had anyone ever asked, I've no doubt he'd have turned all the credit over to me." Trudie smiles, "and I never would have taken it. It may be hard to believe, but I was not very outspoken in those days."

"That is hard to believe." I say joking with Trudie Reed,

struck by the familiar levity that is in the air.

"No, I think it was right the way it was." Trudie walks over to the couch, "I've never told anyone that. Not even my nieces. Nobody knows they were my stories. Nobody but you and Apple."

"Trudie, I don't know what to say."

"Never mind. It all passes. And I had love and happiness. And I must have lost my mind telling you all these sentimental things. I was cleaning out my old things and I saw this and thought, well this is so big it will fit you. I'd made it for Apple. Maybe that's what started me on all this."

She unwraps the cellophane to reveal a gorgeous strapless black vintage dress. A circle skirt that reaches just below the knee, with a fitted top that points at the waist, zips in back and sweethearts at the chest.

"It's beautiful, but I…"

"Oh stop it. I'm too old to fuss around. Put it on in the powder room just quickly, so I know that it fits and try not to touch it to any of your clothes. And for goodness sake, wash your hands before you handle it!"

I follow Trudie's orders and emerge like Cinderella herself, a 34 year old Cinderella. As I stand in the mirror, looking at myself in this dress, that was made for a night at the Oscars, Trudie tugs and pulls at the skirt.

"I think it fits just right. Maybe just here," she pulls at the front. "No, actually, it's right, just as it is." She looks to the mirror then back to the dress, "You know," she says half way between talking to herself and talking to the dress, "I might have liked to be the one to shine." She grabs the dress in the back and gives it a brisk tug, then looks to me in the mirror and says, "if I had it to do again that is, back all those years ago. If it would have been like it is today, I might have liked it if the world had heard me."

I smile and nod and breathe, with Trudie Reed, looking in the mirror at myself, feeling how much I want to shine. I can feel the rumble inside me, awakened by this sweet Johnny Von desire, of a voice that wants to be in the world.

"Then again," she says as she opens a drawer, pulls out a pincushion and clips it to her wrist, "No 'if this had happened…' or 'if that had happened…' could have given me a fuller life. The people that I loved, my friends, knew me."

Trudie quickly stitches the back of the dress with the delft moves of a master.

"Howard knew me. He genuinely saw me and loved me. All those 'if's' couldn't have given me a happier life, so I guess, I wouldn't change it." She peeks up from my shoulder and looks to me in the mirror again, "I wouldn't change a day in Howard's eyes for all the fame on that wall. But it was true love. It was real, you know. You just have to know what's worth having. What's worth keeping and what's worth giving up."

I look at Trudie and then down at the dress and realize she is the first real friend I've had in a long, long time.

That night people do call and invite me to dinner and wish me a happy birthday, but I opt out of all of it. I hang out with Mooch and steam the dress and think about the sweet Johnny Von desire, and feeling powerless, and deciding to think a different story. I get in bed the night of my 34th birthday, click off the lights and stare at the ceiling wondering what I'm going to do with all these feelings that matter only to me. I think about Trudie and Howard and all those famous people; and Johnny Von, down the street behind that giant fence, reading my poem. I think about what it means to shine, to be genuinely seen by one person versus being seen by the world. And then I feel a shift inside me—from wanting Johnny Von to see me—to me seeing Johnny Von.

And I think, *you know, he's just a guy.*

The next day I sign a card, a blank card with a goofy picture of a dog on the front, with a note inviting Johnny Von to walk the dogs with me sometime and my phone number. I walk with my head up and my shoulders square and all the tabloid magazines pushed far, far out of my mind. I put the card into the mailbox next to the shiny metal call box, because this is what I'd do if he were just a guy. Just a guy that I'd met, and talked to once and wanted to get to know. I guy that seemed to like me, seemed to like the poem I'd sent, but was hesitant. I learn that this is what the genuine me does. This is who I am when I let myself be who I am. This is how it is when I shine.

Five days later I've not heard back on the card I left for Johnny Von, but the universe decides to take the lead with me on all this and Mandy Kane, of all people, calls me completely out of breath.

"Tonight" pant, pant, "You and I are going to a party at Lionel Max's estate in the hills. It's a benefit for some African thing, but listen to this, Tracy gave me the invite, the girl that dated Johnny Von's roommate before they did *Kings of Vegas.* I told you about her. She's still tight with all of them. They are all going to be there. Lionel Max and Johnny Von are doing some project together right now. Tonight is a really big, private deal, so it's a great chance for you. Perfect for a second connection."

I did tell Mandy Kane that I was *thinking* about sending Johnny Von a note, but I never told her that I went over that day, or that we chatted by the pool, or that I sent him poetry. I haven't shared. She thinks I stopped walking Valley Glen Drive altogether, and that I haven't had any contact with him since that night at the King King. It just made life easier.

"It's a formal thing. I know, even for L.A. that's not saying much. But Tracy told me it's suits and gowns only. I'm picking you up at seven."

Mandy Kane hangs up as out of breath as she started. She believes Mark Walberg might be there as well. She didn't review my clothes with me, which means she hasn't decided for herself yet, and she doesn't have a minute to lose.

I hang up, call The DryBar and schedule a 4:00 blow out. I take a deep breath. I know exactly what I'm wearing...

The first security gate waves Mandy Kane's Cadillac Escalade forward up a long gravel drive smack in the middle of Beverly Hills. A few moments later a tuxedo clad valet opens the door and I step out into the twinkling fairytale estate of Lionel Max. The night sky is just forming and the starry universe above is a mere faded backdrop to the lights and colors decorating the courtyard. There are pink Chinese lanterns strung throughout the grounds that glow like magic in the dusk. The trees are sprinkled with white lights, as if a million obedient fireflies have come home for the occasion. By the sculptured fountain, a string quartet plays Vivaldi while the glamorous and wealthy step out of their shiny cars, their invitations discreetly in hand. Men in tuxedos with earpieces usher us to the security tables in the main entry to check in.

Mandy and I make our way up the steps to find our place among the bold and the beautiful, the rich and the famous and heads turn. Not to be boastful, but I look stunning in the black dress made for Apple! Thanks to Trudie Reed, I am shining. Men and women alike turn to look at me. I am Cinderella indeed. Mandy has not commented on the dress, which is a pretty good indication of things. Mandy Kane doesn't like to be someone-standing-next-to-the-someone everyone is looking at.

As we wait for our turn to check in by a wall of flickering candles in the entryway, I see the back of Johnny Von's head towering over everyone in the living room. I take a deep breath, my heart pounds, and I can feel all of the sweet Johnny Von desire just bursting out of my skin, but I don't say anything. A man in a tuxedo asks us to move forward and I step out from behind Mandy Kane to the center of the entryway. A halo of candlelight glows around me, my long natural curls brush my bare shoulders, and I feel the moment... the whole room mystified by my radiance. But not Johnny Von, not yet, his back is still to us.

As the line moves up, Mandy sees Tracy through the crowd standing in a small circle of people around Johnny Von. She waves. She calls out. And then Tracy and the little circle of people she is standing with, including Johnny Von, turn.

My experience of time shifts in a way I struggle to describe.

As Johnny Von turns in slow motion, all the experiences of my life that have lead me here, light up, like a single thread running through a temporal tapestry. Suddenly all the marker moments, from the second grade, from meeting the International Playboy, to the coffee shop in London, from waving to the Trans Am on Valley Glen Drive, to Johnny Von by the pool, all the way up to standing in the mirror at Trudie Reed's house—all of them from childhood and adulthood—which until now have been strung together in chronological order, fracture. Unexpectedly, this line of events breaks into just a collection of moments. In this other worldly sensation of time as Johnny Von is turning, all of these moments in my life are randomly thrown up into the air, out of sequence, suspended on the cusp of here and now. Scattered like a deck of cards fanned up to the ceiling, they are all neutralized. I am unable to deem any moment good or bad, important or trivial, without the relativity of time to discern them. They all exist at once in a state of limbo.

Tracy waves back, and now my sensation of time speeds up.

I watch in a fast forward motion Johnny Von's eyes start to scan the entryway, looking to see who Tracy is welcoming in. As I watch, I am acutely aware of the sounds surrounding me, the tinkling of drinks, the mingling voices, high heels clicking on the tile floor, the security man tapping his pen on the clipboard. Johnny Von's eyes look across the room to the table, his demeanor is light and friendly. My skin is on fire. I feel the soft cloth of my dress, the heat of the candles behind me, the cold of the walkway under my shoes, the slight brush of the silk scarf of the woman next me. Johnny Von's eyes move down the line. I'm aware of every smell, the burning candle wax, the heavy cologne of a passing security guard, the musty corners of the entryway, the rose fragrant soap on my skin. He sees Mandy Kane. Still there is a social niceness to his expression. My eyes in this singular flash of time are hyper-sensitive to the light and edges of everything, the white and pink colors glowing from outside, the dimmed pendent over head, the soft lamps in the living room, the sharp flashlight at the security table, the flickering of candlelight all around me. I see, feel and know every detail in the room at once.

Then it all stops.

I feel my heartbeat thump my chest.

Johnny Von's eyes land on me.

And then, in the next thump of my heartbeat, I see this in his eyes: stunned, then scared, then panicked, then angry…then controlled… then flat. Johnny Von turns away.

I feel the room start to collapse around me. I don't understand. It's like I've heard the pop of a gun, someone's been shot, something horrible has happened and I don't know what it is yet. All the moments of my life that have led me here start to rain down and I don't know what to make of any of them. I don't know what any of them mean.

Like a match struck and thrown in brittle dry brush, Johnny Von whispers to someone next to him, who steps quickly and whispers to Tracy, and then moves off to whisper to someone else. Tracy's face drops. It's like I'm watching a line of fire run through the most flammable material known to man, moving faster than you can watch it, fanning out as you look on with horror and disbelief at a wave destruction right before your eyes.

"I.D. and invitation." The security guard calls out for Mandy Kane's attention to scan the barcode on our invitation, but she is too distracted by Tracy's expression across the crowd to notice. "Miss," the security guard says again politely, "I need your name and invitation." He holds out his hand just as the final chain of whispers makes it to his ear from a large bodyguard that has appeared out of nowhere.

"Ladies, can you step to the side with me."

I feel myself begin to implode; all my senses growing distant. I start to go numb.

Mandy looks confused, she begins to wave her invitation in the air while the large bodyguard steers us off to the side. A kind of fog comes over me. I can't really hear what they are saying or make sense of it. Out of the corner of my eye, I can see the people around me begin to point and whisper, but I can't tell if it is really happening or not. I look over one last time to the living room, to find Johnny Von, to have him look at me again and make it different, but he's gone. I see Mandy talking to the bodyguard, pointing to Tracy, who's now made her way over to us.

I feel myself fading back, slipping away, watching a nightmare that I know can't be real, but I can't wake up from either. Tracy pulls Mandy aside, whispers in her ear and they both look over at me like...like.... all those kids in the second grade, like I'm covered in vomit, like I'm a monster. It seems they talk for awhile, but I'm not sure because they feel far away and unreal. I'm only aware of the light and breath draining out of me, my spirit starting to hemorrhage. Horrified to realize, I'm the one whose been shot, I'm the one about to look down and see a sucking chest wound.

Mandy walks up to me and says without a flinch, "He called you his stalker."

As I watch her say this to me, it's like I've been ripped in the chest and now kicked in the soft of my belly, catapulted backwards off the side of a mountain. Her voice is harsh and violent, and filled with distain. Her words are spiked with mockery, establishing a clear distance between us.

I try to speak, to say something, but I can't get anything out. I just shake my head 'no' in disbelief. I feel a shooting pain in my solar plexus and I choke on the air, unable to utter a word.

Mandy Kane just looks at me, letting the word 'stalker' hack its way through my skin, into my chest, all the way to my tender and open heart. She stands in front of me for a moment expecting some kind of apology for the humiliation I am, some kind of admission of my perversion.

I think, *she's lying, they're lying, he doesn't think that, he wouldn't say that...* I scan the room and see the people in line looking and looking away, and I try to find Johnny Von through the crowd, because this is a mistake, but he's nowhere.

Mandy Kane gets nothing from me, I can't form a single

word, so she shoves the valet card in my hand, "Look just take my car and go. I'm staying. Just leave my keys out under the plant at your door and I'll pick up my car in the morning." She turns and walks into the crowd with Tracy.

Just like that, it's over.

The crowd closes me out and goes on as if I'm not there, was never there. The security guard motions me to the door and watches me walk quietly to the valet stand. He stands at a distance in the courtyard, watching me walk all the way down the drive.

I hand the card to the sweaty tuxedo man and he runs off. I sit on a cold concrete bench by a large hedge filled with twinkle lights. I feel tears running down my cheeks but I'm not crying yet, not really. I'm just stunned.

Alone in the night, I wait.

I click my handbag open and closed a few times and see that my hands are trembling. I struggle to remind myself that I am not powerless, that I am going to think a different story about myself no matter what.

I know I look beautiful in this dress. I know I'm a nice girl; sincere and kind-hearted. I know that I can be my genuine-self and I can shine. I know I'm not a stalker! I mean look at Mandy Kane, if anyone comes close to crossing that line…she's probably in there right now sniffing out Mark Walberg's place setting and paying off the waiter to move her next to him. A stalker! I'm not a stalker. I am not that! I'm not a monster. And who cares what those people think, they don't even know me. They are not my friends. I don't need any of those stupid

Hollywood people. Who cares what they think! Who cares what Johnny Von thinks!

I try with everything I've got, but it doesn't work because I do care what Johnny Von thinks of me. And what I saw in his eyes, what he said about me, how Mandy Kane and everyone looked at me—it's breaking my heart. As much as I want to hold it together, as much as I want to say it doesn't matter because I don't really know him, it is, without mercy, breaking my heart. And with every fiber of my being, I don't want to have to kill off the sweet Johnny Von desire that has bloomed my heart open. The sweet desire that animated the world around me, at 34 years old, like nothing else ever has. But I can feel it dying, and taking me with it... and I don't know how to stop it.

It's like I have to go and kill that baby deer, in The Yearling. I'm Jody and that innocent, soft eye'd deer that I've fallen in love with, allowed to trust me and love me, I have to hunt it down and kill it. That's how the Johnny Von desire feels inside me right now, like the yearling. Gregory Peck is standing over me saying, "Take the yearling out in the woods boy, and tie him and shoot him." And I can't do it, so Jane Wyman shoots and hurts him, and now I'm that Jody-boy looking down at the mangled little deer, confused and writhing with pain, the only sweet friend I have, and Gregory Peck is yelling over my shoulder, "Jody, you got to finish him now boy, you got to put him out of his torment."

What a horrible story that is!

I'm sure he tells him, "That's the way the world is, son." I mean, that's the point of the movie right, the cruel world.

Well, fuck the way the world is. Build a bigger pen for the deer, or take him to another forest and integrate him into a wild herd or something! He can't be the only damn deer in the Everglades! Making that boy kill that deer is just plain cold hearted and cruel. It's sadistic. And I tell you what, I'm not killing anything I love!

So I fight for it, here on this bench, like I'm fighting for my life. I fight for my open heart by searching for any thoughts of relief, but I find NOTHING to sooth myself. And before I lose the fight, abandon myself forever and succumb to the way the world is, before I buckle, convinced the universe is a cold hearted and cruel place, unable to find rhyme or reason... unable to see myself in any other way than the "unwanted" way they all see me... I hear Johnny Von through the hedge. His circle of friends has moved out to the patio and he's standing just a few feet behind me, completely unaware that I am here on the other side of the hedge, bleeding out, by his hand, mere inches away.

I turn my head and I can see him through the leaves and branches and twinkle lights. I can see him talking and I can hear him laughing. But, it's a different laugh. A laugh I don't recognize. It's nothing like the way he laughed that day by the pool. It's the laugh of...the laugh of Johnny Von...the Movie Star.

And with that thought, the split second before

my heart decides to fold, before I become invisible forevermore, right before I abandon myself for the third and last time in my life, I remember Trudie and I look down at this dress made for Apple. I think about Howard and all those famous people, and about Johnny, on the other side of the hedge, Johnny Von the Movie Star—all the nights of desire that must have lived inside him to bring his dreams to life. And I think about all the parts we are all always playing.

And then something in me stands up.

All the moments of my life that have led me here, click back into some kind of divine and right pattern and I understand it all, even though I can't yet articulate it, I can feel a rightness return to the universe.

As I hear Johnny Von talking and laughing and socializing behind me through the hedge, my mind plays through all the ways I'd imagined him over these past few months; all the ways I'd envisioned him to be. And instead of trying to sort through the real and the unreal trying to decipher what is image and what is him, instead of my reasoning mind trying to find the truth of him to make sense of all of this, I shift inside to see for the first time all the ways I'd imagined myself to be.

I suddenly see the girl as the lead, not the supporting role. I look at the woman I'd been in all my dreams; her strength and love and ability to live out desire. And I see clearly how the Johnny Von desire bloomed in me that day by the pool because of the kind of heart I have.

And I realize for the first time since this started that
day with the hawk, how all this has everything to do with
Johnny Von, the genuine attraction I have for the man, and
nothing to do with Johnny Von!

Because...I am the Johnny Von desire.

It's in me.

And while Johnny Von may be the muse for the energy,
while he may have been a moment in time, a genuine
exchange that pointed me to the source—the wellspring
inside me I'd capped off—it's all in me. It belongs to
me. And what Johnny Von, or anyone else says or does or
thinks about me can't take that away. No one outside of
me can diminish the sweet Johnny Von desire because it's
mine and I know it.

It's the deep understanding of William Blake. An
inside knowing of that place where love and art are born.
And celebrated. And given full permission to flow out—
everywhere—even when the world scorns it.

And with this knowing, I suddenly love that woman
playing the lead! She is wonderful, wonderful, wonderful.
And she looks fabulous in this dress made for Apple. And
she knows it.

All the people that I love run through my mind, my
friends and relatives, ones with significant others and ones
without, and I think, "I would love it, if someone I loved,
had someone like me. I wish that for all of them."

As if a spell cast over me when I was a little girl is

suddenly broken, in a woosh, I feel all of myself returned. The valet heads down the hill to the gates at the end of the drive in Mandy Kane's ridiculously big Cadillac Esplanade. I stand, feel my feet on the ground, and walk away from the hedge filled with twinkle lights. I walk away from the voices and the laughing of Johnny Von the Movie Star. I hand the valet the card and take the keys, and I hear my heart whisper back, not in the voice of Billy Byrde, but in my own voice , "I knew you'd come for me. I knew you'd come for me, even if you didn't know."

Johnny Von the Scientist

Estella steps into the laboratory as the sliding glass doors seal shut behind her. Underneath the clicking of glass test tubes, the electronic twerping voice of **The Controller,** through the many translucent virtual monitors, Estella sees him. Johnny Von the Scientist stands in the center of the room, his shoulders tall amidst the crowd of subordinate scientists surrounding him. He is radiant as the light bounces off his white lab coat.

In the large room, lit only by a few spotlights shining down, Estella takes a moment in the shadows to study him without fear. She lets her eyes languish on him — the way he touches his hand to his cheek as he listens to his colleagues, the way he adjusts his thick, black-rimmed glasses when he speaks, the passion in his eyes as he reaches to grab an idea out of the ethers.

Johnny Von the Scientist pokes the air in rapid

succession, making adjustments to the virtual model of boson particles they are discussing.

Hidden in the shadows, Estella wonders if he will be the one.

She catches herself slipping into the thought and abruptly stops the sensations inside her. She has not been caught staring, no one has seen her there, but her Pod might detect her increased heart rate, track the euphoric chemicals coming off her skin, record the intensity of her brainwaves and flag her. The data would alert **The Controller**. She has to shut down her feelings, numb herself. She has too many secrets as it is, already breaking more rules than she should. She can't risk being transferred off the floor of intellect workers. Not before she understands what happened that day.

Estella was at her station, an area no bigger than a four by four square of personal space, on the intellect floor. It was a workday like any other. She'd just arrived and was adjusting her settings for her Pod. She remembers the details exactly.

"Ambient, peppermint and rose. Sunny and mild," she whispered in the air. "Work Feed." It was the same setting as most days. The virtual translucent monitors in the air around her blinked off to reboot.

She watched him walk Aisle 8B7 and then turn down her row, on the way to his private lab. Many days he passed behind her, head down, busy in contemplation.

Often she noticed the squeak of his shiny white zylar shoes and heard him whispering possible combinations to Level 16 into his integrated structureless microphone. But on this day, in the moment of the lull — the two seconds that her Pod is non-active as it changes settings — she felt the breeze of him on the back of her neck. In that moment she turned. Against regulation, she looked away from the glass trays of DNA polymers she was sorting and met his eyes. As he walked by, she was overtaken by the wake of his scent. Johnny Von the Scientist, in the lab for eighty-six hours, smelled.

He smelled like a man.

It was a fragrance Estella had never experienced.

She'd had her scheduled appointments, her designated relations, she'd been with men. Men whom she found pleasant and satisfactorily attractive. Her body's biological responses were all normal. But this was something new. Estella's whole body was struck with a tingling, buzzing energy as Johnny Von the Scientist walked past her that day.

When she thought about it later, she realized that he must have gone more than the mandatory eight hours between decontamination misting. Which could only mean that **The Controller** was not monitoring him! And although she could not exactly account for what had come over her, her sudden and intense attention for him outside his intellectual fame, it did occur to her that Johnny Von the Scientist might be the only man outside **The Controller**'s power. That he might really be the one.

"Of course I reversed the Higgs Field and set up the initial vacuum!" Johnny Von the Scientist fires off. "Any school child would start there!" He snaps at the round, bearded physicist, Elmo Trino, famous for his findings in animal life reconfiguration. Elmo Trino was the favored candidate to solve Xbox 6000 before Johnny Von the Scientist hit the scene.

"What about Integrated Derivatives Silicon Theory?" someone else offers from the crowd.

Johnny Von the Scientist shakes his head no.

When Xbox started more than 500 years ago, it was introduced to the public as an amusement. But as it evolved and the Virtual Revolution got underway, it took a more serious role in society. With each new version, what were once games became sophisticated software design problems. With each victorious player, another level of complexity was calculated by the software itself. It then began to reason on its own, based on the accumulated human input. It became the universal think tank for the software that would eventually be known as **The Controller**.

It was evolving nicely until the technology became so sophisticated it reached a tipping point. It was suddenly beyond any one individual's understanding. It was above any one ruling body. The technology was barreling out of control and Xbox was allowing **The Controller** to exist on its own, outside humanity's reach. Even as the World Government came together, **The Controller** was already beyond its sanctions. What was originally hoped to be the great equalizer and protector for the whole of humanity, as well as the individual — a true reader of the majority's intentions and well-being — was now a harsh and limiting electronic overlord.

"Hemp-hum." Estella clears her throat, hoping her presence will be noticed. She is nervous enough without the added awkwardness of not knowing what to do with herself, how to proceed.

Johnny Von the Scientist turns. He sees Estella across the lab. Without expression or acknowledgement, he turns back and continues with his discussion.

"Carbon neutrino particle transference?" another scientist offers.

"Done it." Johnny Von the Scientist shoots down the idea, still shaking his head, his temper escalating.

Normally, Estella wouldn't be this nervous and unsure. She is a good cataloger, confident in her work and secure with her position, even though she was not on track for the intellect floor. Estella started out in the Book Repository, when there were still physical texts to be entered into the World Data Bank. Like everyone else, her career was set on her eighth birthday. She was assigned to the activity **The Controller** deemed appropriate — work chosen according to her monitored likes and dislikes recorded by her Pod. She progressed quickly through the ranks until the Turnovers in 2545, 12 years later.

The Turnovers was a chaotic time, when extremists were insisting that everyone must participate in Pod technology. Everything had to be virtual. Any physical source of information — information that was not being supplied by **The Controller** through each person's Pod — was a threat to the survival of the system. They argued that being exposed to and reacting to information found outside the Pod would skew the results being tallied. It would impinge **The Controller**'s ability to serve humanity's highest good.

So, when the goal of the Turnovers was reached, when every book, every printed page was destroyed over a decade ago, Estella was reassigned to the 673rd floor, cataloging for Gene Duplication and Review. And now she is here, on the vast floor of intellect workers, sorting trays of DNA polymers.

"Blinovitch's Second Law of Temporal Inertia," a scientist shouts.

"No."

"Random quark directional flow? Kerastase Theory?"

"No. No!" Johnny Von the Scientist snaps back, his passion flaring.

"Binary Derivatives with early String Theory!" a small junior physicist offers from the back of the group, not knowing when to stop.

Johnny Von the Scientist throws up his hands. "Get out!"

Estella is unclear if she is included in this direction, or if she should stay? Her morning orders were to report to his lab. But does he mean he wants everyone to leave?

She watches the group grumble and peck the air around them, saving and closing the translucent notes they've been making on the virtual monitors of their Pods. She steps to the side while the glass sliding doors swish open and the group files out in front of her. She looks to them hoping someone will direct her.

"The guy solves Xbox 6000 and he thinks he's a genius," Elmo mutters

"But he is a genius." The junior scientist offers back, too enthusiastic for Elmo's taste.

"He doesn't have to act like the only one. Jeez. Prima donna."

The junior scientist can't help himself. "But he solved Xbox 6000! The guy saved the world!"

"Not yet!" Elmo counters, exasperated with the little man. "There's still THE PROBLEM."

The doors swish shut behind them, but Estella can still hear the two men arguing down the hall. "But no one knows how he did it ..."

To understand the complexity of the situation, Xbox and **The Controller** have to be viewed in light of Pod technology. Pods started evolving the same time in history, when personal space and privacy became impractical and then impossible.

In its modern form, it consists of three infinitely small stitches of electronics found in all clothing, which monitor and set the immediate atmosphere around an individual. In practical terms, it alters the molecular structure within three feet of the body. This translates to settings as basic as sound, smell and climate control, or as complex as an instantaneous force field. Through direct monitoring by **The Controller**, the Pod can project a force field at the nano-second detection of fear, measured from the biological changes of the skin and brainwave activity. It can insulate, protect, and circumvent all injury; it can neutralize any pathogen that would start disease. It is a beautiful technological companion of safety throughout one's life.

And not only does it address the elements and buffer the senses, but it also serves as total communication and information between all individuals and, more important, between the individual and **The Controller**. Within the Pod there is a constant feed from **The Controller**, everything from the World Data Bank can be called up: text, pictures, film, and music. World News and Helpful Official Suggestions stream constantly. **The Controller** is always surveying the choices and responses to all the information coming through.

There is no denying that Pod technology countered the effects of losing the sensations of freedom and private life, it made everyone more comfortable with the transition. Without a doubt, it spawned the Virtual Revolution.

And there is no arguing its place in the unequivocal advancement of humanity. With Pod technology and **The Controller** software, society advanced at an unparalleled rate in the early days because everyone was receiving the same information. Mankind became more homogenous and harmonious because **The Controller** was taking every individual into account, educating and steering the world by the calculated results.

But it also set an unstoppable course. What only Johnny Von the Scientist understands is that it carried the seeds of its own destruction and quite possibly the end of humanity, now at hand. THE PROBLEM arose when **The Controller** calculated its own ending and started to organize plans for the destruction of the world. The only way to stop it was to solve Level 15 of Xbox 6000, the highest level of the software, gain access and control of the software again, and then reroute the system

This is what he did.

This is how she came to know his name.

He played it to the end, staying one step ahead of the game. At the end, Johnny Von the Scientist set up a kind of grand checkmate. He had the last move and Xbox could not proceed without him. The system needed him. But how Johnny Von the Scientist made that final move, no one understood. And what his next move would be to solve THE PROBLEM is what has Johnny Von the Scientist in the lab day and night.

Again, Estella clears her throat, tries to get his attention now that they are alone, but Johnny Von the Scientist does not turn, he keeps his attention on his work.

"I'm Technician 022269," Estella calls out, still not brave enough to cross the room to him.

"I know who you are!" Johnny Von the Scientist snaps back at her, still consumed by the previous discussion. His voice is loud and angry. He does not look away from the virtual model of boson particles he is adjusting in the air.

Estella feels her skin go hot. The last thing she wants is to appear awkward in front of him. Before that day, the day he met her eyes, she only knew him by name and reputation. And since that day, she has thought of him in great detail. She has thought of him with a desire and affection she's never experienced before. She's not thought of him hostile like this.

"Why are you here? It's not time yet! I told the system to request you when I was done. Do I look finished? Do I look like I'm finished to you! How is Level 16 going to engage if there is no Level 16!" Johnny Von the Scientist is yelling across the lab in full frenzy. His face red and cross.

Estella is shaken. She's thrown. "I'm sorry ... I ..." Estella starts to stammer. She's never been singled out like this. She doesn't know why Johnny Von the Scientist is yelling at her. She doesn't know what she has to do with Level 16 or any of this. She's not a scientist, she's a cataloger.

"Oh no." Johnny Von the Scientist's exasperation switches to panic. "It's the default then. I set the default to get you if the countdown starts ..." He begins a terrified scurry, adjusting the virtual model in front of him. "I don't have any more time. I can't talk to you about the sketches." He scrambles to his desk and rifles through the contents. He puts something into his white coat pocket that Estella cannot see from where she is standing, and then empties the rest of his pockets, dumping everything on to the table.

"Come here. Get over here!" He says to her alarmed and distracted by the virtual model in front of him.

Estella is scared and confused. As she crosses the lab, her mind flashes to her large bathroom at home, and the black market Brixtonian pencil she keeps in her make-up case.

Guilt and panic storm through her. She is meticulous in her routine. How could he know?

She thinks of arranging the fluffy bath mat just so on the tile floors. The way she strips off her clothes and puts them in the metal lined hamper so the Pod cannot monitor her. The way she turns on the water before she picks up the pencil, before she takes the illegal, home-made rice paper from the bottom drawer.

For years it's been the same.

On the soft mat she sits, naked and alone, her mind filling with images. Naked, in the only place, at the only time **The Controller** can't determine her exact movements, Estella loses all sense of space and time. As the tub fills and the mirrors cloud with steam, Estella lets herself go, creating places she's never been. With each image sketched, with each imagined place put on the page, her heart opens and sighs with relief. Estella has art in a world that bans it's physical existence.

And every night, when the picture is done, when the bathroom is thick with steam and her large tub of water is full and waiting, she takes the paper and submerges it in the tub as she steps into the warm liquid. Projecting herself into each imagined place, blending with the image in every last detail, she watches the places fade away, dissolving herself into them as the paper disappears.

But why would a famous scientist care about such things? Why would Johnny Von the Scientist be mad at her? Her indiscretions outside the lab would be the domain of the disciplinary council.

Of course it's more than an indiscretion. The punishment for such a crime would be severe. The only thing worse, the only action that would cause immediate shutdown is ...

"Birth Name!" Johnny Von the Scientist shouts out.

...saying her birth name aloud.

During the Turnovers, **The Controller** recommended numbers. It was a platform the extremists took to heart. It was efficient and they claimed it made everyone unique —

no more duplicate names by random chance. Of course the famous or the celebrated were allowed names, but they were needed as characters, as archetypes to steer and occupy the masses.

Why the extremists took this recommendation so intensely, no one knows. Perhaps it is the nature of dealing with extremists not to understand the reasoning in their behavior. Extremists do not deal in reason, they deal in rules. How it came to be the highest rule doesn't matter now, the individuals are numbers and numbers only. Anyone uttering a birth name is immediately shut down, the Pod starts to delete the atmosphere of the individual immediately.

Johnny Von the Scientist makes his final adjustments and screams again, "Birth Name!"

"I ... I can't. **The Controller** ..."

Still slightly turned away from her, he screams, "Lady, you think I care about **The Controller**? In a few hours we are all going to be shut down! Tell me your Goddamn Birth Name ..." he turns to her, meets her eyes, pauses, softens and says, "Trust me." Standing square to her now, just inches from her skin, he says, "Just say it." He holds her gaze. "Say your name outloud."

"Estella." It whispers from her into his eyes. Immediately she feels the pressure change around her. Already **The Controller** has flagged her and cut the oxygen in her Pod. With her last breath, she says it again staring into the eyes of Johnny Von the Scientist. "Estella."

Instantly he reaches out, grabs both her wrists with his big hands, and calls into the air, "Build the room."

The lab goes empty.

In a flash, Estella feels cool air rush into her lungs.

In the next moment, although Estella cannot register a sense of time, she sees Johnny Von the Scientist in front of her. They are alone, standing in neither darkness nor light, although she can see him perfectly. The floor beneath her is neither present nor absent, but she is standing next to him still the same. There is no direction, up or down, backward or forward, but he releases her wrists, takes her hand and begins to walk anyway.

"Let's walk," he says. "It will help your senses adjust."

"I don't understand. I don't understand where we are."

Johnny Von the Scientist smiles, his voice deep and soothing, "Estella, welcome to <u>Level 16</u>."

They walk in silence a few steps and then, not letting go of her hand, he reaches over in a comfortable embrace and kisses her cheek like they are old friends, and then continues forward.

As Estella starts to anchor in the movements and the security of his hand, Johnny Von the Scientist starts talking, "Do you know about me?"

"Of course, everyone knows the results of Xbox 6000."

Estella is woozy, but she tries to focus her thoughts as she speaks. "We all know your story on the floor. The technicians talk about you all the time. How amazing it is that someone like you, without upgrade documentation or programmed birth tracking, solved it, when it was statistically impossible by human means." She spews out everything she knows about the rise of Johnny Von the Scientist. "...and that stopping the software has allowed science to take part in <u>Level 16</u> and address THE PROBLEM before it's too late."

Estella stops abruptly. She feels her mouth go dry, her palms sweaty and her heart race as she catches herself rattling off the famed facts of Johnny Von the Scientist to Johnny Von the Scientist.

He puts his hand on her shoulder, he comforts her as if to say, "It's all right. It's all right to be nervous. I understand."

She is startled by the quality of the contact at her neck, somehow more real than she has ever felt the touch of another person. Estella relaxes under his hand.

Johnny Von the Scientist smiles reassuringly and begins walking again.

"It's a simple thing, really, when you step back. With Xbox evolving on its own, and **The Controller** coupled with Pod technology steering the flow of mankind — not all at once, but over time — humanity lost the ability for ingenuity. With the constant feed from the cradle to the grave, men and woman no longer have imagination, unique perspective, like they once did. There is no contribution of new thought to the system." Johnny Von the Scientist's voice is filled with compassion. "For most this isn't a problem. Most don't know it at all, content in the comfort and safety, the pacification of the Pod. And for the odd few that struggle with it, nature still rules: they either adapt or die out."

"Certainly, people still dream, still imagine, still create?" Estella, in her disoriented state, cannot help herself from cutting in. "I dream."

"I know, Estella." Johnny Von the Scientist smiles. "I know you dream." He looks forward and continues walking and talking, her hand still safely in his. "Through charting the decline in imagination, **The Controller** calculated a point in time with no new input. The design of the software is set up in a way that does not allow it to remain static. So it projected, that at the point of no new input, at the registering of the last of imagination in humanity, it would start moving backwards, start deconstructing, and start ending the world.

"But you had an original thought?" Estella, feeling more grounded, interrupts him again.

"Yes. I did have an original thought. And that is how I solved Xbox 6000. It was a leap of imagination. At the end, I gave up all I'd ever been taught, I gave up all outside reason, and I led my decision by my imagination. And, Estella, knowing how to do that did not come from anything I'd ever received from **The Controller**. Estella, knowing how to do that came from you."

"What?"

Johnny Von the Scientist stops, drops her hand, and reaches into his lab coat pocket. He takes out a worn leather-bound book. "This is how I knew." He hands her the book.

It has been so long since Estella touched and felt the weight of a real book in her hands, she does not immediately recognize what she is holding.

She reads the faded gold title, "Emotional Energy Theory—a thesis by Humphrey Cheeseman." Dated 2460. A flash of recognition and affection washes over Estella, "Cheeseman's work on Intuitive Deliberate Creation. The proofs of imagination over reason. Where did you get this?"

"I started out at the Book Repository, a cataloger in Section 13." Johnny Von the Scientist smiles.

"But what does this have to do with me ... with this ..."

"Cheeseman did the work, articulated the ideas, but ..." he takes the book gently from her hands, flips the pages, and returns it back to her hands. "I believe these notes and sketches are yours."

Johnny Von the Scientist is moved as he watches Estella recognize her first attempts, her own hand, something beloved and lost returned to its rightful place.

Estella smiles as she flips the pages studying the sketches she'd copied from the books of art she was scanning before the Turnovers. She beams with delight that she finally has someone to confess to, finally someone to talk to about something that has been on her mind a long, long time. Her voice is rapid and unselfconscious. "You know, **The Controller** banned this book so long ago no one remembers anything of it. You can't even find Cheeseman's name in the World Data Bank. I found it by mistake, my third year cleaning out Repository 8 when we were moving buildings. It wasn't registered anywhere and I snuck it to my station and poured over every word. I made the notes thinking it would never be seen. The sketches were from a book of art called *Landscapes* — paintings; a two dimensional kind of artwork. They're static images created by colors applied to a flat surface."

Estella takes a breath and studies more of her earlier drawings. "I was fascinated by them. People don't really look at them anymore, they are never called up in the World Data Bank, but I had to scan everything, so…" Estella trails off as she flips the pages, sees the subtitles she'd copied from the books: "Meadow," "Hills," "The Skies of Saint Germaine." She smiles, amused at her sincere efforts to record and duplicate. "I found them mesmerizing. I don't know, there was just something about them, I could sit for hours looking at them."

As Estella talks, she can feel a ripple in the room, a pulse ever so slight.

"They're static you know, paintings, no sound or action to them, so everything is implied — the emotions, the movements, what happens before and after the moment depicted, everything is imagined."

She looks at Johnny Von the Scientist smiling as she says the word.

Estella rubs the cover, presses the worn, violet color of the leather to her lips, inhales, and then looks curiously to Johnny Von the Scientist. "I threw this book in the back of the stacks when the Turnovers started. I watched the fires that same night. How could you have it ..."

His smile is warm and genuine. "I found it in a pile behind the building, my last day." He takes off his glasses and steps closer to her. "It was very intense ... very emotional, for me, reading this book with your sketches and notes. It changed me. But finding the book was easy — it came to me. A stroke of fate. Finding you, Estella, that was much harder."

Estella feels her body buzz, like it did that day. Again she feels a pulse in the room, a wrinkle of energy flashing through.

"All these years," he says, "knowing you were somewhere working in the system. A girl who signs her name, Estella. I longed for you, even though I only knew you from the scribbles and the sketches. I longed to hear the voice behind the words, to be with the girl that dreams such places." He rubs her un-calloused and tender hands holding the timeworn leather-bound book. "I've been looking for you for a long time."

"But how did you know it was me, then? How did you know who I was?"

"I saw it," Johnny Von the Scientist says with confidence. "I saw you turn to look at me that day; I saw it in your eyes. I recognized you." He smiles as he gazes at her. "But I couldn't call you to my lab until I had this completed." He looks around to the space they are standing in, "Until I had Level 16 ready for you."

Estella takes a deep breath, tries to take in everything she's hearing, her mind races to get a foothold on what is going on. "Where are we now then, what is this? What do I have to do with Level 16?"

"Estella, we are standing in the raw fabric of matter." He smiles and tries to explain further, "A kind of Higgs Field." He searches for the right words. "Think of it as God's clay." He puts his arms out with pride, showing her his work, "We are out of the temporal stream." He pauses as if he can hardly believe it himself, "Here … we can create a whole new reality."

Estella is still unable to take in what, exactly, he is telling her.

"Let me show you." He takes the book from Estella's hand, flips the pages to one of her sketches. "What is this?" He hands her back the book. "Talk to me about this."

Estella smiles, unsure but willing. She looks to the

picture and begins to tell the story. "Apparently, at one time the sky was all blue, and the land was entirely earth growth, green and brown and yellow, with flowers of every color that came on their own!"

The room pulses strongly. Johnny Von the Scientist seems to flicker ever so slightly with the pulse. It's barely noticeable, but Estella pauses.

"And what's this?" he points.

She continues, "The skies were open, with pure white puffy clouds that slowly changed shapes and moved with the wind. And it seemed like, in the paintings, you could see the sky from the ground! It wasn't filled with structures and flying cars. It must have felt wonderful and free."

The room pulses twice, and both Estella and Johnny Von the Scientist start to laugh. But again she notices that with the pulses, Johnny Von the Scientist seems to blink with the waves of energy.

"Hurry, what's this?" he says, pointing to something in the picture, in the clouds of the sky.

"Oh! This is my favorite thing. It's the only thing that could traverse the sky, it was a flying animal! They were called birds, and they would sing! They would fly in the sky with beautiful wings and feathers. This kind would hover high over the trees, with grace and skill, I remember reading about this kind, this one ... what was it called..." She looks to the scribbled notes. "A hawk! Oh, yes! I love that one."

As the word forms and hits the air, a blistering screech comes out of the void. A hawk of such beauty, perfectly formed and feathered, swoops down inches above their head. Looking up in amazement, Estella doesn't notice that for the same moment the hawk soars above them, Johnny Von the Scientist is barely visible in front of her. It circles in the vast space for a few moments and moves out again into the darkness.

Estella and Johnny Von the Scientist stare stunned at one another, and then break into ecstatic laughter.

"I knew you could do it!" He laughs and shakes his head, "I didn't have it, I could never focus and concentrate enough emotional energy, but you!" They both cannot stop the giddy, excited laughter, "You!" He puts his hand on her shoulder, pulls Estella closer and kisses her. "I knew you could."

In the embrace, he whispers into her ear, "Now, feel the whole thing, the sky, the meadow, the field full of flowers."

Estella takes a deep breath and finds herself there, in the most perfect rolling hills of multi-colored wild flowers, trees and birds and a house in the distance, the perfect mix of old and new, that she knows is hers. The sky overhead is blue and cool and endless. She is in one of her pictures, one of her favorites, now tangible and real. Instead of dissolving it is manifesting in greater and greater detail around her.

She turns ecstatic and joy-filled to Johnny Von the Scientist, only to see him barely there in front of her now.

Her elation turns to horror.

"What's happening! What's happening to you?"

"Don't be scared. Estella, don't be scared." He touches her shoulder as he'd done before but now she can barely feel his touch with all the sensations of the breeze, the sun on her skin.

Seeing her distress, Johnny Von the Scientist rushes to explain. "The day I found the book, I was trapped in the Book Repository. When the Turnovers stormed the building, I was locked in behind the stacks by accident. My Pod was damaged, my clothes torn in the attack, so no one knew I was there. For three days I sat, before the fires raged, and I read. For three days you were there with me, your words, your places. And in that time, I made myself more energy than person — I applied ... I used Cheesman's Emotional Energy theory. I walked out of the fires a kind of hologram of the man I'd been, with one purpose and one purpose only, saving the world for this," he opens his arms looking to the hills and sky, "... and for you," he says, meeting her eyes. "My wanting, my intention, was so intense, there was no way to tell the difference in the physical world, whether I was energy or biology. Only, I can't hold here. I'm not real. And we're here now ... you're here now." He opens his arms. "All of this is here now."

Estella is spilling with tears. "But you can't leave me. I felt you! You must be real!"

As he is fading, Johnny Von the Scientist's voice is still warm and comforting. "There was a time when I was real. But what you experienced was the energy of me, not the man."

"No. No, I don't believe it!" Estella cries and tries to hold him close even though she can feel the fading of him. "I can't be alone here. Not now. Not after I've finally found a place, found someone who understands."

"Shh. Shh, Estella. It's going to be all right. You won't be alone. Look at me. I'm going to tell you what happens now, how this works."

Estella pulls back from her desperate attempt of embrace and looks into the eyes of Johnny Von the Scientist, fading but still strong.

"You will think of someone, feel inside someone whom you loved, someone you were connected to once. The emotional energy will bring that person over. And then they will think of someone — without even being aware of it — they will feel someone they were connected to with love, they will turn to look for them and there that person will be. On it will go. In a single moment, everyone will be here. None of them will remember any of this. No one will know there was ever a time of Pods and **The Controller**. Brought over with love, they will come with only the best of themselves, to a world of beauty you've put into motion. They will live lives that are led by their imaginations, now inspired, by what you've created."

"Then I will think you! I will think you over."

"You can't."

"Why!"

"Because you did not know me." Johnny Von the Scientist reaches out to her, but his touch has no weight. His eyes now cloud with a kind of sorrow. "My physical self did not even look like this, like what you see in front of you. What you're looking at ..." Johnny Von the Scientist looks to his hands, now nearly gone, with a poignant smile, "...is the essence of me."

Estella's face streams with tears

"Don't cry. It's going to be okay." He tries to touch her cheek as he fades to nothing. "Someone did once, someone loved me, my mother, my father, my friends — someone will think me through."

Estella nods, her body loosens, her tears subside.

"I won't remember," he says. "I won't remember you or any of this."

Estella nods her understanding, now barely able to see him at all.

"But you'll find me." He smiles at her one last time, confident and true. "You'll know me. You'll recognize me in time, Estella."

"Yes," Estella reassures him, wiping her cheeks dry, trying to be brave.

Johnny Von the Scientist uses all the energy he has left to touch Estella one last time, he brushes her forehead and says, "Don't worry. You'll know me, Estella, by the way it feels when we meet again."

And then ...Johnny Von the Scientist ...disappears.

She turns to see people already on the road, walking as if nothing has happened. She looks across the field in the distance and sees figures milling around the house.

Slightly panicked, she turns back to where he was just standing. Estella calls out one crucial last question: "And here, Johnny..."

She looks up to the sky. "Here we can <u>feel</u> what we want?"

"Estella," he says, his voice alive and close to her. "Here we can <u>feel</u> everything."

Chapter 8

"If the fool would persist in his folly
he would become wise."

~ *William Blake*

The days on Valley Glen Drive following what happened that night at Lionel Max's Hollywood estate were quiet. And I was thankful for it. It had been harsh and difficult. Even with the moment of feeling myself totally returned, and knowing what I know now, I needed the time to settle back into the world, to sooth the abruptness of the event. To bring my whole self back and reorganize to the streets and the dogs and the days that are my life.

I didn't want to see or talk to anyone, but not because I felt humiliated or needed to hide, it was just that I felt so very different about everything and I needed time to re-orient myself. I knew I would never see Mandy Kane again, which actually didn't bother me in the least. And I knew I'd never talk about Johnny Von to anyone again. I was a bit unsure how it would feel seeing him the next time he drove by me on Valley Glen Drive but it didn't take away from the feeling that I'd found my way home to myself.

I did want to see Trudie Reed.

I wanted to talk to her and tell her about wearing her dress, about the poetry I was writing and the deep understanding of William Blake—about everything that had happened; especially the sweet Johnny Von desire that I'd discovered lived in me. I had stories to tell, I have poetry and passion in me, to share with a friend that would understand and enjoy it. But for days her house was dark. I rang the bell each day, but I could see through the window of the garage that her car was gone. It wasn't until Friday that I finally saw movement in her house through the front kitchen window.

I tie Moochie in the garage, happy that I will soon be able to tell her my stories. I ring the bell and think about how delighted she will be that the dress she made for Apple pulled me through a moment in time which has changed the course of my life. I want to tell someone who sees me, how I shine.

A young woman I've never seen before answers the door.

Her eyes are puffy and red, "Can I help you?" she says with a formal and well composed sadness.

My heart drops, I know why she's here before she says anything. I can feel the darkness, the heavy emptiness in the house behind her.

"I was looking for Mrs. Reed."

"My aunt passed away last night." She sees my face shadow over, and puts her hand out on my arm. She reports the details in an effort to explain away my expression, "It was very quick. She drove herself to the hospital a little after midnight last Friday with chest pains. Emergency at Cedars admitted her and put her in I.C.U., but she slipped into a coma shortly after she arrived at the hospital."

"Oh." I nod my head as she continues to offer more reason to alleviate what she reads as confusion on my face.

"She was in I.C.U. all week, but she never regained consciousness. She went into severe cardiac arrest last night and they followed her orders not to resuscitate."

"Okay." I say and pat her hand on my arm. I nod yes. "Okay," I say again and turn to leave. I don't know why I say 'okay' like we've just agreed on something. It seems stupid and insensitive as I hear it leave my lips, but it's all I can get out. It's all I can say, so that I don't burst out and tell her! Tell her that I'm the only person who knows they were Trudie's stories. Everything is passed and gone, and they'll box the pictures and divide up the shiny awards from the bookcase, and I'm the only one who will ever know they were all Trudie's stories! I'm the only one who will ever know about the dress she made for Apple, and how I wore it the day I stood up and didn't let my heart break anymore. The moment I decided not to be invisible anymore. 'Okay' is all I can say so I can get away from her, before I betray my friend's confidence in a sudden burst of loneliness.

I'm frazzled and raw as it is. I give my condolences to Trudie's niece, excuse myself and walk to get Moochie. I don't know how I feel, I'm upset, but more dazed and disoriented, until I look down at Moochie to untie the knot in his leash. It's then that a profound calm washes over me. Something in the way he looks at me, shocked that we would be leaving. The way he plants all his weight down, doesn't budge and says with his eyes, "No, you're wrong. We can't be leaving, where's my biscuit? Where's the lady I like, my friend that gives me the biscuits?"

It's in how I have the overwhelming impulse to say to him, like Trudie Reed said to me the first day I met her and then that last day, "It all passes."

I say out loud to Moochie, "It all passes, my baby dog. Don't worry. Trudie Reed's gone on, but it's okay. We'll get you a biscuit somewhere else. Come on."

It's silly words really, to my dog, about a biscuit, but it brings an understanding to me that words between people couldn't have.

I finally get him going, we head down the street and I

find myself crying once again on Valley Glen Drive. But this time it's a clean kind of crying, a washing away of pain. Tears that are not looking for a way out, just crying because the sadness is there and it's okay that it's there. And I feel this way not just about Trudie Reed's passing, I feel this way about all of it, everything that happened on Valley Glen Drive. The wonderful and the terrible, the feelings of love and loneliness, the real and the unreal, it's all okay. It all lives inside my heart.

"Wait." Trudie Reed's niece calls out and catches us as we make our way back up Valley Glen Drive from the dead end. "Is this you?" She hands me an envelope with my name written in script with a red ink pen on the front.

"Yes." I say sniffing up my tears, a bit confused.

"It was on the counter when we came into the house. Trudie must have wanted to give it to you."

"Thank you." I say quietly and keep moving. I don't open it in front of Trudie's niece. It's probably rude, but it's from my friend and it's private. I take my time finishing the walk. I load Mooch in the car, get in the front and sit for a minute. I open the envelope. There is no note or card, just the black and white picture of Trudie Reed and Apple.

"Anyone else? Does anyone else want to read today? We still have a few more minutes left to class."

I feel my heart racing. I have a poem in my hand that I wrote the day I found out that Trudie Reed died, when it was finally all okay inside me. I know I have to read it, and I have to do it now; this is the last class. But even more than that, I have to do it because I know that the universe sent me William Blake not only to understand and revel in desire, the sweet Johnny Von desire, but to also claim it as my own. The universe wants me to feel everything and be my genuine self, knowing I have a voice that wants to be in the world. With that thought I raise my hand and Andrew Banks nods me to the front of the room.

My hands are trembling and my voice is shaky, and I feel stupid for being so nervous about this, but I unfold the paper and I read my poem. It is a poem about time and space and soothing and wanting ... to be alive, to be here in God's creation. A poem about what comes before and goes after, it was for Trudie and Johnny Von and mostly for me.

I hear my voice in the air and when I'm done everyone is quiet. I can feel my face burning.

Andrew Banks looks wistfully out the window. "Yes," he says and sighs. He then turns back to me and smiles. "Can you read it again?"

I read the page again. Again there is a hush in the room.

"Lovely," Andrew Banks says. "Just lovely. I think that this is the perfect poem to end the semester with: eloquent and stunning."

Relief floods through me. The class nods along with Mr. Banks, visibly impressed. I'm sort of shocked by it, but it feels ... wonderful. The grannies beam with pride and Lillian says, "Quiet as a church mouse all semester and look at that, a little poetess in our midst."

Ruthie calls back, "Maybe if someone else could get a word in edgewise with all your talking we'd have heard more."

"Thank you," Andrew Banks looks at me with a sincerity that is found few and far between in Los Angeles; the kind of thank-you that you feel.

He then ends the class.

As everyone packs their books, says goodbye and shuffles out the room, Andrew Banks stops me. He hands me a card outlining a private poetry group he runs; it's a group of writers that gather by invitation only to work on their poetry and other writings. He explains that they don't have students in the group, but he'd like to invite me to join anyway—based on the poems I've turned in and my reading in class today—if I'm interested.

I nod thank you. I'm choked up, overwhelmed with emotion at the offer.

Andrew Banks smiles and tells me he looks forward to hearing more from me.

All the way to my car, I can't feel my body walking through the parking lot. It's like the first time I really kissed a boy; floaty and fantastic, like I might lift off the earth at any moment unfettered by the laws of gravity or the way the world is. I'm as high as I can be. I've found my place to shine.

I don't know how many weeks go by before I see Johnny Von again on Valley Glen Drive. I know that I'd been meeting with the private writing group for a while, and that Trudie Reed's house had been cleared out and put up for sale. It's not like I hadn't thought about it, about seeing him. I'd thought about it a lot; I'd thought about it from every angle of reaction that you can imagine.

I know initially I thought he was a big fat-head. At first, I imagined stopping him on the street and giving him a piece of my mind about what an unkind jackass he was. How sad it was that he was just a self-obsessed, shallow celebrity, one of many in this town, who would inevitably die alone or cycle through one unhappy marriage after the next, emotionally crippled by all the money, women and yes-men kissing his butt and then stabbing him in the back. As it played out in my head, I imagined him regretful, guilt-ridden and apologizing, over and over, until I conceded. But those thoughts didn't stay very long, and they didn't really sit right inside me, although at the time, right after if first happened, they were quite satisfying.

Then sometimes I thought, well, I'll just stop him and tell him that I'm not a stalker. I'll just tell him, person to person, I was just a girl with a crush; shy and awkward maybe, perhaps naïve in my approach, but I was never stalking him. He misunderstood. I had a little speech in my head, but I could never really see it play all the way through either. Stopping someone to tell them your not stalking them is, I imagine, a counter productive action.

Other days, depending on my mood, I ran through the spectrum of "who cares," all the way to "I guess I can see his side of it; why he would misjudge me and say that."

Having imagined so many different responses, I was shocked at how I really did feel when it happened.

It is a clear day, the cold has just snapped and the trees are turning. I remember the big crunchy leaves under foot, and noticing that Moochie is frolicking more than usual, running up into the yards to patter through the yellow leaves.

I stop to play with Mooch in a small patch of front yard belonging to a white brick house across the street, a house or two down, from the giant entry gate of Johnny Von. I'm teasing Moochie on the grass, grabbing his tail, chasing him and winding him up with my voice.

"Show me the moves," I say to Moochie when we play, "show me the moves." He then does a wild puppy scramble all around me. He's big now, but he still flings himself around and zips by and wags his tail as he runs past me, just a hair out of reach. He finds a stick and we tug and toss it a little. And then, given his girth, he drops and squishes his belly into the cool grass to rest for a bit. He lays there grinning and panting.

Just as he does that, a huge breeze blows through
and all the trees bend and sway. The millions of leaves
rustle and dance with abandon. My hair blows wild and
free, and the cold wind rushes over my skin, zooming
down the street. I look up at the big trees and notice the
leaves still holding on. I stop to watch the ones that are
ready to let go take their turn. I sit next to my Moochie
in the grass to watch them fall and twirl around us. I
congratulate and commend each leaf that I can; I bask in
their dance from air to earth. I rub Moochie's head and
tell him what a handsome dog he is. I take a deep breath,
feel the cool air rush into my chest, and I know I couldn't
be an ounce happier than I am right now. I feel right
and blessed and part of it all, I feel like I'm in love—with
everything.

Right then, I hear the rumble of the Trans Am, the
gate rolls open and out comes Johnny Von. I look at him,
straight on, back behind the tinted windows, and I feel…
a rush of love and appreciation in my belly! He's drives
slow down his driveway as Moochie and I are sitting in the
leaves, and I have a spontaneous burst of gratefulness toward
Johnny Von, which is most unexpected. And then, as he
passes, he smiles friendly and soft, looking at the two of us in
the grass, in love with everything.

He waves and zooms off.

It is the last time I will ever see Johnny Von in person.

I have to sit for a minute to register it, and find a place for
it inside.

I feel back inside me to the original Johnny Von desire, and like it was a little pool of water, I dip myself in and swim. I think of him in all the wonderful ways I'd imagined him and the way I felt about him in our ever so brief crossings. And I let myself enjoy it all again.

I think about Mandy Kane and Shelby and everyone else that told me I had to forget about Johnny Von. All the people at the party and the way they looked at me, the way he looked at me. And I know if they had any idea that I was sitting here today swimming in the sweet Johnny Von desire again, after everything that happened, they would really tell me to see a therapist, or take out a restraining order. But now, thinking of all the scorn and rebuff, I have to smile. And I almost feel sorry for all of them.

How little they know of the sweetness of desire and where it can lead you.

As if it were a finite thing. A limited amount that you have to be careful with, have to mete out with caution. As if pouring desire in one direction might cause you to run out and then lose out somewhere else. As if life has a rule where you only get one direction to point this desire that bubbles up like champagne. And more than that even, as if this one direction is bound by what the world thinks is appropriate. That it is contingent on its equal and assured return.

How little they all know.

It's a shame for them.

I wouldn't tell them, but I know in my heart I'm going to like Johnny Von and think of him and all of this for as long as I want to. It brought me to the love I always wanted. It brought me home to myself. I understand William Blake, and I'm no longer bothered by the way the world is. I know in my heart I'm going to think about Johnny Von and the sweet desire it pulled out of me, for as long as it feels good. I look up at these big trees that have lined Valley Glen Drive for decades and decades, and the leaves that come and go, and come and go, always letting go with such ease, year after year. And I look at Moochie, who has no idea of time, or of coming or going; my dog—just happy here today, sitting with his belly in the cool green grass. And I realize, I'd dream of Johnny Von for a thousand years… if this is where it leads me.

A few weeks later, I am offered a job as a writer's assistant. One of the guys in my writing group recommended me. It was more money, better hours, and with a writer whose work I really, really liked. So even though I loved my little dog business, playing outside all day, I decided to close shop and take it. Plus, it was heading in a career direction that seemed to suit me, my talents and my place to shine. Besides, he told me I could bring Moochie to work everyday and he had a big backyard.

On my last day walking Valley Glen Drive, I stop by Trudie's house and peek in the windows one last time. It is still empty but I find it comforting to say good-bye this way. And then, after a slow stroll, saying good-bye to the trees and houses that had been part of our life all these days, Moochie and I stop at the mailbox of Johnny Von one last time.

I have a poem for him.

It's the poem I read in class that day. The poem about time and space and soothing and wanting ... to be alive, to be here in God's creation. The one about what comes before and goes after, the one written for Trudie and Johnny Von, and mostly for me.

And don't worry; I'll let you read the poem. It's still personal, but this time, don't bother about folding it down or tearing out the pages after your done reading it. I don't mind. If it speaks to you, if you like it, you can have it too. If not, well, that's okay with me too.

This is the poem:

In the Twilight of the Babies

They are not rushing.
They're patting soft drums
between your shoulder blades
to calm you.

They know.
Time and Space is difficult.
They know.

They, too, will set courses
to join with joy and pain.

They will be small bodied;
learn to count
and wiggle;
become lost in the thicket
of "when?"
like you and I. They will wonder why
they are here,
what is their part
to play.

In that confused forest
their babies will begin patting,
their babies will whisper
like you whispered
to your mother and father-
something wonderful and clear
and obvious,
something you can't remember,
but know you said.

As I put the poem in a card and put the card in the
mailbox, I notice high in one of the big pine trees of the
house of Johnny Von a large red-tailed hawk. I'm not sure
it's the same one that started the whole thing that day, but
he does look content and satisfied, perched there, staring
down at us.

I take it as a good sign.

I close the mailbox and call Moochie forward and finish
our last walk on Valley Glen Drive.

Acknowledgements

The 3 Gates

I am a writer only because Bruce Gelfand, crossed my path fourteen years ago. In his classes and workshops over the years, I have witnessed many writers born before my very eyes. He is talented beyond his years and a true teacher that leans into one's strengths; however small and hiding they maybe, and invites them to step into the full light and glory they crave and deserve. He is the writing teacher you wish for, and I was lucky enough to find early. www.BruceGelfand.com

I wrote this story, and finished it, only because of Heidi Rose Robbins. She is a poet and teacher who lives to embrace the mystical behind the mundane. Beyond being inspirational in her boldness, her exploration of love and the power of the spoken word, she came to my house once a week and listened as I wrote each new chapter. I will always be awed by that act of friendship. www.heidirose.com

You have this book is in your hands now because of Oprah's interview of Brene Brown, which I clicked on Oprah.com one day, randomly.

www.oprah.com/video_search.html?video_query=Brene+Brown

This manuscript was collecting dust on my shelf for years, filed under "I wrote this novel once..." Brene Brown's book, <u>Daring Greatly</u>, restored my faith in heartfelt things and let me be more of myself, once again, in the world. And Oprah, well, I can't even wrap my head around how much Oprah is a conduit for the uplifting of the world. She's a damn blessing in a sea of media scariness. I hope she lives long and prospers, and creates ...even more. www.brenebrown.com

Other many people helped me along the way, reading and encouraging and moving this project forward. Reader friends: Andrew Heffernan, Gwyn Fawcett McColl, Mary Duhon, Madley Katarungan and Kimberli Waack. Publishing friends: Marcia Ho Adams, www.marciaadamsho.com, Delaine Ulmer, www.studioultimatedesign.com, William Williams, www.alisocreek.net, and Penny C. Sansevieri, www. authormarketingexperts.com. And of course, my family, who knows how I am, and loves me anyway, and always give me stuff to write about.

About the Author

Edith M. Cortese is a freelance writer, a sometime novelist and a mom. She was once, a lifetime ago, a dogwalker. She lives in Los Angeles with her family and an old, good dog named Moochie. She would love to hear from you: hello@trumpetboypress

---

Dear Gentle Reader,

This book needs your help.
We live in interesting times in the
world of book publishing! This
is a self-published title, which
is EXCITING because it's right
out there for you, wholly created
cover to cover, by me, the author. It's one independent, creative
vision. I like to think it is an endeavor that is bold, and cutting
edge, entrepreneurial, and …limitless. So limitless that when
I last Googled it, I discovered that about 800 books a day go
up for sale on the internet. Which also makes this endeavor …
DISCOURAGING.

While I, personally, am okay with the idea of suffering for my
craft, content with the simple act of it's creation, Moochie knows I
used his name and based the chocolate lab character extremely close
to his real life self! He's talking royalties. I can't distract him with
biscuits forever.

Self published books rise in the ranks because readers like
you (yes, you!) go to the internet and post reviews, click Like
and Friend buttons, tweet, blog and talk about it on sites like
Goodreads.com.

If there is anything you like about this work, please post a
review somewhere on the internet, or stop by my website and grab
a widget. If like me, (before I decided to self-publish a book) you
have no idea what that is, please post a simple, friendly word on the
book page for *A Thousand Years of Johnny Von* here: www.amazon.
com

Moochie thanks you in advance. (He has plans to put in a pool.)

Sincerely,

Edie

www.trumpetboypress.com